GIRLS
FROM

ISBN: 978-1-68313-175-5
Library of Congress Control Number: 2018955053

Pen-L Publishing
Fayetteville, Arkansas
www.Pen-L.com

First Edition
Printed and bound in the USA

Cover art by Bob Boze Bell
Cover and interior design by Kelsey Rice

GIRLS FROM CENTRO

BY JUNI FISHER

ACKNOWLEDGMENTS

To Amy Hale Auker, for tossing a match under me,
then guiding me through the fire.

To Duke and Kimberly Pennell,
for taking a chance on a fledging's first flight.

To Rusty, for being patient. You deserve a halo.

And to Florence Ophelia Fisher,
who taught her daughters to love books.

For those who dream beyond borders

THE GATEWAY

She lies half asleep,
one ample buttock on Arizona in the United States
and the other on Sonora in Mexico.
The backbone of the sister cities known as Nogales
is the border that divides two countries.
The gateway between the two countries
rests between those fleshy parts.

1

TERESA 1971

Hole in the border fence

I don't think God was watching when we went through the hole in the border fence like it was the gate in our yard and walked away with our backs to the lights of town. We'd left home in early May so we wouldn't be in the Sonoran Desert in the middle of the June monsoon season. When we got about a mile past the United States border, an early storm crawled over the mountains and covered the sky. The roads and ditches filled with water, and a fast running wash blocked the trail Mama had picked for us to get away from Nogales.

My sister Salma was four. She was hungry and crying. My fourteen-year-old sister Luna held her while my mother took me across that flooded dirt-banked ditch on her back. Rushing water tore the bank away in chunks behind us and in front of us.

Weeds and sticks poked up from the water like hands to grab at our legs. I tried to hold my feet up but my pants got wet all the way to the top. It was raining so hard when Mama got me to the other side I could barely hear what she was saying. Mama looked back at my sisters and waved to Luna to take Salma under a tree, away from the water. Luna squatted under that bent-over tree and shook Salma hard.

"Shut up!" Luna yelled at Salma.

Mama said we'd have to wait for the water to go back down. I asked how long. She said it would drop when the rain stopped.

A half hour later it was still raining but the water didn't seem higher, so Mama waded back to carry Salma across. Thunder cracked over our heads right as Mama stepped into the flood with Salma in a sling she'd made from her shawl. Luna jumped toward them and grabbed Mama's arm. The soft bank gave away and Luna tumbled into that sandy, swirling current behind our mother. Luna screamed and Mama grabbed her by the back of her T-shirt and pulled her onto her feet. Mama yelled at Luna through the rain. She was supposed to wait. Luna shook her head "no" and stayed beside Mama, grabbing at her every time she lost her balance.

I said a prayer when a dark clump of brush swept toward them. I thought God answered my prayer because the snarl of sticks and roots went behind them instead of right into them. Mama stopped, like she couldn't move. She pulled the shawl over her head, and shoved Salma at Luna.

"Take her! Go! Go!"

Luna grabbed our sister and lunged for the bank.

Black-clawed branches longer than Mama's arms rose from the sea that lay between her and freedom and took her under. Luna heaved our baby sister onto the breaking bank, and I dragged Salma away from the edge. I reached for Luna's hand, missed it, scratched her face. She shrieked like a wounded rabbit through a mouthful of dirty water and dragged herself up with her elbows toward Salma.

It was not until she had her knees in the wet sand and was pulling at her pants because they had gotten dragged halfway off, that she looked behind her and saw only water, bobbing brush, and branches. An awful wail shredded Luna's voice like it was ripping open.

No prayers got answered by God that night.

Our mother was gone.

DISTANTLY RELATED HEARTS

Each Nogales is a bustling city,
as alike and as different as a rooster and a hen.
They are the same species and neither perpetuates without the other.
They wriggle and pulse with life
from distantly related hearts.
Nogales, Arizona has City Center,
and Nogales, Sonora has Centro.

2

ANA 1944-1947

The convent

Ana Rosario could cook prickly pear leaves and make jelly from the fruits, and she could simmer a wiry, sinewy rooster into a wonderful, spicy stew. She had helped around her Aunt Pena's house and she knew how to cook on a wood stove or in an iron skillet over a fire. Pena's husband, Ancho, had built churches and schools until he'd had a stroke that rendered his left arm slack and the left side of his face in a permanent look of sorrow.

There was an orphanage at the convent in Centro where nuns took in children who'd lost their parents or had been left there in the night by mothers who could not afford to—or bear to—keep them. Ana went one day, at her Aunt Pena's suggestion, to help the nuns. The stove in the convent's kitchen had burned out from the inside, and the nuns didn't know what to do.

Ana looked at the ruined stove in the convent kitchen, then built a fire outside in a circle of stone, carried some big pots out into the yard, and cooked supper for the nuns and the children. The priest, who had stopped in to give last rites to a dying nun, smelled something cooking not at all like the typical fare in the convent kitchen. He stayed for a bowl of *posole,* a hearty stew, and asked who had made it. The nuns pointed at Ana. He offered to pay her a small amount of money to cook every day, since he was tired of bland food when he stayed for supper with the nuns. She agreed, so long as she could bring her infant daughter, Nina, with her.

Every morning Ana left little Nina in her basket with one of the young nuns and walked out into the desert to find cactus pieces she could cook. She was clever with spices and collected more flavors by bartering with vendors who had shattered chile pods they couldn't sell to tourists. She took the vendors' limes and oranges that had dried out and would have been thrown away and used the flesh and skins for flavoring dishes. The priest was pleased and proud. When priests from other parishes visited, he'd invite them for supper. They praised his wisdom in hiring a good cook, and for taking pity on the young mother whose husband was working in New Mexico and had not sent money to take care of his child.

The priest invited more guests for supper and gave Ana money to get extra chickens for the pots. One day he brought a pair of pigs for the nuns to feed in the pens at the edge of the yard. He suggested the pigs could eat the scraps from the kitchen, but the mother superior told him there were few scraps, since everyone ate the meals Ana prepared.

The priest visited the food vendors at the outdoor market, and said he'd like to have any vegetables and fruit that had gone bad to feed to the convent's pigs. The vendors wanted to look generous in the eyes of the priest, so they kept old produce in burlap sacks behind their booths. The priest sent two of the younger nuns to pick up the full sacks, feed the pigs, wash the sacks and return them to the vendors the next morning. The young nuns were quite beguiling, and the vendors started giving them a few extra items that were still fine to eat but not pretty. This seemed to be a good trade, since the priest often invited a vendor or two to stop at the convent for supper after the market closed. When the vendors came, they'd bring some prime goods along to add to supper.

The store owners who didn't sell produce learned what was happening at the convent and, to be favored in the eyes of God and the church, they asked if they could pay to come to supper. Someone brought a stove they were no longer using to replace the burned-out stove, and Ana moved the kitchen back inside.

Within six months, extra guests were numbering a dozen every night, and the money was welcome at the convent. Guests would ask to see the cook so they could give her tips, saying they wanted to help her with her daughter. Ana saved the money in a wooden box she kept beneath the floorboards under her bed at Aunt Pena's house, and gave some money to her aunt every week in gratitude. Pena was happy to have a little baby to love and was proud of Ana for her reputation as the best cook in the village.

As far as Pena was concerned, Ana was her daughter from the day she'd moved in. As far as the nuns and priest knew, their cook had a husband who was missing or dead and it was their Christian duty to keep her employed in the kitchen, watch baby Nina, collect the extra money that came to the convent, and teach her to speak, read, and write English.

Ana started taking Nina along to collect spices at the market. A vendor gave Ana packets of vegetable seeds, and the orphans helped her plant a garden in an open patch of ground alongside the cemetery. Church goers brought buckets of water to the convent gate. Orphans were put to work watering the garden every morning and picking pests from the leaves to feed to the pen of laying hens in the coop behind the kitchen.

At Ana's suggestion, the nuns brought home a rooster from the market. The problem of buying extra chickens was solved. In a short time, there were more hens and young roosters than the convent could use. The young nuns started taking extra chickens to the market to sell weekly and scurried back with money to hand over to Mother Superior.

The priest had been keeping the number of paying guests at supper to twelve so as not to displace any of the children, but then he had an idea. He had some tables and benches from a classroom brought out and put just inside the front gate of the convent so meals could be served to more guests outside. Ana taught one of the more enthusiastic nuns to cook tortillas. The shortage of plates at the convent was solved by putting stacks of thick tortillas on tables, and letting the guests ladle posole into tortillas.

One day, a pair of well-dressed tourists came to supper. They paid twice the asking price, insisting the food was worth it. The tourists wanted to meet Ana, and she was brought from the kitchen, still wearing her apron, her hair tied up in a scarf. They found her story to be intriguing. Ana was, by the Mother Superior's current account, a young widow with a toddler to care for, who was cooking at the convent to support herself.

The couple wondered, if the convent had a shade over the front yard, over the tables, and more plates and silverware, could they serve more people? Maybe serve lunch as well as supper? The priest heartily agreed, and he could get some of the older orphans to help with serving. The American tourists returned the next day with tables, benches, a roll of slatted bamboo to make a shade, a cartload of plates, forks, and spoons, and six dozen cotton dish towels to be used for napkins.

Within three years, the convent's open-air restaurant was known as the best place for authentic native fare. Vendors who ate regularly at the convent sent shoppers for lunch. Ana's workday started at five thirty in the morning with breakfast for the orphans and nuns. Young postulants with cooking experience were sent to the kitchen in aprons. The orphans picked vegetables and took them to the kitchen door every morning in the spring and summer. Ana was paid extra money for each purchased meal from her kitchen because the priest insisted that she be rewarded for bringing money to the orphanage.

Everyone at the convent, from the nuns to the orphans, benefitted from the extra cash and attention. The children were well fed, happy, and knew how to work. Some of the orphans were adopted by American tourists who took them to a more privileged life in the States. That made more room for taking in new orphans.

A wealthy-looking American couple came for lunch two days in a row and offered to hire Ana to cook for them in Arizona. She told them she couldn't leave because she was waiting for Nina's father to return. They said they understood, but they'd give him a job taking care of the yard and garden if he ever came back. Ana couldn't even imagine a yard of green grass, or a garden whose only purpose was to look pretty. She said she'd think about it and excused herself to return to her work.

When the couple came back the next day for lunch, the man took a seat closest to the kitchen door and motioned to Ana. He handed her an envelope from the pocket of his suit jacket, and she opened it to find more money than she had saved in her wooden box over the past three years. The woman with the man got up from her seat and walked over to Ana, who was starting to understand the power of that envelope full of money.

"I'm Lorene Ormond. My husband, Stan, will pay you that much every week if you come to Arizona with us. Please say yes." The woman put her hand on Ana's arm. Ana shifted her eyes to three-year-old Nina, and back to the envelope. "My husband likes to have things the way he wants them, and I like to have a good cook. If you come, I'll make sure your daughter gets everything she needs."

Ana told the woman she needed to think about the offer, and perhaps she could be ready to go in a week. The man looked sharply at his wife, then looked nice again.

"Tomorrow. We'll come to get you tomorrow, if you want the job," he said. The couple left. Ana tucked the envelope into her blouse and continued cooking.

That night Ana told Aunt Pena about the couple and their offer of a job and a place to live in Arizona. Pena cried, but said "Yes, yes, you should go, it is good you can make so much money and have a better place to live."

Uncle Ancho raised his good hand toward Ana and said, "But are they good people, Ana? Maybe that man only wants you to be his other wife."

"What?" said Pena, "Who does that, Ancho? No one does that."

"Some men do that," Ancho said.

"Oh, Ancho, stop trying to scare Ana," Pena said.

Ana went to her room and put Nina in her crib, then lay on her cornhusk mattress, wondering what she should do. She felt for the place in the floorboards for the box and took it out of its hiding place. The wood was smooth and dark from handling, and the leather hinges were silent when she opened the lid. She put the envelope in the box and closed it, then reopened it, took a few bills out and laid them on her bed. She shook out a burlap sack and folded her few clothes, rolled up Nina's little dresses and placed them in the sack. She tucked the money in the pocket of her dress and left the sack on her bed.

She shimmied out the window of her room and walked to the convent. The kitchen there had been home to her for three years and the priest and the nuns had shown her kindness and appreciation. She wanted to go into the chapel to pray about her decision.

All her life, Ana had been told the Blessed Virgin would help her with any problem. The Virgin's statue was in the chapel, and Ana needed her help.

Ana walked slowly toward the statue of the Virgin, which glowed in the dim moonlight from the chapel windows, then knelt in front of it. She looked up into the face of plaster and paint that she had been taught was holy and serene. The Virgin gazed at the floor behind Ana.

"Will you tell me what to do?" The Virgin didn't answer, wouldn't meet Ana's eyes. Was she angry with Ana for wanting to go to America? Was she upset that Ana wouldn't be cooking for tourists and bringing money to the convent? That might be it. Ana stood up, trembling, took her rosary from her pocket and draped it over the Virgin's neck. The Virgin didn't acknowledge the gift but gazed over Ana's shoulder. Ana took a step back to try to make the Virgin look at her. She refused to look at Ana.

"You think you are good because God gave you a baby?" Ana challenged her. "You are no better than me. He did not marry you. But you lay with Joseph after that, didn't you? You are no virgin." The Virgin had nothing to say.

The Virgin stared at the wooden benches behind Ana, unable to look her in the eye. "No one ever has said that to you, have they? That you were just a woman with no husband who got pregnant," she said, "but you stand there and act like you are better than everyone." Ana snatched her rosary off the Virgin's neck. "You pretended to have a baby with God, to make what you did right, didn't you?" The Virgin looked grim, even ashamed.

Ana took the money from her dress pocket, laid it at the Virgin's feet, then stepped back. "I was going to give you this to give to the sisters so they would think you had performed a miracle, but I am not going to make a miracle for you. You stay here and rot until you fall apart." She snatched the money and dropped it in her dress pocket.

Ana walked toward the door of the chapel. She put the wad of bills in the offering plate that was ready for Sunday Mass and went out the door. Outside, she changed her mind and went back in. Jesus hung at the door, gave her his pity, bled his grief over her leaving, and told her he did not need her money. She picked up the folded bills and, as she pocketed the money again, Jesus rolled his eyes to the God that had forsaken them all.

The next day Ana made breakfast for the nuns and children and watched Nina playing with one of the orphans that the other children teased because of his drooping eye from a botched delivery. He'd probably never be adopted. She knew, looking at that boy, that it was the right thing to take her daughter away from the sadness that blanketed the orphanage.

Ana suspected Mother Superior knew what was going on because at breakfast she'd said an extra prayer of thanks for the good meals that had blessed their tables for three years. Ana scraped the big iron skillet clean for the last time.

When the kitchen was cleaned, Ana sent two postulants out to the market for supplies, then went to the room where the old nun kept a desk for the business of the church. She meant to tap lightly on the door, but her pounding heart made her rap out three knocks that drew a startled "Yes, who is it?" from inside.

"It is Ana."

"Come, then." Ana pushed the heavy door inward. "Yes, Ana, I know why you are here. I know you are going to leave us. We are sad to see you leave. We all love you very much, and Nina is so dear to all of us."

"Yes, Reverend Mother, I . . . " Ana tried to will away her tears. A tearful goodbye was not what she'd planned. "I only decided last night, it is the best thing for Nina. I want to buy her nice things. And she can go to school in America."

Mother Superior waved her hand over the papers on her desk. "School is important, Ana, but bought things are not so important to a child. I want you to know you are always welcome here. You and Nina may always come back."

"Thank you, Reverend Mother." Ana's throat felt like it was trying to crush her windpipe. "I will miss you. Would you like me to fix the noon meal today? I can do that. They will come to get me this afternoon."

"Oh, child, please don't worry. You need to pack your things, perhaps? What will your Aunt Pena do without you? We will watch over Pena."

"Oh, thank you. The Ormonds seem to be very nice, do you agree?"

"Yes, Ana, they seem very nice. I hope you will be happy working for them." Mother Superior rose, embraced Ana lightly, kissed her cheek. "Go with God, dear child. He shall keep you safe."

"Thank you, Reverend Mother, goodbye." Ana wiped her tears on her apron and backed toward the door.

"Thank you, Ana," the Reverend Mother said gently. "Goodbye."

After Ana had closed the office door and her footsteps had faded away down the long hall, Mother Superior lifted the Bible she'd lain over the stack of bills Stan Ormond had brought to her. That much money would keep the orphanage in food, bedding and clothing for the children. She could pay another cook to take over Ana's job.

She bowed her head to plead with Jesus to negotiate forgiveness from God because she knew it was wrong to send Ana with that man and his wife. She'd taken his money to convince Ana to leave the convent, knowing in her heart that he might not be an honorable man. He had offered even more if Mother Superior could convince Ana to leave Nina behind, but Mother had said no. After all, she had to live with herself.

3

TERESA 1971

At the market

Pia was pregnant the first time she showed up in Centro, the village within the city of Nogales. She may have been fifteen, she may have been twenty. It was hard to tell her age with that shawl draped to hide her face. Our mother told us Pia was hiding her harelip. Mama said she kept the tie on her peasant blouse undone so the village men could get a peek at her breasts when she bent over to display the eggs she offered for sale. Pia's best customers were the people whose laying hens she'd stolen the week before.

Two months after we first saw her hanging around on the market street where we sold souvenirs to tourists, she delivered a howling, squirrel-faced baby that looked both gringo and native. My mother's friends at the market said they'd seen babies like that before, from women who drank too much. We watched Pia wandering up and down the alleys on the market street a few days after the baby was born, like she was looking for somebody. Then we saw her talking to Favo, leaning close and holding on to his arm. She took a yellow envelope from him and gave Favo her dirty, blue striped bundle that stank of unchanged diapers and baby vomit.

Favo dealt in every kind of selling that happened in Nogales. Sometimes it was a baby monkey for a rich little girl to play with. Sometimes

13

it was a human baby like the one he bought from Pia for God knows what purpose. And whatever people did with their purchases was not Favo's concern. He found the thing the customer wanted and delivered it . . . for a price.

Lupe sold embroidered blouses she bought by the cardboard box-full. The blouses came from China in huge crates and could be bought for twelve pesos a box when the truck came to Nogales. Sometimes Favo brought them to Lupe for fourteen pesos a box, and Mama said it was probably all profit to him because he most likely stole them.

Lupe draped a faded yellow tape measure around her neck, and a small pair of brass scissors on a cord to snip off "Made in China" tags and stray threads. She hid the boxes under her canvas tarp to make a platform for her blouses and perched a plastic Virgin Mary statue on top. Maybe the Virgin Mary absolved her from wrongdoing.

Tourists watched her arrange the cheap polyester garments and murmured to each other, "We should buy one of her blouses. They're such nice fabric. She probably makes them herself. Embroiders them by kerosene lamp."

They'd ask loudly in their best high school Spanish accent, "Do you sew these yourself? Do you do the designs?" The woman tourist made sewing movements with her manicured hands and motioned to the scissors and tape measure. Lupe grinned at them. She didn't want to lie, so she'd wait. "Sew . . . " the woman said more loudly, "do you sew?"

Lupe bobbed her head enthusiastically, "Oh, si, si." Out came the wallet, and the husband bought one in every color for his wife, never haggling the price. Lupe nodded at the money and said, "Gracias, Gracias." The tourists walked away smiling at each other like they had done a great thing, buying hand-embroidered Mexican blouses from an impoverished woman. Lupe lived in a three-bedroom tract house on the hill with running water and a television. She bought her husband Sal a Toyota pickup. Lupe made a good living, buying low, selling high. I learned from watching her how to smile and not speak English. Of course, we all spoke English, but the better sales came from knowing when to just nod and smile at the gringos.

On Saturdays and Sundays we helped my mother at the market. She'd put on her long skirt with an exploding rainbow of colored ribbons sewn around each tier. The waist tie had tiny bells at the ends of the cords that sang with every move she made, and the fabric swayed in soft shushing sounds. I loved the sound of my mother's bell skirt. She sounded like angel music played on goat bells, far off in the hills.

Every Saturday morning Luna and I loaded the four-foot long, two-foot wide sheet of plywood on the red Radio Flyer wagon with baskets of souvenir maracas and castanets to sell to tourists. We put the loosely woven multi-colored, striped cotton blankets and printed wool felt ponchos over them and covered it all with our green canvas tarp. Mama pulled the wagon. I pushed from behind, going up the hill, and Luna carried Salma. We didn't need a car. It wasn't very far to the market street for us.

Salma probably got more people to stop and look at what we were selling than anything we did. By the time she was one year old, she knew how to sit her chubby little butt on a back corner of the canvas and coo and laugh and point at customers and blink her huge round eyes at them when they stopped to say something to her in Spanish. Mama gave her a single maraca to shake, and a tourist couple would buy a set of them for their own grandbaby, maybe several sets, so all the grandchildren would be able to drive their parents crazy on Christmas morning. If we had more blue maracas that week that was the color Mama gave Salma. If we had more of the grey striped blankets that week, Salma sat on a grey one. She was great advertising, that Salma. She showed off the goods, Mama took the money. I handed over the bag of purchases with a smile and a "Gracias" and Luna rearranged the display, humming "Celito Lindo" to get the attention of the next shoppers, two canvas tarps away. Those tourists loved hearing a melody they knew from an American corn chip commercial. They'd turn toward Luna's voice, and when they stopped at our tarp she'd go silent. They'd look around for the source of the only Mexican song they recognized, and soon as they'd look away, she'd start again and get them to look back at her. Luna's perfectly timed blush was an art form. I think the buyers thought they'd gotten a message from heaven to stop and buy.

Esmelia and Rosalinda were first cousins who made candies to sell especially to tourists. Their candy-making secret was to add salt—two tablespoons to each batch. Tourists tasted tiny samples of salted candy. They'd buy a paper bag full, realize they needed a drink, and pay double for Esmelia and Rosalinda's warm American sodas, or plastic bottles of water the cousins filled from the tap at the public rest room up the street.

People in the States go to a university to learn marketing tactics. Where I come from, every seller on the street knows the game.

Esmelia and Rosalinda had known Pia's mother and would tell anyone who'd listen the story of the woman going to Tubac to work as a housekeeper at a resort hotel. How she'd gotten pregnant by either the manager of maintenance or the gardener. How she'd been fired when her belly swelled. How she couldn't get another hotel job so she headed back to Mexico on foot.

The woman knew nothing but bad luck. She got caught by a border patrol agent who didn't believe she was trying to get out of the United States, not into the United States, and she offered a blowjob to be set free. He accepted her offer, kept her cuffed, and took her where another agent was parked in his truck. That agent took the offer too. The second agent thought she wanted to go to Tubac so he dropped her off near the same hotel where she'd just been fired, and she had to start all over again.

We'd see tourists sitting at tables covered with greasy vinyl tablecloths, cautiously trying an "authentic" tamale. They seemed to think if they sniffed each forkful, somehow they would be saved from food poisoning. Pia walked through the street tables at the cafes. She'd watch for tips left under the edge of a plate and grab them with hand movements so deft it was easy to believe she'd been a street urchin, pickpocketing her way through shoppers.

Esmelia told my mother that the reason Pia had a harelip was because God had punished her mother for those blowjobs. My mother told us that was not the reason. She said harelips ran in families. And that we should not marry a man with a harelip, to be sure our children would be beautiful.

GETTING OUT OF NOGALES

About two hours before dark, the streets begin to empty of gringo tourists.
They quicken their stroll to an almost running pace
once they hit the final corner,
and turn for the border gates.
That's where the street children are.
The kids with eyes ruined at birth
because of syphilitic prostitute mothers.
The poor things with a withered arm or leg or twisted spine,
mauled during delivery by adolescent siblings
who knew nothing about assisting a birth.
The bolder beggars rush the tourists.
The better-faced kids get in front of the women,
knowing that one time out of ten,
they'll be appealing enough to her for an American quarter.
Once the change purse comes out,
a dozen grubby faces close in, hands outstretched.
Some of the children offer a handful of well-worn candy
in dirty cellophane, pleading
"Señora, Chicklet? Chicklet? Penny."
No one pays only a penny for candy
and no tourist takes the trade-worn sweets with them.
Recycled merchandise makes the world go around on the final stretch,
getting out of Nogales.

4

TERESA 1971

Mama got a letter

My mother said she knew Maria when they were girls. They'd gone to the same school. Maria lived on a ranch in Arizona and took care of the home of a wealthy American, doing things so the wife didn't have to do anything but get her hair done, or her nails done, or whatever she could have done instead of doing for herself.

Mama got a letter from Maria and read it to Luna and me. Maria wanted Mama to come to the ranch in Arizona to cook for the rich Americans she worked for. There was a part in the letter where Maria said Luna and I could help too, since I was twelve and Luna was fourteen. When Mama read how much money the Americans would pay, she had Luna read that line out loud so she was sure what it said. Mama folded the letter and told us we would be moving to Arizona.

Maria sent a map with her letter, with a note on it that said when we got to Rio Rico, in Arizona, Mama was supposed to call her on a pay phone at the gas station. Maria would drive down to pick us up.

That night, Mama showed the letter to our father.

"Did she send money?" he asked.

"Why would she send money? I haven't done any work yet," she said. Mama went out the back door, and stood leaning against the fence, looking at the sky. My father copied the map Maria had sent on a paper bag. He put it in his shirt pocket and left.

When Mama came back in the house, she told us to decide what we wanted to take with us to Arizona because we'd leave in a couple of weeks.

She said it would take two days to get there, and we'd sleep outside in our clothes. Luna and I wanted to tell our friends about the adventure, but Mama told us to keep quiet, so we did, or at least Luna did. I told my best friend Paco from school, because I knew he didn't talk to the other kids. Paco said he'd miss me, and he wished he could go with us.

Mama sent a letter to tell Maria she'd take the job, then told our father if it worked out he could come in a few months, maybe get a job at the ranch too.

My father was supposed to be there helping us the night we started out for Tubac, Arizona, but Mama found out he was drunk and holed up in a shack with Pia. Mama tipped the washbasin onto the bed in case he brought Pia back to the house. After that, I don't think she ever wanted to see him again. We left home after dark, so no one would see us leaving with our backpacks.

Four hours later, Luna and I were huddled around Salma, sobbing. Luna stayed with Salma while I walked downstream, hoping I'd find my mother alive, clinging to the tree that grabbed her. The rain stopped like someone had shut off the faucet. By the time I got back where we'd come out of the water, Luna had all Mama's things laid out on the sand. She was using the flashlight to look at the map from Maria. How could she be looking at a map while our mother was missing?

I was trying not to cry. Trying wasn't working. "What do we do now?"

"We need to find Maria. That's what we do now." Luna folded the map and put it away.

"I think we should go back—"

"No, Teresa, we are not going back. Do you want to drown? We keep moving and get to Maria. She'll know what to do," Luna snapped.

"But if we go back, someone can help us and—"

"And what?" she said. "I'm not going back. And if we stay here, the border patrol will catch us. I'm not going to have any harelip babies."

5

ANA 1948

Grey-green-eyed Jesus

Aunt Pena didn't fight Ana's decision to go work in Arizona, but she cried all the same when Ana came from her room with a bag of clothing slung over her shoulder. Uncle Ancho tried to give Ana some money. She refused to take it. She had half the money her new boss had given her in her bag with her rosary and had left the other half on her bed for Pena to find. Ana kissed Pena and Ancho and said, "Time for me to go."

Pena backed away from Ana, feeling for her rosary. Ana was going to the States with people Pena had never met, and as far as she knew, she wouldn't ever see her niece and Nina again. Pena mashed her cotton handkerchief into a soggy clump and set her lips in a straight line. Ancho's stroke-ruined face hung slack, and drool and sadness poured from the left side. Ana hoisted Nina on her hip, swung her bundle of clothes behind her, and walked away.

She hoped the Ormonds would come down this street, see her, and pick her up before she reached the convent so she wouldn't have to go to the place where the blessed Virgin was probably waiting for her to come back, so she could dare Ana to repeat what she'd said. And Ana didn't want to have to face poor, forlorn Jesus again.

21

The Ormond's black car was parked at the convent. Stan Ormond leaned against the hood, looking down the street. His wife, Lorene, sat in the car watching him. Neither saw Ana approach until Nina squeaked at her own reflection in the car's back window.

Lorene smiled and started to open her door, but Stan quickly stepped around the passenger side to push the door shut. Lorene looked at her lap. He opened the back door and motioned to Ana to get in the car while he put her things in the trunk.

"Hello, Señora Ormond," Ana said.

"Hello, Ana," Mrs. Ormond whispered. She didn't turn to look at Ana.

Stan got behind the wheel, put his hand on the rearview mirror and adjusted it to watch her settling into the back seat. Ana could see only his grey-green eyes. Without a word to Ana, or a glance at Lorene, he drove away from the convent. The car lumbered, rocking and complaining, over dirt roads made by human feet, burro hooves, and wooden carts. Ana watched the marketplace slip by. Saw two women she knew. Saw them cover their mouths to whisper to each other as the car rolled away from Centro.

A half hour later he spoke, watching Ana in the rearview mirror.

"I've got something for the baby to make her sleep. We have a long way to go. It's better if she's quiet." Ana glanced from the grey-green eyes in the mirror, to Lorene, and saw Lorene's shoulders stiffen.

"I can keep her quiet, Señor Ormond."

"Yes, of course you can," he answered, "But it'll be best if Mrs. Ormond holds her at the border crossing."

They rode in silence again, Lorene sitting stiffly, never speaking to or looking at Ana. Ana thought that, for a woman who'd been so friendly when she'd asked Ana to work for them, her behavior was odd.

Stan pulled the car off the road at the first border crossing sign and turned in his seat to talk. "We're going to do this right, Ana, so they don't ask questions. I don't want any arguments, all right?"

"Yes," Ana answered.

"I do the talking. Do you know why, Ana? You can't speak. You can't hear. You're deaf and dumb. Do you understand? Lorene will hold your baby. I'll explain that we adopted both of you at the orphanage, and if they ask you anything, you don't hear, or speak, or understand."

Lorene got out, opened the back door and took Nina. Nina laughed when Lorene swung her around to take her to the front seat. Lorene unwrapped something that looked like a chocolate candy and slipped it into Nina's mouth.

"See that white shift?" Stan said, indicating a folded garment on the seat, like the ones the children wore at the convent, "Put that on, and for heaven's sake, cover your chest. You're twelve years old today. Do you understand?"

"But Señor—"

"Hush. Not one more word. Be a good girl now. Let's get this over with."

At the border, a uniformed agent waved for them to stop. He leaned closer to see into the car when Stan rolled the window partly down.

"Good afternoon, officer," Stan began. His voice was cheerful. "What do you need from me today?"

The agent's gold eyetooth glinted and the mole on his cheek sported an oily sheen. He leaned down to consider Lorene holding the little brown baby, then studied Ana. His eyes fell on her chest, mercifully covered by the muslin shift she wore over her best dress. Ana kept her eyes on her bare legs.

"My wife and I adopted this little child," Stan explained, motioning to Nina. Nina played with the collar of Lorene's dress. "The one in the back is the older sister. Poor thing is deaf and dumb. We wanted to give her a better life than being a beggar. Better in our country than yours, eh?"

The agent's eyes met Stan's, and he rested his fingers over the three inches of window. Stan's left hand remained on the wheel, but with his right, he slid folded money under the agent's hand. The agent gazed at Lorene's clean, white throat as his fingers closed around the bills. He tapped the window glass with a heavy gold ring.

"Good day, señor, señora, thank you for visiting Mexico."

Stan drove forward and another agent waved him through.

"Keep still, don't look back," Stan muttered, without looking at Lorene or Ana.

He drove a few minutes then pulled over. "Okay, Lorene, that's enough." Lorene opened the door and slid out, holding Nina close to her. She reached for the back door and Ana tried to help by pushing the door handle, but the door wouldn't budge. "Let her do it," Stan said.

Lorene swung the door open, gave Nina to Ana, then returned to her seat and smoothed the front of her dress. Ana could see the shoulder of Lorene's dress was damp with Nina's sweat and drool. Nina was limp, half asleep. Ana turned her daughter so she was facing forward. Ana didn't look at the rearview mirror. She didn't want to meet those grey-green eyes.

Stan drove another half hour, then stopped at a gas station.

"Leave the baby in the car, Lorene. Take her in when you bring Ana back."

Ana and Lorene walked to the door with the green-and-white hand-painted sign that said "Ladies" with a silhouette of a woman in a dress beneath the word. Lorene busied herself with fluffing her hair while Ana used the toilet first.

"Stay in here with me or we'll both be in trouble," Lorene said, while she shimmied her dress and slip up.

Ana looked in the mirror and saw a girl she scarcely knew in a white orphanage shift. She saw that she did look twelve years old right now. She turned on the tap, and splashed water onto her neck and face.

Lorene came from the stall, adjusted her dress, and used a paper towel from the roller above the overflowing trash basket to dab water on her temples and back of her neck. "Ana, he just knows best, and I need to do better at doing what's best." She fixed her lipstick.

Ana smiled. She'd stay silent. She'd get to her new home, her new job, and it would be worth the strangeness of this trip.

At the car, Ana lifted Nina from her sleep on the back seat and gave her to Lorene. "We'll be right back," Lorene said, as though it were the most natural thing in the world to take another woman's child to the restroom, while the mother was right there. Ana slid into the seat to wait. The grey-green eyes watched her in the mirror.

"You can take that shift off, Ana. You were a good girl to do as I told you. You see, there were no problems. I treat the border agents right, and they treat me right. If you do as you're told, it makes life so much easier." Ana watched the green-and-white restroom door.

Lorene came out leading Nina by the arm. Nina stopped to point to a dog that was picking at a flattened crow carcass on the road. Lorene put her hand to her mouth as though she were surprised, lifted Nina, and Nina squealed happily. Lorene saw Stan watching her and hurried to the car, deposited the child in the back seat with Ana, then quickly got into her place in the front. The black car growled to life and took the Ormonds and their new cook back out to the road. The Ormond car always did as it was told.

They stopped at another gas station an hour later, and Stan let Lorene take Ana to the restroom, while he went to the cafe across the highway and bought food. He handed sandwiches wrapped in waxed paper to Lorene and Ana. He brought a thermos of water and paper cups from the trunk of the car.

Ana wanted to drain her cup of tepid water in one gulp, but saved part of it for Nina. The sandwich was like nothing Ana had ever seen: pale-tan-crusted white bread cut diagonally, stuffed with chopped hard-boiled eggs, lettuce, small bits of pickles, and a white sauce that held it all together. She'd eaten half the sandwich before she noticed Lorene smiling kindly, offering a paper napkin.

"Thank you," Ana said, taking the napkin.

Stan stood outside the car to eat with his hip against the door. His trousers had an odd sheen on the back, shiny from sitting.

Nina woke up sniffing at the air as if she were searching for a scent. She saw the sandwich and moved closer to her mother. Ana tore the last half of the egg salad sandwich and handed a piece to Nina. Ana laid the remaining piece on the waxed paper.

Stan got back in the car. "How's the sandwich?" he asked brightly, not addressing either Ana or Lorene directly.

"Oh, just wonderful, dear. That was so nice." Lorene answered.

"Thank you, Señor Ormond," Ana said. Ormond looked at little Nina for the longest time.

"She needs more. She looks thin to me."

"I think this will be enough, but thank you," Ana said.

"I think in Mexico, you people are so used to starving, you think it looks normal," he said in steady cadence.

Ana didn't know how to answer. Nina was a healthy little girl.

Lorene fished around in the paper sack and brought out the half sandwich she had rewrapped and put away.

"She can have this half of mine. I can't finish it." She handed the wax papered sandwich half to Ana.

The sky lost its colors as the sun slid behind the mountains. They drove north. Nina slept across Ana's lap, clutching a crescent of bread crust to her cheek. Ana let her eyes close, her hand on her daughter.

She was in the chapel at the convent. Jesus had come down from his cross, hands and feet bleeding, to sit beside her. She leaned against him and felt his warmth.

"Ana, you know I will never leave you, but you have to talk to me about things. Do you understand?

"Yes," she tried to whisper, but her lips were sealed over.

"The Virgin is very angry, Ana. She told the Mother Superior what you said to her, and the Mother Superior is angry that you would talk to the blessed Virgin in such a way." Jesus stood. The blood that had pooled in his lap from the wound in his side slithered like a bloody snake down one bare leg. "I never asked to die this way, Ana, but my father didn't stop it. He could have saved my life, but he looked away while they killed me. My mother could have done something, but she let me die. I should have run, should have hidden. They could have stopped it. Why didn't they, Ana?"

Ana wanted to tell Jesus that she too felt betrayed by the Virgin but she was sorry about what she'd said in the chapel.

"My father is rich, Ana, but he lets some people have more than they deserve, and he lets others who work hard suffer. I would give them all everything they need. But the Virgin wants them to suffer. She wants you to suffer."

Ana reached for Jesus's hand, saw that the bloody place where the nail had been was only red paint. Her words came out choked and hoarse.

"I do not want to suffer. I want my daughter to have a better life than mine."

Jesus rolled his head to the heavens, looking for an answer from God, the way he had on the cross when he made one last appeal for his life.

"Why do you not hear me?" he whispered. Ana didn't know if he was speaking to God or to her.

Ana looked for the Virgin Mary's statue. It was gone, and Ana saw her rosary where the folds of the Virgin's plaster robe had rested on the platform. Ana tried to reach for her rosary, but her arm wouldn't move. Jesus held her by her wrist. "That rosary is not going to help you now, Ana."

Ana turned to face Jesus.

He closed his eyes and leaned close. "Only I can save you now."

She raised her eyes to meet Jesus's eyes and he opened them. Her mouth felt glued shut. Her small scream stifled itself behind her lips. Jesus's eyes were grey-green.

She awoke with her heart pounding as the car bounced over the cattle guard at the entrance to the Ormond ranch.

"Wake up, everybody. We're home," said Stan Ormond in the voice of the grey-green-eyed Jesus.

FEATHERS, SPURS, AND BEAKS

Arizona has baseball spring training camp.
Devoted fans can watch the toll as coaches sort
draft picks and minor leaguers hoping to move up to the majors.
Players don't go down in a blaze of wounded glory in baseball.
They are either traded down into obscurity or retire.
Baseball fans don't crave blood.
Sonora has cockfighting.
Roosters win, are wounded, or killed.
There is no retirement plan for a rooster
primed and dosed to fight to victory or death.
Fans who crave betting on feathers, spurs, and beaks
are there for the blood.

6

TERESA 1971

One good rooster

My father raised fighting cocks. He kept a dozen scarred-up roosters tethered in our yard, each with a wood crate or oil drum for shelter from the sun and from the other scruffy birds. They tried to kill each other every chance they got.

He'd owned only one good rooster in his life; a broken-winged, one-eyed old boxer that spurred like a bird half its age and twice its worth. That rooster got stolen and even Favo—who my mother said was probably who stole it—said he could not find it. We heard the rooster was fighting in California, taking down well-bred opponents. That rooster, fueled by cartel cocaine in its life after kidnapping, had become a legend.

My mother, sisters, and I didn't go to cockfights, but we fed roosters and kept their water cans filled. Luna and I sacked the birds going to fighting matches, with the roosters' eyes covered with our hands to keep them from flogging us while we put them in burlap sacks. Four or five birds went to the fights. Sometimes only one or two came home.

There would be new roosters on the tethers the next week, eating chunks of fat and meat mixed in their grain. They'd watch us so closely, I wondered if they were planning to pounce and tear us up with their beaks and spurs. When I was very young, I had nightmares that roosters chased me to the corner of the dusty yard, where no one could hear my screams. Their combless heads jabbed at me, while they screeched death chants.

One night, when she was eleven years old, Luna followed our father to a match. The woman who sold painted wood marionettes at the market was sitting at the entrance, and she waved Luna in without asking for money.

Our father was getting a rooster ready, ruffling and shoving it at the other rooster. It was Luna's favorite rooster. It had a white slash of feathers on one side of its back. That rooster was the only bird that had ever taken food from our hands.

The starting signal was given. Luna saw the roosters rise and fall in a fury of clipped feathers. Barely four seconds had passed when the white-backed rooster Luna had fed by hand stopped flapping and spurring. Its breast was opened up like it was sliced by a razor. The fight was over. The handler of the victor held his rooster overhead. Papa unfastened the fighting spurs and tossed the dying bird in a barrel at the edge of the ring. Even through the din of hooting and jeers, Luna heard the rooster she'd cared for make a final rattling crow.

Mama scolded Luna when she came back to the house. "You should not have gone there, Luna. It's not safe for a young girl. Don't do that again."

Luna never did.

I was sure there had to be some money in cockfighting; my father just didn't know how to win at it. There were other men around where we lived who raised roosters and I knew all their kids, so if their fathers were in the yard tending roosters, I paid attention. He didn't take all the care they did. If my father ever made money fighting roosters, Mama never saw a peso of it.

But he'd show up in new clothes and with food for Mama to cook for him. Sometimes he smelled of Aqua Velva aftershave, and sometimes he smelled like the gutter. Once we came home from the market with our wagon, and as we came in the front door, we heard the back door open. Our father bolted into the front room with no shirt on, and Mama ran toward the back door, cursing. He grabbed her by the shoulders and shook her and told her she was being stupid. Then he grabbed a clean shirt off the clothesline and took the coin purse from our market supplies. He said he'd go get some meat for dinner, and we didn't see him until the next day.

Sometimes we'd see our father talking to Favo and, when he'd see us, he'd turn his back to us. Favo was never up to any good. Maybe our father wasn't either.

One day, after school, I saw my father in an alley giving a paper-wrapped packet to a man in a car with tinted windows. I told Luna to go on, that I'd forgotten something at school, and I doubled back to follow my father. He was easy to spot that day in his white shirt with bull heads embroidered on the back. He went into a bar that had a spray painting on the outside wall of a fat naked blonde woman sitting on a donkey. The donkey had a dumb smile on its face.

The smell of beer and smoke drifted out over the top and bottom of the bar door. I heard laughter and yelling, heard a donkey braying, then grunting, more laughter from the men. I went to the door and could just see over the top. My father was standing with his back to me, hooting, making donkey sounds, waving his beer bottle in the air. A big-bellied man led another donkey, painted like a zebra, into the room. Men pointed and laughed. The donkey stumbled when it lurched up on the platform in the middle of the room. A huge woman was lying naked on a bench on the platform.

I didn't tell my mother. I didn't know how to tell her what I'd seen. But I knew then my father was not a good man. I hoped he wouldn't come home that night.

He did come back that night, drunk. My mother pushed him out the door, saying he stank like beer and smoke. Luna started crying, and that started Salma crying. I didn't cry. I wanted him to leave forever. I wouldn't miss him.

Paco was the quiet kid at school who made good grades. When school let out he'd hurry home to tend two fighting roosters his father had given him to raise. Paco and his father went to cockfights in the building where Luna had followed our father. I'd see Paco helping his father load rooster cages into a trailer behind their car, and he'd tilt his head at me instead of waving, since his hands were full.

"Hey Paco!" I said, one afternoon, "where are you going so fast?"

He slowed down to talk while he walked. "I have to take care of the roosters."

"I'll help you," I said. Paco shrugged. His father was working in a row of white painted A-framed shelters when we got there, and he looked questioningly at Paco.

"This is Teresa, she goes to my school." Paco's father nodded. Maybe he thought since I was a girl, I wasn't going to steal their secrets. He let me stay to help. The roosters in Paco's yard were stronger, with longer legs and clearer looking eyes than the fighters my father kept. I could tell they were good birds. I helped Paco feed the roosters and let my hand brush against his when I passed him the scoop.

We finished feeding, and I needed to hurry home. "Good luck tonight, Paco," I said as I headed for the chain link gate to the street. It would take some time to get in on the secrets, but I was a master saleswoman at the market, and I knew how agreeable boys were when a girl paid attention to them.

Paco showed me his notebook of schedules for putting the roosters in the fly cage to build muscle and endurance. My father had no fly cage. He didn't feed his birds well, and he always let their water get filthy. I paid attention at Paco's house when we mixed hard-boiled eggs and corn with pellets shipped from the States. I dusted roosters for lice, held wings for Paco's father to trim, kept my mouth shut and my ears open.

After I'd been helping a few weeks, Paco's father put two young roosters together to spar, so he could decide which to keep. The rooster he decided to let go for the stewing pot was a far finer rooster than my father had ever had.

One afternoon, Paco told me he was going to fight his best rooster and his father had told him if he wanted, he could bring me if I wouldn't be upset about the fighting and blood. I knew I'd get home later than I was supposed to, so I said, "I'll be right back," and ran to my house. My mother was in her room humming to herself, and came out wearing her nicest dress.

"Ah, Teresa, there you are, Luna and Salma are already at your grandmother's place. Your father and I are going to a party. We'll be late, so you stay overnight at your grandmother's."

"Mama, Paco's mother asked me for dinner. Can I go there first? I'll go to Grandmother's after that." I was sort of lying but sort of not. I mean, I was going to Paco's house.

"Oh, that's nice, have fun," Mama said. "Don't stay too late."

I hurried to my room, put a change of clothes and my nightgown in my pack with my hairbrush and toothbrush. Walking from our bedroom to the living room, I stepped on a lip gloss Luna had bought at the market. Well, if I left it on the floor, someone would step on it and break it. I opened the sticky plastic cap and smelled the oily cherry scented gloss. In the little mirror on the side of the container, I saw that my lips surely should have some cherry-scented lip gloss to go to a cockfight with my best friend. I smeared some on. Luna should be glad I'd picked it up off the floor.

I ran back toward Paco's, but walked when I was two houses away so I wouldn't look so excited. Paco's mother opened the door when I came through the wire front gate.

"Hello Teresa, I hear you're going with the men tonight. Come in, have some dinner with us."

The table in the kitchen was covered with a new cloth. Paco's mother put a stew pot of spicy, simmered pork and hominy posole and a dish of rice on the table. Her plates and bowls were the color of limes, all matching. Paco and his father came in from the back yard, happy and talking about their roosters. Paco's younger sister, Carmen was already sitting at the table, holding a picture of a puppy she'd colored at the special school she went to.

Paco's mother motioned for me to sit beside Carmen, who waved her artwork at me and I told her it was beautiful. Carmen's sharp greyhound face, sprawling teeth and downward tilted eyes were strangely peaceful. She pushed the picture toward me with her boney hand. Carmen acted like she was three years old, not seven. "She wants you to have it." Paco said, smiling kindly at his sister.

"Wuuund," Carmen said. Maybe Carmen had the best life of all. She'd be cared for. Everyone would always love her pictures. She'd always be a child to her family.

Paco's father wasn't drunk the way my father always was. He wasn't angry at everybody in the world the way my father always was. He told Paco's mother how well-prepared Paco's rooster was for his first match, and that he had a few others to take, but we'd be back early. My father never came home from cockfights early.

Paco and I helped his mother clear dishes, then she waved us away from the sink. "I can do this. You two get ready to go." We practically bolted out the back door.

Paco's father's car was parked alongside the gate, with a red and yellow trailer hooked up, and wooden boxes for roosters were stacked with the doors facing out for loading. Paco and I took birds, two at a time to the trailer to box them. Paco stopped to stroke his rooster's iridescent breast then slid the wooden door down and latched it. Paco seemed unsure whether to sit in front with his father or to get in the back with me, but that was solved when Paco's father's friend Chulo arrived and sat in the front seat.

When we got to the cockfight arena Paco and I stayed with the trailer while the older men went inside. Paco kept looking through the holes in the box at his rooster, telling him not to worry. When we unloaded the boxes and took them inside, the smell of chickens, smoke, dust, and blood was so strong it made me gag. Paco coughed a lot and kept spitting while he was lining up the boxes in a row. Chulo checked the legs of the birds that would fight first, wrapped their sanded-down spurs with tape, then as each one was ready to take to the ring, he and Paco's father put on the fighting spurs. They warned us to not let the roosters' feet near our faces or arms once they had their spurs on, and I listened. I didn't want to get cut, and I wanted to prove I was as brave as any boy there.

Paco excused himself to go outside after Chulo helped him get his bird spurred. He came back with the odor of vomit on his breath. It was time to take his rooster to the ring.

He held the bird he'd raised and helped train as loose as he dared, to taunt the other rooster. The opponent was held by a teenage boy with a pock-marked face. They put the roosters in a two-part cage with mesh between them and hoisted it three feet above the sand. The birds were dropped in a blur of neck feathers and open beaks. I held my breath.

The fighters shoved their chests at each other and raised and lowered themselves just like they were doing a dance, until the other bird flew at Paco's. The referee stepped in and motioned to Paco. Paco rushed forward to grab his rooster by the legs. I almost cried with relief that the fight was over.

Paco's rooster had backed away from his competition. Paco's father told Paco it was all right, there would be another day. Paco looked a little sad while he unspurred and re-caged his rooster. That night four of the six roosters Paco's father fought won. One lost when it was injured. Another was killed.

We dropped Chulo at his house, then they dropped me off at my house. I was going to get my things and walk over to my grandmother's but my parents were already back home. My mother was at the kitchen window and saw the car pulling the trailer loaded with chicken crates. Mama waited 'til I'd come in and closed the door to say anything.

"Ah, Teresa, how was dinner with Paco's family?"

"Fine, nice," I said, trying to understand what was going on.

"Good, good, they are nice people. You are probably tired, time to get to bed."

"Yes, goodnight Mama. Goodnight Papa."

I escaped to my room. Mama knew where I'd been but she didn't say anything. I didn't ever want my father to know I'd been helping the Dominguez family with their roosters. I also knew that even if I liked Paco, I didn't want to go to the cockfights with him anymore.

7

TERESA 1971

In the dark

Salma began sobbing in a high-pitched hiccup when we held her between us, crying over our lost mother. She had gone silent by the time I got back from looking downstream. After we decided to follow the map to Rio Rico, Salma stopped acting like a four-year-old and became some child we didn't know. She had shrugged out of her wet clothes and didn't want to wear the extra T-shirt and pants Mama had packed for her. I gave up on getting clothes on her and told her she had to at least wear her shoes and panties.

Luna draped Salma's wet clothes over our packs, handed Salma her red and blue backpack, and told her she had to carry her own things. Salma shrugged the straps onto her bare shoulders without a word. I carried Mama's pack on my chest. It smelled like her hair.

We walked without the flashlight, staying far from the shapes of ocotillo and mesquite. A feral dog, maybe a coy-dog, slunk away from a stinking mound of remains that had been something larger than a jack rabbit. A crow cackled a warning in the dark.

Luna walked ahead and I stayed close to Salma to make sure she didn't get her bare legs into cholla, but then I got one of my pants legs covered with jumping spines. Luna got mad at me when I had to stop and change into my other pants.

Everything we knew was behind us, nothing would ever be the same. Our mother was lost. Probably dead. I knew Luna was right about going on. Maria was expecting us and we had American quarters to use in a pay phone to call her.

We were already at the point of no return.

Every somewhere else
glows with promise of something better.
And beyond the glow
is someone looking
toward yet another somewhere,
hoping for the same.

Luna and I kept our eyes on the lights of a town and walked north. We'd get to the top of a hill and find the lights as far away as the last time we'd seen them. Salma walked for two hours before she got tired and started slowing down. But even then, she didn't whine or cry.

We stopped to rest. Salma tried to walk away from us when we pulled her pack off her bare shoulders. The night was cool, and Luna wanted to get some clothes on her. Salma stared off into the night as we pushed and pulled her into her clothes. Luna told her to lie down and go to sleep, so she lay across her pack on her stomach, looked dully at us, then closed her eyes. We lay down on either side of Salma, and Luna was asleep before I even laid my head on my pack.

I dreamed I was in the kitchen with Mama. She was flipping tortillas on the flat tin sheet she kept by the stove. She had a pan of sizzling, snapping pork pieces on the back burner.

I woke up. We couldn't have slept more than a few minutes. Luna was on her side, curled around her grey and black pack with her hair hanging over her face. Salma's little red and blue backpack was between us, but Salma was gone. I yelled Luna's name and she bolted from sleep like she'd been hit by lightning. I pointed at Salma's pack.

Luna was on her hands and knees, patting the sand around her, like she could find our sister that way. We grabbed each other's arms.

Luna sounded as scared as I was. "You stay here. I'll go around the bushes. I'll find her."

My throat was tight. Luna stepped into the shadows and disappeared like a ghost. I closed my eyes and wished this part—in the desert, looking for Salma—was the dream and what was real was back in Centro, in the kitchen where our mother was cooking.

Luna called to Salma from out in the darkness, and between her voice and where I stood, a branch snapped. Every hair on my arms stood up.

"Luna, is that you? Luna! Stop that . . . Luna . . . "

A whitetail deer bolted from an acacia thicket and bounded across where we'd been sleeping. Its cloven feet punched and sprayed sand across Salma's pack. A dry rustling came from the same thicket and I froze.

"Is she with you?" Luna yelled. I couldn't answer, couldn't breathe, certain there was a jaguar or a wolf chasing the deer. I turned to face death. My pack was at my feet. I swung it by one strap at the parting branches ten feet away. The pack hit Salma right in the head as she walked into the clearing and knocked her down. She sat blinking for a few seconds, and then her face scrunched up. Her wailing brought Luna running.

"Why did you do that?" Luna yelled, and jerked Salma up by her arm.

"I thought . . . I thought . . . " I sobbed. Luna brushed sand off Salma's pants, and said a curse word when she saw Salma had wet herself.

Luna swatted her behind and shouted, "Don't you ever do that, don't you ever."

Salma sat on the ground, maybe to hide her bottom from another swat, maybe to surrender.

Luna crumpled to the ground and wrapped her arms around her legs. She looked up at the clouded moon, cursed, covered her face and cried into her hands.

The sky was lightening when we began walking again, so we finally knew for sure which way was east.

In the light, we saw mountains to the northwest and a white flag moving in the breeze far off in the northeast. Luna studied the map from Maria. Then she showed me that a road lay ahead somewhere, but she could not tell how far it was. The map said a mountain shaped like a sheep's head was our landmark to find the road. All we could see was a range of mountains, and not one looked like a sheep. We knew we were supposed to stay out of sight when daylight came. But Maria's drawing on the map showed a tower that said "AQUA."

The water bottles in our packs were still empty. We'd carried them that way and meant to fill them after we'd crossed the border. We hadn't filled them. My mouth, throat, and eyes felt as dry as a spider web. Luna, bossy as ever, said we were going to the tower for water. I'd have gone anyway.

We'd been told there were people in Arizona who know that people who cross the desert need water even if they are breaking the law. They make no judgment of those who come into the United States. They only wish to be kind. They leave water in plastic gallon jugs at the towers.

We kept losing sight of the tower as we walked. The high brush and saguaro were always hiding it from view. Luna stopped to look at the map and turned around to try to find the sheep head mountain again. I barely breathed while she looked at a trail that went off to one side. I was afraid if we strayed from the path that seemed to go to the tower we'd be lost. I was afraid we'd be wandering until we died and wild dogs came to carry off pieces of us.

Luna began veering north.

"This way," I said. "Let's stay where people have walked."

She slowed down without looking at me, and got back on the path. Salma walked soundlessly between us. We never let her out of our sight.

We walked forever—or maybe only an hour—in the desert, aiming for the tower flag. I wanted to stop to rest, but Luna was marching along like a soldier, following a path littered with clothes, pieces of tinfoil, a child's shoe, a pair of tiny socks, a faded backpack. An empty water bottle. A dead cat.

Salma slowed down, and without a word, pulled her pants to her knees and squatted. "Wait . . . " I called to Luna. Salma whimpered as she peed into the sand, and I smelled sharp, pungent, concentrated urine. She made a small cry as she finished, and stayed crouched, like she didn't want to get up. "She needs water," I said.

"Come on," Luna said. I helped Salma get her pants up and we kept going, but I wasn't trying to catch up with Luna. The sun was high and the sky was blue-green with no clouds. Where was the rain that had changed our lives the night before? I listened to the crunch of our sneakers on the crusty earth, then something else in the distance: a dull metal on metal sound, a thump, the sound of a man's voice. I grabbed the back of Salma's shirt and pulled her into a thicket of creosote and acacia. I heard the shooshing sound of shoes in the sand ahead of us and hoped the person running our way was Luna.

Luna looked around wildly as she came into view. I gave a single, low whistle, and she charged toward us. She dove into the brush and slammed into me, gasping for air. We backed further into our hiding place. A man in a tan shirt and pants came into the clearing from the direction Luna had come. We kept our heads down. Even Salma held her breath. He stopped a few steps from us, looking around the skyline, like there was something at the tops of the trees he was looking for. He took his hat off to wipe his forehead. He wore a gun in a holster. A green water bottle hung in a leather sleeve on his belt. He slid the bottle from the holder, opened the cap, put it to his lips.

There was a crackling sound in the direction he'd come from, and a voice. He put the bottle back in its holder, and walked toward the scratching, muffled voice. Something that had been attached to his uniform shirt slid free, bounced off his holster, and fell to the sand. Its tiny sound was lost in the wind but the little object glinted in the sun. I kept my eyes on it.

We heard him speaking, then heard the other crackling voice answer, and heard the truck's engine start. The wheels crunched away and when we couldn't hear the truck any more we crept out of our hiding place.

"Let's get water and get off the trail," Luna said. Her voice was low, like she thought the brush and weeds might tell on us. I stopped where the object had fallen from the man's uniform and picked up the rectangular gold pin with letters embossed and darkened across the front. The clasp that should have held the pin was open. It said "Sanchez." I slipped the pin into an outer pocket of Mama's pack, fell in line behind my sisters, and hoped there would really be water at the tower.

We saw the flag again, with its fabric popping in the wind, and ran toward it. At the base of the tower we drank half a jug of water each before we stopped. We filled our bottles and Luna took what food we had out of Mama's pack: a tin foil packet of tortillas, and four boiled eggs.

We decided to eat two of the eggs and share bites with Salma. Luna handed me a tortilla and a boiled egg, and she peeled her egg, and handed it to me to give Salma the first bite. Salma looked at me suspiciously and bit the end of the egg. She spat the piece out on the sand. Luna snatched it up, squeezed Salma's cheeks and crammed the sandy egg crumb between her teeth, then clamped her hand over our sister's mouth.

"You do not spit out food, do you understand? Swallow it, or we leave you here."

Salma fought like a wild animal, kicking and clawing at Luna. I sat on the ground, too tired to do anything but watch the struggle. My older sister had gone insane.

"Stop," I said quietly, "she's only a baby." Luna glared at me, shook Salma, and let go of her. Salma crawled away from us to sit among the water jugs. Luna coughed out a dry sob, but no tears came. I handed her a water jug.

I gave Salma half a tortilla to eat. I wrapped the other half in tinfoil and sat in the shade with a boiled egg, a tortilla, and a jug of water. Luna took her pack and the jug to another patch of shade. Salma watched her warily. I didn't want to think how far it was to the highway, and how we would get to the pay phone without being seen, or how we were going to tell our mother's friend Maria about our mother drowning.

I dozed off sitting on the baked ground, under wisps of pale acacia for shade.

I heard the rain, the river, the breaking branches, heard Luna's cries, heard my mother's voice saying,

"Take her."

I snapped awake when an ant found my bare ankle.

Salma poked at a sliver of her tortilla on the ground. I picked it up, and bushed the sand off, put it in her hand. "Please eat, please eat" and she obeyed, keeping her eyes on Luna.

Luna took the map from her pack and turned it three ways, studying it. It seemed her storm had passed. It was like we'd been reborn, from the food, from the water. There was a new-looking wooden ladder nailed to one side of the tower. Without saying anything to Luna, I started to climb. I didn't know anything about the marks on the map, but I needed to see what was out there.

Something Forbidden

Every day they arrive from the United States side of Nogales,
trying to look unhurried,
as though they are on an innocent, unplanned jaunt to the Sonoran side.
But their blood quickens
at the thought of finding something forbidden.
They are here to satisfy curiosity with a seamy adventure.
They bring money and judgment,
and leave both behind.

8

TERESA 1971

Favo

Favo could take you across the border, and it would cost you all the money you had—or it might cost you nothing, depending on what you could do for Favo. Mama hadn't asked Favo to take us over the border, it was our father who'd told him we were going. He told Mama to at least talk to him. Favo came to our house, and Mama made us stay inside while she went outside with her arms folded to talk to him. We could hear them.

"I'll make you a deal. You carry a chicken, I take you for a really good price. You swallow a couple of balloons, give them back when you get there it's half price."

"We won't carry chickens or swallow balloons. We're not mules. How much for me and my girls, to get us to Tubac?" My mother's voice was low.

"A hundred apiece, but you leave that oldest girl with me, it's not going to cost you nothing." When he said that, Luna and I peeked out the window.

My mother put her hands on her elbows. "You get away from my house, and don't you ever come back here." Only my mother could glare like that.

Favo backed away from her, grinning, and got in his cherry-red car.

"I'm offering a good deal. Maybe you should listen to your husband. Think about it."

Favo used people the way some people use a paper towel. I knew something was wrong with the way he did things but it was beyond my understanding when I was twelve. I knew he spent a lot of time with Pia, but Pia spent a lot of time with a lot of men. We'd been told that another woman Favo knew kept a supply of babies coming to Favo. She'd tell the neighborhood women they were nieces and nephews of relatives who had died and they'd left them to her, and she was taking care of them until they went to live with other relatives. She must have had relatives who were white, black, and Chinese. Favo picked them up to take them to their new "families."

In town, at the market, in school, there were whispers about people who went over the border. Some wrote to their families to say the work was good and sent money. Some were never seen or heard from again. We heard about border crossing coyotes that would take people's money, load them in trailers, and promise to drive them over, but would unhook the trailers from the trucks in the desert with people locked inside. Or they'd take their money, take them out in the desert, and shoot them.

"Mama, it won't hurt to carry some chickens, and I can come to Arizona later," Luna said.

"No, we will not and you will not, and don't you ever talk about that again. Never. Do you understand? And we are not mules," Mama said.

Well, that seemed like a dumb thing to me.

"Of course we aren't mules, that's silly," I said.

Mama looked at me, exasperated. "Teresa, it means he wants us to carry drugs for him. We're not going to do that for him or anyone else."

Mama had told us we'd just leave when the time was right. She stitched packets of money into her backpack after every market day for months. We never knew how much was in there.

One day, she told us to be ready to go soon. The next night when my sisters and I were in bed, we heard Mama telling our father he could come to the ranch to work there too. He laughed at her and started slamming things around in the room. Salma woke up and began to cry. Mama came in to pick her up. Mama was crying. She wiped blood off her lip with her apron.

She whispered, "We leave tomorrow night. After school, Teresa, you come right home, don't go to Paco's house. Don't tell anyone."

The next afternoon we saw Favo beside the car lot, leaning against his car. He wore a new shiny brown suit and pointed boots. His sunglasses reflected everything so you never knew where he was looking, but that day I knew he was looking at Luna and me. He jerked his chin at us as we went by.

"Hey Luna, want to make some real money, better than selling junk to tourists?" Luna stiffened, and slowed down a little.

"Keep walking," I whispered.

"It's only a matter of time, little *puta*," he said.

I grabbed Luna's hand and made her walk faster so she wouldn't answer. We stopped when we got around the next corner. She had tears running down her face.

"Why did he call you a whore?" I asked her. I knew it had hurt Luna. From then on, I hated Favo.

That night I saw Favo's car going really slow by our house. Maybe he thought Mama would change her mind. I told Mama he was out there, and she told me to stand out in front of the house, and whistle if I saw his car, but he didn't go by again. We went out through the back yard. Mama carried Salma, and Luna and I carried our four backpacks. Our market friend Lupe's husband, Sal—picked us up behind the church to drive us to a place where we could get through the fence and the wash. Mama tried to give Sal some money but he shook his head and patted Salma's cheeks, waved goodbye, and left us there.

Mama pushed us into the cover of brush. She looked at the night sky, looked at her map with her flashlight, and we started to walk.

The stars disappeared behind black and blue clouds, and we kept moving. That path took us to the gap in the fence, then to the wash.

That was where the early rain moved over us, and when the rain began God stopped helping and everything went wrong.

From then on, Luna, Salma, and I were on our own to either get to the place on the map in Arizona or give up.

And we didn't give up.

9

TERESA 1971

Another racetrack job

Our grandmother gave birth to our mother south of Juarez. The father was working as a racetrack groom at Sunland Park in New Mexico and our grandmother told her family he'd been detained when he slipped into Juarez to buy drugs for the racehorses he took care of, and maybe that was the truth. Or maybe he got another racetrack job further north, and it was easier to keep moving than to go back to his pregnant teenage girlfriend. He never did come back. Grandmother's family sent her to live with relatives in Centro.

Grandmother did get married, when I was eight years old, to a nice man who smelled like soap and aftershave all the time. He had a clothing store that sold party dresses and wedding dresses. I think our grandmother got her wedding dress for free when they got married. She opened her jewelry box and gave Luna and me each a rosary made from manzanita berries on her wedding day. Luna ran to show our mother.

I saw a plain gold ring in the box. I asked if it was a wedding ring and she said it was, that she used to wear it when our mother was little and then she gave it to me. She put it on a piece of string so I could wear it as a necklace. I always wore that gold ring, hidden under my clothes. It made me feel special, that I had her ring, like I was her favorite.

When Luna and I would see her, she'd ask us if we made good grades in school. She said she had enough money in the bank for us to go to a university, if we had good grades.

10

ANA 1948

The center of a valley

Lorene Ormond turned in the car seat to speak to her husband while Ana held on to Nina, who'd awakened and was fidgeting. Ana watched Lorene's profile against the dashboard lights. Lorene listened to her husband saying something in a low voice. Lorene's eyes flicked on Ana for a moment, then riveted on her husband's face again.

When the car left the main highway, Lorene turned to look at Ana, and began to speak in a low whisper Ana couldn't make out. Lorene raised her eyebrows as if to ask "Yes?" Ana studied the woman's face, so pretty in the moon and dashboard light. She had no idea what the woman had asked her but nodded "yes."

"Good," mouthed Lorene's lips.

The ranch house that lay in the center of a valley was aglow in the pale moonlight. Stan Ormond drove around it, stopped and got out. He tugged at the bottom of a wall, and a wide door swung upward.

"Stan is such a gentleman. I'd get the garage door, but he never lets me," Lorene said. Ana had never seen such a thing, a door for a car and people who put their car in the house.

Stan opened the trunk, got his and Lorene's bags, and left it open. "You can manage your things, can't you Ana?" Ana slid out, got her bag of clothes from the trunk and went back for Nina.

"Oh, I'll take her in, Ana," said Lorene. She had Nina awkwardly balanced on her hip. Nina jabbed her arm toward Ana, grasping at her. Lorene reached up, encircled Nina's wrist with a manicured thumb and first finger and brought the child's arm back. She hugged Nina tighter.

"Look, darling, she already knows me," she said to her husband.

Stan dropped the suitcases beside the door. "Give her back to her mother, Lorene. You're tired."

Ana took her daughter from Lorene, shifted her belongings so they hung from her forearm, and waited. Stan held the door open and Lorene went in.

"Here's the kitchen, where you'll work," Lorene said, beaming. The kitchen was the size of Aunt Pena and Uncle Ancho's whole house. "Let's get you settled in your room," Lorene said, taking a bracelet-sized key ring from her husband. She led Ana across the kitchen to another door and slid a key into a lock.

Ana followed Lorene down a carpeted hall with two doors on each side, and one at the end of the hall. Lorene pushed a door open. "This is your room, and there, see, we have a crib for your baby. The bath-room is at the end of the hall; you share with two other girls. You'll meet them tomorrow. One has a son a little older than your daughter. You'll like the other girls, you have so much in common."

"Oh, yes, thank you, Señora. Are they from Nogales? Centro?"

"Oh, gosh, I don't remember, but they're Mexican, so you'll all get along. See you in the morning." Lorene left, pulling the door shut be-hind her. Nina heard the door to the kitchen close, then the muffled metal sounds of the key ring, and the lock sliding into place.

There was a soft tap on Ana's door, and she opened it cautiously. A pregnant woman in a pink nightgown stood barefoot in the hall.

"We heard you were coming and got your room ready. I'm Suela."

"Hello," Ana said, not sure if she should ask her in.

"I'm coming in, and Maya will be here in a minute."

Ana backed up, holding Nina. Suela came in and sat on one of the wooden chairs at a small table.

"Where did you come from?" Suela asked.

"Centro," Ana said quietly, glancing at the open door to the hallway.

"It's okay, they lock the doors to the house, but in here, we keep ours open," Suela said, smiling at Nina. Another woman, perhaps thirty years old, was at the doorway.

"Shhh, I just got Rudy to sleep," she said in a loud whisper. "Hello, I'm Maya." She took a seat on the narrow bed.

"I'm Ana, this is my daughter, Nina," she said.

"Oh, so pretty," Maya said, "Will you get to keep her?"

"Keep her? She's my daughter." Ana replied.

"Oh, I just meant—" Maya started.

Suela shot Maya a hard look, and said, "Ana is the new cook for Señora Ormond, and she brought her daughter with her. With her from Mexico." She inclined her smooth brow toward Maya.

"Oh, that is wonderful! My Rudy will be happy to have a new friend to play with." Maya smiled broadly.

"You'll meet Gabriella in the morning. I work at the laundry and sewing room. I leave for work when she comes to open the kitchen," Suela said, getting up from the chair.

"What time should I go to the kitchen?" Ana asked, shifting Nina's drooping weight to her other hip.

"Gabriela will come get you, Ana. The door is locked anyway."

Suela and Maya moved toward the bedroom door.

"You can keep your door open at night, if you like, in case you need us. I hope you stay," Maya said.

Ana felt the long day in her shoulders and neck.

"Thank you. Will I get a key tomorrow?" Suela and Maya exchanged a look again.

"Good night, come to the door across from here if you need anything," Maya said, resting her ample hip against the open door. "You won't get a key, Ana. Only Gabriella and Señor have keys."

"Señor Ormond?" Ana whispered, laying Nina on the bed.

Maya smiled at Nina, "Yes, him. Are you a good cook?" she asked.

Ana thought to herself, what a strange question, I was brought here because I'm a good cook and answered "Yes, I am a good cook."

"Good," said Maya. "I'll see you tomorrow. I'll be working in one of the other houses, but I'll be back when my son is out of the nursery."

"He does not go with you?" Ana asked.

"No, he goes to the school, there are other children there whose parents work here, your daughter will go too, there is a place for the little ones," Maya said.

"Oh, my Nina can stay with me. She does not get in the way," Ana said, pulling a nightgown over her daughter's head.

"Señor will not allow that in the kitchen," Maya told her. "It's not done here."

"I am sure if I talk to him—" Ana started.

Maya interrupted, "Don't . . . don't start out asking for favors and you will not have problems here. I just want to help. You need to sleep now. Good night," Maya said, on her way out.

Ana heard Maya's door close and pushed her own door closed. Nina was draped on the bed, as though she'd melted there. Her round black eyes were half closed.

"Come on, little one, time for you to get in your own bed." Ana put Nina in the crib, pulled the light blanket over her and touched her forehead with one finger. "Sleep now. Tomorrow we have much to do."

Ana undressed and put on her plain cotton nightgown, picked up the towel and washcloth from the bedside table, and headed to the bathroom at the end of the hall to wash her face.

She looked at the tired woman in the mirror. The woman who, only the day before, had a good job for an unmarried woman, and hadn't had any plan except to survive. Now she was in a nice house with her own room, with walls and doors. It had a bathroom just for her and the two other women to use, instead of a communal ditch where buckets from houses were sloshed out twice a day.

Life was going to be very good for her in America.

11

TERESA 1971

Mama's things

"What are you doing?" I asked Luna. We'd drunk all the water we could hold, and our bottles were filled. "We're supposed to stop and find a place to hide when the sun comes up." Luna was stuffing things from Mama's pack into hers.

Luna pushed a pair of thin-soled shoes, a cotton blouse, a hairbrush and a water bottle toward me. "You take these." Mama's things.

"Why are you doing this? I'll carry Mama's pack. Stop it," I said.

Luna stopped for a second. "We need to lighten up. We'll take her things, but the pack is too much."

"No! it's not, I'll carry it!" I pleaded. She grabbed my wrist firmly.

"One pack each," she said. I understood. I emptied the pack I was carrying and loaded my things into Mama's pack.

Salma's little pack smelled sickeningly sweet and foul. I turned it over, and a dead yellow and brown chick plopped out with her things. Salma tried to grab it, but I beat her to it, and flung the body off into the brush. She made a face like she'd start screaming. Luna made a sharp hiss at her. Salma stared at Luna and me, made a fluttering noise when she sucked air through her mouth, and decided not to cry

We dumped sand into Salma's pack, and shook it around to get as much of the smell out as we could. Luna dropped in some sprigs of creosote weed before she put Salma's things back.

From the tower's ladder, I'd seen a break in the brush that looked like a road. The map showed a canyon near the tower, and the writing said, "place to stay during day."

"We'll keep walking," Luna said.

"And what if someone sees us?" I asked.

She shook her head. "Nobody will see us. We need to keep moving." Luna put her pack on and started out without waiting. I had no choice. I followed her. Salma stopped pouting over the dead chick and trotted to keep up with us.

When we stopped to rest, we crawled under the overhanging bank of a dry wash where someone had left an empty water bottle and a greasy pair of pants. I wondered why someone would take his pants off and leave them behind. I dragged the pants to one end of the wash and put the bottle in my pack.

"You and Salma rest, I'll watch. Then you watch while I sleep," Luna said.

The dirt bank wasn't cool, but it was shaded, and Salma nodded off with her head on her pack. I watched pale dry branches twitching in the hot gusts of wind. I wished for sleep and then I was home.

I was walking to school and saw Paco ahead. I ran to catch up. Paco turned and spoke in a voice that was not his at all. There was an ugly wound on his face from forehead to cheek, like a slash from a rooster's spur. The cut was black with dried blood at the top, but at the bottom, brown blood and pus oozed and dripped onto his collar. My hand went up to touch his face. He snarled like a street dog and ran away from me down a side street. At the end of the street a gang of children circled two roosters. One had its comb and feathers trimmed for fighting. The other, not trimmed, not a fighter, more like a rooster from some old woman's yard. The fighting rooster threw itself forward and sliced the air with its spurs, but its beak was bleeding. The gentle rooster stood, watching its death rush toward it. The fighter hit the yard rooster and fell over, gasping in its own blood. Its broken beak hung to one side of its head. The peaceful rooster looked down at its dying attacker, then raised its head to crow. It emitted a low screech, then another and another. Paco grabbed my arm and started shaking me, whispering, "Shhh, shhh, wake up." He touched my forehead and his hand felt dry and hot. His voice became Luna's and when I opened my eyes, the street was gone, the children were gone. Only the sound of the shrieking yard rooster remained.

"There's a windmill and a water tank. We're near a ranch or something," Luna whispered. She pointed up, and the sound of the windmill turning somewhere beyond the rim of the bank became clearer.

"There has to be a road that goes to the highway," Luna said.

"It might only go to a ranch and they might turn us over to the border patrol," I said.

"Come on," she said, shaking Salma awake.

We followed the sound to the windmill. The water in the tank was ugly clouds of dark green. Tire tracks circled the tower, and the brush opened to a road on one side.

"We'll walk on this road. If we hear anyone, we'll hide," Luna said. I looked at the painted markings on the windmill's rudder. We were tired, and as soon as we'd eaten our last two eggs and five or six tortillas, we'd be out of food. We dipped our cotton bandanas in the water. Luna took the map out of her pack and studied it. I knew she had no idea where we were. I offered to climb the ladder to see if I could find a paved road. Luna shook her head, shrugged her pack off and began climbing.

When she was half way up she stopped to look at her hand, like she'd gotten a splinter in her palm. Luna hung her elbow over the rung and used her teeth to pick at the palm of her hand. Salma sat down beside her pack in the little bit of shade beside the water tank.

A gust made the windmill shift direction, and Luna looked in the direction the blades had swung. She froze there for a second, then came scrambling down the ladder as fast as she could. When she hit the ground, she grabbed her pack, jerked Salma up by her arm, and said in a low, frightened voice, "Run!"

She never looked back. Salma pulled back but Luna clamped her grip on our sister and yanked. She dodged her way through brush and ran alongside a rusted out pickup frame.

"Down," she said. She pushed Salma against the truck's rotted tires. "Shhh . . ."

We waited. Luna waved her hand at me to stay down. She tilted her head to peer over the truck's door. She snapped back down, panting. Salma flopped over onto her pack and stared at Luna through tousled hair. Luna crawled to the side of the truck bed. She looked again, in the direction of the windmill.

When she ducked down again, she motioned for me to get the packs. I felt helpless but I hooked my arms through the straps. She jabbed her finger at the open truck door. I understood. I put the packs on the floor of the truck's cab. The door was open, though. They wouldn't be hidden. Neither would we.

Luna pulled a tumbleweed toward the truck door. I heard a low cough, then smelled the sulphur of a lit match. Then the scent of a cigarette. Two voices followed the cigarette smell. Luna looked frantic. She put her hand on mine, and mouthed, "Favo."

"I don't think they made it this far," said one of the men.

"Maybe not, but somebody wearing kid's shoes came this way, so we keep looking."

"Favo, there's lots of girls. Let's get some other ones."

"What? When did you ever pass up a girl, Victor, my friend? I say they are somewhere out here, and that mother of theirs isn't. No tracks for her. Those two older ones are mine, you can have the little one."

I tapped Salma lightly on the arm to get her attention and put my finger to my lips. Luna motioned to an opening in the brush, and I shook my head "no." We heard the grind of sand as the men walked around the tower.

"Climb up there and look around, Victor . . . you have to go higher than that." Victor muttered something. We heard a dull crack of wood, and Favo was laughing, and Victor was cursing. A sharper splintering sound. The thud of something hitting wood. A groan.

"You want to see, you climb, asshole," Victor shouted. "My arm is broken."

"You look like shit, Victor."

"Shut up." The voices moved further away.

"I'll drive." Doors closed, and the car started. I thought Luna was going to bolt, but she stayed with Salma and me. We flattened ourselves against the dirt, listening to the car moving away.

Luna closed her eyes for a moment; when she opened them, she said, "Stay here. The way they went is the way to the road." I watched her walk to the tower, and it was like she was sniffing the air. She went up four rungs on the ladder, to the broken one that hung from the frame and looked around. She motioned that we could come out.

"The road is that way," she said, "They turned on it. They're gone." We pulled our packs from the truck cab. A lizard scurried from under one of them.

Luna pulled one of the water bottles from her pack, drank, then handed it to me. Salma took it from me when I was finished, tipped it to her lips, and handed it back empty. Luna put the empty bottle in her pack. We each ate a tortilla. This time Salma didn't play with hers. I thought about the two eggs in Mama's pack, imagined the taste and feel. I started to say we had them but Luna was already putting her pack on.

We stayed on the edge of the rutted dirt road. I had sand in my shoes and socks and needed to stop to shake them out. A blister had already broken on my heel. I rinsed it with water from one of my bottles to soothe the sting. When I put my sock back on, it was worse. "If you don't hurry, I'm going to leave you here," Luna said.

Salma had been quiet all morning, but she shuddered and pleaded, "No, no, no."

"Come on, we're not leaving her, but you won't stop and take your shoes off, will you? Salma swung her head back and forth. No, she wouldn't.

I was mad at Luna for making us move in the daylight, right on a dirt road, when everything we'd been told was about hiding from roads and staying out of the sun. The part about staying out of the sun made sense now. My lips felt like pieces of cardboard, and even with my bandana tied over my hair, the tops of my ears were hot and felt crisp. I knew then, we could die out in the desert and no one would ever find us.

THE QUIET

In the desert, the quiet is full of sound.
Wind breaks free of the sky, forces low notes through saguaro,
and screeching tones through cholla.
Roadrunners fling grains of sand against rocks and drying cactus
as they buzz their way to a feast that might be this afternoon,
or day after tomorrow.
The desert is littered with dried remains of those who didn't plan.
Those who ran out of water.
Crows and vultures pick the bones clean.
Larger animals carry skulls away from dry limbs
to extract the brains in private.
A crow overhead, thrashes beaten-up wings, moves from branch to rock
to cactus, stays just ahead, always watching with a flicking eye.
It clicks its roadkill-greased beak, and flies ahead again,
marking its departure with a short stream
of black-grey slime that spatters the sand
with the sound of meat frying in oil.
The crow stops abruptly to cock its head at the slap of shoes on pavement.
The crow's clicking slows, then stops,
and the wings make muffled thumping sounds.
It circles and lands on top of a saguaro, cocks its head,
reports the situation with one sharp "caawk."
It makes a low noise like pebbles rolling on a piece of tin.

12

TERESA 1971

The edge of the road

In the village where we'd lived, when cars rolled along the street, with the shops holding the sounds close, you could hear the engine, the turning of the wheels, the groans and sighs as the car came to a stop. But out in the open, cars hide from your hearing. We had to go all the way to the edge of the road, where we could be seen, before we could see cars coming and run back to the brush to hide.

It looked like water on the road in the distance in either direction. A car was floating above the water toward us. It took a minute for the car to get close enough to see the windows and the two women inside. One woman was looking at a piece of paper, and the other—who was driving—was talking.

I was standing in the shade, not really hidden by the acacia trees, and even as the car passed, I couldn't hear the car sound I thought I'd hear. It was more of a scraping noise on the road as it went by. The leaves behind me fluttered. The woman holding the paper looked up just as they passed, and I knew from her eyes and her open, red-painted mouth that she'd seen me. I jerked back and waved my hand to Luna and Salma to move away from the road.

The car went on. The red-mouthed woman was looking back to where she'd seen me. Her hands were waving. She was either excited or angry. The car slowed down and started to turn around. I didn't wait to see more. I ran in the direction Luna had taken Salma.

I heard Luna whistle and stopped, listened again for her, and saw her. She was waving toward a clump of brush. I looked where she was motioning and saw two young men in dirty clothes crouching with their packs beside them. One of them shook his head "no" slowly. I pointed at the road, trying to make them understand that someone was coming. I scratched my way into the brush where my sisters were.

We heard tires leave the road, and brakes squeak when the car stopped.

"Here, right here, I saw her, here, I swear," one of the women said. From their hiding place, the two young men bolted like rabbits from a coyote, crashing through dry branches as they ran. "There! There!" the woman said. "No, wait—come back!"

The other woman's voice was lower, and she didn't sound excited.

"We won't hurt you."

"Please, please let us help you," one woman called while they walked in the direction the two men had run, away from us. Luna motioned toward the road, and started creeping out of our hiding place, with her hand clamped on Salma's wrist. I was afraid to speak, but I followed. Luna stopped beside the car, and looked in. The car was the color of green turquoise. The metal trim shone in the sun like a bracelet. The windows were open. The cloth seats smelled like soap and perfume. There was a store-bought map, and a red leather purse on the front seat.

Luna put her hand on the backdoor handle.

"Luna! No—they're coming," I whispered. Luna glared at me, opened the car door, and pushed Salma in. She followed, folding herself over her pack, into the space between the back seat of the car and the front seat.

"What are you doing?" I cried.

"I'm not walking anymore," she said. "Maybe they'll take us to Tubac."

"Get out of there! Are you crazy? They're coming. Come on! Get out!"

She gritted her teeth and said, "Leave me alone. They'll help us." I heard the women's voices and jerked the pack out from under Luna. She clawed at me. "Give me that. It's mine!" I shoved the car door closed, crossed the road, and crouched down behind a bunch of acacia trees right before the women came out of the bushes.

The women got into the car. I hoped they wouldn't see my mother's pack. I'd left it in the brush when I went to stop Luna and Salma. The driver looked out into the desert where we'd been hiding while the other one with the red mouth put on more lipstick. The driver combed through her short hair with her fingers, and they drove away. They took my sisters with them.

I crossed back over the road to get Mama's pack and put the things from Luna's into it. It didn't make sense to carry two packs so I left Luna's under the trees. Now, all I had was Mama's pack, some clothes, two boiled eggs, three tortillas, the map, and a half bottle of water. I was all alone in the world.

I walked in the direction the blue-green car had gone because, even if my sisters were stupid, I had to find them.

HE KNOWS HORSES

He hears about a horse breeder in Arizona who needs barn help.
He knows horses. He can do more than clean stalls.
His father is a charro, a great horseman.
He helps his father with breaking the two-year-olds to ride,
with grooming their horses at the charreadas,
the Mexican rodeos where his father competes.
He dreams of building a herd of horses sired by the breeder's stallions,
far better than the ones he could find in Mexico.
He dreams of showing his fine horses to his father.
Of making his father proud.
His brother Manuel is also good with horses, but in a different way.
Manuel has always been different.
Gentle, graceful like a ballet dancer.
A pretty boy, maybe too pretty, with wavy, too long hair.
"Maybe a change would be the best thing for Manuel," his mother says.
"Get him out of Nogales, away from the city. Too many things can go
wrong in the city, can pull a boy in a bad direction. Take him with you,"
she says, "it will be good for him."
He promises Manuel the prettiest horses to break
if he will come with him.
It will be a better life.
"But we have no papers," Manuel says.
"But we speak English," he tells Manuel.

13

TERESA 1971

I could tell by their eyes

"Hey," said a man's voice. "We saw those girls get in that car."

My heart was pounding so hard I could hear it beating in my head. I didn't know what to do. They might be just men who were trying to get somewhere, the same as my sisters and I were doing. Or men who take people across the border and take their money and kill them.

"If you want to walk with us, fine. If you don't, fine. I am Miguel, my brother is Manuel. We are from south of Nogales. We are going to Green Valley to work." One of the men stepped into view, and the crow cautioned him with a splatter on the top of the saguaro. I got to my feet.

When we sold goods at the market, the others who sold goods were part of us, and we were part of them. These men were the same as me, the same as my family. I could tell by their eyes.

I walked toward them, and Miguel said "Good. What is your name?"

"Teresa."

"And your family name?"

"Espinosa, from Centro, the north part. I don't know what my sister was thinking."

"We saw her," said Miguel, "we saw her push the little one in the car. Is she your sister too?"

"Yes. Now I have to find them. I took her pack to make her get out of the car. But she wouldn't get out."

Miguel's clothes were dirty, but his shirt was good cloth, the ivory cotton shirt of a charro. His belt was stitched with the designs of a charro's belt. I wondered if he was really a charro, or if he had bought the shirt to impress girls. Manuel, the quiet one, had curly black hair that hung to the neck of his T-shirt. His face was smooth. Handsome in a soft way. Manuel's black T-shirt had a huge pair of red lips on the front. He had a cut on his bottom lip, and a bruise on the side of his nose and under one eye.

Manuel hadn't spoken. He walked with his eyes on the brush, on the road, and when the crow rattled and croaked, he jumped a little.

"He is nervous," Miguel said. "Do you want to know why, Teresa?" I didn't answer. Miguel touched his brother's sleeve, "Tell her why, Manuel."

"Shut your mouth," Manuel said.

"Manuel got in a fight," Miguel said. "A coyote tried to take his shoes. He didn't let him have them."

We walked two hours until we came to some buildings and a gas station. One building had a wide glass window across the front. The turquoise green car was parked there.

"Hey," Miguel said, whispering so loud he might as well have talked, "that's the car. Let's go see if your sisters are in it."

"No," I said, "I'll go."

The car's windows were open. I walked closer. I looked up when I was beside it and caught my breath, because I could see my reflection in the window on the building, and that meant anyone inside could see me. I turned my head to look where Miguel and Manuel were hiding and wondered how fast I could run.

When I moved a step closer, the reflection cleared in the window. There was Salma, standing on the red plastic seat of the booth, spooning something from a tall glass into her mouth. Luna was across from her, pushing a wadded paper napkin toward Salma. And there was a plate beside Luna's arm with food on it. I could smell meat. They were in a restaurant, eating, while I had been walking. The two women sat in the booth, the driver beside Salma, and the red-lipped one beside Luna. They seemed happy, smiling, and had pushed their plates to the center of the table. Luna was drinking from the glass in her hand . . . was that cola? . . . with a straw. My head was hot and I felt dizzy. Maybe it was because I hadn't eaten any of the food in my pack. Because I'd been saving it for when I found my sisters, to share with them.

Luna looked out the window and her eyes met mine. Her mouth opened and the red-lipped woman turned to see what Luna was looking at. The woman who wore lipstick slid out of the booth to let Luna out, and followed her. I wanted to hit Luna with my pack, but I'd left it with Miguel and Manuel. Luna pushed out the door and stormed toward me.

"You stole my pack and ran! What kind of sister are you?"

"Stole it? I was trying to save you, because you're so stupid!" I yelled at her.

"Who's stupid? We have a ride to the ranch, and we have food. What do you have to eat? Rotten eggs and tortillas, and dirty water. Who's stupid now?"

I started to cry.

The woman with red lips spoke. "Who's this, Luna?"

"My stupid sister, Teresa," Luna said.

The woman turned toward Luna and put one finger to her red lips to make her be quiet.

"Teresa, are you hungry? Come in and have some food." Even when I looked into her eyes, I couldn't tell if she was a good person.

"I have to get my pack. I left it over there," I said, pointing to the line of brush across the road. I didn't mention the two men who'd walked with me.

"All right, you get it, and we'll order some food. Yes?" the woman said. Her voice was soothing.

Miguel and Manuel had hidden behind a clump of trees. I crossed the road to get my pack. "Are you here?" I called to them in a whisper,

"My sisters are here, and there is food. I can bring you something."
There was no answer.

The crow lifted from his perch above me, flew to the next branch
that would hold him, and noiselessly peered down at Manuel, with the
huge red lips on his T-shirt, and then I saw Miguel. Miguel shook his
head "no" and they were gone. I walked back to where the woman and
Luna were waiting.

The woman at the table smiled when I slid in beside Salma. Salma
was licking the sides of her glass. The table smelled of meat and milk
and sugar, chocolate and onions. A woman wearing an apron came to
the table and set a plate in front of me. It had a hamburger and fried
potatoes on it, some lettuce and a slice of tomato.

"Eat, Teresa," the lipstick woman said. She squeezed red sauce onto
my plate from a plastic bottle. "Do you want ketchup?"

She picked up one of the fries, dipped it in the ketchup, and put it in
her mouth. Luna had a tall, frosty glass like Salma's in front of her. She
sucked at the straw like a pig. I ate the hamburger like I hadn't eaten in
days. Maybe I hadn't. The woman who'd been driving had short brown
hair, almost like a man's, but she had a tanned, pretty face. She sort of
looked Mexican. The red-lipped woman was also nice looking, and
she had chin length reddish-brown hair. There was something familiar
about her. She cleared her throat.

"Teresa, we came looking for all of you and your mother. Luna
told us what happened." My eyes snapped up to meet Luna's while she
sucked the straw. I frowned at Luna. "Teresa, maybe you don't understand. We knew you were coming. When your mother didn't call yesterday, we knew something had happened. We drove out to look for
you. I thought I saw you in the desert, but I saw the two men run away.
And when we got in the car we didn't know your sisters were in it."
Luna's eyes dropped to the napkin beside her arm. "Luna," the woman
asked, "why didn't you tell us Teresa was with you?"

"You told them it was just you two?" I said to Luna.

"I wanted to get to the ranch, where we'd be safe . . ." her voice was
trembling with the weight of the lie.

"Well, you're safe now, all of you are safe," the red-lipped woman said. "We'll get you to the ranch."

"Thank you, but we have a note from someone, and we're supposed to call her from Rio Rico," I said, still watching Luna.

"This is Rio Rico, Teresa. Do you understand? I am Maria."

Salma tipped her glass over. The last of the shake slid onto the table.

"And I'm Angela," said the other woman, "I work at the ranch too. We're here to take you home."

"As soon as we get back, we'll see if the agents . . . well, maybe they've found your . . . " Angela's voice trailed off as Maria motioned to the woman at the counter.

"Do you like chocolate?" she asked me, pointing at Luna's glass. "Another chocolate shake, please," she called.

I was so tired. The sound the ceiling fan made was like the beat of crow wings over our heads. The sound of the machine mixing the chocolate shake was like the screeching of an owl. I was too tired to talk, too tired to sleep. The lady from the counter brought over a tall glass with stiff whipped cream and a cherry from a jar on top. I thanked her. I closed my eyes as I held the spoon in my mouth. Luna grinned at me, and Salma started to slump forward. She fell asleep right there. The lady from the counter came to clear the rest of the dishes. This wasn't so bad after all.

There was a grind of gravel when a car stopped outside the cafe. Angela's face grew dark and angry. She mouthed something to Maria, and Maria waved one hand toward the rest room door. Angela hefted Salma onto her hip.

"Girls, come with me to the rest room right now. Please, just come now. Bring your packs."

Luna scooted out of the booth. I left the spoon in my shake, shoved my arms into my pack straps and followed. I wanted to run. Something was wrong. I didn't want to be trapped. Now we had to trust this woman who was here with the woman who said she was the Maria we were supposed to meet. I followed her to the rest room. She pushed us into one of the two stalls.

"Stand on the toilet seat. Hold on to Salma. Shhh. Scoot back. Make room for me." She latched the stall door and perched her bottom on the edge of the toilet. A man's voice was moving around in the cafe.

"Yeah?" said the voice, "But I better look for myself." We heard footsteps behind the counter. "Little girls . . . are you here? Your Papa sent me to find you. He wants you to come home."

Luna caught her breath. "Favo," she barely whispered. Angela reached back with both hands and squeezed our legs, I guess to keep us quiet. The restroom door swung open and a shadow showed at the open bottom of the stall. The shadow's legs came closer, bent, and went back out. Angela stood, and reached back to flush the toilet. She looked at us and held her finger up in front of her lips.

"Lock the stall. Stay here 'til I come for you. Got it?" Luna and I nodded. Angela opened the stall door, ran some water in the sink, and went out the door.

"Favo. Well, well," we heard her say. "What are you looking for? A goat? A donkey? Or something nastier? What? I can't hear you. I asked you a question, you creep. You go back to that shithole you crawled out of. We're trying to have lunch here and my shake is melting."

Luna's eyes bulged out at me. She held Salma tight because she was starting to squirm.

"You heard her, dingle balls," Maria said, "go back to Mexico. You missed those girls by two days. We took them back home to Mexico yesterday. If you had the brains a rat has in its ass you'd know that." The bell on the cafe door jingled, and then the door slammed. There was a rumble of a car motor.

A half minute later, the restroom door opened.

"Okay, come on out. Let's get you girls to the ranch," Angela said.

We walked to the car. I looked at Maria, then Angela. I'd only heard language like that at the cockfight and in front of the donkey bar. But those women had made Favo go away with their talk.

They put my pack and Salma's in the trunk of the car.

"Where's mine?" Luna asked.

"I put your things in my pack. I couldn't carry both."

She huffed through her dry, cracked lips and climbed in the back seat. Maria opened the door on her side of the car, and I got in and sat as far from Luna as I could.

"Come on, little one," Maria said to Salma, "You ride with me in the front." Maria turned to us in the back seat, and her face seemed softer, more kind. "It's a good ways to the ranch. Why don't you try to sleep?"

Luna slumped against the door and closed her eyes as the car rolled onto the main road. There was too much to see, so I willed my eyes to close only long enough to rest them, then told them to open again. They didn't listen to me. I could hear the car, the road, the voices of the women in the front seat, but my eyes refused to open. I let them stay closed, holding the afternoon sun back with my eyelids. The red darkened to purple, then deep blue, then black, and . . .

I was in the marketplace, holding coins in my hand, and in my dream the coins were warm. I knew I was supposed to spend them for something, but I couldn't remember what it was, and my mother would be mad if I came back without that thing she had sent me to buy. I turned around to look at the vendors and saw my mother, wearing her market day skirt with the singing bells. Her hair was in a long, thick, beautiful braid.

She was looking for me. I tried to call, but my voice wouldn't leave my mouth. She was walking away, looking all around her, asking people where I was. No one was stopping to answer her. She stopped moving, turned around, and stared at my face. She looked so young. Like she was a teenager, just a few years older than me. She held out her hand, and I reached for it with my hand that held the coins. She walked away from me and into the crowd.

When I tried to follow her, it was as if my feet were chained to the ground. I looked down, and they were not feet at all, but a round base of plaster, like the statues at the church. I looked at my hands, and saw that they were made of plaster too, the fingers all joined together like paddles. The paint was peeling from my fingers. I wanted to put my arms down but they were extended from my painted body, palms up, waiting for something to be placed on them. I couldn't bear to look at them so I willed my eyes to close, but my eyes were painted open, gazing at something just beyond my outstretched hands. My plaster eyes tried to push out tears, but only tears of paint appeared on my cheeks. I felt so sad. The other people in the market around me had become statues. They were all stuck in their places. I gave up, and my statue slept, eyes painted open, hands waiting for something. Or nothing.

Angela pulled off the highway onto a gravel road and drove several minutes until we saw lights. I thought we were driving into a small town. When we were closer I could see a huge, lit-up adobe house, bigger than the church yard in Centro. At the end of the gravel road, at the next to last house, Angela stopped and opened her door. She lifted Salma without waking her from the front seat. Luna and I followed Maria to the trunk to get our backpacks.

"Do you live here too?" Luna asked Angela.

"That one's mine," she answered, pointing to another house on the road.

Maria pushed the front door open and flipped some light switches. I stopped on the doormat and looked down at my shoes.

"Don't worry, we're all used to desert dust. You won't hurt anything," Maria said.

Salma woke up when Angela walked onto the tiled floor of the front room. At the end of the room was a television twice as big as the one Reynaldo Torres had at his cafe where people watched soccer games. The table with six chairs around it had so many candles in clay holders at the center, if they were all lit, you could warm your tortillas and cook your food right there. The kitchen was beyond a set of swinging doors. Maria swiped another light switch.

"Sit, girls. I'll fix us something to eat." Angela plopped Salma down on a tall stool at the counter in the middle of the kitchen. Luna and I sat on either side of her. Angela looked over the contents of the refrigerator. Maria came from the pantry with a loaf of store-bought bread.

"Peanut butter and jelly okay?" she asked, and Luna nodded.

Angela set sandwiches and corn chips on small plates and slid them toward us.

"I'll get milk."

I didn't know I was hungry again until I started eating. Angela and Maria were talking about plans for the next day when Salma started wiggling on her seat. The smell coming from her was awful. Angela started to laugh, but saw Salma's tears welling and said, "Oh, honey, it's all right . . . " She looked to Maria for help.

"Come on, kiddo, let's get you out of those clothes," Maria said. Luna rolled her eyes at me while Maria took Salma down the hall.

Maria came out a few minutes later holding Salma's pants at arm's length, walked through the laundry room at the back of the kitchen and went outside with them.

"Good plan," Angela said, and went down the hall to the bathroom where Maria had left Salma in the bathtub. I was so embarrassed. We had just met our mother's friend and her friend, and Salma messed her pants in the kitchen. Maria hosed the pants outside on the grass, then brought them in and dropped them in the washing machine.

"When you girls finish eating, I have another bathtub. One of you can use it, the other one can use the one Salma's in when Angela gets her out."

Luna slid her chair back, picked up the plates and headed for the sink. "You can just put those on the counter, hon. Come on, maybe you can help Angela with your little sister. Teresa, you come with me." We followed. I was tired down to my bones. Maria led me through a room with three beds, to a door on the side of the room.

There was a shining white bathtub, toilet, sink, and a huge mirror. The filthy girl in the mirror was me. I worried how I must smell. Maybe as bad as Salma. Maria turned on the faucets and squeezed a plastic bottle over the water. Scented pink foam appeared and grew.

"Leave your dirty clothes outside the door. I'll get them in the wash and bring you back a T-shirt to sleep in," Maria told me, and left.

I peeled off my clothes and folded them. That seemed silly to fold dirty clothes but it felt impolite to put them outside the door on the floor in a heap. I heard Maria's footsteps in the hallway and heard her speaking to Luna or Angela, or Salma, I couldn't tell which. I turned the faucets off, and the foam in the tub sounded like a soda that had just been opened. I stepped in and let the water and bubbles close around me. I used a big round sponge to scrub myself. Then I leaned back and let the water take away the two—or was it three?— days of crossing the desert.

I felt more alone than I had ever felt. I cried.

Angela came in with Salma wrapped in a towel and sound asleep. I put on one of the three T-shirts she'd left on a bed. Angela smiled kindly while she put a T-shirt on Salma.

"Okay if she sleeps with you tonight?" she barely whispered. I slid between the smooth sheets with my little sister.

"Goodnight, honey. This will all work out, okay?" She turned the light out and left. I didn't hear Luna come in. If she turned the light on, I never knew it.

Luna was there in the other bed in the morning, face down. Her pillow was wrapped around the top of her head. One foot stuck out from the covers. She had angry blisters on her heel and instep. I could hear voices down the hall and wondered where my clothes were. Since the T-shirt came down to my knees, I decided to go down the hall to find Maria.

I stopped outside the kitchen door when I heard a man's voice, then a short laugh. Maria came out with a covered platter.

"Oh, good morning! I have clean clothes for you." She went into the other room and came out with a stack of folded garments. "Take these in to your sisters for me. And breakfast is ready." She tipped her head toward the kitchen. She wore a green robe that looked brand new. The bottom edge of a lacy nightgown showed at the hem. I thanked her and hurried back to the bedroom. I put Luna and Salma's clothes at the foot of Luna's bed and got dressed. Maria had washed our sneakers.

I hurried back to the table for breakfast with Maria and whomever the other person was. It seemed odd that she had company over for breakfast while she was still in her nightgown and robe.

There was a man at the table in a tan uniform. I was about to sit down when I saw the border patrol truck through the front window. Maria had turned us in. I started to back away from the room. Maybe I could get to Luna and Salma. Get them up. Get them out a window. We could hide. We'd get away.

"Teresa, this is David. He was out looking for you, when we didn't hear from your . . . " she hesitated. I knew she didn't want to say, "from your mother."

"Hello, young lady. You must be good at hiding. I only found your tracks," he said.

"It's fine, Teresa, officer Sanchez is my . . . " she flicked her eyes at him, and he poured coffee in cups on the table ". . . boyfriend."

So, my mother's friend who lived in Arizona had a boyfriend who was a border patrol officer. I didn't know if that made me safe, or if I should still plan to run. I saw his profile when he looked at Maria, and that was when I knew I'd seen him before.

It was at the tower where we found water. He was the guy who went back to his truck. I remembered the heavy gold name badge I'd found. He didn't have a badge on his shirt. There were two embroidered holes where it should go. I wondered if I should go get it and give it back to him.

Maria handed me a glass of cold milk. "I'll check on the other girls, don't wait for me." She went down the hall in a cloud of clean-smelling green robe. Officer Sanchez lifted the cover off the platter of scrambled eggs and sausages. He scooped some of each onto a plate and put it in front of me. I must have looked scared to death because he stopped while he was filling his plate.

"You're safe here, kid. Nobody's going to turn you in. You're Teresa? The middle one? The one who showed up later at the cafe?"

He had a kind face. I wondered how he had learned all of this just coming over for breakfast. And he must have showed up unexpected, because Maria hadn't had time to get dressed yet.

Maria came back from her room, carrying a gun in a holster and a belt.

"Oh, thanks, babe," the officer said.

Why on earth would she have his gun belt in her bedroom? Had he lost it, and she'd found it the way I found his badge? I thought he must be very forgetful, no matter how nice his smile was.

A door clicked down the hall, and Luna appeared, dressed in clean clothes. Salma was behind her, still in the T-shirt that dragged on the floor and sagged at her small round shoulders.

"Come sit down. I'll get you some milk. There's more food warm in the oven," Maria said. "David, this is Luna and Salma." Luna looked at him wide-eyed.

David lifted the cover on the platter and said, "Let's finish this off." Salma gleefully picked up a sausage with her fingers and poked it into her mouth.

"So, today," Maria started, as she set a second platter down, "I need to get in touch with your father and let him know you're here." Luna stopped picking through her eggs, and looked up at me. I was sure our mother would not have wanted our father to know where we were. Mama was through with him the night we left Centro.

"Maybe we could call our grandmother. She lives in Centro too. She has a telephone at her husband's store." Luna offered. I nudged her leg with one foot, under the table. "What?" she asked.

Maria poured more coffee. "Maybe," she said, "but is there a number to reach your father?"

"We don't have a phone, but there's a phone at the bar where he goes," Luna said.

"What's the name of the bar?" Maria asked.

"Dorado-something," Luna answered. I pursed my lips tightly and nudged her leg again, this time she just looked at me instead of saying "what?" I didn't want Maria to call our father. He might come get us. If our mother really was dead, he might get a new wife. It might be Pia. I wasn't going back to Centro so Pia could be my mother.

"Can we go look for our mother?" I asked.

"Sweetheart, David sent someone to look around the crossing, soon as he found your tracks and knew she wasn't with you."

"Did they find her?" I asked. Maria set her cup down.

"Yes, they did."

"Where is she?" I asked.

David rotated his coffee mug a half turn in front of him. I could hear his breath whistling low, like a breeze pushing through the woodpecker holes in a saguaro.

"We sent her back to Mexico, Teresa," he said.

My heart began to pound, but I still didn't want to ask. Because for that moment, it was possible that she had lived through the floodwater at the crossing, and I wanted that feeling that we were getting her back to go on longer.

Luna broke the spell.

"She's alive!"

"No, sweetheart," Maria said, reaching across the table for Luna's hand.

"Then where is she?" Luna shouted. She shoved her chair hard against the wall behind her and ran to the room where we'd slept.

"I'm so sorry, honey," Maria said to me. Salma tipped her milk over and David jumped up to get a towel from the kitchen. I'm sure he was glad to be doing something besides bringing bad news and watching people cry. I didn't cry. I already knew she was gone. I had already lost her, prayed for her, and cried for her.

"Please," I said, "can you tell me where she is now?" David mopped the milk with a towel and used a paper napkin to finish. He glanced up at Maria, looking for help I suppose. Maria's hands curved into crescents in front of her, her finger tips barely touching.

"The border patrol sends people they find to a place where they keep them for a while, and if the family wants to come get them, they can bury them," she said.

"Then we can go get her and bury her," I said quietly.

"No, you can't, Teresa, you crossed the border illegally, and if you go, you have to show your documents."

"But you can go get her," I said.

"Well, no," she said, "I can't because they would ask how I knew she was there. It would tell them that I was helping her cross illegally. I'd be in trouble. David would be in trouble. They won't know you're here if we just let it be for now."

"Then what happens to Mama?" I hoped my voice didn't break.

"Your father can claim her, Teresa, if you can help us reach him," David said. "As far as I'm concerned, you were born here, and you've always lived here." I understood. I asked to be excused from the table. I noticed how dark David Sanchez' eyes were.

I said, "I have something."

In our room, I dug through Mama's pack. Luna lay on her bed, staring at me with red rimmed eyes.

"I'll be back." I assured her. She didn't answer.

I hurried back to the table. Maria leaned close to David, speaking quietly, and stopped when she saw me.

"Here," I said to him, "you dropped this." He took the gold name badge.

"Ah, I know where I lost this. I got called away, you know, or I would have found you." He fastened the badge into the stitched holes on his uniform.

"You might have, but you didn't." I answered.

He lifted his flat brimmed hat from the chair beside where he'd sat.

"Better I didn't," he said.

14

ANA 1948

Better than some things

Ana shoved the tangle of sheet and cotton blanket to the foot of the bed with her heel and swung her legs over the side. She checked Nina, found her sprawled on her back, snoring like a nightgown-clad brown frog. Ana headed to the bathroom door at the end of the hall, and absently turned the knob. Suela was on the toilet.

"I'm sorry," Ana apologized. Even at the convent, where there were hardly any secrets, a hook and eye on the bathroom door kept one's privacy private. Ana waited in the hallway, cringing and clamping when the toilet flushed and water ran into the sink. She practically rushed the door when Suela emerged.

When she got into the bathroom she was glad she'd worn panties under her nightgown. She'd started her bleeding, but had not bled through her gown. She knew she had nothing to staunch the flow in her bag of things. Still sitting on the toilet, she opened the cabinet beside her. There were four boxes of sanitary napkins stacked along the cabinet wall closest to the toilet. When she opened the cabinet door again to drop the paper wrapper in the trash container, she saw a dull red rubber bag with a round plug in the top, and a hose coming out the bottom. She'd seen that kind of bag before, in the bathroom used by women who came to the convent to have babies. The bathroom would smell like vinegar when they had used the bag. Ana closed the cabinet, embarrassed that she had been so nosy.

Back in her room, she found Nina standing in the crib looking like she was ready to cry. She lifted her to keep her from making noise. A door opened and shut out in the hall, and there was a light tap on her door.

"Ana, I have some crackers here for your daughter. I meant to bring them last night and forgot." the voice said. Ana opened the door to Suela and thanked her. She poked an orange cracker into Nina's pouting mouth.

"Is this going to be your first baby, or do you have others?" she asked Suela, who stood in the doorway watching Nina.

"My first, but I hope I have more," Suela said. "Are you married to Nina's father?"

Suela was pleasant, no accusation in her tone. Ana glanced at the wedding band she'd bought for herself, four years ago when she was pregnant with Nina.

"I was, I think he must be dead, though," Ana said, regretting the lie as soon as it left her lips.

Suela sighed. "Oh, well that is better than some things."

What things? thought Ana. Better than being unmarried and abandoned? Better than being raped and left for dead?

"I mean," said Suela, "if you loved someone and they were married to someone else, and you had his baby, that would be even worse wouldn't it?"

"Yes. That would be worse than him being dead," Ana said.

There was a rattle of cabinets down the hall, behind the door to the kitchen. Suela's posture changed.

"Gabriella is in the kitchen. She will be here in a few minutes. If Nina is ready, she can go with Maya to the nursery at the school. She will take good care of her. You were at a convent, right? Safer here than at a convent for her. No mean nuns to spank her."

Ana hurried to button her dress and put her hair in a bun.

A key clicked in the hallway door lock and heavy footsteps on the carpeted floor came to Ana's open door.

"I'm Gabriella. I'm the manager of the house. You're Ana?" the woman said.

"Yes, I'm Ana. This is my daughter, Nina. She is no trouble at all. She is used to playing alone when I'm working," she began.

"Good, she'll do fine here," said Gabriella. "She can play alone or play with the other children at the nursery, it doesn't matter. MAYA! Are you ready?"

"Coming," Maya called from her room. Gabriella turned her square-shaped face to Ana and tilted her head. Ana saw in the light from the hallway that the woman's hair was colored, and the roots were laced with grey.

"We like things simple here, Ana. If I let you keep your baby in the kitchen, I'd have to let Maya's son run like a little wild man all over the house, and it would not be a peaceful place here. Do you understand? The children must be kept together where they can learn to be quiet, and be happy together. The same will go for Suela's baby when it's born."

"Si. I understand," Ana said. "Suela gave me some crackers to send with her."

"No need to do that," Gabriella said. Her face softened. "They have plenty at the nursery. We'll bring some here for you too, to keep in your room. And Ana, we speak only English here."

Maya was standing in the hallway outside her door, holding the hand of a boy about five years old. His face was round and solemn. He stared at Ana, and she smiled at him. He ducked his head, looked up at Maya, and tugged at her arm.

"Yes, we're going, Rudy," she said. "He loves school."

Ana had brought two little dresses for Nina, and slid one of them over Nina's arms, and wrestled the tie at the neck into a bow. "Okay, ready," she said, and kissed Nina's forehead. "You go with Maya, she is like Sister Bertia, very nice." Nina bubbled and chirped and skipped toward Rudy. The good in her having been raised among nuns and orphans was, Nina trusted everyone.

"Ana, I'll get you a uniform. Señor and Señora won't have breakfast until later. Are you two coming?" Gabriela called back to Suela and Maya. Little Nina was holding Rudy's hand and blowing kisses at Maya as they all headed to the kitchen door. "The children eat at the school cafeteria, and they know she's coming. They have some baby food ready. I think they didn't know she's already three. She eats regular food, yes?" Gabriella asked.

"Yes, yes, she eats everything." Ana followed Gabriella to the door to the kitchen. Gabriella had left her keys in the outer lock. She waited with her hand on the key ring until the others came through, then shut and locked the door behind them.

Maya and Suela went outside through a door on the side of the kitchen. Rudy's hand was clasped in Maya's, and Nina's hand was in Rudy's.

"This way," Gabriella said stiffly. They pushed through a swinging door into a room across the kitchen from the outside door.

There was a long metal sink with three faucets on the back wall of the room, and two long, Formica covered tables stood in the middle. Gabriella indicated for her to turn to the left, and they went through another swinging door into a short hallway, which ended in a closet full of starched grey dresses on clothes hangers. Shelves at the end of the room held more than a dozen pairs of shoes, freshly done with white shoe chalk.

"Find your sizes, take a pair of shoes, and three dresses. Make them last if you can. Laundry is once a week. Take an apron for every day too." She indicated another shelf across from the shoes. "They're on that shelf, all one size. If you shave your legs, you can go without stockings. Otherwise, stockings are here," she pointed to a wide drawer below the shoe shelf. "Keep your hair out of the food. If Señor finds one hair on his plate, you won't forget. I'll be in the kitchen. Come out when you're dressed. I'll put your extra dresses and aprons in your room for you while you start breakfast."

Ana took a dress she thought was her size to the curtained dressing room and it fit so she picked two more, then selected seven aprons, and a pair of chalk-white shoes. She folded her own dress neatly, laid it on top of her extra aprons, and put her scuffed shoes from the convent on the same pile. With the uniforms and aprons over her arm, and her dress and old shoes pressed to her chest, Ana pushed through the swinging doors to the kitchen.

"Good. I'll take those," Gabriella said, taking the pile from her. "You get these eggs separated, and I'll show you the rest as soon as I get this put away." Gabriella rattled her way through the lock, and into the hallway to Ana's bedroom.

Ana glanced at the clock in the kitchen. There were red lines painted on the glass at eight, twelve, and six. It was now seven fifteen. She separated the four eggs that had been set on the counter into a glass bowl she found in the cupboard. Not seeing a place to put the shells, she stacked them, nestled into one another on the counter beside the wire basket that had held them.

Gabriella came back, jangling the keys as she locked the door. "If you need to use the rest room while you're working there is one for household help in the room where you picked your uniforms. Wash your hands in the sink there, never in the kitchen."

"Trash goes here," she pointed at a round metal can with a shining top. Gabriella pressed the toe of her pointed shoe on a pedal, and the top swung up with a sharp squeak. Ana dropped the shells in and Gabriella released the pedal. "Can you read English, Ana?"

"Yes."

"Here is what you cook today. Meal times are marked on the clock. I'll let you know if they change the mealtime, and it will be on these notes for every meal. See, here above what's on the menu is how many people to cook for. Make an extra plate at breakfast and lunch, and after everyone is served, you may take your plate to the back room. Be quick, in case someone wants something more, you need to be ready to fix it for them. They'll ring a bell. Dinnertime, make enough for the other two women and the children, and you can eat in the back room, or in your rooms. I lock up a while after dinner."

Ana nodded, and looked at the handwritten slip of paper.

Breakfast for 2, 8:00
French toast and sausage
Water and orange juice

"If there's not a recipe I've laid out with the menu, cook things your way. I'll let you know if it's not to their liking."

"Yes, all right, what is in this?" Ana asked, indicating the first entry on the paper.

"Whip those egg whites with a little milk and dip two pieces of bread in that for Señora, then put the yolks in. Dip four slices in for Señor and one or two for you if you like. Fry them in a pan with butter," Gabriella gestured at the stove, "until they're light brown. Understand?"

Yes, Ana understood.

"Sausage in there," Gabriella pointed at the steel doors of the refrigerator. "Two on Señora's plate, six on Señor's. You'll learn how much each wants. I'll be here to help, so it will all go smoothly at first."

"Oh, thank you, Gabriella, it is kind of you to help me get started," Ana said, reaching for a skillet on an overhead rack.

"It's all worked out so the Ormonds don't have anything to be unhappy about. It's my job to take care of them. Your job is to cook what they want, have it ready on time, and clean up after yourself. If you do your job and aren't any trouble for anyone, you'll do fine here."

"Yes, of course," Ana said. "Shall I make breakfast for you too?"

"Oh, no, I don't eat in the house." Gabriella flapped one hand toward Ana and said, "I'll take care of their juice today."

"Should I make coffee?" Ana asked.

Gabriella stopped and turned sharply.

"No coffee. These people don't drink coffee."

15

TERESA 1971

First day

Maria fluttered her eyes at David and made him laugh. We'd finished breakfast and he'd poured the last of the coffee. Angela came in the kitchen through the back door talking loudly and stomping her feet.

"Come on in," Maria called from the table. David stood.

"I've got to get going," he said. Maria went over and hugged him. He looked at me, and seemed uncomfortable. She kissed him on the cheek, then patted his arms.

"Thank you for your help."

He gave her a serious look. "Yes, ma'am, that's my job."

Angela swung through the door from the kitchen.

"Well, HERE you all are."

"Are you finished?" I said to Salma, and didn't wait for an answer before I picked up her plate. Angela held the door for me and motioned for me to come with her.

"Come on kids, time for you to learn to do dishes." Salma beamed, and climbed down to follow me into the kitchen. "We have a LOT to do in here," Angela said loudly, as the kitchen door closed behind her. She winked at me and made kissing noises into the air. That made me laugh. It was the first time I'd laughed since the day before we'd left home.

I took the dishes to the two big sinks and reached for a sponge.

"Here, let me show you," Angela said. She pulled on a metal cabinet door and a rack rolled out, with plates standing on their edges. "In the dishwasher, Teresa."

"I'm not going out to get those cups 'til all the kissing is over," she said. Salma imitated the kissing sounds and Angela laughed. "I have some boxes in my car. Let's go get them."

Salma and I followed her out to the car. She gave us each a box to carry. Salma tried to set her box on the bumper the way Angela had when she closed the trunk.

"No, you carry that, you have to work to eat around here," but she said it laughing. Salma clutched her box to her chest and walked toward the kitchen door. I saw David Sanchez's truck going out on the gravel road.

Luna was sitting on her unmade bed, digging through our mother's pack, since everything we had brought was in it and Salma's pack. Now, in daylight, Mama's pack looked old and ragged.

Angela set her box on my bed. I was glad I'd made it before I went to breakfast. She pried one of the boxes open and lifted out a green dress to hold up to Salma's shoulders.

"Shall we put this on?" Angela knelt to the floor. Salma held her arms up and let Angela peel off the T-shirt she'd slept in. "Well, my goodness, you need panties, young lady," Angela said.

"Here." Luna handed Salma's underwear to Angela.

"In you go," Angela said. Salma stepped in then held her arms up for her new dress. "There's shoes in that other box," Angela said to Luna, while she did the row of white buttons on the back of the dress. Luna emptied out the shoes on my bed, and all of them were a lot better than the ones we'd been wearing.

"There should be some hangers in the closet. You can also use the chest of drawers for your things," Angela said.

Luna went to Angela and put her arms around the woman's waist.

"Thank you. Thank you for finding us. Thank you for bringing us here," and then, Luna was crying. Angela patted her back.

"You'll be fine here. Maria and I will make sure you're okay. All right, girls, whatever doesn't fit, put back in the boxes, and I'll pick it up later."

The blue skirts and white blouses in one of the boxes were all the same. Luna and I held the tan canvas shoes up to our feet and tried on blouses and skirts. In the second box were nightgowns, and two dresses: one yellow with an orange sash at the waist, and the other had splashes of colors like a basket of fruit, and a bright pink sash, and there were two grey skirts. I claimed the yellow dress because it looked like my size. Luna and I put things on the hangers and folded the other clothes.

"See, your clothes are in here, Salma."

"My dress!" Salma said, twirling around.

"Yes, your dress. Here, let's get you some shoes." Luna handed me shoes and socks for her and Salma plopped down on the floor to wait.

I wrestled the white socks onto her feet, then slid one of the black shiny shoes on. It had a strap with a buckle, which delighted Salma. Those were grown up shoes to her. She put the other one on by herself, stood, and twirled again.

"All the skirts and blouses are the same," Luna said.

"Maybe they're what we wear for work," I said. She shrugged. Maria tapped on our door.

"You girls dressed yet?"

Luna and I looked at each other. We'd been dressed for a while. Of course, we were dressed.

Maria opened the door a crack and poked her head in. "Oh. I see."

Maria came into our room in a grey dress, the color of a dove. She looked very different from the Maria in the flowered blouse and blue jeans who had brought us here last night. Her short reddish-brown hair was pushed back in a headband, with three hairpins on each side behind her ears.

"Are we going to both work at the same house?" I asked her.

"Oh, no, sweetheart," Maria said, tilting her head, "You're going to school."

Maria put her hands on Salma's shoulders and turned her around. "So PRETTY!"

"We can do the job Mama was going to do," Luna said. "We can cook. We'll help you."

"Not just yet. When you're older, if you stay, maybe. But school 'til then," Maria said, while she looked at the things we'd hung in the closet.

"Put on the navy skirts and white blouses please, and the espadrilles. Those are your school clothes." I looked down at Maria's white rubber-soled shoes. She was wearing stockings. "Today I'll show you around and we'll go over to the main house for lunch."

"Are we going where Mama was going to work?" Luna asked.

"Yes, of course. Come out when you're ready. Salma can wear her green dress, she doesn't need to wear a uniform yet." Maria left us.

Luna found two rubber bands in the pocket of Mama's pack and after she braided my hair, I braided hers. The skirts had zippers instead of ties. When we put them on, the fabric made a pouch in the front.

"Maybe that goes in the back, over your behind," Luna suggested.

"Maybe it's big for YOUR behind," I said. Luna laughed and twisted the skirt around and the fit was better.

"Do we leave the blouse out, or tuck it in?" she pondered.

"In, I think. Maria's was in," I said.

"Maria had a dress on. You can't tuck a dress in," Luna said, while she unzipped her skirt. She smoothed the blouse in and zipped the skirt again. "I think in." Luna seemed pleased with the way she looked.

Salma was in front of the mirror on the bathroom door, making her skirt sway back and forth while she twisted to see herself. She grinned and curtsied like Shirley Temple in the black and white movies we'd seen at the Centro theater. It was the first fancy dress she'd ever had. We'd never seen her act like that before, swishing around and staring at herself.

"Come on, movie star, time to go," I said, taking her hand.

"Pretty!" she chirped. She took one last look in the mirror before she let me lead her away.

90

Angela was at the table with Maria. Maria stood up quickly when we came in. "Here you are, all ready for your first day!" she said

"Why don't I take Salma to the nursery, and you girls can go with Maria to see the rest of the ranch," Angela said.

"Nursery? What is that?" Luna asked, looking to me and then Maria.

"All the young children go there while their mothers are working, some are just babies, and some are Salma's age. They have good ladies there to take care of them. I promise."

"Oh," said Luna, "There must be lots of people who live here to have a place just for the little kids."

"There are twenty families in all who live here. At the other ranch, there are another fifteen. Angela, how many in the nursery now?" Maria said.

Angela tapped her wristwatch lightly, and answered, "I think two babies, and ten or so between two and five."

Luna looked at me, then Maria. "How many at the school?"

"I think there are thirty-five or forty who go to school here. More than when I went to school," Maria told us.

"YOU went to school here?" Luna asked.

"Yes, I did," Maria said, "So did Angela. I was born here. Your mother went to school here until she was fourteen. Didn't she tell you that?"

"Luna, Teresa, did you ever wonder why your mother spoke good English? At school, here we spoke only English. Do the other kids at your school in Centro speak English as well as you do?"

"No, but we have English class in school."

"It helps us at the market when we go—when we went—with our mother," I said.

"Yes, of course it does. You'll do fine at school. Here, you speak English," she said. "You go to school for the rest of the semester. Then if you decide you want to go back to Mexico, we'll get hold of your father, and get you back home, okay?"

"Or we could call our grandmother, and she can drive her car and get us," I said.

Maria smiled at us, and glanced at Angela who was hiding her eyes from Salma with her hands, and opening her fingers to peek out.

"Yes, of course she can." Maria stood and smoothed her dress again. "Ready to go? It's not far. We'll walk to the school. Then we'll go to the main house. Mrs. Ormond will want to meet you," she said. "Better get a move on, Angela, I think she's coming by the nursery late this morning."

"Maria," I asked, "may we go see where Salma will be?"

"Yes, yes, of course you may," Maria said. "We'll go to the nursery first."

Luna took two steps toward the door, stopped and said, "Did our mother want to come back here because she wanted us to go to school here too?"

"I don't know. I wrote her and said there was a good job here, and that you could go to school here. She wrote back and said she wanted the job. She said . . . well, it doesn't matter now. I'll take care of you because she'd want that. And, if you don't want that, I'll help you go back to Mexico. But I hope you stay. I want you to be here. I have missed her."

"We'll stay, won't we, Teresa?" Luna nudged me.

"Yes, we'll stay," I said.

Maria put her arms out, and we went to her, and put our arms around her. She smelled of nice soap. I could see why she and our mother had been friends. I liked her reddish-brown hair, and her eyes. Her eyes were a different color than anyone's I'd ever seen.

For Salma, everything was shining and happy and wonderful because she had her new dress.

Angela shook Salma's arm playfully. "You look SO pretty."

Across the gravel driveway, we crossed a line of white-painted rocks, onto green grass. There was a place like this in Centro, a park surrounded by shops and places for tourists to eat, with grass cut short.

You could see the snakes if the grass was short. This yard was as big as the whole school and playground where Luna and I had gone in Centro.

We went through a glass door into the school office. A round faced woman with pale skin and freckles, about Maria's age, came out and leaned against the counter.

"Maria! I was hoping you'd bring the new girls from Centro today."

"Here we are," Maria said. "This is Luna, she's fourteen, and Teresa, she's twelve. We're taking Salma, here to the nursery. Aren't we Salma? We'll come back to get enrolled for school tomorrow."

"Fine, fine," the woman said. "If you girls want to wait here," she motioned to a row of four chairs against a wall, "while someone takes Salma over to the nursery—"

"Thank you, but we'll go with her," Luna said. I was glad she said that.

"Oh, yes, of course," the woman said. "She's going to love it here." She leaned over the counter to look at Salma. "And such a pretty dress!"

"I'll stay and visit with Miss Connie," Angela said, "while you take Salma over."

"Okay, we'll be back in a few minutes," Maria said. We walked from the office building on a shaded cement sidewalk and at the fifth door, Maria stopped to check Salma's dress and socks, then opened the door.

The room was bigger than I expected. On one side were five rows of wooden desks and a huge green chalkboard, twice as big as the one in our Centro school. A door beside the chalkboard opened. A woman came through and held the door for an older woman and a group of children. Some were about Salma's age, and some might have been about five years old. Behind the children, a girl Luna's age pulled a cloth-hooded wagon with two babies in it. The younger woman smiled at us and said something quietly to the older woman.

"Hello, Miss Maria!" said the older woman. She was pretty in the way grandmothers are pretty, with a smooth face and halo of grey-streaked black hair held with a tortoise comb on each side. Our grandmother had combs like that. The woman reminded me of our grandmother, and for that, I liked her.

"Hello, Miss Suela," Maria answered. The woman looked at my sisters and me, using eyeglasses that hung from a silver chain on her neck.

"These are the girls? Very pretty," Miss Suela said, "They look like their mother."

Maria looked down at the sleeve of her dress.

"Nina is . . . "

"Yes, Angela called this morning. I'm so sorry. Well, girls I'm glad you're here. Do you speak English?"

"Yes, we do," Luna answered. Miss Suela smiled kindly at us and turned toward the other woman.

"Wonderful, isn't that wonderful, Miss Rosa?" The younger woman had told the children to sit on the floor on pillows.

"Yes, it is. Is our new student going to start with us today?"

"Yes. Come on, Salma, you can pick out a pillow," Miss Suela said, and held her hand out to our sister.

"It's good she's starting now, she'll get adjusted to the nursery."

Salma looked up at Miss Suela and yelped "Grandmother!" The woman laughed and steered Salma toward the other children.

"Oh, Salma, you are a beauty, aren't you? Here, you can sit with Eva and Tomas. Good, good."

Salma plopped down between the boy and girl who looked like twins.

"Well, that was easy, wasn't it?" said Miss Suela. "When will these girls begin school?"

Maria put her hand on my back.

"Maybe tomorrow. I'm showing them around first."

"The sooner the better," said Miss Suela, tilting her forehead toward Maria. "Yes?"

Maria placed her other hand on Luna's back, and said, "Yes, maybe tomorrow." Salma was already leaning against her new friend Tomas, looking at a picture book.

We went out to the hallway. Six children who were probably seven or eight were coming our way. The girls wore white blouses and blue skirts like the ones Luna and I had on, and the boys were in white short-sleeved shirts and blue pants. One girl and boy had hair so blonde it was almost white. They walked a little apart from the other four, two black haired boys, and two girls with reddish brown hair.

"Second and Third grade, I think," Maria said. The children walked down another hall, opened a door and went in. She looked at her watch. "They must be coming from recess. Let's get Angela and go over to the main house. Mrs. Ormond will want to meet you."

Angela and Miss Connie were leaning against the counter studying a cloth-covered green book when we went in. Miss Connie closed the book and put it on a shelf with other green books.

Maria and Angela said goodbye to Miss Connie.

"See you tomorrow?" Connie flapped her fingers up and down in a wave. We smiled at her. We walked back across the grass.

"So, do you know what Connie told me?" Angela asked Maria. Maria kept walking as Angela talked. "She said there was a new family on the west ranch, and they all had the flu, and the baby had to go to the hospital for fluids and both parents had to take time off. Now isn't that a good way to make a bad impression when they're new on the job."

I thought to myself that our mother must have made a really bad impression by drowning instead of coming to work.

We walked between two buildings in our path, and almost ran into a man pushing a wheelbarrow loaded with flowerpots.

"Hello, Rafael, doing some planting, I see," Angela said.

The man swept his soft-brimmed straw hat from his head. "Yes, Señora has a party, she wants new plants. Hello . . . " he said, making a slight bow toward Luna and me. This man with the wheelbarrow was sun baked as dark as a roasted chile pepper. His hands were long and callused, and the cuffs of his shirt were frayed. He was thin, but seemed strong for an old man. His eyes were as round and bright as a crow's. He took in everything about us with those eyes. It was like he meant to remember something important.

"I am Rafael, nice to meet you," he said.

Maria was in a hurry, I guess, because it seemed she didn't want to stop very long to talk to this man.

"These are Nina's daughters, Luna, and Teresa."

"Nina's daughters? Where is she?" he said.

"Raphael, we'll talk later," Maria said. That was kind of her, I suppose, to not tell him, in front of us, that our mother was dead.

16

ANA 1948

Unspoken greeting

The Ormonds sat at the huge polished table; Señor Ormond at the head of the table, and Señora four feet away, on the long side of the table. He wore a white shirt with a grey monogram stitched on the left cuff and a blue-and-grey striped tie. Señora wore a pale rose-colored dress with sleeves to her elbows. Her hair was arranged in coils behind her ears, and she wore face powder.

Señora's sharply arched eyebrows were drawn with an eyebrow pencil. Her lipstick was perfectly lined, and there was already lipstick on the rim of the juice glass in front of her. Ana knew Centro women who wore eyebrow pencil and lipstick in the morning. They worked in the bars, keeping the men happy and getting them to buy drinks. Those women brought clothing and bedding to the convent, and put money in the offering plate every Sunday. The nuns would not speak to them or look at them, as if they were unclean.

Señora smiled sweetly at Ana as she followed Gabriella into the dining room and Ana nearly ran into Gabriella's heels, returning the unspoken greeting. Gabriella nodded sharply toward the empty space in front of Señor Ormond. Ana knew then that she was to set his plate down first. He glanced at the plate, but not at her.

Señora Ormond said, in a small quiet voice, "Thank you, Ana." Gabriella's breath drew sharply. Ana guessed she was not to respond. She inclined her head and kept her eyes lowered. Señora said nothing more.

"Will there be anything else, Señor?" Gabriella asked.

"That will be all, Gabby. Make sure breakfast is on time tomorrow," he said. Señora Ormond's shoulders stiffened. She kept her eyes on the napkin in her lap. Ana felt the sting of disapproval from her new boss, who'd complimented her cooking just a few days before, and had given her an envelope full of money to come to his home to cook. Gabriella took two steps backwards and Ana followed her back to the kitchen.

"I am sorry, I will not be late tomorrow," Ana said when they reached the kitchen.

"Hush. Don't worry, you weren't late. I wasn't late either. Sometimes he says things like that. Don't respond, that's my job. You did fine. Go eat something. They'll ring the bell if they want something else, and I'll go in. I'll come get you if I need you."

Ana took her breakfast into the room beside the kitchen. The door swung open behind her.

"Forks are in that drawer on the side of the table," Gabriella said. "Napkins there." She pointed at a basket.

Ana nodded her thanks.

Gabriella whisked back into the kitchen, and Ana heard cupboards opening and closing. She wished she had coffee, but maybe if the Ormonds didn't drink coffee, it wasn't allowed here. She'd ask another day.

She filled a glass with water from the sink and ate breakfast in silence. She washed her plate, fork and glass in the sink where she was to keep from making any noise in the kitchen. She cleared her throat as she re-entered the kitchen. Gabriella was leaning on the wood-topped cutting table, writing on a tablet. She looked up from her writing and placed her finger lightly to her lips. Ana understood.

Ana motioned that she'd begin cleanup, but Gabriella placed her finger to her lips again.

"Wait until they have finished and gone before you get their plates, and before you do anything in here. They'll ring a bell when they leave the dining room." She motioned to Ana to sit on the stool beside the sink.

Gabriella continued with her writing, then strained to hear something. She nodded toward the dining room door, where Ana saw the silver bell suspended on a curved metal arc. Gabriella pointed toward the bell, just as it sang out one thin, silvery note.

"Okay," she whispered, "but check that they're out of the room."

Ana pushed the door cautiously and peered into the dining room. The Ormonds were gone. Just plates and glasses on the table.

"Take this," Gabriella said, handing her a tray. "Dish cloths and soap are in the cabinet right under the sink."

Ana washed, dried and put everything back where she'd found it. She tucked a stray lock of hair behind her ear.

"You did fine, Ana. I'll be back with a menu for lunch in about three hours. These drawers need to be cleaned with vinegar and water, and the things in them washed and dried. If you want the things arranged in those drawers so you know where everything is, that's fine, but use only these three drawers for cooking utensils so I can find things too. If you finish that before I get back, the stovetop needs to be washed and polished. After that, you could clean the cutting board with salt and put a coat of oil on it. You may go in the room where we keep uniforms to use the bathroom there, but don't stay in there longer than you need to. You need to be in here working."

"Si, I understand," Ana said softly.

"Oh, and remember, only English here. They want a cook who understands them, and who they can understand. They don't speak Spanish. You address them only as Señor and Señora, never by their names. That is the only Spanish they want to hear," Gabriella said, flipping her notebook shut. She slid her pencil behind her right ear. "Tomorrow, part your hair in the center, instead of on the side, always in a bun. I'll bring you some hair pins if you don't have any."

"Yes, I understand," Ana answered. Gabriella went to a drawer for a sheet of paper and a pencil.

"If there's anything special you need in here, that you don't find, write it down. Do you write?"

"Yes, I read and write," Ana said. She hoped her English from the convent would carry her.

"All right, I have to go to the market. I'll be back at eleven thirty to help you start lunch. I think it will be simple, and it might just be Señora today. I'll let you know." Gabriella took the keys from her dress pocket. She opened the door, then closed and locked it again from the outside. Ana wondered what kind of dangers were outside, that the doors had to stay locked.

She started on the drawers she was to clean. The utensils were as clean as though they'd just been washed and put away. Ana emptied the drawers and wiped them with vinegar she found under the sink. She washed and dried the long-handled spoons, forks, ladles, whisks, and a few things she didn't recognize. In the pantry, she found a box of white candles and used one of them to smooth out the runners on a sticky drawer.

The clock on the wall said it was nine forty-five. She had plenty of time to clean the stovetop and scrub and oil the cutting board. Like the drawers, the stove seemed clean to her, but if it was this easy to clean, she wouldn't mind cleaning every day. The cutting board needed a little more work. She'd need sandpaper to get the surface more even, but she'd ask for that when Gabriella came back. She was putting a coat of oil on the cutting board when she saw a movement out of the corner of her eye, at the door where Gabriella had gone out.

The door's four glass panes glinted in the morning light. At first, she thought it was the sun's flash that caught her eye. She walked to the door and leaned to one side, then the other to see if there were something moving outside. There was nothing. She heard a car start. Heard the crush of gravel under wheels.

The car she'd ridden in from Centro was backing up, away from the side of the house. Stan Ormond was behind the wheel, looking over his shoulder as he backed the car toward the driveway. He didn't look toward the kitchen door. She was glad he hadn't seen her standing there. Ana watched him drive away toward a group of buildings close to the hills.

She looked down at the latch Gabriella had locked as she'd left. The heavy beveled window panes sloped to where they met the wood frame. At the corner of the pane nearest the lock were two smeared fingerprints. Ana tried to wipe them off with the corner of her apron, but they were on the outside.

It was eleven o'clock.

17

TERESA 1971

I always knew Paco

I guess I always knew Paco, because we went through school together. He was shy of girls, but not so shy around me. My sister said it was because I acted like a boy, but that wasn't true. I didn't act like a boy. I wore dresses and skirts and blouses like the other girls did. I did like to play kickball at recess and most of the girls didn't. Luna made fun of me in front of Mama, that my underwear had shown at recess, and Mama told me to wear shorts under my dress.

She told me she used to play kickball with a boy she knew. I asked her if the boy grew up to be our father. She said no, it was not the same boy, but maybe she should have married that boy she played kickball with instead. She didn't smile when she said it.

Paco sat near the back of the classroom, and I'd sit a row in front of him. I'd turn my head to watch him concentrating on his lessons and he'd always catch me looking, and he'd smile. He'd sit across from me at lunchtime with his shredded chicken or eggs, or beans in a tortilla and one long green pepper, and sometimes a piece of cake his mother had baked. He'd share his cake, and if I had an apple from the market, he'd cut it with his pocket knife and I'd share with him. We were best friends. I loved him the way friends love each other.

When it was Christmastime our teacher brought white tissue paper, thin and easy to tear, and we tore it into pieces and pasted them on the windows with water. She said it would look like snow. Snow. We were wondering why she wanted us to make white spots on the windows. She was a nice teacher from California, in the United States. She came from the mountains, where she said it snowed in the winter. Well, we'd seen mountains in Sonora but not snow. She showed us a picture of the mountains in California, said it was near where she grew up. There was a white frosting on the mountains and the trees, and on the roofs of the houses. She pointed to the windows of one of the houses, and there was a white border around each of the window panes.

"That's snow on the window," she said. Then we understood where to put the white tissue paper, to make our windows look like they had snow.

Paco folded a piece of the tissue paper into a little flower and gave it to me. I hid it in my pocket so Luna wouldn't see it. When I got home, I put it in the drawer beside my bed where I kept the rosary my grandmother had given me.

Later, when I was helping Paco get his roosters ready to fight, he was more serious than he had been in school. He didn't smile as much. I wondered at first if he was mad at me, but that wasn't it. He wanted me to come to his house to help him, and I always wanted to go. He was always glad to see me, and I was always glad to see him.

I think that is what love means. I think love is like snow on the mountains and trees and houses and windows. You have to see what it looks like first, to know what it means.

18

ANA 1948

Lunch

"Hello, Ana, how are you doing with the kitchen?" Gabriella asked brightly. She carried a brown paper sack against her chest, and the smell of fried chicken wafted into the kitchen.

"Fine, I have cleaned and found where things go."

"Good, good. Señora Ormond is having lunch at her mother's house, and Señor is in town. I brought over some food from the school. They always make too much. We'll have lunch, and I'll go over the dinner menu," she said, taking packages from the sack. "There's enough here for lunch and some leftovers. We have mashed potatoes and green beans . . ." She filled two plates with food.

Ana followed Gabriella into the back room to the table. She wondered if Gabriella would pray over the food the way the nuns always did. Ana hadn't uttered a prayer since the day she'd spoken in anger to the Blessed Virgin in the chapel. There was no prayer from Gabriella, and Ana was glad. The potatoes and green beans were as bland as baby food, but the chicken was crisp and spicy.

Gabriella picked up the second piece of chicken from her plate.

"I'm glad you're here, Ana. Señora Ormond was most happy with the breakfast you made. I'll be here for the next few days to help. She'll always let you know what she and Señor want to eat, and if it's something you don't know how to cook yet, don't worry. I'll help you. The last woman who cooked, well, she made a lot of mistakes."

"I will try not to make mistakes," Ana said.

"Yes, I'm sure you will, Ana," Gabriella said, putting a bone on the edge of her plate. "Ana, I was wondering, did your husband leave you and your daughter, or did he die?"

There it was. Now she was trapped, and she knew she couldn't lie to this woman. She'd probably guessed the ring on Ana's finger was one she'd bought for herself at the market. That she and Nina's father hadn't been married at all.

"Oh, Gabriella, the Mother Superior may have told Señor Ormond something that was not true." Her small voice caught in her throat. "I am not ashamed of my daughter. I was not married to her father. He left before she was born."

Gabriella laid her smooth hand on Ana's arm.

"That doesn't matter, Ana. Señora Ormond loves little babies. She'll visit the nursery to hold them and pretend they're hers. She is . . . well, she isn't like other people, but she means no harm. Señor Ormond lets her hire girls who have babies, usually younger than yours. Señora only wants to play with them."

"Oh," Ana said softly. "Like Maya and her Rudy?"

"Sort of like that. Maya didn't have Rudy yet when she came here. The Ormonds must have liked you, because Nina is older than a baby."

"But they told me they wanted me to cook," Ana said.

"They do. Don't worry."

Ana stood to take the lunch dishes to the kitchen and felt a warm sogginess that reminded her she'd started bleeding that morning, and she hadn't brought what she needed with her from the bathroom in the living quarters.

"I am so sorry. I will need to go into the hallway, to the bathroom there," she told Gabriella, hoping she didn't need to further explain.

"Ana, there's a bathroom in here."

"Yes, but, I need something in there." Her face turned red.

Gabriella nodded, her face showing she comprehended that this young woman might need things from the women's quarters that were not stored in the kitchen and house staff bathroom. "Of course, and bring whatever you need to keep in that bathroom."

Gabriella unlocked the door, and Ana hurried to the restroom, pulled her dress to her hips, and inspected her underwear. She changed the pad and put three more from the box under the sink in her apron pocket. She hurried to her room for her comb, parted her hair neatly down the center, frowning at how white her scalp looked where her hair parted, and put her hair back up. She made sure it was smooth and tightly in place. Gabriella was waiting just outside the door.

"Thank you," Ana said.

"Yes, of course," Gabriella said, "and do wash your hands, we wash our hands here a lot."

Ana put the pads in the bathroom cabinet. Her face was burning from embarrassment when she went to wash her hands.

She wondered what happened to the babies Señora Ormond had played with when they were no longer babies.

19

TERESA 1971

Running the house

Rafael pushed his wheelbarrow toward a flat-roofed shed after Maria told him she'd talk to him later about our mother. At the shed, he looked back and raised one hand in a half wave, then put it quickly to his wheelbarrow handle again.

"It's okay to talk to Rafael, but don't take him from his work or he'll get in trouble, and we wouldn't want that to happen," Maria said.

We walked toward the big house. Luna asked, "Maria, what's your job here?"

I looked at Luna like she was stupid, because that was a stupid question.

"I help with running the house, and Angela and I both help in the kitchen when the Ormonds are having company."

"Do you cook for them?" Luna asked.

"Sometimes. Right now, they have a part-time cook, and they want someone full-time, that's why I sent a letter to your mother."

"But our mother was not a cook," Luna said.

"Ah, but she was, she used to help in the kitchen when she lived here. She helped until she and her mother left for Mexico. She was fourteen, and she was a good cook already."

Luna gave me a funny look, and turned to walk backwards, so she could face Maria while we walked and said, "She was a cook? She never told us."

"She probably didn't talk about growing up here, because of her mother," Maria answered quickly. It sounded like she'd already thought about that answer and had practiced it.

"So," Luna said, "were you born here?"

"Yes, I was. I was adopted by the Ormonds," Maria said.

"Did your parents die?" Luna was so nosy.

"Well, no, but my mother didn't want me."

"Why?" Luna asked, with a surprised look.

"Because . . . it's hard to explain," Maria said.

Luna's face clouded for an instant, but she could not just stop talking.

"I can cook, so instead of going to school, you can show me how to make the things they like," Luna said. She'd jumped so quickly to a new subject that Maria looked startled.

"We can talk about that later. Angela and I are both cooking over there. And you can come help us, but you need to go to school." Angela hummed and nodded in agreement. I didn't say anything because I knew Luna could cook, at least for our family she could. But I also knew she didn't want to go to school any more. She'd told me that in a couple of years she'd be married with a baby and she didn't need more school to do that. She had snuck off and kissed a boy after school once. I saw her. They looked like two chickens pecking at each other.

Maria used a big ring of keys to open the door at the side of the main house. She had us wash our hands in a room behind the kitchen. She said we'd wash our hands a lot here.

Angela took out store-bought bread, thinly sliced chicken, slices of cheese, and jars of mustard and mayonnaise.

"We'll make sandwiches, and there's soup to re-heat here," she said. Maria came to take the pot and set it on a stove.

"Hey, Luna, will you keep an eye on this soup and stir it?"

Angela handed me a rubber spatula. "Mustard on one, mayo on the other."

"Lettuce," Maria said, when she'd looked at a paper on the refrigerator under a magnet.

"Lettuce," Angela repeated. She slid a cutting board and knife toward me. "Cut on the diagonal," indicating with her hand that the cut was to be from corner to corner. I cut each sandwich, and she made another motion. "Cut again. Four pieces. Always four." Angela went to a cupboard for dishes.

"I'll check on her," Maria said, more to Angela than to Luna and me, and went into another room. She came back to the kitchen. "She's ready."

Angela and I put four sandwich pieces around each of the five plates. Maria put soup in bowls. Luna and I each picked up a plate, and Angela and Maria took the other three. Angela hesitated at a swinging door that went to another room.

"I'll go in first and get Mrs. Ormond served, and you'll come in with Maria. If Mrs. Ormond greets you, you say 'hello, nice to meet you, thank you for inviting me,' or something like that. If she asks you a question and it's a yes or no answer, say 'yes ma'am' or 'no ma'am.' Wait for her to start eating before you touch your silverware. Put your napkin in your lap. Here we go." Angela pushed the door with her elbow and slipped through. We waited for about ten seconds, then followed Maria to the dining room.

THE GUITAR PLAYER

Every Saturday a man wearing white pants, a white shirt,
a wide brimmed sombrero and huaraches on his feet
appears on a corner of the market street in Centro, Nogales.
He sits on his simple wooden folding chair and begins to play his guitar.
He removes his hat and sets it upside down at his feet.
A few coins are glued to the inside of the crown.
When the number of tourists who have stopped to listen to the guitar
player reaches ten, he begins to play a faster tempo.
More tourists gather and drop coins in his hat.
His wife watches from across the street with a simple long shawl
draped over her hair and wrapped around her shoulders.
She counts the people.
When there are twenty people gathered,
she walks slowly across the street.
She stands at the back of the crowd, as though listening,
and little by little,
works her way forward until she is standing in front of the guitar player.
She begins to sway to the music.
He increases the tempo.
She opens the shawl a little and begins to turn slowly.
The tourists think she is a peasant, caught up in the music.
Someone begins to clap.
Her arms come free of her wrap and raise over her head.
She rolls her castanets and fixes her eyes on the person who is clapping.
She slides a shapely leg out to one side and holds the pose for a moment.
There is always a small gasp from the crowd.

She spins herself out of her shawl.
Beneath the guise, she wears a sparkling black skirt and a
white blouse pulled down around her shoulders.
And she begins to dance.
She shakes her beautiful black mane of hair free.
There is a rose behind one ear.
She is easily in her fifties,
still alluring to the tourists who thought they were watching a passerby,
and now realize they are seeing a professional flamenco dancer.

20

TERESA 1971

Expensive dress

The woman wore a marigold-colored dress that shimmered in the light. Her mahogany-colored hair was swept up at the sides, held with gold clips above her ears, and soft curls fell to her shoulders. She seemed young to me at first, because her skin was smooth, but her eyes looked old. The fabric of her dress was two layers, the marigold color underneath, and a top layer the same color, but you could see through it. I knew it was an expensive dress.

The woman sat in a high-backed chair on a long side of the table. Maria whispered, "Teresa, go to one side. Luna, to the other." Angela was standing to one side of the woman, holding her lips tightly as we came in. She leaned forward to hear something the woman was saying. Angela answered, and the woman looked sharply up at her, then at us. We set our plates down.

"Luna, Teresa, this is Mrs. Ormond. Mrs. Ormond, these are Nina's daughters, Luna and Teresa" Angela said.

Late that night, I lay in my bed, remembering how the woman stared for a long time at Luna, then slowly turned her head to look at me.

How her lips lifted into a smile that showed on her mouth, but not in her eyes. She moved like a painted marionette they sold at the Centro market.

"How do you do?" she said. Her head turned from side to side when she looked at each of us.

"Yes, ma'am," I said. I didn't know the answer to "how do you do?" I looked at Maria and hoped I'd said the right thing.

"Ma'am, the girls have come here from Centro. They are staying with me for now. They have a younger sister who is four," Maria said. It was like the woman in the marigold dress was half asleep, until Maria told her about Salma.

"Four!" the woman said brightly, "Oh, where is the little one?"

"She's at the nursery. We can meet her later if you like," Maria told her.

The woman looked at Maria in the strangest way. Maybe she had gotten dizzy, because she put her hands on the edge of the table. It was hard to tell if she was pale, because she had a lot of makeup on her face. Maria picked up the white cloth napkin beside the woman's plate, and spread it over her lap, just like she was a child who needed help.

"Thank you, dear," the woman said.

Luna was reading a magazine in our room that night, turning the pages so hard they sounded like they were ripping. Maybe Luna was thinking about how Maria had shot a look at her when she asked Mrs. Ormond a question.

"Did you know our mother, ma'am?" Luna asked. I looked at her, wishing I could say "will you just stop asking questions?"

Maria drew in a soft breath. The woman seemed unable to under-stand the question or else unable to speak.

"Luna is asking because their grandmother was here years ago. Their mother was Nina," Maria said gently.

"Nina!" the woman exclaimed, "Oh where is my baby? Where is she?"

Maria shot Luna a look that told her to shut her mouth and eat her lunch.

Maria nudged my leg under the table and told me with her eyes to eat my lunch and say nothing. I did.

"Ma'am, these sandwiches are that chicken left over from yesterday, and I sliced it up extra thin for you," Maria said.

"Did you? Did you?" the woman asked. Her face kept the same ex-pression. Her eyes didn't change. She picked up one of her sandwich pieces and ate, in dainty bites.

I couldn't get the strange lunch with the woman out of my head when I tried to sleep that night. I just wanted to get out of that room when the woman's head jerked up like she'd heard a balloon pop and stared at Luna.

"Nina, I've missed you. I'm so glad you're back. And Maria is all grown up now, as you see," The woman said.

"Yes ma'am," said Luna. Angela must have kicked Luna's leg under the table because Luna sort of jolted and looked down at her plate.

"Ma'am," said Maria, "Luna is Nina's daughter. Isn't she pretty?"

"Oh yes, yes, I knew that, yes, she is so pretty." The woman's eyes fell on me. After a few seconds of not knowing what to do, I set down my spoon and smiled at her. Something was wrong with her. I wondered if she was drunk, but I don't think that was it. No wonder she had to have someone like Maria and Angela cook for her. She was pretty, but her head was not working right.

"My husband will be home this evening," the woman said.

"Yes, ma'am," Maria said, and touched her hand to the woman's dress sleeve.

"He'll be so happy there's a new baby coming . . . how old is she?" The woman was looking far away out the window behind my chair. I looked up at Luna, because I knew Luna was staring at me, wondering the same thing I was wondering: what was wrong with Mrs. Ormond?

"She's four, ma'am," Maria told her.

"Oh, that is perfect," the woman said, looking at me, and then Luna for agreement.

"Yes, we all agree on that, don't we?" Maria said, nudging me with her leg.

"Yes, ma'am," I said. I'd finished my lunch.

Maria lifted her napkin from her lap, folded it twice, and laid it beside her plate. We followed Maria to the kitchen with the dishes. Maria checked our blouses and skirts for bread crumbs and spots. "We'll go back in and thank her for lunch."

When Maria pushed the door to the dining room open, the woman was holding on to Angela's hand, leaning in to talk with her like Angela was her best friend in the world. Maybe Angela was her best friend.

"Thank you so much for having us for lunch," Maria said, nudging our shoulders gently.

"Thank you, ma'am," I said. Luna did the same.

Mrs. Ormond rose gracefully from her chair and went toward a door at the far end of the dining room before she spoke.

"I hope you'll come back and meet my baby daughter. Perhaps you might like to play with her?"

The sun shining through her hair was like a crown of light I'd seen on a painting of a saint. She looked beautiful for that moment.

I thought of Paco's sister, Carmen, that night. Carmen always had someone to take care of her, to tell her what to do and when to do it. Carmen was always happy because she didn't know any better than to always be happy. I was just about to ask Luna what she was thinking, when Luna put down her magazine.

"What do you think is wrong with Mrs. Ormond?" Luna's eyebrows made a perfect set of quarter moons over her forehead. She looked just like our mother.

THE DANCE

She seems lost in the passion of the dance,
but really, she is counting the crowd.
She keeps the audience building around her
until there are forty or fifty people.
She swirls and draws them toward the hat on the ground, gesturing.
They put more coins in the hat.
Her husband drops from the chair to one knee on the ground,
still playing his guitar.
She leaps onto the chair to demonstrate her finale,
her shoes tapping a rapid staccato on the wooden seat.
The crowd responds with whistles and cheers and a final shower of coins.
A young girl who helps her mother and sister, selling cotton blankets,
maracas, and castanets on the market street in Centro
watches the dancer every week.
Today, she has a coin to put in the hat.
One of the dancer's gold hoop earrings
flies out into the street as she twirls.
The girl picks up the earring, holds it and the coin
and waits for the dance to finish.
As the crowd gives up the last coins, the young girl approaches shyly.
The dancer puts out her hand for a coin, and
the girl gives her the earring first.
The dancer scowls at the girl in disgust.
And the girl changes her mind about giving her coin to
a woman who seemed beautiful
but is not beautiful anymore.

The girl walks quickly back to the green canvas tarp.
When her mother walks toward her,
her mother's bright colored skirt, adorned with tiny bells makes music.
"Not everything that looks pretty is pretty when you get close, Teresa,"
the mother says.

21

ANA 1948

The offending toast

Breakfast for 2, 8:00
Grapefruit
Toast and marmalade
Bacon
Fried eggs

Señor Ormond rang the bell for Ana before she'd gotten back to the kitchen.

"Why is this toast so dark?" he asked.

Ana's face burned with humiliation. She took the offending toast back to the kitchen and made two lighter slices. She slipped back into the dining room quietly and set the plate in front of Stan Ormond. When she went back to clear the table, the new toast was untouched.

Every two weeks Gabriella brought three envelopes of American money. Suela and Maya talked about buying pretty dresses, and sometimes went to town with Gabriella for shopping. Ana put her envelopes in a rubber-banded bundle in the bottom of a drawer in her room. She could not think of a thing she needed from town.

Ana asked Gabriella if she could help her with mailing letters and money to her Aunt Pena in Mexico. Gabriella said there was a bank in town, and she'd help set up a bank account to keep her money safe. Ana gave that some thought. She trusted Aunt Pena but didn't know if Uncle Ancho might spend it betting on cockfights.

The three women in the hallway wore uniforms from early morning until midafternoon, when Maya brought Rudy and Nina home. Then they'd change into clothes they'd brought when they came to the ranch or something from the boxes of used clothing Gabriella brought to the hallway rooms. Some afternoons, if she was around the house, Gabriella would leave the side kitchen door open so the women and children could be outside on the grass. When Suela got home from her sewing job, Ana put her kitchen uniform back on and fixed dinner.

Rafael brought vegetables from the garden and eggs from the flock of chickens he kept and left them at the kitchen door for Gabriella to bring in. But when Maya and Ana were in the yard with the children, he'd push his wheelbarrow over to bring vegetables and eggs, so he could visit for a while.

Ana only heard from her employers through menu notes, or special instructions from Gabriella. In the three months she'd been cooking for the Ormonds, Señora had called her to the table because she wanted a different fork, or she'd dropped her napkin on the floor, or because the store-bought jam was too sweet, or because the soup she had not tasted yet was too salty, she could just tell by the smell.

But the toast was different, because *he* spoke to her.

The day Señor Ormond sent his toast back because Ana made it too dark was the day Suela went into labor. Gabriella and Ana were getting in the car to go to the bank when Maya came racing across the lawn.

"She has had one of them, but another is not coming out."

"I know how to help," Ana said quietly.

"You take care of Nina after school, we'll go help Suela," Gabriella said. "Ana, get in the car. Maya, is she at the workshop, or at the midwife's house?"

"The midwife's house," Maya said. "I'll come there when the children get out of school."

"Right," Gabriella said. "Let's get going Ana."

Gabriella drove across the yard to a house enclosed within an adobe wall. An old Mexican woman waited at the door. Ana heard whimpering cries from behind the wrinkled old woman and pushed her way into the dark room. Her eyes adjusted to the dim light as soon as she saw movement deeper in the room. She walked toward a gringo woman in a white dress beside a cot. Suela was on her back on the cot. The woman in white and another woman were holding her arms. A contraction slammed Suela into the bloody sheets, and she shrieked, cursing in Spanish at the soulless mothers of whores who held her.

"Ana can help," Gabriella said to the women.

"Let her go." Ana held back her own fear when she saw how pale her friend was. She rolled Suela onto her side and tugged at her blood-and-sweat soaked blouse. "Help me get this off her," she said without looking up. The two women stepped away from the bed.

"She cannot be indecent in front of Heavenly Father, not even while she births," one of them said.

"What?" Ana snapped.

Gabriella began pulling at Suela's blouse, ignoring the protests of one of the white women. The old woman who'd let them in shut the door and came closer.

"I need lard," Ana said in Spanish. The old woman hurried away and came back with a lidded tin pail. "Now, Suela, we are going to help you get on your knees."

Suela focused her bloodshot eyes on Ana and muttered "thank you." They helped her onto her knees, with her head against Gabriella's lap. Ana scooped a handful of lard and smeared it over her right hand and wrist.

"Suela, amiga, I am going to feel this baby. It is going to hurt."

Ana slid her slender fingers through the distended cervix, and felt only the buttocks of a baby. "Ah. This baby is backwards."

Suela buried her anguished face against Gabriella.

"Just do it," she whispered hoarsely in Spanish, "Because if you don't these whores of Ormond will get to watch me die."

When Ana's arm was in to her wrist, she looked up at Gabriella. "Let's roll her over slowly."

She kept her hand in place, pushing against little buttocks. She felt the baby slide. Ana scooped past a tiny foot and found a knee. She felt her way over the legs, guided them towards the chest, then slid her hand back to the feet, which were mercifully together, and pushed both feet upwards.

"Suela, don't push yet—" Ana's words were cut off by another contraction. She kept her arm in place. When the squeeze on her arm softened, she told Gabriella, "Now, on to her other side."

Ana didn't know how long it had been before the two women who'd held Suela down on her back had panicked and sent for help, but Suela was getting so weak that she wouldn't be able to push.

Suela came to rest on her right side, Ana felt the baby roll so that it's spine lay along Suela's, with the legs coming down the birth canal. "This baby is coming out feet first, but it is coming out," Ana said as the next contraction hit Suela.

The feet, legs, and buttocks of the tiny boy were out and Ana watched Suela's face as the contraction ended. This baby needed to get out before he suffocated. There was not much room to get her hand in, but she could feel that the umbilical cord was under one of the little arms, and around his neck. Suela shuddered with another contraction and cried pitifully. She shoved the baby out in a slosh of dark blood.

The two white women backed away from the bed. "Oh Heavenly Father, we ask for your mercy."

Ana slid the coil of umbilical cord from the neck, held him upside down in her ungreased hand, and shook him. There was no movement.

"My baby, my baby . . . " Suela began keening in Spanish. Gabriella held on to her hands when she tried to grope her way to Ana.

"Hush, Suela," Ana said firmly. "I'm not through with him." She gave the limp body a slap on the back of the thighs. He hung like a dead, skinned monkey from Ana's hand, and she squeezed his tiny chest twice with her free hand. The lips were darkening.

Gabriella murmured a prayer.

One of the white women put her hands over her face and whined, "You're hurting the baaaby."

"Oh, I can't bear to watch," said the other woman, who had retreated to the corner furthest away from the cot. The tiny mouth opened. A glob of mucous flopped and landed on Suela's leg with a soft slosh.

"He is going to cry now," said the old midwife. Her wrinkled face glowed strangely, like a burned down candle in the dim light.

Ana stuck her finger into the open mouth, scooped out another blob of sticky mucous and squeezed his chest again. The thin little cry sounded like a kitten's, but it was a sound, and he gasped air into his lungs when Ana put her greased arm along his back and swung him upward.

"I need some string," Ana said softly to the old woman, who hurried off to another room. She was back in seconds with a ball of twine.

"Tie here and here." Ana then realized this woman had assisted many births. She knew where to tie the cord. The old woman took a pen knife from her apron pocket, folded the tied-off segment of umbilical cord around the blade, and severed it by pulling the fold tight against the blade.

"Where is the other baby?" Ana asked, wiping her hands on a towel Gabriella handed her.

"We put her in a crib," one of the white women answered.

"Who took care of her?" Ana asked, laying the tiny boy on Suela's bare chest.

"I did," answered the old woman, in Spanish.

"I'm sorry I was telling you what to do. You know what to do," Ana said.

"Yes, I do," said the old woman, "but not how to push a baby back in so it can come out."

"Bring the other baby in here, please," Gabriella said to the gringo woman in the white dress.

"You don't give me orders, you're just a . . . a maid," the woman sputtered.

Gabriella left Suela's side, walked to the woman and backed her against the wall.

"Go get the other baby," she said in a low voice. "If you don't want to, how about if I tell Mrs. Ormond about how you—"

The woman scurried away and returned with a swaddled infant.

"Unwrap her and put her here," Gabriella said.

The woman took a step back from the cot. She stared in horror at Suela's bare chest where the newborn boy lay limp but breathing.

"I'm not putting her on that mess," said the woman, indignantly.

Gabriella took the baby from her, unwound the swaddling, and laid the tiny girl on Suela's chest. Suela wept, exhausted, with her hands on the heads of the two infants. The little girl's mouth began to move.

Ana guided the mouth toward a nipple and stroked the baby's cheek with a finger. The baby girl began to nurse. The two white women huffed loudly and went outside.

Suela was exhausted, but at peace, in a sticky, sweating way, gazing at the tiny girl who was latched on and sucking like a healthy piglet.

"Do you have a breast pump?" Ana asked.

"Yes. And some bottles." The old woman padded to the kitchen and came back with an ancient breast pump in her apron pocket, then ran back to the kitchen to a whistling kettle. While Ana and Gabriella changed the sheets and put fresh bedclothes on Suela, the midwife clattered around and returned with four steaming mugs on a tray. Hot milk sprinkled with cinnamon for the new mother, and aromatic tea for the rest. The tea smelled like sage and tarweed, licorice, and vanilla. The baby girl had fallen asleep, and the boy had not nursed.

"You drink this, then I will help you save some of that milk, *chica.*" The old woman tenderly patted Suela's cheek.

"And you," she said to Ana, "You drink this tea, and after you leave, I will read the leaves." The old woman's eyes had a bluish cast in the dim light, and Ana realized she was nearly blind.

"How do you read them?" Ana asked.

"With my fingers, and my heart. For people who have souls. Not those two who were here when you got here. They have no souls. They—"

"Thank you for the tea, Esme," Gabriella said quickly, "I'll be back for Suela tomorrow. Do you need anything for her for tonight?"

The old woman held her mug close to her face, breathing the steam. "I have all I need here. I will take good care of them until you come to take them from me." she said. She turned her rheumy eyes from Suela and the babies to Ana's face. "I hope you don't have any babies."

"I have a little girl," Ana said, confused. The woman looked past Ana, to the window that illuminated the room.

"I hope you don't have any more, because it will only break your heart, and you will not be able to love them."

Gabriella spoke with a harder edge in her voice. "Thank you for the tea." The old woman withdrew to her tea.

Gabriella sat on the chair next to the cot, and patted Suela's arm. "I'll get you some things for tonight. We'll go home tomorrow."

"Home?" Suela asked, dreamily. "We'll go home with their father, and we'll be a family."

"Do you know where we can find him? To let him know you have had your babies?" Ana asked.

Gabriella turned to see the front door standing open, and no sign of the two gringo women. She squeezed water from a washcloth in a basin the old midwife had brought, and gently wiped Suela's face.

"He knows by now," Gabriella said.

Dinner at 6:30, 4 adults, 1 child
Family style, spaghetti and meatballs and a salad
Ice cream for dessert
High chair beside my chair, please

"Where is Nina?" Ana said, as much to herself as to Gabriella. Gabriella stopped the car and Ana was striding toward Maya before the engine stopped. Maya waited at the kitchen door with Rudy. Rudy was pulling and twisting away from his mother's grip.

"Hurry, Rudy is going to wet his pants." Maya turned to Rudy. "You do not piss on the grass, you just wait."

Gabriella turned the key and Rudy bolted from his mother. He pulled at the locked hallway door, then ran to the bathroom in the kitchen's side room.

"Where is Nina?"

"Nina? You don't have her?" Maya looked puzzled.

Ana's voice rose. "You were supposed to bring her to the midwife's house." If Maya was joking, it was not funny. She spun to look around the yard. Nina must be hiding, playing a game with her. That must be it. "Nina! Come out."

"Ana, she is not with me. When I got to the nursery they said Señora picked her up. You did not know?"

Gabriella pocketed her key ring. "Maya, what's going on?"

"Oh, Gabriella, I went to the nursery to get Nina. They said—"

"Never mind," Gabriella said. "I'll find her, Ana." She picked up the menu from the counter.

"Where is my daughter?" Ana shouted, rushing into the kitchen. "Nina!"

"Ana, shhh. Please don't," Gabriella said. "I know where she is."

Ana stopped cold and turned to face Gabriella. "Then tell me where my daughter is!"

"Ana, I promise she is here, I'll get her." Gabriella read the note. She sighed and put the note down. Ana snatched the rose-colored paper from the counter.

Ana spoke evenly as she held the note out to Gabriella. "This one child that is coming for dinner, is this my daughter?"

"Ana, she has done this before. I'm so sorry. But Nina is safe. Please, Ana, please. Get cleaned up and get dinner started, and I'll check on Nina. I promise she is fine."

Ana's fury rose and nearly choked her.

Maya wailed tearfully, "Oh, I wish I'd gotten there first."

"Maya, please," Gabriella sighed. "Please get cleaned up, Ana. I'll be back with her."

Ana looked down at her bloodied uniform. She felt like her chest was caving in from the sob she held down in her lungs.

"I'm going with you. No one can just take my daughter."

Gabriella shook her head firmly. "I'll be back. Please, Ana, don't make this worse. Just get cleaned up. I need to change clothes before I go in the main house. But I'll find her. I promise you." Ana glared while Gabriella spoke quietly to Maya. Rudy came back to the kitchen.

"Come on, Rudy, let's go find your book." Maya grabbed Rudy by the hand.

"Use the shower in the kitchen bathroom, Ana, and get a uniform there," Gabriella said, looking at the blood and lard on Ana's arms. Ana watched in disbelief while Gabriella closed Maya and Rudy in, then locked the kitchen door behind her. Her Nina was missing, and now she was trapped in the kitchen while someone else went looking for her.

Ana ran through the back room to the rack where uniforms hung. She jerked a hanger from the bar and took the dress to the bathroom. The shower curtain rings screeched when she ripped the curtain aside.

She shoved a towel over the towel bar and turned on the water. Pipes shuddered and water came pouring out, splashing on the floor. She'd wash up, get changed, and then she'd go into the main house and find Nina. That's what she'd do.

Her bloodied uniform went in the laundry basket in a wad. She scrubbed her arms and hands and under her nails with the brush. When the water ran clear, she shut the faucets off and reached from behind the curtain for a towel she'd hung on the bar. It wasn't there. She pushed the curtain aside and picked up the towel from the floor.

She put her underwear and slip back on, then the fresh uniform. She was re-pinning her hair when something in the mirror caught her eye. It was the bathmat on the floor behind her. The one she'd just stepped on coming out of the shower.

There was a faint shoe print on it, the size of a man's shoe. She stared at the image in the mirror, trying force her racing mind to reason. Ana retraced her steps to the shower and looked down curiously at the damp mat. Maybe one of the men had been working in the house, maybe he had fixed something in the shower. Then she spotted the other shoeprint, pressed into the towel she'd just picked up off the floor and used.

Her skin went cold.

Dinner at 6:30, four adults, 1 child
Family style, spaghetti and meatballs, and a salad
Ice cream for dessert
High chair beside my chair, please

Gabriella came back from changing her stained clothes and found Ana staring at Señora Ormond's note again. She drew a deep breath.

"Ana, please don't be angry. Mrs. Ormond has had Nina in the house with her all this time."

"Why? Why would she do that without asking me?" Ana struggled to keep her voice from exploding.

"She loves little children, Ana, and she means no harm. But I'm sorry she didn't let us know what she was doing. She'll bring Nina to the dinner table, and I'll make sure she—"

"I am not allowed to say who has my daughter?" Ana's expression went flat.

"Please, let me handle it with Señora Ormond," Gabriella said. "I'll make sure it doesn't happen this way again. The other two at dinner will be the women who were at the midwife's house. I'll handle things. Please let me." She disappeared into the dining room.

Ana started the requested dinner and extra for Maya, Rudy and herself. She was whisking salad dressing when she heard her daughter's squealing laugh from the dining room. She grabbed the countertop hard to keep from running in, grabbing her daughter, and running home to the convent. She wanted to feel safe again. Instead, she tossed the salad.

Gabriella came in, grim faced, took the salad, then motioned from the dining room door for Ana to come with the spaghetti.

"Oh, here we are," said Lorene Ormond. She wore a peach-colored blouse and tan skirt, with her perfect hair and peach-colored nails. "Thank you, Ana."

Ana nodded.

Nina waved her chubby hands from the high chair beside Señora Ormond. Nina wore a new pink dress, with a pink bow around her head that pulled her dark hair away from her face. On the tray of the high chair lay a blonde-haired doll with painted lips, and a dress that matched Nina's dress. Gabriella poured water for the two women across the table from Mrs. Ormond and Nina.

Ana rushed back to the kitchen. Her face burned with anger at the arrogance of the woman who had taken her daughter from the nursery and dressed her up like a doll. She was waiting when Gabriella came into the kitchen.

Ana spoke in a hiss under her breath. "What is going on? Where are Nina's clothes I sent her to the nursery in this morning? Who gave her the right to do that?"

"Ana, I know how it seems, but listen to me. She'll buy her some dresses and nice things and when another little girl comes along that she can spoil, she'll leave Nina alone. She's done this before. She wants a little girl. I won't let anything happen to your daughter. She'll be safe. I promise."

Ana pressed her fingers into her eyelids, but it didn't help her see the reason for Señora taking her daughter. "Will I get her back after dinner?"

Gabriella touched her arm gently. "Probably."

"Probably!" Ana said, incredulously.

"Let me finish. Showing her to the guests will be all Señora wants. But, please, don't say anything, it's not the place—"

Ana waved her hand at Gabriella to say no more. She made a tray for Maya and Rudy.

Ana could hear the conversation at the dinner table clearly, not at all like the silence when it was just Señor and Señora. One of the women from the midwife's house was talking loudly.

". . . and thank goodness we were there or we'd have lost both babies."

The other voice said, "So sad about the little boy, isn't it? These girls don't eat properly, that's the problem. They don't know anything about the will of our Heavenly Father."

Ana still tasted bile from her discovery of footprints on the bathmat and towel. Now she gave Gabriella a questioning look.

Gabriella leaned over to whisper, "The little boy. He isn't doing well yet."

"What? Why?"

"Those two told Esme, the midwife, they thought he was cursed. They went back, after we were gone."

"Cursed? How would they know!" Ana whispered, "That baby was upside down, that was all. He was fine."

"Yes, he seemed to be," Gabriella said quietly. "I'll go over tomorrow first thing and see Suela. Let's go after breakfast. You can go with me."

A half hour passed and Ana quietly cleaned up the kitchen, seething at the voices of the two women, and the sounds of Nina laughing along with Señora Ormond when she laughed. Ana's heart felt like lead in her chest, to hear such talk like that about poor Suela and her babies. Especially by those horrible women in the dining room. She heard Señor say "I trust you'll make all the arrangements for the baby, Rosemary?"

One of the women answered "Yes, of course, Stan, as always."

Now, Ana's heart was pounding again. Arrangements? For Suela's baby? The bell for dessert tinkled, and she realized she hadn't dished the ice cream.

Gabriella said, "I've got it. You go clear dishes, I'll get that ready."

Ana smoothed her hair, then slid silently through the door. Nina had spaghetti sauce on the front of the new dress, and even more on her face. She held a handful of noodles in one hand and half a meat ball in the other, and she was about to fall asleep into the rest of the food on her tray.

"Shall I take this girl to the kitchen and clean her up, Señora?" she asked quietly, pushing the tray out so she could lift Nina from the high chair.

"Oh, that would be nice, thank you. She did make a mess of herself. And get that dress clean, if you can, Ana, it's new."

"Yes, she certainly is a messy little thing. No one has taught her manners yet," said the voice that must have been Rosemary.

"Now, Rosemary, the poor thing is probably an orphan. You don't expect her to have manners, now do you?" said the other, the one with the big lipstick-lined lips.

"Rosemary, Rayleen, I will not have you speaking like that to Lorene about that child, do you understand? When you have your own to raise, let's see how you do," Stan Ormond said sharply.

Ana's mind was reeling. There had never been discussions going on with her in the room before, and she didn't want to be in the room with these women for this discussion now. She lifted Nina from the high chair, closed a free hand over Nina's fist that held a strand of spaghetti and rushed back through the kitchen to the back rooms. She thrust Nina at Maya.

"She has had dinner, as you can see," Ana said.

Ana went back to finish clearing dinner plates. Gabriella set dessert down, and quietly took the high chair into the kitchen.

Ana scraped dishes and piled them into the sink with a bit more clatter than usual.

"I think that was all right for you to take Nina away to clean her up—" Gabriella started.

Ana interrupted in a shrill whisper. "She is my daughter, not a doll for anyone to play with and dress up. This cannot happen again. I will not be quiet about this again."

131

Gabriella reached for Ana's hand to stop the rattling plates. "Ana, I am so sorry. If Nina were my daughter, I'd be very upset too. I'll be sure this doesn't happen. I'll explain to Señora Ormond. Thank you for not saying anything."

Gabriella helped Ana finish the after-dinner cleanup and carried the tray with plates for Maya and Rudy to their room.

"I'll see you in the morning, Ana. I'll take care of this, I promise."

Ana took her plate from the oven where she'd left it to stay warm and scraped the food into the trash can. She went into the hallway, to Maya's open door to find Nina in her nightgown, stacking colored wooden blocks on the floor with Rudy. She heard the deadbolt slide shut behind her at the hallway door.

"Maya, have you seen Suela since you left the midwife's house to get me and Gabriella?" Ana said, sitting down beside Nina.

"No, why?" Maya was unpinning her hair.

"Because those two women went back to the midwife's house and now they say the little boy is cursed," Ana told her. "I hope it's not true, but I will go over with Gabriella tomorrow to see Suela. Who are those women? I know Gabriella does not like them."

"Those women are witches. Terrible women," Maya said, picking up her hairbrush. "They are sisters, that is what Señora calls them. Señor calls them that too," she said.

"Sisters? Nuns? They are not nuns!" Ana said.

"No, sister-wives," Maya said. Rudy tossed a block toward Nina, and it bounced off her bare leg. "Rudy, don't throw the blocks."

Ana picked up the block and pressed it into her palm, feeling the edges, while Nina tried to pry her mother's fingers away from it.

"What does that mean, sister-wives?" Ana asked.

"It means they are sealed to a man by the church, and they can't get married to anyone else, but they are not married to him either," Maya said.

"What does sealed mean?" Ana asked.

"It means they can have children with a man, and it is all right in their church," Maya said.

"For a man to have three wives?" Ana asked, not believing what Maya was saying.

"One wife, but he can have other women sealed to him, so they can have children who will have his name. The church lets men do that," Maya said, looking at her work worn hands.

"How can that be?" Ana asked. She hoped Rudy was not old enough to repeat things he was hearing.

"I thought you knew. Suela's babies are with a man who is married to another woman, and that woman does not know it."

Ana stood shakily. "The father of Suela's babies is married to another woman?" she asked.

"Yes, I thought you knew," Maya said. "He told Suela he would love her and take care of her."

She patted Rudy's head when he carefully handed a block to Nina instead of tossing it.

Ana swallowed hard before she spoke. "No, how would I know that?"

Maya sighed and put her hairbrush down.

"Ana, it's the way of their church here, and to them it is the way to heaven, so that sounds good to the man, even if we think it is wrong in the eyes of God."

"Maya, it IS wrong. It is wrong. What happens to Suela now?" Ana blinked as she looked at the children.

Maya looked closely at Ana and sighed. "She will stay at the midwife's house for a few days, and if one of the babies is damaged, that is sad. But maybe Suela will get to live in her own house, without locks on the doors. You have seen the small houses to the west of the main house? The ones with the fences around them?"

Ana nodded.

"If the man is pleased with one of her babies, she will live there, and have others. If not, she will come back to live with us, and that leaves the houses free for women who have babies he wants."

"Babies he *wants?*" Ana asked. "Why would he not want them?"

"If they look white enough, he will want them. If not, their mothers can keep them if they don't get in the way. I got to keep Rudy, because he looked too Mexican."

"Maya, you are saying you had Rudy with the same man?" Ana said, picking up her daughter.

"Do you want me to tell you or not?" Maya said. "Ana, it is different here. If you want to know, I'll tell you, and if you don't want to know, I won't."

"I don't know if I want to know," Ana answered, feeling in the pocket of her uniform for anything to hold in her hand. Her stomach clenched into a knot that gripped her tightly. Ana twisted the cheap gold wedding band on her ring finger. She had not thought much about the man who'd run away from her when she had gotten pregnant until now. Now she wished he had come back from the racetrack and married her, so she would not be here, listening to Maya explain that the same man had made Suela and Maya pregnant, and was not going to marry either one of them because he was already married.

"He said we were sealed in the eyes of his Heavenly Father. That's what he calls God. And it was approved for us to have a baby. But he said Rudy was born with the mark of Cain, and it was my fault. He said after Rudy was born that I could still work here. And maybe someday I will have another baby. I get paid good money, and Rudy can go to school here. It's not like you think."

"Maya, you'd have another baby with him after he said that about your son?" Ana got to one knee and picked Nina up.

Maya seemed at peace, happy, even, to Ana. Ana backed toward the door with Nina in her arms.

"I don't know, maybe. It's not like you think," Maya said.

"I don't even know what I think," Ana said.

Ana felt as if the blood had drained from her head. She took Nina into her room and shut the door. She put Nina in her crib and went into the bathroom down the hall to put her nightgown on, since it was the only door other people didn't just walk through. She hurried back to her room. Maya's door was still open. Maya was on the floor, showing Rudy how to make a pyramid stack of blocks, just as if their conversation had never happened.

Ana lay on her narrow bed, on her side so she could see Nina's crib. The Ormond's kitchen and servant's quarters were locked up for the night. Gabriella saw to that. But Ana didn't feel safe, even with all the locked doors, because somebody with a key to the kitchen had used it today to come into the bathroom while she was in the shower.

Ana drifted off to sleep.

The blessed Virgin appeared before her, in a pale blue, blood stained dress. Her hands and feet bled from holes in them. The Virgin held a blue-faced baby in front of her while she wailed at Ana to help her. Ana groped at the blue baby, and pulled the umbilical cord from around its neck, and as she did, the tiny boy's grey-green eyes opened and blazed at her.

"Whose child is this?" the Virgin demanded.

Ana knelt in front of the plaster woman, staring at the baby.

"I don't know," she answered. Her voice was a choked gasp in her throat.

"He is the child of Satan, Ana, and you let him live," the Virgin whispered hoarsely.

Ana's own "No, No, No, No," brought her back to her room and her little bed. She was sweating, and Nina was whimpering in her crib.

Maybe everything that had happened that day had been part of the bad dream. Because what the horrible women said, and what Maya had told her, couldn't possibly be true. Ana lay in the darkness and listened to the night winds push at the window panes. "Better not sleep, better not sleep," they said. Ana turned her face toward Nina's crib and considered picking her up and bringing her daughter to her own bed, but Nina had quieted herself. She'd let her daughter sleep, and try to sleep herself, even if she had to face the Blessed Virgin holding up her devil's spawn in her dreams. And she knew what she'd do if the Virgin tried to hand her that grey-green-eyed infant again.

22

TERESA 1971

Pretty people

Maria didn't say anything until we got to her kitchen door. "Girls, when you go to school, don't talk about Mrs. Ormond. There are things about her that you don't understand. She's a nice lady. That's all you need to say if another kid or a teacher asks."

In our room, I laid my clothes I'd worn from Centro on my bed. "You're not going to wear those, are you?" Luna asked.

"What else am I going to wear?"

"You have new clothes to wear, Teresa." She opened the closet and counted her blouses and skirts. "You wear whatever you want, but I'm going to dress nice so I can get a job and make some money."

"Maybe we should go home, Luna."

"Home? I'm not going back! Pia is probably in our house right now!" she shouted. "You want Pia for a mother?"

"Stop yelling. Maria will hear you," I said. My throat was starting to hurt. Luna shuffled the hangers in the closet and pushed hers further over to her side.

"I'm staying until I make some money," she said, "I'm going to get my own house."

"Luna, you're so stupid," I said to her. "You think you can buy a house? Houses cost a lot. You're fourteen. You can't buy a house."

"Well, I can cook, so I'll do like Grandmother did and cook," she snapped.

"Let's just tell Maria we want to go home."

"I'm going to make some money. These people are rich. They can pay. Don't say you don't know they have money."

I gave up talking to her. Maybe I needed more sleep. Maybe she was right about not going back to Mexico right now, but I wasn't going to tell her if she was.

Luna looked in the mirror and held her hair on top of her head.

"Help me fix my hair," she said.

I got the brush and some of our mother's hair pins out of the pack.

"I think Maria will hire me to work in the kitchen instead of making me go to school." she said. I made sure when I hit a tangle in her hair I pulled extra hard.

"You are going to regret that," she said, under her breath.

I put her hair up in the same kind of soft roll I would do on Mama's hair.

Luna looked at it and said, "There, you did fine. See how easy it is to be nice?"

I slapped the brush down on the dresser, picked my old clothes up, and went into the bathroom. I slammed the door behind me, and heard Luna laugh. I didn't really want to wear those old clothes, but I didn't want to wear the same clothes as Luna the crazy person. I waited until I heard her go out of the bedroom, then sat on the edge of the bathtub with my old clothes from Centro in my lap and cried a little.

After I changed clothes and washed my face, I walked to the living room. Luna was sitting on the sofa, watching the television. The people on the television were pretty and white and they all had fancy clothes and perfect hair. Maria came in from the kitchen and sat on the arm of the sofa to watch. She talked to Luna like she knew those people on the television.

This woman was married to this man, but she used to be married to the other man who was a doctor, until she found him cheating with the woman who just put on her fancy fur coat and left, and their daughter they had while they were married was about to get married herself, but her boyfriend was in the hospital because he had amnesia. Luna asked what that meant, and Maria said it meant he couldn't remember things, and he was supposed to marry her, but he had married someone else. I stood behind the couch listening to Maria's explanation of the television people's lives. They might be pretty people, but they had ugly lives.

The clock on the living room wall made a musical sound.

"Three o'clock," Maria said. Now, there was a man on the television who was sad because he had his white uniform and his cap on, but no one had called him to fix their washing machine.

Maria stood. "Salma will be out of the nursery in fifteen minutes. I need to go get her. Anyone want to go?" Luna was glued to the television, watching the pretty people.

"I'll go," I said, then looked down at the old clothes I'd just put on. Maria glanced back at the ugly lives people, then looked at her watch.

"You're fine just like you are." she said. Luna looked sideways at me and made a face. I followed Maria out the door. She didn't lock the door behind her. Maybe she hoped somebody would steal Luna. I hoped somebody would.

It took less time to walk to the school than it had in the morning, I guess because we weren't talking and Maria was in a hurry. We saw a few women coming out leading small children. "Ooo, I didn't want to be late . . . " Maria said, more to herself than to me.

All the children except Salma were gone, and the woman who had been in the office that morning looked up from the desk and closed a yellow folder and smiled. Salma sat straddle-legged on the mat where I'd last seen her, looking up and laughing at a woman who sat on a low stool beside the play mat with her back to us. The woman in the shimmering marigold dress, with mahogany colored hair. The woman we'd fixed lunch for, that was who it was. She was holding out animal crackers for Salma who waved her hands like the monkey that used to beg from tourists on the market street in Centro. Salma was stuffing crackers in her mouth as fast as she could take them.

"Oh, *there* you are," Mrs. Ormond said to Maria. "My little Salma and I were just about to go home, but Suela said you'd want to come see her, didn't you, Suela?" Mrs. Ormond looked back at Salma and laughed when Salma wiped her hands on the front of her green dress. Miss Suela pushed her glasses up on her nose and gave Maria a look that said she did not want to talk about this right now. Connie, from the front desk took her yellow folder and left.

"Yes, we wanted to see her, and Teresa would like to take her back to my house and give her a bath for you, wouldn't you, Teresa?" she said. Her voice rose sharply at "wouldn't you?"

When Maria's forehead pushed up in a crease, I said, "Yes, Ma'am."

"Oh, lovely, that is wonderful. You know I can't have my girl be a mess when she meets Mr. Ormond, now can I?" She stood and backed away from the cracker crumbs scattered around Salma. "When will you bring her to my house?" Mrs. Ormond asked, coming toward me. "I assume you know how to wash her, and that you can get some clean clothes on her, too?" she said, looking at me like she'd never seen me before, and it was barely two hours after we'd fixed her lunch and eaten with her. She had to be older than she looked, because she certainly was forgetful.

"Yes, ma'am," I answered, taking Salma by the hand and pulling her to her feet. Salma started to whimper, and I squeezed her arm to let her know she needed to hush right now and come with me. Bad enough Luna was acting crazy. I wasn't going to leave Salma with this crazy woman.

"Someone has come a long way to see you," David Sanchez said when he came through the door between Maria's kitchen and dining room.

School had let out for the summer that day, and Maria had picked us up after school to go to the grocery store with her.

"Hey, Luna, Teresa, I have a surprise for you," she'd said.

"What's the surprise?" I asked when we were on the road to Tubac.

"It's a surprise," was all Maria would say. She stopped at the market and bought some packaged meat, sugar and a gallon of milk. "Let's get back and get dinner started. David will be here at six thirty."

Luna rolled her eyes at me and whispered, "He's always there at six thirty."

By the second week in June we knew all the other kids at the school, except for the white-haired, white-skinned twins, who didn't eat lunch outside with the rest of us. Luna had done well in school, and even helped one of the other Mexican girls with her English. We'd never realized, until we went to school in Arizona at the ranch, that we really did know more English than other kids from Mexico.

I didn't like school at the ranch. I hated the way the teachers told us that we needed to read some different Bible she was always talking about, and told us what "Heavenly Father" wanted us to do to earn our way to heaven. I'd liked going to school in Centro, but here it made me feel like I'd done something wrong. Every morning the teacher would talk about what was expected of us, how we would have to learn to be good girls. There was some different underwear the teacher told us we needed. When I asked Maria about that she said we would not need different underwear. Luna had weird ideas, but she wasn't as weird as that teacher. I was glad when Maria told us we wouldn't have to go to church with the other kids on Saturdays.

I was setting the table at Maria's house while Luna helped in the kitchen. David Sanchez's patrol truck pulled up outside the back door. David came through the door to the dining room and that was when he said someone had come a long way to see me.

The door from the kitchen opened, and there he was. Paco. My best friend Paco. I shrieked with happiness and rushed to him and put my arms around him. He felt bony and dried out, but he was Paco. His cheeks and lips were chapped, and his hair looked like he had been in a windstorm, but he was Paco. I held him by the shoulders and looked at him. I wished I could kiss him without everybody seeing.

We gathered around the table set with a platter of beef and a pot of gazpacho. Paco ate as if he hadn't eaten in a week. He ate everything Maria pushed his way. She brought flan from the kitchen and set two dishes in front of Paco. Finally, he looked up at Maria and said, "Gracias."

"Well, Paco," Maria said, "I'm glad you ended up here, however it was you got here."

"What did you do, run away from home?" Luna said, leaning toward Paco.

I snapped a look at her that told her to shut up. Paco took a shallow breath, like he was thinking how to answer. Luna was not going to shut her mouth. She was so nosy.

"Who brought you, a coyote?" she asked. Paco was scooping flan from the second dish. He stopped for a second, holding the spoonful of quivering flan in front of his mouth.

"A man said he'd help me," he said, "I made a deal with him. But," he put the spoon in his mouth, "he didn't bring me here like he said he would."

Paco told us that the man had been waiting for him when he came out of school one day, a few weeks after my mother and sisters and I had left Centro. The man told him he knew where we'd gone. Did Paco want to visit? Paco asked how much it would cost to go to Arizona, and the man said he'd seen Paco's roosters, and he'd trade one of them for a ride. Paco knew he couldn't trade off one of his roosters because his father had given them to him, and he told the guy that, so the guy said he'd get Paco in some good cockfights in Arizona and they could be partners. He'd give Paco a ride for half the winnings if he brought a rooster with him.

Paco knew his parents wouldn't let him go, so when the guy came to the school again and told him they'd go that night, he snuck out his bedroom window with a sack of clothes, got his rooster, and met the man on the next street over from the school. He said the man talked a lot about me and my sisters, so he thought the man really knew us. The man had pulled off on a dirt road about an hour after they'd crossed the border, saying he needed to piss. Paco got out to do the same, and the man drove off with Paco's bag of clothes and his rooster.

Paco didn't know where he was, so when he saw lights he walked toward them. He didn't know where he was going, but he went to a ranch house and drank water from the hose in the yard. He was afraid to knock on the door to ask for help. He walked all night, and in the morning, that was when the Border Patrol agent came driving down the dirt road and saw him before he could hide.

"That was me," David Sanchez added.

"Who was the guy who gave you a ride and stole your rooster?" Maria asked. Paco looked down at his empty dessert plate.

"Favo," he said, almost in a whisper. David and Maria looked at each other, then Maria started picking up dishes.

"FAVO!?" Luna screeched, "Favo doesn't know a thing about roosters and fighting except how to gamble on them!"

Oh, now Luna was an expert on cockfighting, and on what Favo knew.

"Shut up, Luna," I said.

"I picked Paco up near Patagonia," David said. That was where Favo left him. Paco told me he was trying to get to his friend Teresa Espinosa in Tubac. So, I brought him here."

Maria's voice was low. "Favo wasn't bringing him here." She had stopped in the kitchen door to look across the table at David.

"No, he wasn't bringing him here," David said.

"Lucky for you, Paco. One of the other agents would have turned you in," Maria said.

"Maria, I could get in a lot of trouble for transporting him here," David said. "I could lose my job."

Maria set the dishes she was carrying on the kitchen counter and came back to put her hands on the edge of the table. She leaned close to David.

"You didn't know he came from Mexico. You were being a nice guy. You gave a lost kid a ride," she said.

"Yeah, like you gave the girls a ride, except I have a patrol truck, and I have a uniform and a badge that says I work for the Border Patrol." He leaned back in his chair and looked at Luna and me. "You girls don't talk about this at school, okay?"

Luna picked up her spoon and stabbed it through the quarter inch of caramelized top on her flan. "We're out of school for the summer. And I'm not going back." She looked at Maria like she was challenging her.

"No, we won't tell. Salma, you won't tell, either, will you?" I said.

Salma waved her spoon above her flan. "Won't tell. Won't tell."

David helped Maria clear dishes, and said to us, "My guys know who Favo is, and we know what Favo does, and it's a good thing he left Paco where he did. That was why I found him."

"He didn't seem so bad, until he stole my rooster," Paco said.

"When was Favo ever not bad?" Luna was mocking my friend, and I hated her for that.

"He seemed okay. He said he knew all of you, and he knew where you were," Paco answered, looking at me.

"Ugh. He's a liar. You were lucky he didn't kill you, not just dump you," Luna said, like a know-it-all. I wished she'd go away. Maybe go get lost in the desert.

In the living room, Paco sat on the sofa beside me while Luna twisted the television knob to get a show she wanted. I wanted to sit close enough that our legs would touch, but I knew if Luna saw she'd have a big mouth and tell everyone.

We watched "Happy Days" and I remember thinking that it would be happy for me now, with school out, and with Paco here. David and Maria were talking in the kitchen, and I heard her yell, "Favo! You know what he is!"

I nudged Paco's leg. I wanted to ask him which rooster he'd brought, but his head was tipped forward, and his eyes were closed. He was asleep. David came into the living room from the kitchen.

"Come on, little buddy." He half carried, half led Paco down the hall.

"Tomorrow we'll work on getting him back home. We need to let his parents know where he is," Maria said. She stood behind the sofa, watching the television.

"If they know Favo took him they probably think he's dead," Luna said.

"You shut your big mouth!" I shouted at her. I stomped down the hall to our room and slammed the door hard.

I tapped on the door and went into the kitchen. Maria was looking in the freezer, and stopped what she was saying in the middle of a word when I walked in. David was sitting on the counter with a beer in his hand.

"Yes, Teresa?" she asked.

"I'm sorry to interrupt," I said, "but I was wondering about something that happened the day you found us."

"Yes?" She closed the freezer door.

"Favo came into that cafe, looking for us, and you and Angela hid us from him. But how did you know we were hiding from him?"

"I didn't know," she said.

"But you *know* him?" I asked.

"Yes, I know him," she said.

"But, if he lives in Centro . . . how do you know him?"

"Favo is from here, Teresa."

"HERE? From Tubac?" I was a little scared, even in Maria's house.

"No, honey," she said, "from here, the ranch. He hasn't lived here for a long time, but he was born here."

"Born here," I repeated. "His mother lived here?" Maria watched David peeling the label off his beer bottle.

"She still does. She's a good lady. She works in the nursery. She takes care of Salma."

"Miss Suela? Miss Suela is his mother?" I could barely keep my voice from cracking.

145

"Yes, she is. But it's not her fault Favo was a bad kid. She tried," Maria said softly.

"Suela told you that?" I asked.

"I grew up with him, Teresa," she said, her voice even softer, almost a whisper. "He was a bad kid when he was in school. He was just born bad."

David set his empty bottle on the counter and swung his legs. "Teresa, I knew Favo was looking for you, we saw him around out there when Maria was waiting for you to get here."

I remembered when Favo called Luna a puta in Centro. Favo had been looking for us in the desert, too, when Luna, Salma, and I were trying to get to Tubac. He was at the windmill. In that cafe where Maria and Angela had stopped with Salma and Luna, where I had found them, Maria and Angela talked to him like they knew he was a bad guy. Now, he'd found Paco and made an offer to take him to us. That meant Favo knew where we were.

"He knows we're here," I said, watching David, because his face was easier to understand than Maria's.

"Yes, he does, but he won't come onto the ranch, even Favo won't do that. We won't let anything happen to you, Teresa. Favo can't ever come back to the ranch."

"Why?" I asked.

"He hurt a girl at school," Maria said. She leaned against the counter, close to David.

"Maria, I think—"

Maria glared at David and pointed a finger at him like she wanted him to stop talking. But he kept talking.

"Maria, she needs to know why she can't go off, trying to go back to Mexico, alone. She has no idea what Favo would—"

Maria's eyes flashed.

"Then why don't you arrest him when you see him? You use him to find the other coyotes. Like it's okay to do that because he does you favors."

"I can't arrest him just for being in Arizona, Maria. He has his papers. He's a citizen," David said.

146

Maria yanked a clean dishtowel out of a drawer and poked it through the handle on the refrigerator door. I knew this kind of talking had happened before, between her and David, the way he put his head down while she talked. I'd seen my father do the same thing when my mother had yelled at him for letting her down, which he did a lot.

I walked to the back door, pushed the lock button in, then went out the swinging door into the dining room. I looked at the windows beside the table and checked the levers that locked them. Luna was watching some dumb commercial for hairspray, and Salma was trying to fit a Barbie doll into a toy truck. I pushed the lock button on the front door then went to our room. There were window latches on those windows, and I snapped them closed.

I was wide awake when Luna brought Salma in. I closed my eyes tight. She started to open the window latch. "It's too hot in here," she said.

"No!" I shouted, "Leave it closed. Leave it."

"You're so weird," Luna said.

I didn't want to tell her I was scared. And I didn't want to tell her what Maria and David had said in the kitchen, either, because Luna would have something mean to say about it.

"Just leave it, please, Luna, just leave it locked." For once she didn't argue. From down the hall I heard Maria tell David she was tired. I heard his engine start and the tires on the gravel.

I must have slept, because I woke up when something made a flapping noise outside. I sat up and looked toward the window. Something big and white was coming right at the glass, and I yelled "NO!"

I stared at the round yellow eyes and the wing feathers, and the sprawled grey wings of a little bird the white owl had caught against our window. Luna jumped up when I yelled.

"What was that," she whispered hoarsely, "a ghost?"

I told her I thought it was an owl, and she went right back to sleep. I guess I went back to sleep too because I dreamed about a yellow eyed ghost.

I was wide awake a long time before the sun came up.

THE GHOST

The ghost of the desert rustles softly from her lair
to stalk the creatures on the floor of her world.
She is all-seeing.
Her eyes see the fearful, the stunned.
Her ears hear their heartbeats.
Her wings flare instead of cupping, so she can drop silently,
but they know she is coming.
They feel her yellow eyes on them.
They feel the rush of the white wings pushing them to the sand.
The ghost carries them back to her nest to feed her young.
While she hunts tonight, the snake visits and takes an owlet.
A fair exchange for the mouse he was eyeing
when the white ghost covered it with her moon shadow.

23

TERESA 1971

Clean clothes

"Buenos días!" Paco looked like he felt better already, sitting at the table ready for breakfast. He was wearing clean clothes that Maria must have already had at the house. They weren't the same clothes he'd had on last night. Maria came out of the kitchen with a pitcher of orange juice and poured him a big glass.

"Good morning to you too, Paco. You want juice, Teresa?" she asked. Salma came running down the hallway in her nightgown. "Morning, little sunshine, want some eggs?" Luna got to the table about the time Paco was mopping up the jumble of egg yolks and bacon with a piece of toast. I tried to eat, but my head hurt so bad it felt like it was trying to push my eyes out.

"Paco, do your parents have a phone?" Maria asked. Paco stopped chewing and nodded slowly. "Do they know you're here?" He shook his head "no" and set his fork down.

"No, they wouldn't have let me. I snuck out and—" he stopped when Luna shoved my shoulder hard.

"Teresa has a boyfriend," she said in a sing-song voice that I knew was meant to embarrass Paco and me. Paco's cheeks flushed bright red. I hated Luna for being so mean.

"That's enough, Luna," Maria said sharply. She leaned toward Paco. "I'm sorry for her bad manners, Paco. I'm going to need to call your parents to figure out how to get you home. Officer Sanchez, who brought you here, can't be the one who takes you. Maybe I can take you, or your parents can meet me in Nogales. Do they have a car?"

Well, here I was in this place with my rude sister and I didn't like the school and my best friend in the whole world had just gotten here. And Maria was trying to send him away already.

"Paco just got here!" I said to Maria, "He needs to rest, and Favo might be out there."

"Favo!" Luna exclaimed, "What does Favo have to do with Paco going home? Favo probably thinks he's dead."

"Mind your own business, Luna, we weren't talking to you," I said. Luna slapped strips of bacon on a piece of toast, wrapped her napkin around it, and went back to our room. Paco looked even more uncomfortable.

Maria helped Salma put butter on her waffle but no syrup. Salma didn't like syrup on anything. Such a funny little girl.

"Let's talk about this later," Maria said when she had Salma eating, "and Paco, Teresa can show you around. I'll wash your clothes from yesterday. You keep the things you're wearing. We have plenty of clothes around here."

"Gracias. Thank you," Paco said.

I started stacking plates to take them to the kitchen. I still had a headache and felt like throwing up. Could everybody just stop talking for a while, and just let Paco be here?

"I'll be right back," I said, walking toward the hallway. I needed to wash my face with cold water. Luna was on her bed, looking at a magazine Maria had given her. The pictures were of women wearing a lot of eye shadow, and clothes that looked like they couldn't have even walked in them. She didn't look at me or speak to me when I went into the bathroom. I shut the bathroom door, ran cold water on my hands and tapped them on my forehead and neck. The wave hit me when I raised my head to look in the mirror, and I barely made it to the toilet to vomit. I rinsed my mouth and brushed my teeth again.

When I came out, Luna was gone from our room, and when I got back to the dining room, I knew she'd told Maria I'd thrown up. Maria's eyes looked worried, like my mother's eyes used to when I was sick. She put her cool hand on my forehead.

"I'm all right," I said, "Just a headache. It's better now." I was lying to Maria. My headache was still there.

Paco set down his glass of milk and put a warm brown hand on my arm. "Teresa, I don't want to make you feel worse, but I need to tell you something."

I swallowed the next wave of sickness.

"All right, tell me," I said. I laid my head on my arm, against the cool wood of the table.

"See," he said, "I knew you were going to Arizona, and then . . . " he traced a line on the table with his fingertip, "Favo came to school and waited for me to come out, and he told me he knew where you were, and he could bring me to you."

"You told us that. But he didn't bring you here."

"No, he lied. He said there were good cockfights here, and if I rode with him, and shared the money I won, well I already told you that part. But he lied about the cockfights. And I think he lied about you too. He said you told him to bring me here. You didn't tell him to do that, did you?"

Paco's eyes were sorrowful, and I wanted to touch them, and make him close them, because it hurt to look at such sad eyes.

"Favo said he'd bring me right to the gate of the place where you lived. Then he said your grandmother was sick, and you and Luna needed to go home and take care of her."

I looked across at Maria. She'd been quiet while Paco talked.

"My grandmother?" I said. "She's sick? How does Favo know my grandmother?" Maybe I had a fever, and that was why things didn't make sense.

Maria took a quick breath, like she was about to speak, then her eyes rested on Paco.

"Paco," Maria said, "Did you see her? Teresa's grandmother?"

"No, he told me he went to see her, and she was really sick, and that she needed Teresa and Luna to come back. He said if I brought them to him, he'd bring us all back home. But he got me out of the car and drove away."

"Then David found you?" Maria asked.

"Yes. The next day. I hid in the bushes when he got out of his truck to look around. He left for a while but he came back and said, 'I know you're in there' and 'no sense hiding, it's worse if I have to come find you,' and I got scared he might shoot me if he had to come find me, so I came out, and he asked me what I was doing out there alone, and I told him, and he . . . " Tears slid down Paco's cheeks.

"Then he brought you here," Maria said.

"Si, he brought me here, and I'm going to be in so much trouble when my father finds out," Paco said, pressing his palms against his wet cheeks.

"Okay, well, if Teresa is feeling better, you two can watch TV, or go play at the school yard, and then we'll get in touch with your father later today. I'll talk to him, all right? You write down the phone number for me, and I'll call your house. What is your father's name?"

"Enrico," Paco told her, "Enrico Dominguez. Like my name."

"All right, please write that down, and your number. Maybe he'll let you stay a few days. I'll tell him what's happened, and that you can stay here. You don't worry about that part. But don't you leave this ranch without me or Officer Sanchez, understand?" she said.

Paco's lips pressed together, and he nodded that he understood.

Maria went into the kitchen, and came back with two aspirin tablets. "Take these, Teresa."

I swallowed them with water. "Maria, can we call my grandmother? Since she's sick?"

"I have a feeling she's not sick. She's too mean to get sick," Maria said, and stood up.

"Can we call her?" I asked.

"I don't have her number, Teresa, do you?"

I didn't know it by heart, but maybe it was on the paper that had been in our mother's pack. I excused myself from the dining room and went to the closet in our room. Luna was sitting on her bed, looking at the magazine again. Mama's pack was in the back of the closet, but was empty.

"Where is that map we had? Did it have Grandmother's phone number on it?" I asked Luna.

She slapped the magazine down on the bed as though I had asked her to do some huge impossible thing and rolled off the bed. She yanked the top drawer of the dresser open and tossed out a pile of socks and underwear then threw the folded paper from the bottom of the drawer at me. It fell on the floor. It was the map. There, on the bottom of the map, in my mother's handwriting was Maria's phone number in Arizona. Below that was "Ana Lopez," and a phone number. Really, it was the phone number for her husband Alisio Lopez' clothing store. He sold fancy clothes for people who could afford them, and they had a nice apartment above the store where he and my grandmother lived.

I took the note to Maria and she slipped it into her pocket. "It's too early to call a store yet, so we'll call during business hours. In about two hours." She tapped her arm lightly, where she usually wore a watch. "I have some work to do, you two entertain yourselves, I'll be back in a couple of hours, so don't you call yet. Wait for me."

I said I would.

I wanted to hear my grandmother wasn't really sick, that Favo had lied, the way he'd lied about everything else.

And I knew Paco sure wasn't in a hurry to go back home to face his father.

24

ANA 1948

A new day

Was it all as bad as she'd thought it was the night before? Ana regretted she'd confronted Gabriella in the kitchen. She'd apologize when Gabriella arrived today to let her into the kitchen, that's what she'd do. It wasn't Gabriella's fault. In the light of a new day, she knew she'd been worn down from Suela's difficult delivery and listening to the horrible things said by the two women who'd been at the midwife's house and dinner.

In the early morning light, Ana lay still, listening to the music of Nina's voice. Her daughter was telling her new doll, in unaccented English, that they'd get ready for school now and there would be pancakes with butter. The incident with Nina being taken without her permission had made her consider leaving her job, but maybe Gabriella was right; there was no harm done, and Señora Ormond simply didn't know better.

Maya coughed across the hall, so Ana hurried to take Nina from her crib and ran her to the bathroom. "Come on, Nina, time for a bath." Nina sputtered in her almost four-year-old's glee, standing in the spray to catch water in her open mouth. Ana soaped and rinsed Nina and herself quickly, wrapped towels around them and hurried back to her room just as Rudy bolted from Maya's door, tugging at his pajama bottoms while he ran down the hall.

Ana saw that Maya had washed Nina's new pink dress and hung it in the open space of Ana's closet. It was already dry. She touched the lace collar. So pretty, probably almost a week's pay for Ana. She would try to see it as a gift instead of an intrusion. She could do that.

At six twenty, she heard the hall door open and said, "Come on, Miss Gabriella is early." She packed Nina's little bag for school with a picture book Nina loved and the new doll. The hallway door to the kitchen stood open.

Ana called to Maya "We will be in the kitchen."

"I'm coming," Maya answered from behind her door.

Ana picked up the note on the counter to see what to fix for breakfast. She hoped it wouldn't be for the Ormonds and the two women from the night before. It wasn't Señora's fancy handwriting with loops and turned up ends on every word, and it wasn't Gabriella's large firm printing. The writing slanted backwards, small and pointed.

Breakfast for 2, 8:00
Waffles, with maple syrup
Strawberries in the sink
Juice, whatever sounds good

Ana could smell the sun-touched strawberries in the slatted wood basket in the sink before she saw them.

"Nina, you sit right here until Maya comes out." She handed Nina a strawberry from the basket. "Shhh, don't tell," she told her. The strawberry disappeared into Nina's mouth, crown and all.

She heard Maya and Rudy at the hallway door to the kitchen, and said, "Gabriella must be in the back room or the pantry."

"Why is the outside door open?" Maya asked.

Ana headed to the pantry for flour and shortening.

"Hello?" she called into the back room. "She must be in the dining room," she said.

"If I take the kids to school for breakfast early, maybe I can see Suela on my way to work," Maya said, while she tried to smooth Rudy's bristling hair.

Ana peeked into the dining room, knowing the Ormonds wouldn't be there for another hour. No Gabriella. But surely she was close and would walk in any moment. Ana turned back to the sink, rinsed and drained the strawberries.

"One for you, because you are so good," and handed one to Rudy. Maya was leaning out the open kitchen door.

"Have you seen Gabriella?" Maya asked someone outside.

Rafael stopped trimming the bush under a dining room window and came closer. He took off his hat before answering.

"No, Maya, I have not seen her."

"Then who opened this door?" Maya said, exasperated.

"I don't know. Maybe she opened it while I was not looking," Rafael offered in his kind and simple way. "Good morning, little one," he said to Nina, when she peeked around Maya's skirt. Nina hid in the folds of fabric.

"Is her car out there?" Maya asked.

"I will go see," Raphael said, and jogged around to look. He stopped at the corner of the house and shook his head back at Maya.

"Well, where could she be?" Maya said to Ana. "I might get in trouble, but the door is open and I need to get these children to school and get to work." Ana glanced at the clock.

"Yes, you do. It will be all right."

"Come on, you two," Maya said. Rudy took Nina's hand and led her out. Maya started to shut the door behind her, but stopped when it was at the halfway open position she'd found it. She looked back at Ana and waved.

Ana, hands busy with flour sifter and mixing bowl, raised her chin to acknowledge her. She sifted some cinnamon into the bowl and tapped the glass lightly with the gold ring on her left hand. Vanilla . . . a few scrapings of vanilla bean into the flour would be her way of forgiving Señora Ormond for not asking if she could take Nina from school.

She'd have Gabriella ask Señora what had happened to the clothes Nina had worn to school the morning before. She added two extra eggs to the batter when she realized she had more flour and spices in the bowl than she needed. That was all right, she'd make extra to send to Suela and the old midwife, Esme, this morning. Maybe everyone would like bacon. Yes, that would be good with waffles, even if the note didn't ask for it. She cut thick slices of bacon from the slab in the refrigerator and put them on the griddle. The note said "Juice. Whatever sounds good." Pineapple juice with a sliver of strawberry on the edge of each glass would be pretty with waffles. And she'd garnish the sliced strawberries on the waffles with a sliver of fresh pineapple to finish the effect. She'd make this breakfast special. She'd remember to check that her hair was sleek before she served breakfast. Gabriella had taught her well.

At ten minutes to eight, she put two plates in the oven to warm, and set out two metal pie tins to put breakfast in for Suela and Esme. At seven minutes to eight, she slipped into the back room to check her hair and wash her hands again. She'd mention the footprint on the bathmat and towel to Gabriella this morning. She lifted the laundry hamper lid. The bloody uniform, towel and bathmat were gone. Gabriella must have taken the kitchen laundry last night after Ana had gone to her room. So, maybe she'd already seen them. She'd probably have an explanation.

The silver bell in the kitchen made a double "ting-ting'" as she entered the kitchen. She went to the counter, plated the waffles, strawberries, and bacon, added the garnishes, and put everything on the tray. She turned her back to the swinging door to nudge it open with her hip and swept silently into the dining room.

Stan Ormond sat with his back to the kitchen door in his usual place. Both arms rested on the table and, as usual, he didn't look at his cook when she brought the plates. Ana set his plate down from his left side, as Gabriella had taught her, then placed Señora Ormond's plate at her usual place.

"Mrs. Ormond will not be here for breakfast, Ana," he said, adjusting his silverware.

"Oh . . . " Ana replied, surprised enough at his speaking that she'd forgotten her vow of silence in the dining room. She reached for the edge of the plate to take it back to the kitchen, thinking "Well, Suela's breakfast will look very pretty, then."

In a smooth, casual movement, Stan Ormond reached toward the plate and his hand brushed Ana's wrist for an instant.

"Please, Ana, leave it, and you sit down. Please eat breakfast here with me this morning." Ana was about to quietly decline, wondering what Gabriella would tell her to do, when the man looked up at her with a softness in his eyes. She hadn't seen the tiny gold flecks in his eyes before. The grey-green color was less like slate, and more like the leaves on the olive tree near the kitchen window. She looked back at the kitchen door, hoping Gabriella would come back right now and say there was something she needed her to do in the kitchen, because this did not feel like something it would be all right to do, to sit at the dining room table and have breakfast with her boss.

"Please, Ana, sit," he said, motioning to the chair. "Mrs. Ormond went to town early this morning, and Gabriella had to go to town. An emergency," he said. "One of the girls, the one who had a baby yesterday. There were complications. They took her to the hospital."

The blood drained from Ana's cheeks. She and the midwife had done everything right. She remembered delivering the afterbirth. Her shallow breath grappled at her throat.

"Oh, yes, I helped Suela. Everything was all right yesterday . . . " she said, and already regretted that she'd said more than her position as cook and food server allowed.

"Please, eat with me this morning, it's all right. I'll like having some nicer company, after last night. I'm sorry you had to hear those women talk the way they did."

He placed his napkin in his lap. "Will you pray with me, Ana?" He motioned for her to place her hand on the table, and he placed his over it gently. "Heavenly Father, bless this food you have provided, and let it nourish and strengthen our bodies today for the tasks before us. Let Gabriella be wise in her decisions as she helps one of your lost souls with her trials today. And let this dear woman who feeds our family feel more a part of my family from this day forward," he said, giving her hand a gentle squeeze. "We ask this blessing in the name of Jesus. Amen." He gave Ana's hand one more pat as he released it.

"Please, Ana, I know you are not supposed to talk, but today, I'd like you to." He picked up his fork and reached for the syrup. "May I?" he asked, with an unfamiliar kindness. He held the pitcher of maple syrup above her plate.

She didn't want syrup. She was not capable of speaking just yet, still wondering about the sudden change from the odd indifference of meals at the Ormond table.

He poured a swirl of warm amber over her waffle and did the same over his.

"This looks wonderful," he said, picking up the thick bacon with his fork. "We've been so happy with your cooking, Ana."

Her eyes dropped to her plate and she blushed. She was feeling the gnaw of not eating dinner the night before, and she picked up her fork.

"I'm glad you could join me today so I could tell you that," he said.

Maybe she had misread him. Maybe under the surface he was appreciative, beyond paying her wages, after all. She ate her breakfast in quick bites.

He was halfway through his plate, when he speared a slice of strawberry. "I found these in town yesterday, and they looked so good. I hope you don't mind that I left them in the sink."

Ana looked at him in surprise.

"Oh, Ana, Gabriella didn't see you this morning before she had to leave, did she? You must have wondered why there was a basket of strawberries in the sink, and the door was open. I told her I'd take care of the doors today. I hope that was all right with you."

"Yes," she said. "Maya and I wondered."

"I also opened the hallway door, but didn't say anything. I didn't want to startle you ladies. Did Maya come out first, or did you?"

"I did."

"Good, of course you did. I'm happy you could make sense of my note about breakfast. I know my handwriting is just terrible sometimes."

"Oh, Señor, it was fine, I just did not recognize it."

"But you read it and you made breakfast and you took care of getting everyone off to school and work. You see, Ana, that is what makes me glad I hired you," he said, adding more syrup to his waffle.

Ana's face was burning. "Thank you for having me here, Señor."

They finished eating in silence.

He folded his napkin and laid it beside his plate. "I need to go to town," he said. "I'll call and see how things are going and if it's all right for the girl to have a visitor, I can take you to see her and the baby."

"Yes, I'd like to see Suela," Ana said. She wondered why he was calling one of his employees who lived in his house "the girl" and why he was saying "the baby" instead of "the babies." Ana rose to pick up the plates.

"I'll come by the kitchen in about an hour, after I make a few phone calls." He stood. "I'll make sure your daughter is taken care of this afternoon, if you want to spend more time with the girl, or do something in town."

"Oh, I won't be able to stay long," she said, backing through the kitchen door. "I think Señora told Gabriella she might have someone over for lunch."

"Don't you worry, I'll take care of that. I'll see you in an hour," he said.

Ana took the dishes to the sink. Well, this was certainly a change. She'd thought that Señor just didn't like her, despite Gabriella's telling her that they were pleased with her cooking. Today, he was so thoughtful to tell her himself. Maybe he was a nice man after all. She did the dishes quickly and put the extra food in the refrigerator. Her uniform was still clean, and she went into the back room to remove her apron. She re-pinned her hair and made sure her bun was centered.

She sharpened two kitchen knives while she waited. At nine thirty, Stan Ormond appeared at the kitchen's side door.

"Are you ready to go?" he said cheerfully.

She waited outside the door while he fished a set of keys from his pocket.

"My car is around front," he said.

Rafael was pushing a wheelbarrow of tree trimmings to the compost pile. He hesitated when he saw Ana, but didn't wave. Ana saw him looking and felt bad for not waving or speaking to him, but thought she'd get Rafael in trouble if he stopped working. Outside of the women she shared quarters with and Gabriella, she knew no one here besides Rafael. She hoped he would understand. He continued his trek to the leaf pit and raked leaves onto his compost pile. She continued to the car, went to the back door, and waited for her boss.

"Here, you sit in the front, since it is just us today," he said, opening the car door for her.

Stan Ormond started the car, then backed up to the ranch road. Ana saw Rafael had stopped pushing leaves and trimmings around, and was watching the car. She'd have to explain her silence to Rafael next time she saw him.

Ana recognized nothing of the passing scenery on the ranch's winding driveway to the main road. The row of mailboxes outside the gate looked as though it was for a small town. Her boss stopped, rolled down the car window to put a bundle of letters in one of the boxes, and then left the window open.

"Is this all right?" he asked. "The weather's so nice this time of morning." He turned onto the road and Ana's shoulders were pushed back into the seat as he accelerated. She didn't answer about the window, out of habit.

She felt a strand of hair escape her bun and wanted to pin it back down, but didn't want to do it in front of him. She'd have to fix it when he wasn't looking.

"We'll stop at the hospital first. It's a few more miles," he said. Ana kept her eyes on the forest of saguaro, ocotillo, and cholla along the road. Stan Ormond fiddled with the radio dial and turned the volume up when violin music came through the speakers.

"Do you like music?" he asked.

Ana knew she should answer. "Yes."

"What kind of music do you listen to?" he said.

"I do not listen to music."

"Not in your room?"

"No, Señor, I don't have music there," she said, and wished she'd answered differently. He turned his head and looked at her for a second.

"I see," he said. At the edge of town, he turned on the first road.

"Here we are. I'll go in for a few minutes and see how the girl is, and then you can visit. I need to run an errand. I can leave you here while I do that. Will that be all right with you?"

"Yes," Ana said.

Gabriella's dust-coated car was in the parking lot. Ana waited 'til Señor Ormond opened his door to get out. Before she'd opened her own door, he was on her side of the car, reaching for the door handle. She was embarrassed to have him do that.

"This way," he said, heading toward the hospital's glass doors.

She followed. He pulled one of the doors open and stood holding it for her, triumphantly. She ducked her head and walked through.

"Have a seat, Ana, I'll talk to the doctor, and then you can go in," he said, heading toward another glass door, down the short hallway.

Ana sat on one of the green vinyl covered chairs. She heard the muffled voices of two men, then heard Ormond's voice and Gabriella's. Another minute passed. Gabriella came into the waiting room. She sat sideways in the chair next to Ana and began to speak.

"Ana, Suela had a terrible night, and she's sick. I know you understand."

"Yes, I have seen difficult births," Ana said.

"That boy tore something in her, and she's been bleeding. She got a fever overnight, and her milk made the little boy sick," Gabriella said.

"What about the girl?" Ana asked.

"The girl," Gabriella said. "Oh, Ana, I didn't see you this morning. The baby girl died this morning. So sad. They gave Suela something to keep her quiet. I don't think she understands her baby is dead yet, so don't say anything about the girl. Right now, she only remembers having one baby."

Ana's breath went out of her in a hot shudder. Her arms and hands felt disconnected from her body.

"Oh, poor Suela, poor Suela," she said softly.

Gabriella touched Ana's arm. "Señor Ormond is seeing her first. After the doctor has seen Suela again, we can go in. I hope for her that she won't even remember."

From behind the glass door in the hallway, Ana heard a high laugh, and then both a man and woman's voice. A door opened and closed, a nurse in a white uniform rushed out of a room, three doors down from the glass door, carrying a pink-blanketed bundle, and Ana wondered if it was Suela's dead baby girl.

Stan Ormond came out of the door across from where the nurse had come out, with his hands in his pockets. He looked jovial and lighthearted. A strange way to look, Ana thought, when Suela had lost one of her babies. Another man in a white shirt, with his sleeves rolled to his elbows followed him out of the same room. Stan turned to him, they spoke quietly, and then shook hands. Stan looked through the glass door at Ana and Gabriella, and motioned to them to come in.

Gabriella and Ana rose and walked to the glass door. Gabriella whispered, "Remember . . . "

Stan Ormond waited at the door to the room. "She's resting now, but she's lost blood, so just keep things quiet. Keep her lying down. She'll be all right. Doctor's orders."

"In there?" Ana asked, indicating the first door in the hallway.

"Yes. I'll be back soon. Gabriella, will you stay here with Ana 'til I get back?" he asked.

"Yes, sir," she said. He pushed through the first glass door and went quickly through the waiting room. An older man who was helping his wife into the building held the door open for him.

The room smelled of disinfectant and bleach and milk and blood. Suela looked so small and grey-skinned that Ana wouldn't have known her friend if she hadn't known who she was visiting. A glass bottle hung upside down from a hook clamped to the head of the hospital bed. Suela stirred and opened her swollen eyes. She closed them quickly and turned her head away.

"Look who's here," Gabriella said. Suela didn't respond, and Gabriella motioned to Ana to sit on one of the chairs close to the bed. Ana slid her hand over Suela's and was surprised at how cold her friend's fingers were. Gabriella sat on the other chair, leaning forward to brush Suela's hair from her cheek.

"The doctor says you need to rest," Gabriella said, "and maybe tomorrow you can go home."

Suela's dry lips parted. She rolled her head from side to side and made a rattling sound before her voice came out. Her voice broke from pale lips.

"You were there," she said. Ana nodded and closed her hand over Suela's fingers.

"Yes, I was there," Ana whispered.

Suela struggled with forming the words she wanted. "You helped me."

"Yes."

Gabriella nudged Ana's foot with her shoe. Ana didn't look at Gabriella.

"Did you see him?" Suela asked. "He was here. I saw him. He was here."

Ana nodded, because she didn't know how to answer.

Suela closed her eyes. "I knew he'd be here."

"Yes, honey," Gabriella said. She touched Suela's chest with her open hand, and patted her, "Of course he was. Of course, he was."

"He will love me, won't he?" Suela's face crumpled, and she closed her eyes.

"Of course he will, he's your son. Of course he will," Gabriella told her.

Ana looked at Gabriella's face. So calm, so at peace with all this sadness. Ana wanted to cry, and hold Suela, and Gabriella's face wasn't showing anything that looked like sadness or pity. To Ana, she looked like the mother superior at the convent. Serene, that was what she was. Serene. She knew the answers. She always knew what to do. Maybe she'd been raised in a convent by nuns, and that was why she was serene now while this poor woman cried pitifully.

"I can have the nurse bring him in," Gabriella said, "would you like to see him?"

Suela's eyes were like two bruised peaches. When she opened them, they were glassy slits within the dark skin.

"See him? Will he come back today?" she said, reaching for Ana's hand.

Gabriella got up quickly. "I'll go see, all right? Ana will stay here with you while I go ask." Gabriella slipped out the door and closed it with a click behind her.

"Ana," Suela groped at Ana's hand, "they took my baby."

Ana's breath stopped low in her chest. "Gabriella went to get him, she'll bring him back." Suela seemed to struggle with consciousness.

"Is she bringing him back?" she asked.

"She's bringing your baby back," Ana said. She wondered if Suela had become addled from loss of blood.

"She will? She will, won't she?" Suela said when Ana squeezed her hand.

A nurse in squeaking shoes came into the room. She checked the fluid in the bottle hanging from the hook, and took a syringe from her uniform pocket. She pinched the clear tube that went to the crook of Suela's elbow and slid the needle into it.

Ana watched in silence as pale amber fluid flowed into the tube, and saw it disappear under the white tape that held the tube in place in Suela's vein. Ana saw what little air Suela had in her slide away and leave a sagging, barely breathing shell where her friend had been. Ana's mouth dropped open, and she looked up at the bland faced nurse. The nurse's eyes shifted to the bottle.

"She needs to rest now."

The nurse's white shoes squeaked away.

"Suela, can you hear me?" Ana said. She was afraid of the faint gurgling noise Suela was making. "Suela?" she gripped and shook Suela's arm. The door opened, and Gabriella came to sit beside Ana again.

"Let's let her rest. Come with me, Ana," she said.

Ana followed Gabriella down the hall, to a window in the wall. Six tiny glass boxes rested in white metal cribs. Three of the glass boxes held babies: one brown skinned with a surprising shock of black hair, and two pink skinned and bald.

"There he is, the one you saved. He lived because you knew what to do, Ana."

Ana pressed her forehead against the glass and watched the little brown baby struggle to get his fist to his mouth.

"Is he going to be all right?" Ana asked.

"They'll keep him here and give him extra oxygen today."

"What happened to the little girl?" Ana said, with her brow still on the cool glass.

"She wasn't meant to be in this life, Ana. Suela will be all right, she'll have her son," Gabriella said.

"That nurse, she gave her something," Ana said, not taking her eyes from the babies.

"Yes, something to make her sleep. Let's go see if Señor Ormond is back yet."

Gabriella and Ana sat in the waiting room's green vinyl chairs. People came in, talked to the woman at the desk, and went through the glass door and into the hall. A large woman in a blue dress, wearing a tiny pillbox hat with a veil that covered her eyebrows came in, followed by a rail-thin man in a seersucker suit. He wore a yellow bow tie that hung away from his skinny neck. The hat woman carried a bouquet of carnations tied together with a pink ribbon. The woman heaved her frame against the desk while the receptionist looked at some papers, then marched to the glass door. The woman bustled through, dragging the skinny man by an invisible thread of duty. They stopped at the windowed room down the hall, where the woman pointed, and even through the glass door, everyone could hear her say, "Will you look at her? Isn't she just beautiful? She looks just like her mother, doesn't she, Sheldon?"

"Good God," Gabriella said. "Good thing Suela is sleeping." Ana leaned back in the chair and fixed her eyes on the front door. She wasn't tired, she was empty, like her lungs had gone flat.

"Will there be a funeral for the baby?" she asked.

"That might make it worse for Suela," Gabriella said.

Ana ran Suela's pleading through her mind. "She was talking about the baby when she asked about 'him,' wasn't she? She asked me if he was coming back today. I didn't know what to say."

"I know, that's why I went for the nurse," Gabriella said. She picked up a magazine from the low table in front of them and started turning the pages.

"You told the nurse to give her more medicine? You told Suela you were going to get her baby."

"I told Suela what I needed to tell her to quiet her down while I went to get the nurse. She doesn't need to talk or worry right now. You didn't say anything about the girl, did you?"

"Oh, no, no, but when she is better, she will want to know."

"Yes, of course, when she's better," Gabriella said. She dropped the magazine on the table.

"I wish she had been brought to the hospital to have her babies," Ana said, "instead of those women holding her down, and calling us after the trouble started. Maybe they did something wrong when the girl came out."

"Oh, Ana, the midwife was there, she took care of Suela and that baby. She's taken care of a lot of girls having babies," Gabriella said, patting Ana's arm the way she'd patted Suela's.

"But if she had a doctor . . . " Ana said.

Gabriella closed her fingers on Ana's wrist and squeezed. "Ana, I know you are upset by this, but please. We don't do that. We don't bring women from the ranch to the hospital to have babies. We have the midwife. And now, you too. Esme and you have probably helped with more births than any doctor here, don't you think?" she said.

Gabriella smiled, but it didn't look like a smile to Ana. Ana didn't answer.

"Babies can look just fine, and then they're not fine. You saved the boy. Suela is young. She can have another baby."

Ana could not look at Gabriella, but nodded to show agreement. It was just that, a show of agreement. She didn't agree.

Ana stared out the glass doors of the waiting room, into the parking lot. She no longer heard the phone at the receptionist's desk or the squeak of nurses shoes when they came to take visitors to hospital rooms. The woman in the pillbox hat dragged her little husband behind her like a scrawny dog, back through the waiting room without her bundle of pink carnations. They went out the door and Ana watched the man open the car door for the woman. The woman squeezed herself in, rocking the car as she did. He got in behind the steering wheel and Ana could see the woman's mouth moving, no doubt giving him instructions about how to drive the car and where to take her next. The man adjusted the rearview mirror and the woman reached up to put it back where it had been. He looked over his thin shoulder and backed the car up, then drove it out of the parking lot and, for as long as Ana could see the car, the hat woman was still talking and pointing her finger at the man.

Stan Ormond's car rolled into the parking lot. He tossed a cigarette onto the ground as he got out. He smoothed his hair with both hands, using his reflection in the glass door as a mirror. His tie was perfectly centered, but he straightened it in the reflection before he entered the waiting room. "Here you are, did you have a nice visit?" he asked.

Gabriella smiled kindly. "Yes, we did. I need to go grocery shopping. I'll take Ana with me."

"You go do what you need to do and take some time off this afternoon. I'll take Ana back. That's all right with you, isn't it, Ana? Things are quiet at the ranch, Gabriella, and you've been doing a lot. You deserve some time to do what you want to do. Lorene is at the spa, and she'll be staying with her sister, afterwards. I'll pick her up tomorrow morning, so take the day off," he said.

"Yes, sir, thank you," Gabriella said.

They followed Stan Ormond out the door. He opened Gabriella's car door for her, handed her some cash, said something to her Ana couldn't hear, then tapped on the roof with a grin as she put it in gear.

"Well, Ana, since we're in town, is there anything you want to do?" he said.

"Do? No. Oh, I was going to go with Gabriella and she was going to help me put my money in the bank."

"We can go to the bank now, then," he said.

"Thank you, but I did not bring the money with me. I can do it another day."

"Nonsense, Ana, it's not that far back to the ranch, just a few minutes. We'll go and I'll help you open a bank account. Then I'll take you back home."

Ana got into the car and remembered she hadn't fixed the loose strand of hair that had come free of her bun. She re-pinned it while her boss walked to his side of the car. He drove back to the ranch, and when they got to the house he said, "I have to open those doors, don't I?" He led the way, and she stood aside as he keyed the kitchen door, then the hallway door open.

"I will only be a moment. Thank you, Señor," Ana said, and hurried down the hallway to her room.

She was replacing her clothes in the drawer where they'd covered the pay envelopes when she heard the creak at the door to her room. "Maya?" she said, turning to look.

Stan Ormond was standing in the open door.

⫝̸

"Sorry, I didn't mean to startle you," Stan Ormond said from Ana's bedroom door when Ana gasped. Ana stood up so fast she banged her knee on the dresser drawer. She felt like she was the intruder who'd

169

been caught when she saw her employer standing in the doorway of her room. She put the pay envelopes in her dress pocket and closed the drawer with one foot.

"I went back to the car for this, and you weren't in the kitchen." He held a paper shopping bag with handles under one arm. "I got something for you in town. I wanted to give it to you before we went to the bank."

"I didn't mean to take so long," she said, then wondered why she was apologizing. She'd only been in her room for a minute.

"You said you like music. I wanted to get this for you, as a way of saying thank you." He held the bag by the handles, in front of him. "Come on, Ana, take it, it's a gift. It's all right."

Ana stepped forward and reached for the handles.

He drew the bag closer to him. "We're glad to have you here, Ana, and we want you to stay for a long time. You want to stay, don't you?"

Ana lowered her hand, embarrassed that she had reached for the bag.

"Don't you?" he said. He tilted his head. His face was softer in the light of her room.

"Yes, I want to stay," she said.

"Good. This is for you. You can have music. Don't play it too loud. We don't want the other girls complaining," he said.

Ana unfolded the top of the bag cautiously. The white plastic radio in the bag had rounded corners, and a round domed window with a pointer for the numbers, a knob on top of the box, and an electric cord wrapped around it. "It runs on house electricity. You can plug it in beside your lamp," he said, taking the bag from her as she lifted the radio out.

"I do not know what to say, Señor. It is very nice."

"You don't need to say anything but thank you, Ana." The light shone across his grey-green eyes. They were translucent in the shaft of sunlight from the window. "Now, set that where you want it, and let's go to town and get your bank account."

"Thank you, Señor," she said.

She felt as shy as when she was eight years old, and her mother had told her to dance with her uncle at a wedding. Her uncle lifted her up and held her close. Too close. His hands were on her butt and he squeezed her. Too close. Too much. She had hidden from her uncle for the rest of the party.

Ana put the white radio on the top shelf in her closet and smoothed her hair again.

Stan Ormond talked and pointed out things along the road, driving back to town. She'd grown used to him ignoring her when she served meals and picked up dishes, and now his talking, being so friendly, was a surprise. He took the main street through Tubac, turned up the car radio, and tapped his fingers on the steering wheel.

"Here we are," he said, at a parking spot across from the bank. "I'll go in first and get things set up. It's a little tricky, because you're not a citizen, but I'll take care of all that. I'll come back out for you, okay? Be back in a little bit," he said, and walked briskly across the street. He took the stairs into the bank two at a time.

Ana leaned back in the car seat and let the late morning sun wash the thoughts of birthing babies and nightmares about statues from her mind. A breeze lifted the collar of her dress gently. Her eyes closed. She opened them again when something touched her arm, and she jolted wide awake.

"Oh, there I go, startling you again," Stan Ormond said. "Sorry."

"It's all right," she said.

"They're all set up. Let's go in," he said, and opened her door.

She followed him into the two-story sandstone building. The cool tile floor echoed their steps. Someone leaving the bank said "Hey, Stan, how ya doin'?"

"Right here," he said, indicating that Ana should approach the counter, where a middle-aged woman waited on the other side of a frosted glass partition.

"Hello, welcome to the Bank of Tubac. How may I help?"

"Marsha, this is my cook, Ana. Max and I just set her up with a savings account." He used his thumb and middle finger to pull a slender black book from his front shirt pocket. "Here's her savings book. Will you take good care of her while I go sign some papers with Max?"

"Yes, of course, Mr. Ormond," Marsha the teller raised the eyeglasses that hung from a silver chain and slid the earpieces over her salt-and-pepper temples.

"I'll meet you at the front door when you're done, Ana," he said.

"Yes sir," Ana said.

"Will this be a cash or check deposit?" Marsha asked.

"Well, I . . ."

"It's all right, Miss Ana, when other girls come from the ranch it's usually cash. Is it a piece of paper saying an amount or is it money?" the teller asked.

"Money," Ana answered.

"Very good, I'll make a deposit slip. How much?" Marsha said, looking over the top of her blue framed glasses.

"I think six hundred dollars."

"We'll count it. Here, let's see that account number," Marsha said, and opened the black book to the first page. "We'll do a signature card, so when you want to take money out, you can do that any time you come in. Here's that form. I am guessing you live at the Ormond ranch?"

"Yes."

"Good, I have that address right here on file. And what is your full name? All that's in the book is Ana."

"Ana Rosario," Ana said, and the woman wrote that down, and filled in the address.

"Here you go, sign your name here," said the woman.

Ana signed her name.

"Fine," the teller said. "You can count the money, or I can."

"It's fine if you count," Ana said, and emptied her pay envelopes onto the granite counter.

The woman counted with the speed of a street merchant and raised her eyes to Ana when she laid down the last ten-dollar bill. "You must not have spent much of your money. You have more than six hundred dollars here. It's six hundred and fifty. Does that sound right?" she asked.

"I guess it is," Ana said.

"Do you want to keep any for spending out of this?"

"Should I do that?"

The woman's eyes crinkled at the corners when she smiled. "I would, if it were me. Why don't you save out ten dollars, in case you need some cash?" she said, sliding a ten toward Ana.

"All right," said Ana. She folded the money and put it in her dress pocket.

"Then I'll make this deposit for six hundred and forty, and see, I'll put it in the book," Marsha said. She wrote in the numbers as neatly as any of the nuns who taught school at the convent. "And now you're all set to go, Ana Rosario. Thank you for doing business with us."

"Thank you. But I wonder, what if someone else is coming to town and I want to send my money with them to put in the bank?"

"Oh, that's simple, just send your book. I'll put some deposit slips in it for you. Put the account number, this one here," she said, her smooth pale finger pointing to the account number in the book, "on the deposit slip in this space, and put the amount. Then someone can make a deposit for you. They can put money in, and nobody but you can take it out."

"Yes, I understand," Ana said. She took the black cloth-covered book and slipped it into her dress pocket with the ten-dollar bill. "Thank you for helping me."

Ana listened to her work shoes tapping the tile as she walked to the front door of the bank. She felt important, and very wealthy. She had a bank account and it had money in it. She had a book that proved she had her own money, and money in her pocket. Stan Ormond, her wealthy and very kind employer, liked her, and had given her a gift of thanks. She had a pretty little daughter, and a place to live.

Stan Ormond was talking to a man in a short-sleeved plaid shirt, saying his goodbyes when Ana approached the door. "All set, Ana?"

"Yes, sir," she said. He led the way to the car and opened the door for her.

"You know, it's so close to lunchtime, why don't I take you to lunch at a restaurant? Let someone else cook," he said.

Ana put her hand in her dress pocket to touch the money and the bankbook. "All right," she said.

She felt like a sixteen-year-old girl at a party where the handsomest boy there wanted to dance with her. She knew it was different, because this was her boss, and he was married, but it was nice to have someone being attentive to her, even if it was just that he was grateful that she could cook and deliver babies.

"Tell you what, let's leave the car here, and walk down a block. There's a cafe there," he said.

She tried to follow him, but he kept hesitating as he walked so she had to walk beside him. He pointed to the courthouse, the bakery, the hardware store, telling her about the people who had businesses in town. She became comfortable walking beside him as he talked to her.

"They have tables inside or outside. How about inside?" he said, pulled the screen door open, and stood back so she could go in first.

A blue haze of cigarette smoke hung from the ceiling to the tops of the tables. The man behind the long bar at the back of the room watched them in the mirrored wall, turned his towel over to the cleanest side and mopped at the bar.

"Sit anywhere ya want," the bartender rasped in a gravel voice. He turned his head toward an open window into the kitchen and shouted, "Greta! You got customers!"

"Here, Ana, this is good," Stan said in a low voice. He turned to look at the bar. "I'll get us something to drink," and walked to the bartender.

The bartender listened, nodded at Stan, then looked at Ana and grinned ghoulishly, showing gapped yellow teeth. He dumped a scoop of ice cubes into two glasses, poured something green from one bottle and something clear from another, then topped off both glasses with water. Stan brought the glasses back to the table.

Greta limped from the kitchen door and stopped to set her cigarette in an ashtray on a table. She snapped her order book open and groped in her piled-up orange hair for a yellow pencil. "Know vaat jou vant?" she asked. It was an accent Ana had never heard.

"Bring us two steaks, medium. And fries," Stan said.

Ana had started to say she'd just have soup if there was soup, but she guessed she was having a steak and fries. She smiled at the woman with orange hair. Greta's housedress was sweat-stained at the armpits, and the threadbare apron tied over it was splotchy with grease. Greta crammed the tattered order book back into her apron pocket. She scuffed away in her house slippers to pick up her smoldering cigarette and hung it back between wrinkled lips. When she'd gone through the kitchen door, Ana let out a short laugh. She put her hand over her mouth, embarrassed at herself.

"Oh, I should not laugh," Ana said.

"I know, she's something, isn't she? I eat here just to get to see Greta. She's a good cook, though."

The man behind the bar rattled empty bottles into a box. "Hey, mister," he said, "two plays on the juke box, on me, got any requests?"

"No, whatever you want," Stan told him.

The bartender leaned against the shuddering, pale lit juke box and pushed some buttons. A warped and scratchy Lena Horne sang "Stormy Weather" and this time Stan laughed out loud.

"Oh, that's a good one Ernie," he said.

Ernie the bartender coughed like he was dying and went back to his box of bottles.

Stan picked up his glass. "To good cooks and good food." He touched his glass to the side of hers, just as she reached for it. He kept his eyes on the front door and took a sip. "Ernie! You are the master!" he said loudly, not looking over his shoulder at the bartender.

Ana tasted her drink. She had snuck communion wine from the altar at the convent, something half the nuns did on a regular basis, but this drink was cool and minty and reminded her of a pie she had made for the mother superior, with fresh limes and meringue. She smiled at the bartender, and he touched his eyebrow in a drunk-looking salute.

"This is nice, isn't it, Ana? To get away from the ranch? Sometimes I get so busy I forget to even speak to the people who help me. Like you. You understand, don't you? How that is?" He rotated his glass and slid it closer to him.

"Yes, we are all busy sometimes," Ana said, but she wasn't sure what she was supposed to understand.

"It's not me, Ana, it's my wife, Lorene. She sees Maya with her son, and the girl, Suela, about to have a baby, and she sees you, and your pretty daughter, and you can cook, and that's hard for her to accept. Did you know that?" he said, staring where his thumb pressed the side of the sweating glass.

"Why?" Ana asked.

Stan looked toward the kitchen. Ernie carried his ragged box from behind the bar to the pool table.

"Lorene, well, she wants children and she can't have them. She thinks if she can't give me children that she's of no use to me, and I'll leave her and find another woman who can have children. She knows that jealousy is a sin, but she can't help it. She's jealous." His shoulders remained stiff. "That's why I don't talk to any of you when she's around. Ana, I want to apologize for that. You must think I'm not a nice person," he said, then lowered his head. "I'm so sorry. I want to change that."

Ana took a sip, then another from her drink. She traced her finger down the side of her glass, from top to bottom. This explained his strange behavior in the dining room at home, and now she understood that he was trying not to hurt his wife's feelings.

"It's all right, I understand," she said quietly.

"You do? Oh, good," he said, and raised his glass to her, then drank deeply. "I'm glad you came to town today. I'm glad we could talk."

There were no words for the relief Ana felt, so she took another sip from her glass. Lena Horne lamented that she and her man weren't together, and it was raining all the time. Lena held the last note and the song ended. The jukebox hummed and clunked and asked her to sing it again. Ernie the bartender swayed his way from the pool table back to his grimy bar towel. He mopped at a glass mark in the slanted light.

Greta limped from the kitchen with silverware wrapped in paper napkins and dropped the white bundles in front of her only two lunch customers.

"Steaks ready two minutes, hokay?" she said. She rolled her cigarette to the corner of her sagging lip to keep it stuck in her mouth.

"Yes, that's great," Stan said.

"You two having party here?" Greta said, pressing her fists to the small of her back.

Ana started to say "No."

Stan's voice slid over Lena Horne's and Ana heard him say "Yes we are, Greta. Ana here just opened a bank account and decided to stay."

"Goot, you two make nice couple," Greta said.

Ana snapped into coherent thinking, and said, "Oh, no, I am the cook."

"Goot, you can cook, you keep a man hoppy," Greta said. She reached for the unused ashtray on their table.

"I'm not—" Ana protested.

"Sure, you and rest of girls. Hope you like steak, got some beeg ones in there this week." Greta said. The long cigarette ash fell against her apron, then to the floor.

Greta hobbled back to the kitchen. There was a clattering racket behind the door, and she returned with two platters. "You put ketchup on my steak, you don't come back," she said. She dropped a glass bottle of ketchup from another table in front of Ana. "Hokay for fries, but don't on steak," she practically growled, and lingered at the table.

"I won't. Thank you," Ana said, and Greta took her cue to retire to the kitchen. Ana laughed again as the kitchen door swung shut. She hadn't felt like laughing in a long time.

After lunch and another set of drinks, Stan Ormond walked with his cook up the street to the car. "I think I'm not ready to drive yet. Ernie made those drinks too strong," he said.

Ana tried to glide as she walked because she was afraid she'd sway from side to side otherwise. She was a little embarrassed that she'd finished the first glass, not to mention the second. She felt like she was treading water on the sidewalk beside her boss's car.

"Let's sit a while, okay?" he said waving a hand toward an outdoor table in front of the drug store.

Ana navigated the rolling sidewalk to one of the chairs and sat on the edge of it carefully.

"I'll be right back," he said. He went through the drug store's door in a clatter of bells.

He was back in front of her a few minutes later, holding two ice cream cones.

"I hope you like ice cream." He sat down across the table from her. "I'm glad to see you happy, Ana."

She bit at the crumbling, light golden edges of the cone. She looked away when he licked at a drip on his cone. It seemed wrong to watch him. Across town, the bell in the Holy Church of Our Lady of Immaculate Conception announced that it was one o'clock with a single tone.

"My day's shot, it's one o'clock and I haven't been to the warehouse yet today," Stan said, wiping his hands on his handkerchief.

Ana's head was riding the swells and waves of the drinks she'd had, but she rose to her feet, and kept a hand on the metal table until she was standing.

"Good thing Lorene isn't here, she'd be mad at me for having a nice lunch and ice cream," he said. "Sit down, Ana, I'm not in a hurry to get back, and I don't think you're going to get much work done if I take you back."

She sat back in the chair, relieved she didn't have to walk to the car just yet. She'd hoped the stop at the outdoor table would help her get her legs working better, but she felt more unsteady than ever.

"I gave Gabriella the rest of the day off. Lorene is staying with her sister. So, you don't have to fix dinner. You have the day off too," Stan said, folding his handkerchief.

"Maya will be home with Rudy and Nina though," Ana said.

Stan leaned back in his chair. "I told Gabriella to take them all to Nogales to see a movie. Everybody gets the day off today," he said, winking. "Tomorrow, back to work."

Ana blushed.

"Ana, how old are you?" he asked.

"I am twenty . . . no . . . twenty-one. Twenty-one."

"And do you mind me asking? Where is your man?" he said, in such an easy way that she knew she had to answer.

"I don't know," she said. "He went to work at the racetrack and didn't come back." She lowered her eyes, embarrassed that he'd asked.

"Well, shame on him for doing that," Stan said. "He would be lucky to have you. I wish Lorene was as strong as you are."

Ana swallowed a few times, and let him talk, even if his talk was probably fueled by the drinks.

"Lorene can't have children. I already told you that, didn't I? I wish I knew what to do, she's just not the same girl I married. She doesn't want to be my wife, you know, be my wife," he said, resting his cheek against his hand, and leaning across the table. "She went to Tucson and ordered separate beds for us right before you came here to work. Can you believe that? I don't know if she loves me anymore."

Ana worried her face looked as red as it felt. She'd never expected to have Stan Ormond talking to her, and now he was confessing his troubles with his wife. It didn't seem right. She knew she could never tell Gabriella or the other girls about this day or the things he was saying.

"I have tried. I don't know . . . it's like she's empty. I give her everything she wants, and she still isn't happy. You aren't like that, are you, Ana?" He looked off down the street and leaned back in his chair.

Ana cleared her throat. She meant to say, "I'm sorry to hear that," or "Señor Ormond, I don't think I should hear this" but nothing came out. When his gaze returned from watching a couple walk into the drug store, his eyes bored right into hers. She swallowed and looked away.

"Lorene can't cook. She can't clean the house. She can't even drive. Somebody has to drive her everywhere."

"Well, Señor, I don't know how to drive either," Ana said.

Ormond laughed loudly and wiped an eye with his fist. "Then you'll learn to drive. Would you like that, Ana?" he said.

"Yes. I. Would," She answered in punctuated words. Stan laughed again, brushing his hand on one of hers. She didn't pull away from the touch.

"Okay, I guess I'll take you home now," he said. He stood close as she rose, as if ready to take her by the arm if she swayed on the way to the car. He drove slowly out of town, watching his rearview mirror for the one policeman who cruised the streets of Tubac.

On the ride home, Ana dozed off twice to the sounds of the wheels on the road and the wind sucking at the windows.

Stan stopped the car in front of the house. "The kitchen and hall doors are open. Will you be all right?"

"Yes," she said. "Thank you for lunch and the ice cream. And for the radio." Ana pushed the door open and tested the ground for movement as she got out.

"It was my pleasure, Ana," he said, and backed the car out the driveway.

From the kitchen door, she watched him drive out to the gravel road. Through her fog, she wondered if he was going to the warehouse to work after all.

Ana went to her room and lay down. She could smell the smoke from the cafe on her clothes and hair, so she propped herself up on her elbows despite how heavy her head felt and swung her legs over the side of the bed. She stood long enough to peel her uniform and shoes off, then lay back down in her slip. She didn't want to get up to change or to shower just yet, and she drifted off to sleep, letting a dream take her where Lena Horne still sang that she didn't know why there's no sun up in the sky.

Something was lifting her from the blanket of sleep, something was breathing in rhythm with her breathing, someone was stroking her hair, someone's hands were on her shoulders, her neck, her breasts. If it was a dream, she didn't want to wake. She was only a little startled when she opened her eyes and saw Stan sitting on the edge of her bed with his tie loosened.

"Ana . . ."

She opened her arms.

25

TERESA 1971

Calling home

"We're leaving, so watch Salma." I needed to get away from Luna. She'd make my headache come back if I had to be around her.

"Where is she?" Luna asked, while she sorted through her stack of magazines.

"Playing with her dolls in the living room." Paco and I went out the front door.

The June sun fried the front of the house but there was good shade on the side where the orange tree grew and in the grove of trees around the pond. I wanted to show Paco the pond and the school if there was time. I could see Maria's house from both places, so when I saw her car, we'd go back to the house.

"Are you going to stay and live here?" Paco asked.

"Well, we don't have a choice right now, until Maria figures out what to do." We sat on the stiff grass in the morning shade of the orange tree.

"But your mother's job, it's a good job? She likes it?"

It felt like the grass and the dirt under it had been pulled out from under my legs. My arms felt heavy, and my stomach got hot.

"Paco, didn't you know?" I put my hands flat on the grass to steady myself.

"Know? Know what?"

"That my mother drowned the night we left Centro?" I searched his face to see if he understood me. There was no flicker of recognition, no understanding.

"Yes, I bet you got wet, it rained a lot that night," he said, almost like he was teasing.

"No, Paco, she drowned. She died. I saw her go under the water, and she didn't come up. Officer Sanchez found her body two days later." I was surprised how calm I was, telling my best friend that my mother was dead. Paco sat cross-legged on the ground in front of me with his knees almost touching mine.

"Quit doing that, Teresa, that's not funny," he said.

"Paco," I said, "why would I tease about that? Officer Sanchez didn't tell you?"

"No, he didn't. Why didn't you tell me last night?" he said. He looked at his clean, borrowed sneakers.

"Because I thought you knew. You didn't hear about her funeral?"

"Funeral? No, Teresa, I didn't." His face looked pale, and mine was hot from held-back tears, because I realized no one had claimed her body. Maybe no one besides Luna, Maria, Angela, David, and I knew she was dead. Maybe my father didn't know. My mother had told us not to tell our grandmother that she was going to work at the ranch in Arizona for Maria's boss. She'd told us that her friend Maria in Arizona and our grandmother didn't like each other. Luna asked why and our mother said it didn't matter why.

Paco sat there without saying anything for a long time. I guess it took me telling him about my mother for me to remember the other things and for them to start making sense. Now I understood why Maria hadn't asked for a phone number to call our grandmother.

"Teresa, I don't know what to say . . . I don't . . . " Paco croaked.

"I know. It's okay. You don't have to say anything," I said. "Come on, I'll show you the pond. There are fish in there that can swallow whole frogs." We got up from the grass and walked to the grove around the pond. Two white kids from school were there, so I told them, "This is my friend, Paco. He's here to visit."

We threw dirt clods in the pond, and watched dragonflies dip their mouths to drink. Sparrows swooped at the water and caught beakfuls of fat dragonflies. One of the kids, a redheaded boy, threw a dirt clod at a sparrow on a branch with a dragonfly clamped in its short beak.

"Hey, don't hurt it, it just wants to eat," Paco said.

"Who's gonna stop me, wetback?" the boy said.

"We have to get back to the house," I said. "Let's go." Those two boys from school were kind of mean to other kids. I didn't really like them, and I didn't want a fight to start. All I wanted to do was get away from there without anybody getting beat up.

Paco's arms were stiff at his sides and his hands were clenched. He looked ready to hit one of the boys, and I was afraid if one of the boys hit him first, he'd have to fight both of them.

"Come on Paco, we have to get back."

"Yeah, go eat some beans and tortillas, you greasers," the redheaded kid said. Paco picked up a clod the size of his fist and threw it right into that kid's open mouth. The kid gagged and spat and turned and ran.

The other kid yelled, "You're gonna pay for that!" and ran after his crying brother.

"What a big baby," Paco said. He dusted his hands on his pants.

"Thanks, Paco, now they'll pick on me," I said, but I was trying not to laugh at the stupid redheaded kid who acted so tough, then ran off crying with his mouth full of dirt. Now I just wanted to get back to the house before those kids got brave and came back.

Maria's car wasn't there yet, but Angela's was in the driveway, so we went in the house. She'd brought over another box of clothes, and Luna was going through it, holding things up to her shoulders. Salma loved the orange and green polka dot shirt that looked like a clown shirt and Luna told her to take it, but not to wear it.

"Whatever you don't like, leave it in the box. Somebody somewhere will want it. Hello, Teresa!" Angela said cheerfully. "I heard you have a visitor."

"Yes, this is Paco," I said.

Paco shook hands with Angela. I think she was impressed he had such nice manners. I didn't tell her about the dirt clod.

Maria came in through the laundry room and kitchen, set a paper sack on the kitchen counter and said to Angela, "Lunch at the house is cancelled today."

"All right. Cancelled or postponed?" Angela asked.

"Cancelled. Maybe even dinner. They're in Tucson. Three more doctor's appointments, so they may stay in town tonight and come back tomorrow. I'll know late this afternoon." She put milk and a cantaloupe in the refrigerator. "So, Paco, let's call your father and let him know you're fine here. Maybe he'll let you stay a few more days, if you like."

Paco's shoulders dropped.

"Why don't you stay in here with me while I call, the rest of you can go watch TV," Maria said.

I nudged Paco's arm and he nodded.

Angela and I went into the living room. I could hear the dial turning on Maria's yellow wall phone. She talked to the operator for a few seconds, and then she was quiet again, until I guess somebody answered the phone.

"Yes, hello, Enrico Dominguez? Oh, good. I'm glad your English is good; my Spanish is not. This is Maria Ormond. I'm calling from Tubac, Arizona. Yes . . . it's about your son . . . oh, no, he's fine, he's here with me. Nina Espinosa's daughter, Teresa . . . Yes, Teresa Espinosa. No, she's here at my house. It's a long story, but a friend of mine brought him here. No, Paco is fine. He's not in trouble, but he had some trouble getting here. Yes, I understand, I'd be angry with him too, but . . . yes, he says he brought a rooster. No, he doesn't have it any more. Well, yes . . . someone gave him a ride, and took his things, and the rooster, but Paco is fine. Do you want to talk to him? Okay, hold on." She told Paco his father wanted to talk to him.

Paco's voice sounded smaller. "Papa? Please don't be mad. I wanted to see Teresa and school was out, and I knew you would say no . . . I know . . . but, Papa . . . but I was going to pay my own way with Caesar. Because the guy said he could win fights. No, in Arizona . . . yes, it was

Favo . . . well, now I know he is . . . yes, I know, but he told me Teresa's grandmother was sick and needed help . . . yes, but they came up to Arizona last month. Yes, her mother too. No, not her father. I know . . . but, Papa . . . yes, I understand, and I'm sorry . . . yes . . . but listen . . . but Teresa's mother got killed. Yes, she did. Drowned. I don't know. That's what Teresa told me . . . she told me today . . . it was last month. But I didn't know until this morning. Yes, I'm sure. Teresa saw. I don't know. The border patrol—um, someone from here who helped me get here. I told him I was looking for Teresa . . . I know . . . Yes, but may I stay here with Teresa for a while? Yes, she's fine, but . . . Okay."

I knew he'd handed the phone back to Maria because I heard her say, "Yes, oh, of course, I'm glad I reached you. It's no trouble at all for him to visit for as long as he wants . . . if you . . . yes, I can meet you in Nogales with him, but can it be later this week? Oh, that's good news. Yes, I'll tell him. No, I'm sure he won't do this again, but he's safe here. Ormond. Ormond Ranches, Ormond Manufacturing. Yes, that one. All right, I'll call you later this week and we'll make arrangements . . . yes. All right, thank you."

Paco came into the living room and gave me an okay sign. I went to the kitchen. Maria was sitting on the kitchen counter looking at the note with my grandmother's number. She'd told Luna and me she was twenty-five years old. That was only four years younger than my mother, but she seemed so much younger than that. Maybe it was that her hair was mahogany colored and curly and short, instead of long and black. Maybe it was because she had not raised three girls and had a bad husband.

"I'm going to call your grandmother now. Does she usually help at the store?" she asked.

"Sometimes, but they live above the store, so her husband can call her to the phone."

"I didn't know she was married," Maria said.

"Luna and I got to be in the wedding, Salma wasn't born yet. I guess my mother didn't tell you."

"I got something in the mail from your grandmother a few years ago. Maybe it was a wedding invitation." Maria kind of laughed, but not like it was funny. "I didn't open it," she said, looking at the phone number.

"Why, Maria? Why didn't you open it?"

"Because . . . because . . . I'll tell you sometime. It's hard to explain why." She handed me the paper. "You call her, you tell her where you are, and that you and your sisters are fine, and that I can bring you to Nogales when I bring Paco, or another time." Maria poured a cup of coffee and went out to the living room.

I could hear one of those contest shows on the television. I dialed the numbers on the note, and the sound of dialing was louder than the television. When I told the operator the number she said, "please hold." The phone rang once.

"*Hola*, Moda Lopez," in my stepgrandfather's voice. My mouth was dry. I had forgotten how to talk.

"This is Teresa Espinosa, is my grandmother there today?"

"Oh, Teresa!" Alisio Lopez said, "Where are you? Your father came here last month looking for you girls and your mother. He said you had left Centro and he didn't know—"

"Is my grandmother there?" I asked again. I didn't want to explain everything to him.

"Yes, yes, I'll get her."

The second I heard her voice, I started crying. "Grandmother? It's Teresa."

"Where are you?" she asked in English. She must have had some locals in the store and didn't want them to listen.

"Luna and Salma are with me, we're at the Ormond Ranch."

"Why are you there? How did you get there? "Her voice became sharper, like she was angry. "Let me talk to your mother." Oh, God, she didn't know.

"Grandmother, have you been sick?" I asked.

"No, I am fine. Let me talk to your mother. Why didn't she tell me where she was going? Why did I have to find out you had left in the night from your father?" she snapped.

"My mother—" the door from the dining room swung open, and Luna stood in the kitchen with her arms folded.

"Let me talk to her," Luna said, taking the phone from me. "Hi, it's Luna. I know . . . yes, but she told us not to tell you . . . no, she isn't . . . but Grandmother, didn't you hear what happened? No, you didn't." Luna looked at me, and I saw Luna's pain again, the same look she had the night our mother died.

"Grandmother, no . . . listen to me . . . she is dead. Yes, she is. She . . . the river was high. She drowned. No, a storm and the water . . . no, we didn't. We couldn't. Because we were supposed to meet Maria, and come to the ranch, and we were scared. Do you want to talk to Maria? I know . . . we're all sad . . . please, don't cry . . . I'm sorry you didn't know. Yes, Maria knew, but she didn't know you didn't know . . . here? I don't know, let me ask." Luna cupped her hand over the mouthpiece. "She wants to come here to pick us up right now."

I shook my head "no" because I knew Paco could stay a few more days.

"We'll call you again soon. No, nobody is telling me to get off the phone. Stop being so . . . I'm sorry, but we're fine. I might have a job here. In the kitchen. No, at the Ormond's house. Why? No, why? You're not making sense. We'll call you later. Yes, I think Maria's going to drive Paco down to Nogales to meet his father. Okay. I'll tell her. Bye." Luna hung the phone on its chrome hook.

"She's crying," Luna said. "Give me the note back." I handed it to her. "Grandmother heard from our father that Favo brought us to the ranch."

"Well, he didn't," I said.

"Why would he say that?" she asked.

"Favo lied, he always lies."

"Right," she said. "I'm going to stay here and cook at the big house. I'm not going back to Centro. Our father probably has Pia or somebody there. I hate him."

"But," I said, "we could go live with Grandmother and—"

"And what, live in that stupid apartment over the store and work in the store for nothing?" she said.

"It's not stupid, there are three bedrooms in that apartment. You're stupid," I said, and turned to go back to the living room.

"You're the stupid one," she spat. She went down the hall, and I heard the dresser drawer open and close. I knew she'd put the note away.

I knew that redheaded kid who'd gotten a mouthful of dirt wouldn't be anywhere near the school, so I took Paco to see it. There wasn't anyone in the office building, but the door wasn't locked either. We stood in the open doorway and could hear our own breath echo in the quiet.

"What's in here?" Paco asked.

"Just the office. School records," I said.

"How many kids go to school here?"

"About forty I think. If the office ladies were here we could ask them."

"What are those books?" Paco went over to the row of green ledger books on the shelf.

"That's where they write down who goes to school," I said, "but I don't think we're supposed to be in here."

"So, you are in one of these?" he said, reaching for one of the books.

"The lady who works here wrote us in the book," I said.

"Where?" Paco said, turning some pages.

"I don't think that's the right one," I said, reaching up for the book that said "1970-1971 Enrollment." "We're in this one." He leaned against the counter while I turned the pages. "Here, it shows we started school here. There's the date and our names."

"What's that other number, F Index five?" he said.

"Where?"

"There." He pointed to "F Index 5" written on the last column, to the right of Luna's name, and mine.

"I don't know," I said, looking at the other names on the page. "This one is F index four. This one is M Index seven." I turned more pages, then turned to the front of the book to see if those were some kind of chapters in the book.

"Hey, look!" Paco said, pointing to a set of two dark blue books that were on the shelf above the green books. On the spines of those books were "F Index" and "M Index." Paco scrambled up on the counter to reach for the book with "F Index."

"You're going to get me in trouble." But I didn't stop him.

"Who is Susan Ormond?" he asked.

"I don't know," I said, leaving the green enrollment record book on the counter to lean over the blue book Paco had opened.

"Well it says 'b, 1950,' and 'mother, Priscilla Markley. Blonde hair. Blue Eyes. Father fifty.'"

"Fifty . . . what?" I said, trying to pull the book closer.

"Fifty, what does that mean?" he said. "Fifty is on this one too, he said, pointing at another name two entries down. "This one says 'black hair, brown eyes,' see? 'Matilde Vargas.'"

I looked where he was pointing.

"There's more," he said. "See below that name? It says 'b, 1949.' Oh, b is born. Born, Mexico. Arrived, March 12, 1955. So, she was six. Mother, Rosalinda Vargas, Father UK. What's that? His initials?"

I shrugged.

"What was your number?" he asked.

"How do I know?"

"Look it up in the green book." He pulled the green ledger to him. He turned to a page that said 1970 to 1971 at the top. There was the list of all the kids in school. There were the blonde twins, the redheaded brothers, other kids we knew, and their index numbers. Luna and I were at the bottom of the page, probably because we had started school almost at the end of the school year.

"Here's you," he said, "'Teresa Espinosa, arrived May 14, 1971, born 1959, Mexico. Mother, Nina Espinosa. Father, Carlos Espinosa.'"

"Yes, that's it. I don't remember telling them all that," I said.

"Well, maybe your aunt told them."

"My aunt? What aunt?" I said, looking up at Paco.

"Your aunt Maria, silly."

"Maria? Maria isn't my aunt, she's my mother's friend, they went to school together," I said, looking over the names of my classmates.

"Oh, I must have heard it wrong," Paco said. "Here's Luna. 'Luna Espinosa, arrived May 14, 1971. Born 1957, Mexico. Mother Nina Espinosa, Father UK or fifty.'"

"Fifty? Our father wasn't fifty when she was born, and he's not now."

"I don't think it means an age, Teresa, I think it is something else. See, some of these other kids, same thing. 'Father 50,'" Paco said, running a finger down the ledger page. I looked, and he was right. Some had names for fathers, some said the number 50 and there were more with 50 listed as the father's name than there were with real fathers' names.

"Hey . . . let's look for your mother." Paco's voice softened when he said, "your mother."

"Why?"

"Because, I don't know, so you know more about her. Where she went to school, where she was born. Was she born here?" he asked.

"I don't think so, I think she was born in Mexico. She never talked about here. She only told us about her friend, Maria, I guess because they were friends. But Mama went to school here. Maria told us that. I didn't even know," I said, holding something back in my throat that felt like a cough. I cleared my throat twice.

"Let's look. How old was she?" he asked. When I drew a sharp breath, he touched my arm and his eyes looked sad.

"Thirty-five, I think."

"Okay," he said, "so she was starting school when she was six maybe . . . so maybe that was twenty-nine years ago . . . so, 1942?"

"I guess," I said, sniffling. He reached for the ledger with 1942 on the spine, opened it, and ran his finger down the page of about twenty names.

"No, not here," he said. "Are you sure about the year?"

"You said the year, I said how old she was," I said. He reached for another ledger.

"Okay, now I'm dumb, she would have been born in 1942 and started school in 1948." He looked through the next ledger. "Not here."

"Maybe she didn't go to school here," I said. Paco reached for 1950 and traced two fingers down a page.

"Here's a six-year-old girl named Nina. Is this her?" he said, and I leaned closer to look. Nina. An index ledger number was written beside her name. We got that book off the shelf. And there she was: Nina Rosario, Mother, Ana Rosario. Father UK.

"There's UK again," I said. "and look, there's some other ones with that same father, different mothers." We looked at each other, and back at the ledger.

"Teresa—" Paco started.

I interrupted, "Hey, maybe UK isn't a person."

"So, what is it?"

"Maybe it means unknown," I said.

"Let's look for Maria, she went to school with your mother," Paco said.

Maria wasn't on the list for 1950, 51, 52 . . . but we found her when we got to 1954. I told Paco the index number beside her enrollment, and he found the right book.

"No Maria." he said, "but there is a Mary Ormond. Born 1948. Ormond Ranch, Tubac, Arizona. Mother Ana . . . it doesn't give a last name. 'Father, 50,'" he said.

"But what does that fifty mean?" I saw more kids with the number 50 listed as their father's name.

"Do you think the mother is the same Ana?" he said.

I pushed up on my elbows to look at the whole page. "Paco, I'd know if I had an aunt."

"Let's see how long your mother went to school here," Paco said. He looked for another green ledger. "She would have been seventeen when she finished high school."

"I don't think she went to high school," I said. "I think she dropped out."

We jumped ahead eleven years, and there was no Nina, but there was Mary Ormond again. I went back two years and found Nina listed as a fourteen-year-old, and then not again.

"That must be when she dropped out," I said.

"Hey, look in the upper grades, all the classes are smaller," Paco said.

"So?"

"Well, classes at our school don't get smaller."

"They do if kids drop out," I said.

"Look, it's just the girls that stop after the ninth grade," he said.

"They do? Oh, they do. Maybe all of them drop out."

"The boys don't, see, the boys here are seventeen, eighteen years old," he said, holding his finger on the small group of boys' names.

"What made you think Maria was our aunt?" I asked him, turning the next page of the school ledger.

"Something that guy Favo said."

"Favo? Favo told you that? He's a liar. How could you believe anything he told you?" I didn't understand Paco's thinking.

"He told me he knew where you were. He told me he'd get me to you, and I got here."

"But he didn't get you here, he left you."

"Yeah. And he was also a thief." Paco said. "Let's show Luna these books, maybe she knows more stuff about your mother."

"What for? She only wants to make eyes at the boys at school and watch television. She's the oldest, not the smartest," I said, and put the ledger back.

We left the school office, and I showed Paco the hallway and classrooms. We got in front of the nursery where Salma went, and something thumped in my head. Not like a headache, more like "hey!" and I stopped.

"Let's go back and look at those books again," I said.

We went back to the school office and found the same book that showed where Luna and I started school.

"What are you looking for?" he asked. I didn't answer until I'd found the page for the nursery.

"Salma." I said, "May 13, 1971."

Paco's brows creased together. "She got here before you?"

"Well, she started school before Luna and I did."

"Oh," he said, "what is the number for her?"

"It says Index A seventeen," I said. There were no ledgers with an A.

"What's that?" Paco said, pointing to a filing cabinet. I shrugged. He went to the cabinet and studied the labels. "These top three drawers have A on them, here, fourteen through seventeen."

"Open it." I said.

Paco slid the drawer open. It was full of yellow folders. The colored tabs on the tops each had a first name. We found the folder with Salma's name on it and took it out. Paco pulled the folder in front of it up a little to mark where it went. There was a printed sheet on top.

Name: Salma.
Mother: Mexican, Nina Espinosa.
Father: Mexican, Carlos Espinosa.
Hair: Black. Eyes: Brown.
Age: 4 Years, 3 months.
Language: English and Spanish.
Date of Availability: June 1971.

I stared at the paper for a long time. "What do you think this means?" I asked Paco.

"I don't know," he said, "what else is in there?"

I turned the first page over and looked at the second one.

Eyes: Clear
Teeth: Normal, slight overbite
Height: 37 inches
Weight: 38 lbs.
Notations: Salma is a bright, curious child, who loves to play with other children. She will thrive in a good learning environment. She plays well alone as well, entertaining herself with toys.

"It's her report card, I guess," he said.

"Maybe," I said. I turned that page over, and there were three photos of my baby sister in the green dress she'd worn her first day at the nursery. One was her against a white background, facing the camera. The next one showed her from the side, and the third one was just her face and shoulders. In the photo of her face, I could see a woman's hands, with long, painted fingernails, over Salma's shoulders. Was that person holding her still to have her picture taken?

"This is . . . I don't know what this is," I said.

"Maybe they have a thing like this on all the kids here," Paco said.

"No, they didn't measure Luna or me, and they didn't take our pictures."

"I wonder why?" he said. He tapped on a photograph of Salma. "They got your parent's names right on her file."

"Yes, so? They have them right on mine too."

"But not on Luna's. They have her father as fifty," he said.

"Maybe they made a mistake," I said.

"Maybe," Paco said, as he looked back at the ledgers on the shelf. "They had that same number on Luna's file as on that girl Mary's file. Do you think Mary and Luna are related?"

"Well, if they were, I'd be related to Mary too. So, no, they're not related." I wondered why Paco would be trying to tell me who was in my family.

"Teresa, Mary and your mother both had Ana for their mother's name,"

"There can be two different people with the same name!" I said. Paco was starting to sound as crazy as Luna.

"But they could be the same Ana. Maria looks kind of like your mother. Except she has kind of red hair," he said.

"Except that, my mother, she was Mexican. Maria isn't Mexican. She has red hair. And she looks . . . "

"Half Mexican." Paco finished my sentence for me. My head was starting to hurt again. I wished I had some more of the aspirin Maria had given me earlier.

"Right, so she's not my mother's sister," I said.

"Teresa, maybe she's your mother's half-sister." I slapped Salma's file shut and put it back into the cabinet. I wanted to slam the whole drawer closed but was afraid I'd break it if I slammed it as hard as I wanted to right now.

"Stop it," I said. "My grandmother had one daughter. My mother. With her first husband. I have the wedding ring," I said, pulling on the string I wore around my neck under my blouse. I held it out at the end of the loop of string for Paco to see. I don't know why I thought that proved anything, but it was all I had.

"Did she tell you that?" Paco asked. "Did she tell you she only had one daughter, or did she have two daughters and you only got told about one, or did you only know about one and you never asked, so no one told you?"

It was his patience that made me hear what he was asking. He was asking me to think that my grandmother had another daughter that Luna and I didn't know. That my mother had a sister we didn't know. I looked at Paco's face carefully, and saw he wasn't teasing. He was asking me something important.

"Yes," I said.

"Yes, she told you that, or yes, she never told you?" he asked.

"Maybe I just thought that. Come on, Paco, let's go." We let ourselves back out the office door.

Just after we'd left the office and had gone around the corner, we heard a car. We hid against the building, behind the oleander bushes, and peeked around. Miss Connie was getting out of the passenger side of a dark grey car and turned back to lean into the open window and we saw her kiss the man who was driving. She hurried to the office, and the man drove away, toward the warehouse. Paco and I waited 'til we were sure no one could see us, and got away from the school.

"I'll show you where they keep the chickens," I said. "They're just hens for eggs. But they're chickens."

I saw I'd hit a sore spot when I brought up the chickens. But Paco had hit a sore spot on me when he brought up my mother. So, we were even.

HE IS RUNNING

He is running.
He is running toward the lights of a ranch house in the distance.
He's been running for close to an hour,
and hopes the people in the house will help.
Will bring a car or a truck to help his brother.
His brother has stepped on a rattlesnake. The leg is swelling.
He told his brother to stay put.
He promised to get him a doctor.
He has lost his matches, lost his knife,
and he will lose his brother if he does not get help.

He approaches the ranch house door, sees a woman inside.
He taps on the screen door.
"Please, señora, my brother is hurt."
She screams.
The rancher rushes in and sees him standing at the screen door,
dirty, disheveled, in filthy pants and a charro shirt.
The rancher raises a shotgun and points it.
"No, no, please, I need help."
"Whadda ya want?"
"My brother is hurt."
"Beat it, wetback, or I blow a hole in you,"
the rancher says through clenched teeth.
"Get away from my door. Vamanos!"
"Please, my brother, he is dying."
He backs away from the light of the kitchen, weeping.

The woman is dialing the phone in the kitchen.

"Yes, Luther Randall's ranch here, we have an illegal trying to break in . . . You do? Oh, good. Glad you're so close. Yes, come on, he's still here," the woman says into the phone.

The lights of the border patrol truck top a hill two miles away.
He runs toward the rancher's truck.
He is desperate to get back to his brother.
He reaches for the door handle.
The back of his charro shirt explodes from the shotgun blast.

26

ANA 1948

Keep a secret

"Sober up, Ana," her brain warned. Her body ignored her brain. Her pounding pulse told it, "Shut up, mind your own business."

She didn't dare look at him once his mouth covered hers. She felt as if the breath had been sucked out of her and she clung to him so that she wasn't looking at his face. The man she had thought was cold and uncaring held her, asked her, with his kisses and rhythm, to respond.

He had spoken her name just once, as she woke to him touching her. She knew she could have pulled away, refused him. But generosity and kindness from a man were not something familiar, so she went along, as a dreamer will, falling off a cliff, and vowing not to wake, because the dream might take her somewhere away from the ordinariness of her life.

She hadn't been touched the way he touched her. She hadn't been with a man since she'd last been with Nina's father. The moments of what she'd thought was love with Nina's father had been hurried, on a pallet on the floor of a friend's house with her dress pushed up, and him groping at her. Whatever those moments were had ended when she told him she'd missed her bleeding, and that she might be carrying a child. He was gone the next day. By the time she turned seventeen, as pregnant as an overstuffed goose, fond memories of him were long gone.

And now here he was, the man who'd confided in her about his unhappy marriage this afternoon, how his wife did not act like a wife to him. And he'd chosen Ana as his friend, his confidant, his lover. His hands told her what she wanted to hear.

He didn't remove his trousers and thigh length underpants completely, or his undershirt. Ana told herself it had to be that he wanted her so much that he couldn't even take the time to undress. When they'd consummated his betrayal, and she was wondering what he'd say to her now, he rose and hurried to the hall bathroom, holding his trousers around his thighs.

She lay with sheets tangled beneath her, listening to water running in the sink, on sheets that smelled of sweat and sin. She dragged the top sheet from under her sticky thighs and pulled it over herself.

She imagined when he returned from the bathroom, she'd lift the sheet, and welcome him back in, and she'd hold him and listen to him talk. That was what she'd do. That was what she imagined lovers would do.

The door opened quietly, and he entered her room again. His trousers were zipped and he was buttoning his shirt, then sliding his still-tied necktie over his head and under his collar. He sat cautiously on the side of her bed. She silently vowed she wouldn't be needy. She'd be serene. His lover who was serene. She sat up with the wrinkled sheet clamped under her arms so her breasts were covered. Her hands went to the necktie and adjusted the knot until it was straight. She hoped he would kiss her, but he didn't.

"Ana," he said.

She couldn't meet his grey-green eyes just yet. There was too much chance of saying something ridiculous if she did, and she knew it. She stopped her eyes on his chin. It made her feel the stubble burn that was already heating her jawline and cheek.

"I let myself get caught up in this," he said. "This isn't who I am. You were so beautiful, and you listened. I hope you don't hate me for coming here."

Her cheeks were on fire. She lowered her eyes to his tie. "No, I'm glad you did."

"Are you? Oh Ana, you just make me feel . . . like I'm alive and I haven't felt this alive before."

She wouldn't risk sounding lovestruck now, so she didn't say anything.

"I have to get to the warehouse. They'll be back from the movie about six thirty. That's," he looked at his watch, "two hours from now. I have a meeting in town tonight, and I'll stay there and pick up Lorene in the morning. You don't need to go to the kitchen to cook until tomorrow. I have to go."

Ana was still sitting up with the sheet stretched across her chest.

"God, you're beautiful," he said, and kissed the top of her head.

She let her eyes focus on his face for fraction of a second and stopped some foolhearted words before they came out of her mouth.

He put both hands on her bare shoulders. "Tell me I can come see you again. May I do that? This has to be our secret, it wouldn't do for the other women here to find out you and I are . . . friends. You wouldn't want that either, right? Having those women minding your business?"

Ana shook her head.

"That's my girl," he said. He kissed the top of her head again.

He was out the door, and through the hallway. The door to the kitchen groaned open. His steps at the outer kitchen door, the creak and thump of heavy wood. The sound of the key in deadbolt outside, the tumblers turning.

She rose to wash herself. She couldn't give her secret away with the scent of aftershave and semen. She peeled her slip off in an inside out roll of fabric and took a shower. But how would she explain the smoke smell on her uniform she'd worn into the cafe? She filled the sink with water and squeezed some shampoo over the uniform as the sink filled. She washed, rinsed and blotted as much as she could. She hung the dress in her closet to dry. She put on clean underwear and a fresh uniform. She made her bed.

It was too risky to pull the sheets off and put them in the laundry basket today. It wasn't laundry day for another two days. Someone doing washing might wonder why her sheets were in the basket, might smell the mingled scents. She needed to keep the secret.

Ana knew how to do that.

Ana's heart jumped when she heard the lock on the kitchen door rattle open. She'd been watching Nina grasp at sunbeams streaming through the heavy window panes in her bedroom for close to an hour. She heard Maya's door open, rose from the edge of her bed, gathered up her daughter, and followed Maya to the kitchen. She knew it would be Gabriella, and not Stan Ormond, leaning over a note in the kitchen, tapping a pencil on the paper, humming, looking up, smiling, saying "Good morning." But she felt a throb of disappointment anyway.

"Maya, I'm picking Suela up this afternoon at the hospital. Would you like to ride along?" Gabriella asked. She dropped her shopping list in her purse. "Ana, can you watch the children this afternoon? I'll leave the doors open. They can be just outside where you can see them or in your room while you work. We'll be back before dinnertime." Ana reached for the note on the counter. She hoped to read her lover's pointed, backward slanting handwriting. It was Lorene Ormond's instead. She pocketed the note without reading it.

"Yes, I will watch them."

"Mrs. Ormond wants something special this morning. I already set the table. She'll give you the lunch and dinner menu," Gabriella said.

"All right," Ana said, touching the note in her uniform pocket.

Gabriella checked a shelf in the refrigerator. "I'll bring groceries when we come back. Could you change the sheets in Suela's room? You and Maya may have to help her for a few days. She's still weak."

"Yes, we will," Ana said.

Maya pulled on Nina to get her walking. Rudy, as always went placidly and peacefully to school. Gabriella pulled the outer door closed without locking it and raised her hand in a short wave.

Ana felt for the menu note in her pocket and unfolded the expensive scented paper.

Breakfast for two, 8 AM
Cinnamon Rolls with icing (Mr. Ormond's favorite, so be sure not to burn them)
Poached Eggs
A layer cake, with white icing and this in pink icing:
Happy Anniversary Darling, love, Lorene
Please be careful of the spelling.

Ana looked at the clock and hurried to the pantry for cake pans and flour. She'd be lucky to get something baked, cooled, and iced by eight. She turned the oven on to heat while she got the batter made and in the pans. She beat out a dough for cinnamon rolls and let it rise, then went to work on a cake icing smooth enough to spread and firm enough to take decorations.

She found some cake decorating tips in a drawer. She'd learned to manage a cloth icing tube from one of the nuns at the convent, whose family had a bakery. Everything in the kitchen was under control.

The cake had five minutes to go when a wisp of smoke seeped out the oven door. She jerked the door open and burned her thumb getting the pans out. Both pans were scorched on one side. She fanned the smoke, sprinkled baking soda into the oven, dumped the rest of the box of soda into another cake pan and set it on the cutting board. The cinnamon rolls went into the oven next, and when she adjusted the temperature, she saw she'd set it too high for the cake. She'd have to do something with the burned edges.

She chipped ice from the freezer into a set of pie tins, and set the cake pans in them to speed up cooling. The cinnamon rolls began to fill the kitchen with a buttery spicy aroma and, thankfully, rose well. She double-checked the temperature. She made cinnamon icing with chopped nuts while they baked. Thirty minutes 'til breakfast.

The cake pans had cooled, so she turned them out on waxed paper, and saw one of the pans wasn't turning loose. A chunk of cake crumbled onto the counter. She looked at the clock. She put the better cake on the bottom for a base, iced the top, and eased broken second layer on it. She studied the edges while she sharpened a thin-bladed knife. If she made it round it would be too small for the message. But she could carve it into a heart shape.

She iced the heart-shaped cake, pulled the cinnamon rolls out of the oven, and drizzled them with icing. Ten minutes left. She squeezed food coloring into the remaining cake icing and used the note as a guide to painstakingly apply the "Happy Anniversary Darling" message to the cake. She stopped between that and the signature to choose two perfectly shaped brown eggs from the wire basket on the counter, put the eggs on to poach, and finished the cake decoration. She looked at the clock when she heard voices in the dining room. It was two minutes 'til eight.

Eggs in cups, cinnamon rolls on plates. Thank goodness, the table was already set. She hadn't seen juice or water on the menu but poured two glasses of pineapple juice. The voices rose in the dining room, a gasp, a squeal of surprise.

Hers: "Oh, how gorgeous!"

His: "I'm so glad you like it. I saw it at the jewelry store and I knew I had to buy it for you." The silver kitchen bell called Ana to service. She made her practiced, soundless entry, and placed the dishes. Lorene looked up at her in horror and mouthed "cake" and Ana nodded meekly, slipped back to the kitchen, and returned with the cake. She wondered if Señora Ormond thought she had two extra sets of hands.

Lorene waved an arm that sported a sparkling diamond bracelet, indicating to Ana to put the cake beside the open jewelry box on the table between them. Stan glanced at the message Ana had written on the cake.

"Really, Lorene, you shouldn't have!" He leaned over to kiss the glowing cheek his wife offered as Ana returned to the kitchen.

Ana picked up the pan of cinnamon rolls that were left and looked at the mixing bowls, cooling rack and icing tube on the counter. She wanted to smash the pan on the tiled counter, but set it down silently, lifted two rolls onto her plate with the spatula, and went into the back room. She tore at the coils of pastry and shoved the pieces into her mouth, barely chewing.

She drank water from the faucet in the back room. She returned to the kitchen and looked at the four rolls left in the pan. *Be sure not to burn them*, the note had said. Ana wanted to burst into the dining room with the white plastic radio and throw it at him.

The bell rang three notes for her to return to the dining room. Lorene was holding up her half empty juice glass.

"Ana, what is this?" she asked sweetly.

"Pineapple juice, ma'am," Ana whispered.

"Did I have it on the menu?" Lorene asked, glancing at her husband for support.

"No, ma'am."

"So, you thought it was a good idea to just bring it in anyway?" Lorene said. Her tone was sugary. Ana would have stammered an answer, had she not been so angry. "That is all." Lorene set the glass beside her plate.

Ana turned and went back to the kitchen. She transferred the remaining cinnamon rolls to a glass dish, covered it with waxed paper and set it aside. She waited for the sounds of the two in the dining room to move away, then peeked through the door. Both juice glasses were empty. The rolls and eggs had been eaten. But the cake she'd rushed to make on two hours' notice was untouched. She cleared dishes.

The velvet-covered jewelry box had been left beside Lorene's plate. On Ana's next trip to the dining room to get the cake, Lorene appeared at the door.

"Oh, there it is, I almost forgot my pretty box," she said, grabbing it as though she were saving it at the last moment from theft.

"Ana, you're lucky Mr. Ormond is so agreeable about juice because I know I asked for grape juice this morning."

Ana said nothing.

"If you have trouble with notes written in English, maybe you should have Gabriella read them for you," Lorene said, then smiled as she looked at the new bracelet on her wrist. She closed the jewelry box with a snap and left the dining room.

Ana picked up the cake plate and took it to the kitchen. She slid a crown of toothpicks into the icing and covered it with waxed paper. Her stomach churned sour while she finished cleaning up.

She got linens from the shelves beside the bathroom door, piled the worn and mended sheets from Suela's bed on the floor and remade the bed. A tiny time-scarred crib waited beside the bed. Gabriella must have brought it in yesterday, Ana reasoned. She hoped it hadn't been while Stan Ormond was in her room.

Ana carried the sheets to the laundry bin in the kitchen's back room, then remembered the scented paper breakfast menu note in her pocket. She pulled it out and glanced at it. There was no grape juice on the note. There was no juice at all on the note.

Ana walked over to the counter where she'd set the heart shaped cake and lifted back the waxed paper just enough that she could spit on it.

Lunch 1:00 for 4
Mexican stew like you made at the convent, but not too spicy
Torteeyas with butter
My Anniversary cake with sherbet.
Have the cake on the table when we come in this time.

A delicious shudder ran across Ana's hipbones when she remembered how Stan Ormond had eased her slip out of the way to hook a hand over the waistband of her panties and pull them down.

That morning she'd picked up her underwear from the closet floor and sniffed them. She'd entertained the idea of folding her white cotton panties into his lunch napkin. She didn't wash her hands after she carried towels and her sex-scented underthings to the laundry hamper.

There was nothing about a beverage on the menu, but Ana decided she'd put water glasses and a pitcher of ice water on the table and Mrs. Ormond could decide if she'd let her guests go thirsty. She browned a four-pound package of stew beef for a base. Vegetables were in good supply from Rafael's garden. She had just one green chile pepper Rafael had brought, which she sniffed to confirm it was a mild cubanelle. She looked back at the note: *but not too spicy.* When had she served anything spicy since she had arrived? She wished she had a couple of habaneros to show Lorene Ormond what spicy was.

It was quarter 'til eleven when Stan Ormond appeared at the kitchen door with his hand pressed against the window pane beside the lock. Ana continued to make dough balls for tortillas, watching him. He looked behind him, and both ways before he opened the door and motioned for her to come closer. His face was lined.

"Ana, I'm so sorry," he said.

Ana put her hands into her apron pockets.

"About this morning. One of Lorene's friends saw me driving you to town yesterday to see the girl in the hospital. She saw us go into the hospital together. That was all. But she told Lorene, and Lorene was in a terrible mood this morning when I picked her up at her sister's. She accused me of all kinds of things."

Ana tilted her head slightly and stared into his grey-green eyes.

"Oh, she doesn't know a thing but she's not reasonable," he said.

Ana's teeth ground beneath her smooth brown cheeks. "Your anniversary is today?" she asked.

"Yes, it is. Did you see the bracelet I gave her? Just . . . act normal. I won't be able to drive you to town any time soon, I'm afraid." He glanced at his watch. "She'll be back in an hour. Gabriella drove her to a doctor's appointment. We have time." He entered the kitchen and locked the door behind him.

Ana's hurt and indignation slid away when his hand brushed hers.

"I need you, Ana." He guided her to the servant's quarters.

She knew she shouldn't; that no good would come from letting him have her like this again, but she backed toward her narrow bed, while he undid her uniform buttons. He dropped his trousers to his knees. He groped at her wildly, lifted his weight off her for a second to drag her panties off and plunged into her. They panted like animals. She wanted to claw at his back. To bite his neck and shoulders. To leave marks. She'd give Lorene Ormond something to be jealous about.

He finished quickly. "I'm sorry I have to leave. Do you understand, Ana? Please, say you understand."

She gripped his back tightly, wished he'd stay inside her another minute. But then he was up and off to the bathroom to wash, and he didn't return to her room. She heard the hallway door close, and the kitchen door opening and closing. She gathered her clothes and went into the bathroom to clean up and dress.

Ana returned to the kitchen. It was five minutes 'til eleven. She saw that she had barely enough lemon sherbet in the freezer for dessert, but remembered a bottle of lime juice in the pantry, and located the rock salt and ice cream mixer. Lime sherbet would be better than lemon, with the cake.

LITTLE DEAD RATS

The packrat's seven babies blink newly opened hazy blue eyes,
and sniff for their mother.
She has not brought crickets and scorpions for them tonight.
They snuffle toward the moonlight to wait.
Three packrat babies are eaten by the kit fox.

The fox carries four little dead rats in her mouth
and trots toward her den.
The fox's kits are hungry, and one of them stumbles from cover before
she arrives with supper.
The owl flares her wings soundlessly and drops from the night air.
She flaps back to her nest to feed a fox kit to her four owlets.

27

TERESA 1971

Rafael

"Hey look." Paco was pointing at a chicken against one side of the pen. She wasn't moving.

"I think she's stuck," I said. But she wasn't just stuck in the fence, she was dead. Four neck bones poked out through the wire, and there was a mess of neck feathers and blood outside the pen. I guess a coyote had ripped off her head when she got it through the wire. The rest of the laying hens were cackling and purring. They got louder when I picked up a handful of scratch that had spilled outside the wire and tossed it through for them.

"There's two more cages around there," I said. "I'll tell Rafael about the dead hen." Paco and I walked around the shaded adobe coop to see the rest of the chickens.

"Who is Rafael?" Paco asked.

"He does gardening and stuff. Takes care of these chickens and brings eggs to Maria's house if they have more than they need for the big house."

I saw Rafael pushing his wheelbarrow toward the chicken coops. A shovel and hoe handle stuck out the side. He was always pushing that wheelbarrow, full of dirt, full of trimmings, carrying a wire basket of eggs, or vegetables, or trash that had blown onto the lawn from the desert. Rafael was friendly, he'd wave and smile, but had not talked much to Luna and me since we'd been there. I think Maria must have told him our mother was dead, and he may have been afraid to talk to us after that. He raised his old head higher and veered our way.

"Buenos días, Teresa," he said, touching the brim of his straw hat.

"Buenos días, Rafael," I said. "This is my friend Paco from Sonora, we go to school together in Centro."

Paco grinned at Rafael, and stuck out his hand. I'd seen him and his father do that when friends came by their house.

"There's a hen that got her head pulled off by a coyote or something in one of the pens," I said.

"Oh, that is bad," Rafael said. "I'll go to see."

"Sorry to tell you," I said, and he waved a hand to dismiss that.

"Are you going to live here?" he asked Paco.

"I don't think my parents will let me stay very long," Paco said.

"Paco had a good fighting cock, Rafael, and a guy named Favo stole it," I said.

"Favo? In Sonora?" Rafael asked, and adjusted the shovel handle in his wheelbarrow.

"He brought Paco across the border in his car and lied to him that he was bringing him here, and he left him in the desert somewhere else. And he stole his clothes and his rooster."

Paco glanced at me, and I knew he was embarrassed that I'd told Rafael.

"Favo is a very bad man," Rafael said. There was sadness in his voice.

"You *know* him?" I asked.

"Si, I knew him long ago. He was always in trouble. Born bad, cursed." Rafael stooped to lift the handles of his wheelbarrow. "I'm glad he is gone, and I hope he never comes back." He stopped and set the wheelbarrow back down.

"Teresa, you know Favo too?" Rafael asked, with a face that looked like he was about to sing a sad song.

"Yes, I would see him in Centro. Yes." I said. Rafael touched his tool handles again.

211

"You know that scar on his face, where his cheek bones are caved in? I put that on him a long time ago. I had to hit him with my hoe one time to stop him from hurting his mother. I wish I had killed him then." Rafael looked toward the chickens. "Buenos días, Teresa. I am glad I met you, Paco." Rafael left with his wheelbarrow to deal with the headless hen in the wire.

"I think that's the most I've ever heard Rafael say," I told Paco.

We walked back to Maria's house, and through the front door. Luna was sitting on the edge of the sofa, wearing one of the grey skirts and white blouses Angela had brought with clothes for school. We'd put those grey skirts in the closet and had not worn them, since at school we wore the blue ones. She had her hair in a bun, with four hair pins on each side of her head. "What are you dressed up for?" I said.

"I'm going to work, and I don't want to be late, so you watch Salma now," she said.

"Work? Where?"

"The main house, they need someone to fix lunch for Mrs. Ormond's friends, so I'm going."

"Is that where Maria is?" I asked.

"I have to go. You watch Salma now," she said, and she was out the front door. I watched her walking quickly toward the house, holding her hands at the sides of her head to keep her hair in place.

Paco and I flopped into the furniture in the living room, after I moved Salma's toys she'd left on the sofa and chairs. On the TV, a big yellow bird with a long neck was teaching children to count, and Salma counted with him. Maria came in right as the wall clock clicked onto eleven thirty. "Hello," I said, "is lunch over already at the Ormond's house?"

"Lunch?" Maria said, looking at her watch. "They're having lunch at two, when Mrs. Ormond gets back from town with her friends," Maria said.

"Oh," I said, "Luna just went over there, she said they needed her to fix lunch."

"Needed her? What?"

Maria was out the door like a mad hen and headed for the main house. Paco and I looked at each other and he said, "Trouble."

"Serves her right," I said.

Ten minutes later, Luna came back and glared at me before she stomped to our room and slammed the door. I made sandwiches for lunch for Paco and Salma and me, but not for Luna. If she was such a good cook, she could make her own lunch. Maria didn't come back until almost three o'clock.

"Where is she?" Maria asked, when she came in.

"Room," I said. I knew whatever had happened, Maria was mad about it. Maria went to our room, and we heard her knock on the door hard enough to make it rattle, and then heard her yelling.

"Don't you ever pull a stunt like that again. Do you hear me? You could have gotten in a lot of trouble."

Luna's voice got higher pitched. "But you weren't here, and he said there were two extra coming, and—"

"AND YOU DIDN'T TELL HIM HE WASN'T TALKING TO ME!" Maria shouted. "Did you?" She didn't wait for Luna to answer. "Luna, you must never go over there unless I take you. You don't know things. It's not just about cooking, you don't know how things work here. Do you understand?" she was still loud. "I didn't hear you. Do you understand?"

We heard a muffled, "yes." and two doors slammed down the hallway. I guessed Maria had gone to her room.

"Oh, man, that was bad," Paco whispered.

"I know. I hope she gets grounded. She's been acting really dumb," I said.

On the television, two policemen were talking to a woman whose husband had not come back from a fishing trip. "Just the facts, ma'am," one of the policemen said. Maria came out, went into the kitchen, came back out with a glass of water, and sat down in her favorite chair.

"Were you here when someone called from the main house?" Maria asked. She was still mad.

"No, Luna told me they called and needed her to come over," I said.

"Okay," Maria said. She set her glass on a coaster on the side table. "I don't mind if you girls answer the phone, but Luna is in trouble for letting Mr. Ormond think he was talking to me. She also took my key to the kitchen from the hook by the back door. She let herself into my boss's house. Do you understand why I'm really mad at her right now?" Maria clipped her words off like fingernails.

"Yes, ma'am," I said. I was embarrassed that Paco had heard all of that, and Paco looked embarrassed to be there.

Maria watched television for a little while, and didn't laugh at anything funny, not even the commercials.

"Paco," she said, "I talked to David, Officer Sanchez, about the best way to get you home without getting anyone in trouble. He thinks that I should take you to Nogales and have your parents meet us. Not right now. But you could call your parents and let them know we're working on it."

Paco's cheeks sucked in and out a little, and he said, "Okay. I'll call them. Is tonight okay?"

"Yes, of course. You're welcome here, but I bet your parents would like you home."

"Okay," Paco said.

Later in the afternoon Paco and I went back to the pond to see if we could watch the whiskered, frog-eating fish. We sat on the sandy berm and listened for the croaks, so we'd know where to watch when the catfish grabbed frogs from the reeds. Paco had been quiet for most of the afternoon, but there by the pond he said, "I want to stay here and go to school here." I wanted that too, but I couldn't say it out loud.

When Paco and I got back to the house Maria said she didn't know what Luna was making but she was letting her fix dinner.

Paco asked to use the phone, and I overheard him telling his mother that he was fine, and that I was fine, and he asked her if he could stay for a few days. He waited for a while, and I knew the answer couldn't be that long, and then I heard him say, "Yes, hello, Papa, did she tell you what I asked?"

He listened, then said, "Yes, I know. I promise, I did not mean to . . . yes, well, I did, but . . . just a minute." He set the receiver down and came into the living room. "Excuse me, ma'am, my father wants to talk to you."

Maria went to the phone. "Oh, yes, of course, it's no trouble. I know the girls are glad he's here. He's welcome to stay for a while . . . yes, I know, I would be concerned too, but I assure you he's safe here. Oh. Well then, I'll tell him that, and we can talk again Monday or Tuesday . . . all right, thank you, goodbye."

"Your father will meet us in Nogales. I have time to drive down there next week," she said.

"Okay," Paco said, but didn't look at her. The phone rang, and Maria went to answer it, and took the receiver and coiled cord around the corner into the dining room to talk.

When she hung up she went to the kitchen door and looked in, then came back to the living room. "I think dinner's almost ready," she said.

That was my hint to set the table. Paco helped, and I laughed at him trying to measure how far apart to put the knife and spoon with his finger.

Maria came from the kitchen with a salad. Luna followed with a pan of enchiladas and set it on the trivet.

"Very nice, Luna," Maria said.

Salma picked up salad with her fingers, and I grabbed her hand and shook it until she let go of the lettuce.

"Eat like a person, not like a monkey with your hands," I scolded. "Use your fork."

She laughed and stabbed at the greens.

Luna stood to slice the cheese between enchiladas with a spatula. She had done a good job, with shredded chicken and green chiles, a thick layer of white Oaxaca cheese, melted and browned just the right way.

"How did you get the cheese to brown all over without the edges getting hard?" Maria asked.

"I put foil around it for the first part of baking, and took it off the last five minutes," Luna said.

"I always burn my edges a little. Who taught you that? Your mother?"

"My grandmother. She taught me a lot of things about cooking," Luna said.

"Did she," Maria said. But she didn't say it like a question.

I'd been thinking about what Paco and I had seen in the ledgers at the school office, and just let the words come out.

"Maria, what's your mother's name?" Maria kept eating, but her fork made a sharp sound on her plate every time she touched it.

"Lorene Ormond. Why?" she said.

I didn't answer why I'd asked, but Maria talked anyway.

"I was adopted by the Ormonds when my mother left me," she said.

"Left you? Why would your mother leave you?" Luna asked.

"I don't know. One day I came home from a trip to town, and Mr. Ormond told me my mother had left me and gone home to Mexico."

Luna and I looked at each other.

"What was your real mother's name?" I asked.

"I don't remember," said Maria.

"How can you not remember?" I said. I didn't believe that Maria didn't remember her mother's name, so I asked what I was afraid to ask: "Was it Ana?"

Maria set her fork down beside her plate and folded her hands on the edge of the table. "What makes you ask that, Teresa?" she said. Her voice was like ice cubes.

I had screwed up now, and I knew Paco would not lie to cover for me. Luna had gotten in trouble today, and I was going to be in trouble too, and so was Paco.

Paco said, "We saw the books at the school, and we looked up everybody we knew, just for fun."

"I see," she said. "And where was Miss Connie, who works in the office?"

"She wasn't there," he said. He didn't jerk his head to look at me when I kicked at his foot under the table. Maria looked at me for a few seconds.

"She wasn't there," she said.

"No, ma'am," I said.

"So, you went through the records in the office?"

"Yes, ma'am,"

Maria exhaled. "I want to help you girls, but you make it hard for me to help you if you go doing things you shouldn't do."

I felt ashamed that I'd let curiosity get the better of us in the office. But I had said this much, and I might as well get an answer.

"Was her name Ana?"

"Yes, it was," Maria said. Luna's back went straight as a board.

"Our mother's mother is Ana too," Luna said. Luna pressed her lips tightly together.

"Yes, it is, Luna." Maria said.

"Where was your mother's husband? Was that why she left you behind, to find him? Our grandmother's husband disappeared." Luna said.

"Is that what your grandmother told you? That her husband disappeared?" Maria said, as her cheeks began to get redder than I'd ever seen them.

"Well, not exactly," I said. "She told us our mother's father went away to the racetrack and never came back."

"You girls need to know something. No one else is going to tell you. But you're old enough to know. Your mother and I are half-sisters." Maria said. She put her arms on the table and looked at us.

"Sisters? But why didn't our mother tell us?" Luna cried.

Paco shifted in his chair uncomfortably. Maria folded her napkin and placed it beside her plate.

"Your grandmother left me behind. I was ten years old. She took your mother with her, back to Mexico, and she never came back for me. Never. The Ormonds adopted me. They're my parents, and your grandmother isn't in my life, and I don't want her in my life. You do as you please. Go back to live with her if you want to, but you need to know what kind of mother she was to me."

Luna and I looked at each other, stunned.

"What about our mother's father, and your father?" I asked.

Maria thought for a second, and I could see she was deciding what to say.

"Your mother's father left your grandmother in Mexico when she was pregnant with your mother. My father was not the same man."

"She was married twice?" I asked. I was twelve years old and still hopeful that there was something that made sense.

"No, she was never married," Maria said.

"She's married to Alisio Lopez. He has a store in Centro. We went to the wedding."

"She may be married now, but she was not married to your mother's father or to mine, and it was not the same man. My father was white. So, I'm sorry if that's not what you wanted to hear," Maria said. "Thank you for fixing dinner, Luna. You can help at the big house tomorrow. We have a new cook. You can be her helper. Just until school starts back. You'll make a little money for that, if you want to work. Now, excuse me," she said. She pushed her chair back and went to her room.

Paco, Luna and I sat in silence for a few seconds. Luna's eyes pooled with tears.

"I can't believe our grandmother did that, can you?"

"I don't know, Luna," I said.

"I want to see the books you saw," Luna whispered loudly. "Please."

Something told me to be nice to her.

"Okay, if we can get in there," I said. She and I cleared the dishes, and Paco put foil over the leftovers.

"What about Salma?" Paco asked.

"We'll have to take her with us. Luna, tell Maria we're going for a walk."

"There's a window on the side, behind the bushes," Luna said when we found the school office door locked. "I'll check it." She went between the oleander bushes.

"I never saw that window before," I said.

"You never cut class either," Luna said from behind the oleander leaves. "It's not locked. I have a skirt on, so you have to climb in."

I hefted myself up to the ledge, and Paco put a hand under my knee to help me wiggle through.

"Meet me at the door," I said. I turned the door latch in the front room, and let them in. The moon was enough light. "Lock it behind us."

Luna flipped the light switch.

"NO!" I said.

She flipped it back off.

"That room, go in there. Close the door. I'll get the books," Paco said.

Luna and I took Salma in the room at the left of the office to wait for Paco. Luna picked up a stuffed dog on one of the chairs and gave it to Salma to play with. Paco came in with the whole stack of green ledgers, then went back for the blue ones. I locked the door before Luna turned on the light switch.

"Where's that window from here?" Paco asked.

"Through the other door, to the right of this one. If someone comes, you put these books back. We go out the window," I said.

"Show me," Luna said.

Paco and I started opening books to show her the columns of names and dates and indexes. She studied them without saying anything until she asked, "Who is this? S-O?"

"S-O? Where?" I said.

"Here," she said, holding a finger under a student's record, to the right of "Name of Father."

Paco leaned in, then straightened up.

"Oh. We thought it was fifty. We wondered what that meant," he said.

I looked at other names in the book.

"But see," Luna said, "the person who wrote this makes an S look like a five. It's an S. It's S-O. There's a lot of them."

We went back to the ledger where we'd found our mother's school enrollment. "Her father is listed as U-K," Luna said.

"So are others, I think it's for unknown," Paco said.

"That might be right. Are there any where there's a name?" she asked. We turned some pages.

"Here's D-O." I said.

"But that's not a name," Paco said, running his finger over columns. "Here," he said, "Matthew Roberts. He is the father of Ester Roberts, and Stephen Roberts, and Charles Roberts . . . and Tom and Sofia Roberts." Paco studied the page. "And here's nine kids with the same father, Richard Crawford," he said, and showed me the names of nine students, entering school over ten years.

"And Maria?" Luna asked.

"We think she's this one." Paco turned pages until he found Mary Ormond's birth record. "Father, S-O," Luna said.

"Could that be for Señor Ormond?" Paco asked.

"His name isn't Señor. Stan Ormond," Luna said,

We all looked at each other.

"That can't be right," I said, "half the kids on the pages have that S-O. It has to mean something else."

"Look up our classes again," Luna said. Paco opened the enrollment book.

"Here, so start with Lucinda Torres," he said.

Luna took the index number beside Lucinda's name and found the blue book. "Mother Matilda Torres, father U-K," she said.

"This one now, Ramon Becerra," Paco said.

"Mother Celinda Becerra, Father Ray Becerra," Luna said. "Ramon's mother works in the laundry at the other side of the ranch, and his father works at the warehouse."

"Is Ramon Mexican?" Paco asked.

"Umm, Becerra, that's Mexican," Luna said.

"But is he really Mexican or is he part white?" I looked at Paco for a long time.

"Mexican. Ramon is Mexican," Luna said. "Lucinda is Mexican."

I looked at the list, and started pointing to names to show Paco what he wanted to know. "Half Mexican, white, white, I think half Mexican, Mexican," I said.

"So, these white kids where the mother and father are different names, who are the fathers?" Paco asked, looking from Luna's face to mine.

"Roberts, and D-O and S-O." I said.

Paco tapped on the page he'd been reading. "And the ones you think could be half white?" he said.

"Same? Roberts, D-O and S-O?" Luna said.

Paco nodded.

Salma tossed the stuffed dog on the table.

"Let's show Luna the file for Salma," Paco said. He slipped out into the office and came back to the room with a bundle of files from the cabinet. We opened Salma's file.

Salma crawled into a chair and stood on the seat to see what we were looking at.

"Me!" she exclaimed, pointing at the photographs of her.

"Have you ever seen any of these kids?" Paco asked. He fanned out a dozen folders, opened to show the photos in them.

"No, but these kids here are from nursery school," I said.

"Yes," said Paco, "The photos are from nursery school but some of these are old files, so these kids would be your age now. Are they in school now?"

"Maybe they moved," Luna said.

"Maybe, but most of them have D-O or S-O for their fathers. Do they look Mexican to you?" Paco said, tapping on one of the photographs.

"They look half Mexican," Luna said.

"Half Mexican. Mexican mothers. White fathers. So, where are they?" he asked.

I shrugged.

"See, some of them have the same mothers. Twelve of them right here, from five mothers, two fathers," he said. He turned another page over.

Luna turned one of the files around and leaned over it. "Why do they have Salma in that file?" she said, "She's our sister, and no one is going to adopt her. We should take this with us to show to Maria."

"No, no, don't do that, they'll know we came in here." I took the folder away from her. "If Salma's file is gone, they'll know it was us."

"What about Mary Ormond? Look. Mother Ana. Father S-O. Adopted March 3, 1958." Paco said, running his finger across the line on the ledger. "She was ten years old."

"Who adopted her?" I asked. "Mr. and Mrs. S. Ormond." Paco read from the ledger. I was twelve, and I was not catching on. But Luna got a funny look on her face.

"So, does it mean our grandmother had a baby with Señor Ormond?" she said.

I looked at Luna, but was embarrassed to look at Paco. I knew our grandmother was a good woman who cooked wonderful things and she was married to Alisio Lopez, and he loved her, and she helped in his store, and she gave me rosary beads and her old wedding ring, and I couldn't accept that it was the same Ana who was our mother's mother.

"Let's get out of here before we get caught," Paco said. He took the files and ledgers to put them back. I let them out the front door and latched it behind them. They met me at the window. We snuck away in the moon's shadows of school buildings.

A triangle of yellow light on the ground marked the tool shed near the chicken coops. We went as close as we dared. Rafael was sitting in the tool shed, filing the edge of his shovel.

Luna motioned furiously for us to follow her into the shadows. Rafael's head lifted from his work and he stared out into the moonlit yard. I froze, and Rafael went back to his sharpening. He hadn't seen me.

I could still hide when I needed to hide.

Moon shadow of mountains

The moon and sun are trading places;
each lights its own horizon.
An indigo saguaro forest stands backlit against
the lights of Tubac, a few miles away.
The moon shadow of mountains
sets the dry grass
ablaze in glowing violet.
Night birds whir in the darkness.
Frogs that have escaped the mouths
of catfish at the pond warm up their
chorus of groans and love songs.

28

ANA 1949

A jangling summons

"This cake was my surprise for Stan. Isn't it fun? Elder Bradley, would you like to sit there by Stan? Jane, you sit by me, so we can compare notes about our handsome husbands."

The voices of the Ormonds and their lunch guests filtered into the kitchen from the dining room. The silver bell jangled and set Ana in motion.

"Well, whatever you've planned, Lorene, it smells wonderful," said the woman beside Lorene.

Ana glanced up as she adjusted the tureen. The woman beside Lorene Ormond had the most unnaturally black hair Ana had ever seen on a white woman. It draped in waves over her shoulders and back from a plastic headband. Ana wondered if the hair came from a horse's mane or tail. She dismissed such thoughts and served posole and tortillas.

"Thank you, Ana," Lorene Ormond said.

"Thank you, I mean *see, grassias,*" the black-haired woman intoned.

"Really, Jane," the man beside Stan Ormond said, "aren't you carrying this a little too far?"

"Oh Brad, let me have my fun, I'm practicing for the baby."

Ana set the last bowl down in front of Stan Ormond. He smelled like soap and aftershave. She didn't dare look at him.

Brad spoke loudly to Stan. "My wife seems to think the baby will understand her if she speaks Spanish."

Ana wiped the edge of the tureen, replaced the cover, and retreated to the kitchen. She dutifully cleaned the griddle, listening to the black-haired woman's nasal voice.

"Stan, what do you think? You've had Mexican servants, are they good people? I mean, we'll raise our little Gracie to know Heavenly Father, and she'll get the teachings of the book, but I worry that she'll, you know, just be inclined to sin."

"Why would you think that, Jane?" Stan Ormond said.

The other man spoke, "I think what Jane is trying to say is that even a child that's raised right could be touched by the mark of Cain, being from a Mexican mother."

Ana stopped what she was doing and put both hands on the counter to keep from going back into the dining room.

Stan Ormond answered, "We've never had a problem. I wish I had twenty more like our house manager and our gardener and our cook to work at the warehouse. Isn't that right, Lorene?"

"I suppose," Lorene said loudly, "but I wish they could be taught to drive. Honestly, they have to be taken everywhere." Brad and Jane laughed heartily along with Lorene.

When the laughter stopped, Stan said, "There we have it. Advice on managing household staff by Princess Lorene, who has our house manager or me, drive her everywhere." There was more laughter.

Ana heard the door between the living room and dining room open, and Lorene exclaimed, "Oh good, Gabby's brought her early! Jane, Brad, this is my personal assistant, Gabby. And this is, hold the basket higher, Gabby, so they can see her. This is Gracie."

"Oh, *hole-la*, little baby," the ridiculous black-haired woman screeched.

"I'm sure she will be a blessing to our home," Brad said.

"Is there a bottle for the baby, Gabby?" Lorene asked.

"Yes, Señora, I'll get it warmed."

Gabriella came into the kitchen with a bottle. "I need to warm this."

Ana set a saucepan by the sink for Gabriella to use.

Gabriella set the bottle in the water. "How long? Two minutes?"

"Whose baby is that?" Ana said.

"That couple is adopting her. She's named Gracie," Gabriella said. Ana checked the bottle temperature on the back of her hand and handed the bottle over. "Thank you, Ana." Gabriella disappeared into the dining room. Ana heard her say, "If that is all, Señora, I'll be going."

"Yes, Gabby, that is all," Lorene said.

"Oh, look she's hungry. Momma, yes, I'm your Momma," said nasal-voiced Jane.

"I don't think she knows you yet, Jane," Brad said.

"Oh, she knows me already, did you see her look at me just then?" The baby emitted three short squeaks and started crying.

"Oh Gracie, don't cry, I'm here," Jane wailed. The bell rang a jangling summons. Ana entered the dining room and stood near the door, hands folded in front of her.

"Ana, can you take this child to the kitchen and *do* something?" Lorene said. "Ana has a little girl of her own. Isn't that right, Ana? We never hear her baby crying, do we Stan?"

"That's because her baby is three years old and goes to the nursery every day," Stan said to Brad. Both men laughed.

Ana wanted to vomit.

Ana took the baby, the basket, and the full bottle with her to the kitchen. She held the tiny girl against her shoulder while she rechecked the bottle temperature, then dribbled a little of the formula from the nipple to get the baby to take it. The little girl sucked and pulled the bottle empty, then wriggled and fussed. Ana burped her. Instead of putting her back into the basket, she laid the child over her left shoulder, and kept doing quiet work in the kitchen, one handed, until the baby went to sleep. Ana took her to the basket and saw that the swaddling had loosened, so she laid the little girl on the side table to unwrap and rewrap her.

The umbilical stump was still attached. This baby was only a day or two old. She touched a finger to the perfectly formed, tiny hands. So much like Nina's had been. The fine downy hair was the color of milk chocolate. Ana leaned close to breathe in her sweet milk baby scent.

Had the mother of this baby died in childbirth, or was she a young, unwed mother, like so many who left their newborns at the convent, desperate to hide them from disapproving families? Ana had her Aunt Pena to take her in with Nina, or she may have faced the same decision.

The baby girl opened her eyes and arched her back as tiny fingers curled and uncurled on the edges of the pink wrap. Such a sad thing, Ana thought, that this child's mother, for whatever reasons, couldn't keep this baby girl, couldn't change her mind and take her back. The thought of the awful woman in the dining room taking care of an infant was beyond any comprehension. The bell on the kitchen wall rang through Ana's thoughts. She set the baby in the basket and moved it against the wall. She took bowls of sherbet in on a tray.

"Ana, I just can't cut into my pretty cake, will you do it for me?" Lorene asked. Ana picked up the knife and rotated the cake. She made sure that Lorene and Jane each got a piece of cake from the side she'd spit on.

Ana hurried back to the kitchen after she served cake and lime sherbet and checked on the baby peacefully sleeping in the basket. Maybe the awful black-haired woman would forget she was adopting her, and would leave her behind. Ana had a moment, imagining the possibility: she could give the baby girl to Suela, tell her, *Here, Suela. There was a mistake at the hospital. Your baby girl is here, Suela, here she is. We found her, she was just lost for a day, but she is fine.*

Jane's whining voice jerked Ana's attention back to the dining room. "I wonder how our little Gracie is doing? She's not crying anymore."

"Silence is golden."

Jane said in a loud whisper, "If she's sleeping I don't want to wake her."

"Ana, is the baby sleeping?" Lorene called out. Ana opened the door a crack to respond, in a whisper.

"Yes, she is sleeping."

Lorene tented her perfectly manicured white hands. "Good, you can bring her back in to her parents now." She smiled across the table at Brad. "My Ana has more talents than cooking. Maybe you need to hire some help for Jane. I can ask around to see if there is another girl like Ana who needs a job. There are plenty like her in Mexico."

Ana took the basket by both handles and leaned in close to the baby girl who opened her eyes again and turned her head to yawn. In the side light, Ana saw that her eyes were hazel, instead of the nearly black color of the scores of Mexican infants she'd seen. This baby was light skinned, but Mexican. Or part Mexican. She headed to the dining room, silently apologizing to the little being in the basket for these people fate had chosen for her.

"Oh, there she is, did you miss your mommy, Gracie?" Jane squealed.

Ana set the basket on the floor, where Lorene pointed.

"Thank you, Ana," Lorene said, "Stay for a minute, would you?"

Ana waited beside the baby's basket.

"Ana made this nice stew for lunch. Ana, tell Jane the Spanish word for it," Lorene said. Jane looked at Ana expectantly and Ana could see the comb that held Jane's hairpiece in place behind the headband was coming loose.

"Yes, do tell me, maybe I can learn to make it when Gracie gets older."

"It is posole, ma'am," Ana said.

"Thank you, Ana, that will be all for now," Lorene said.

Ana inclined her head and turned for the kitchen door.

"Jane, dear, maybe we do need a Mexican girl like that. She could cook and take care of our daughter," Ana heard Brad say.

Ana wrapped her arms around herself and wished for the Ormonds and their horrible guests to leave the dining room. She thought about the envelopes of money she'd taken to the bank, and she thought about her Nina who would be able to go to school when she was older, and she thought about the Ormond's kitchen, where everything was nice and worked well, and her quarters where she had her own room.

And she thought about the scent of her grey-green-eyed lover that she'd carried on her skin into the dining room, while she served lunch to his unknowing wife.

Ana was called to the dining room two times to change the baby's diaper, three times to quiet her crying, once to prepare another bottle so Jane could practice feeding her, and once to change the tablecloth because Jane was upset when she found a long black hair beside her water glass. The Ormonds and their guests left the dining room at four o'clock. When Ana went in to clean the dining room, she swept up scattered black hairs from Jane's hairpiece that lay like little dead black snakes around her chair.

At five o'clock, Gabriella and Maya came in through the side door. Rudy led and Nina followed, wearing a paper hat Rudy had made at school and given to her.

Gabriella said, "I have the dinner menu here, the Smiths, that couple from lunch, have gone back to Colorado City."

Ana regarded her, weighing her expression.

"Ana, I can only guess how rude they may have been to you, and I'm sorry. But thank you for doing your job," Gabriella said.

"Yes, ma'am," Ana said.

"People like that have no business adopting a baby. I hope it goes all right. Maybe Gracie will be lucky and they'll bring her b . . . " Gabriella hesitated. "Maybe they'll move closer and bring her to the nursery. Some people who live close bring their children to the school to be raised in the ways of the church. It's a private school, you know. The children of employees get a free education, but other people can pay to send their children here."

"Is it a lot of money to go to the school?" Ana said.

"That's what pays for the school," Gabriella said.

Maya had taken Rudy and Nina to her room. She called out, "Ana, would you like me to change Nina into play clothes?"

"Yes, thank you, Maya," Ana called back.

"Where are her pants?" Maya asked

"In the middle drawer, in the closet."

"Here's what they want for dinner," Gabriella said. "Pork chops, whatever vegetables we have fresh, some kind of rolls, and salad. And juice," Gabriella said.

"What kind of juice?" Ana asked.

"Pineapple. Tell Maya I'll be back in twenty minutes to get her," said Gabriella, as she headed out the door.

Ana thought about what she'd fix to offer Suela when she got home.

"I'll have dinner ready when you get back from town," Ana said, when Maya came to the kitchen for water for the children.

"Yes, good, but if it gets late, feed the kids," Maya said, picking at the side of a cup. Maya held back for a few seconds before she spoke again. "Ana, did you take a radio out of Suela's room and put it in your closet?" Maya asked, with a brooding look on her round face.

Ana froze. Maya had seen the radio.

"No, that is mine," Ana stammered. She couldn't tell Maya it was a gift, or who had given it to her. "Suela has a radio?"

"Yes, in her room by her bed. She only has it on late at night," Maya said slowly.

"Show me," Ana said. Maya led her to Suela's room. A pillowcase covered a rectangular shape on the shelf. Maya peeked under the pillowcase.

"Oh, hers is here. I didn't know." She gave Ana a wry smile. "I didn't know."

Ana lifted the pillowcase. Suela's white plastic radio was exactly like hers.

Gabriella and Maya left for town to bring Suela and her new son home. Rudy and Nina played with a toy boat with a ramp and carved wooden animals, shoving the smaller figures through the portholes. Rudy was a nice boy, so kind to little Nina when they played. He held her hand when they walked to school and let her pick the toys she liked when they played.

Ana was grateful for Maya looking after Nina and for the extra groceries Gabriella brought to the kitchen so the three women and two children in the servant's quarters always had nice dinners together. She was paid well and assumed Suela and Maya were paid well too. But the curt treatment by Mrs. Ormond that morning at breakfast, and the things she'd said to her lunch guests that sounded nice, if one hadn't heard the way she said them, jabbed at Ana while she cleaned shelves and rearranged cans in the pantry.

She replayed the conversation in the car when Stan Ormond had asked her if she listened to music, and she'd said she didn't have a radio. Then, he'd shown up in her room with a radio. She thought about the matching radio in Suela's room, and the firstborn, the girl, of Suela's twins. She thought about the complexion and hazel eyes of the newly adopted baby she'd cared for at lunchtime.

Ana regretted what she'd done when Stan Ormond came to her room, but she reasoned his surprising kindness and strong drinks at lunch in town had blurred her judgment. But then, she'd been sober and more than willing to shrug off her uniform and underwear for her boss's advances the second time.

Two hours later the kitchen door opened, and Gabriella was there, saying she'd make sure there was extra milk in the refrigerator, and that she'd check on Suela in the morning. Maya led Suela in.

"We're home, look at this handsome baby boy Suela has brought!"

Suela looked dazed. She held her new son clutched to her chest.

"Let's take him to your room, Suela, so you can lie down," Ana said.

Maya gently told Suela, "Let Ana have him. She will put him right beside you."

Ana put the little boy, still in a hospital blanket, on his back in the crib. Maya helped Suela out of the new robe and into bed.

"I have some posole, and tortillas, and lime sherbet. We can all eat in here with you," Ana said, looking to Maya for confirmation.

"Yes, I'll bring chairs. The little ones can sit on the floor," Maya said. Suela rolled her head toward the crib where her dark-skinned baby slept. Maya reached out to stroke his short mop of black hair. "My Rudy had hair just like this when he was born," she said.

Ana touched Suela's arm. "I'll get dinner. You'll feel better when you eat something."

Suela pushed her food around while Ana and Maya ate and talked about Rudy's grades in school and what flowers Rafael was planting in the garden, and how many eggs the chickens had been laying. Suela set her plate on her bedside table and asked for her baby so she could nurse him. From her dress pocket, Maya produced a pill bottle from the hospital.

"I am to make sure you take two of these after dinner," Maya said. Suela obediently took her medication, then returned to gazing at her new son.

"What did you name him?" Ana asked.

Suela closed her eyes for a moment, one hand protectively on the baby's head. She opened her eyes and looked down at him again.

Maya shook her head at Ana and mouthed "Not now."

Suela cleared her throat. "His father told me I was his favorite. I named him Favorite." Then, Suela wept.

She was different. He told her so. Even if he hadn't said the words, she knew he must love her. Why else would he take the risk of coming to see her so often?

Stan Ormond showed up at the kitchen door a few times a week, when he'd sent Lorene with Gabriella for a hair appointment, or a manicure, or a shopping spree in Tucson. Ana welcomed his attention whenever he made time for her. She reasoned it was too late to turn back anyway. She turned her head away while he was pressed against her, to keep from getting a whisker rash on her face. And she didn't rake his back when she held on to him, no matter how much she wanted to. After all, his wife might see.

Six weeks after the first time they'd coupled on her little bed, she realized that her bleeding hadn't come two weeks earlier, as it should have. Ana put that worry aside and let herself stay caught up in the secrecy.

When the affair had been going on for three months, she knew, buttoning her uniform, that she was pregnant. She kept her apron on when she served meals. She hid her morning sickness by running water in the sink. Ana selected a uniform in a larger size one day, then saw she'd need one two sizes larger to button it with no gaps at the waist. When her belly became visibly swollen, Stan Ormond stopped coming by.

Suela had gone back to work, and Maya was taking Suela's son and Nina to the nursery when she took Rudy to school. Ana had worried what would happen when her thickening midsection became obvious, but if the other women noticed, they said nothing. Her biggest concern was Gabriella, who she was sure would fire her for getting pregnant, even if she didn't know about Ana's affair with their boss. But Gabriella never looked at her questioningly.

One day, after she'd chosen a larger uniform and tied her apron a little higher, she'd served breakfast, then heard shouting in the dining room between the Ormonds. Gabriella came by to serve lunch and dinner, and breakfast the next morning. By ten o'clock the next day, Gabriella came to the kitchen with a woman about Ana's age.

"This is Juanita, Ana. She'll help in the kitchen. I want you to teach her to cook. She'll be setting the table and serving meals. When she's trained, she'll go work at Mr. Ormond's brother's house."

Juanita was pleasant looking, and tidy. She'd come from Juarez where her father was a used car salesman, and her mother worked as a domestic for a family in El Paso. She'd been engaged to a man who went to her church, but he'd broken the engagement and moved to Mexico City. She'd seen an ad for someone looking for a cook's assistant in Arizona and had called the number. Juanita was grateful for the job away from Juarez. Gabriella had hired her on the phone a month earlier than she needed her, and asked her to be ready to come to work soon, when the time was right. When Lorene recognized that Ana was pregnant, the time was right.

So, Ana had a helper and apprentice, and she knew exactly why. Juanita was given a room in the hallway, and she made herself useful in the evenings, watching the children.

Gabriella had a telephone installed in the hallway and in the kitchen, and left her phone number displayed by both, for emergencies only, she reminded them sternly. That day was the first time she'd openly looked at Ana's belly.

Ana didn't hold it against Juanita that she'd been hired to replace her in the dining room, but she made sure Juanita wasn't going to take over her job.

"Is there anything more I can do to help you today, Miss Ana?" Juanita asked anxiously, on her third day of work.

"Yes," said Ana, "the toilet in the kitchen bathroom has a stain in it. I wish I knew how to scrub it out."

"Where are the cleaning supplies?" Juanita said, with untainted enthusiasm.

29

TERESA 1971

A movie

"I just heard Favo sold a rooster to a man in Sonoita, and I have a feeling it might be yours." I watched Paco look up from his plate of waffles and eggs to David Sanchez' face and I wondered if he'd heard, because he didn't say anything. Maria stopped pouring coffee in David's cup and set the pot on the table.

"So, you can get him back?" I asked.

"I don't know, Teresa, a lot of roosters change hands at those places. Paco's may not even be there anymore," David said.

"Okay, we are not going to talk about cockfighting on Sunday morning at breakfast," Maria said. She poured the last of the coffee in her cup.

"How far is Sonoita?" Paco asked.

"Don't get any ideas, Paco. It's not like it is down in Sonora. That's not the best bunch of guys that fight birds in Sonoita," David said.

After breakfast, Paco asked me, "Do we have to go to church here?" and I told him what I knew: that the Ormonds went to a different kind of church than we did, on Saturday, and that only people who were approved by that church could go, and if your parents weren't in the church, you couldn't go, and they had very strange ideas, like thinking that Jesus had told men to have children with lots of women, and he left special stones under a tree and that's how one man could read the tablets Jesus hid in the man's yard. And coffee is against God's will. Some of the kids at school had told me all that, anyway. And I told Paco that some of the white kids had told me I wouldn't be able to go to their church because I had the mark of Cain. Paco asked what that was, and I told him what the kids had told me: "If you're not white, you have the mark of Cain."

"Who wants to go to a church like that?" he asked.

I said nobody did.

"David wants to take us to a movie," Maria said when she came out of the kitchen. Would you like that?" Well, we were happy about that, because there was only one movie place in Centro and most of the time, except when they had Shirley Temple or the Three Stooges, they were movies that only drunk men wanted to watch.

"The matinee is two o'clock, so we'll leave at noon. I'll pack a lunch and we can eat at the park near the theater," Maria said.

We were so excited to get to go to a real movie that we didn't care what it was about. We went out to throw clods into the pond for a while and saw the redheaded kid and his little brother there. The redheaded kid grabbed his brother by the arm, and they left in a hurry. I guess he didn't want another dirt clod in his mouth.

We were walking back to Maria's house, and Paco said, "I have to go back to Centro next week. I hope Officer Sanchez can find my rooster, Caesar, before I go. If he finds him after I leave, would you know what he looks like?"

I said I would, and that I'd keep him for him until I could bring him back, or until he could come get him.

"I wish I could just stay," Paco said.

"I wish you could too," I said.

It was eleven thirty when we got back to the house, so Paco went to wash his hands and face and comb his hair. I changed into one of the pretty dresses in the closet, and Luna tried on three before she decided which one she'd wear. We let Salma pick out her own clothes. She wanted to wear green pants and a pink dress over them, and we let her. Luna and I went to the kitchen to help make sandwiches for lunch, and Paco helped David put ice water in a jug. Maria dug around in a cabinet and brought out a stack of plastic drinking cups. David carried the cardboard box we'd packed with sandwiches, pickles, and potato chips to the car.

David drove Maria's car, and Salma sat in front between them. Paco sat in the middle in the back seat. We hadn't been anywhere but the grocery store in town, so the way to the park and the theater was new. Luna watched her window, deep in her thoughts. Paco and I hung halfway out the window on my side like little kids.

"Here's the park," David said. "Paco, you help me with the lunch, and you girls pick where to sit." Maria grinned at David. We wandered from tree to tree, looking for a place where the shade had kept the grass from drying. David and Paco walked behind us until Maria stopped walking and pointed to the ground at her feet.

"I'm still stuffed from breakfast," David said, while he helped get the food out. "If I keep eating at your house, I'm going to get fat," he said.

"Nobody makes you eat," Maria told him, but she said it in a nice way. I thought they seemed like a nice couple. I wondered why they didn't get married. Maybe I'd ask Maria about that sometime. But today we were going to a movie.

After lunch, we packed up the box and put it back in the car while David went to get tickets. We met him in front of the theater, just as the lady in the ticket window slid two red and three blue tickets out toward him. Maria looked at the blue tickets and started to say something, but the lady said, "Kids five and under are free."

David pulled the tickets apart so we could each hold ours. I tore off a piece of my ticket so Salma had a ticket to hold too. We gave them to the man inside the theater door. "Movie to your right, restrooms to your left," he said six times as the six of us went by and handed him our tickets. He tore them in half and gave us half back, even Salma.

Luna sat next to David, with Salma beside her, and Maria sat on David's other side, then I sat next to Maria, and Paco sat by me.

The movie was about two bank robbers who were good friends, and they would always escape. One robber had a pretty girlfriend, and the other one took her for a bicycle ride but the first robber found out and got mad. Then they all got on a train and then a boat and went to South America, and the two robbers got shot there. Well, they didn't show them getting shot, but it looked like that was the end of them. In the dark theater, Paco held my hand. I wished there had been another movie after the one about the robbers.

On the way home, David asked Maria if she'd talked to Paco's father. She told him she had, and that she'd probably drive to Nogales and meet Paco's father there. All the air in the back of the car just went flat. Even Luna seemed forlorn that Paco was going to have to leave. Maria told David she'd call again on Monday, to decide the best day.

We watched television in the late afternoon, and David said he had paperwork to do. "If I don't see you before you leave, buddy," he said to Paco, "you be good. And if I find your rooster, I'll get him back to you." He shook Paco's hand.

Paco said, "Thank you," then turned his face away so no one would see that he was crying.

After David left, Paco motioned for me to go with him down the hall to the room where he'd been staying.

"Do you know how far Sonoita is?"

I said I didn't, but we could look at a map.

"Do you have one?" he asked.

"No, but Maria does, in her car." We told Maria we were going outside to walk around, and made sure Maria was watching television and not looking out the window at where her car was parked.

"Here it is," I said, when I found the folded map in the glove box. In the afternoon shade of the house, Paco unfolded the map. We found Tubac, and Patagonia, and then Sonoita.

"It's not that far to Sonoita," Paco said.

I looked at the map again. "It's not that far if you can just fly over the mountains. It would take a long time to walk there," I said.

"I could hitchhike. I could get there," he said.

"Why?"

"Because if my rooster is there, I know I can find him.

"How would you find him? You don't even know for sure it was him that Favo sold, and you don't know who bought him either," I said.

"Have you got some paper?" Paco asked, "I want to copy this map."

Paco was my best friend, and even if what it sounded like he was thinking was not the best idea he'd ever had, I wanted him to be happy, so I went and got him a pencil and paper from my school binder. He traced the roads as best he could, and lifted the paper to see if he'd put the roads and mountains in the right places. I convinced myself he just wanted to see where Sonoita was, and imagine David going there to find his rooster. That was why he wanted a map.

We still had plenty of light when we snuck to Maria's car to put the map back. We saw Rafael walk across the gravel road, toward the pond with a long bamboo fishing pole. I think it was the first time I'd seen him without his wheelbarrow.

"Let's go see if he can catch a fish," I said.

Paco and I headed to the pond in the last yellow light.

"Hey, Teresa," Maria said.

I sat up in bed.

"Can you manage breakfast for you and Salma and Paco? I need to go over to the main house to get your sister going."

"Yes, ma'am," I said.

"I've created a polite monster," she said, then called toward the bathroom, "Fifteen minutes, Luna, and I'm leaving. White blouse, grey skirt, hair in a—"

Luna came out in her pajamas, hair already pulled back, a mouthful of bobby pins, and was winding and pinning her hair up on her way to the closet.

"Good girl. I'll be in the dining room. Be good, Teresa," Maria said, and gave me a little wink. "Don't you and Paco run off and get married or anything while I'm gone."

I rolled my eyes.

Luna dressed in her white blouse and grey skirt faster than she'd ever dressed for school. She was wearing a training bra Angela had brought, with an undershirt over it. The bra straps and undershirt showed under the white blouse. I wished I had a training bra to wear too, but Luna unkindly pointed out that it only worked if I had something to put in it.

"Here, help me get this," she said, backing up to my bed, so I could do the zipper and button on the back of her skirt.

"This is too small for you," I said while I pulled the fabric.

"I know, but it's all I have that's grey. Here I go." She was out the door.

I heard her canvas shoes slapping down the hall. The back door opened and closed, and I knew she and Maria were walking across the grass to the main house.

I waited until seven to get up, get dressed, and go to the kitchen. I decided I should make coffee, even if I didn't really drink coffee. But that day it seemed grown up to have coffee. I dumped out the grounds in the basket and found the red Folgers can. There was a tin scoop in the can. Was it one scoop, or was it more than that to make coffee? The basket had been half full when I dumped out the grounds, so I filled it half full, and put water in the pot and put it on the stove. Would Paco like bacon or sausage? I put both in the frying pan. I mixed eggs and milk to scramble when Paco and Salma were ready for breakfast.

The bacon and sausage were browning when the coffee started bubbling into the glass knob on top of the pot. I guessed that meant it was done, so I turned the burner off. Surely the smell of breakfast would bring everybody to the table. I went to our room, and put my head in.

"Salma, get up, breakfast is ready. You want sausage, don't you?"

She stretched her arms above her head.

"Come on, get up," I said.

She lurched up and said she needed to go potty first.

"Okay, you do that, and then come to breakfast." I hurried back down the hall to the kitchen and put a few sheets of newspaper down to put the bacon and sausage on. When Salma and Paco got there, I'd scramble the eggs.

"Hey, breakfast is ready!" I yelled down the hall. I set out two coffee cups from the shelf and poured a glass of milk for Salma.

"Come on, I'm putting the eggs on," I called again. Salma appeared at the end of the table and climbed into her chair.

"Paco! Salma's going to eat all the sausage!"

"Sausage!" Salma said. The grease splattered a little when I dumped the eggs in, and smoked up the kitchen, so I opened the door through the laundry room to the one outside. There were enough eggs and bacon and sausage for six people on the platter I carried into the dining room. Salma rocked in her chair with her fork ready, but no Paco.

"Okay, here, you want eggs? Bacon too? Just sausage? Use your napkin, not your arm, Salma," I said.

I didn't want to embarrass Paco, but I decided to knock on his door. He didn't answer. After I knocked four times, I turned the knob and peeked in.

His bed was made, and the clothes Maria had loaned him were folded on his pillow. I ran back down the hall, and looked in the dining room, where Salma sat alone, happily eating her scrambled eggs. At the bathroom door in the hallway, there was no sound. I opened the door just a crack.

"Paco?"

He didn't answer because he wasn't there. He wasn't anywhere in the house.

"Keep eating, I'll be right back," I told Salma. I went out the back door, around to the front of the house to look. He might have gone to the main house with Maria, that might be where he went. That was what I told myself.

I went back in the house, sat down with Salma and ate the breakfast I'd fixed. The coffee was terrible, so it was good Paco didn't show up for that part. When Salma was finished waving a piece of bacon around like a sword, I wiped her hands with a kitchen towel, put the dishes in the dishwasher, and scraped the rest of the eggs and sausage and bacon into a glass bowl to put in the refrigerator. Surely Paco would be back before long and I'd reheat everything but the coffee. That, I dumped down the sink.

I went back to Paco's room and knocked again. I don't know why I did that, because he wasn't in there before, and he hadn't come back in. But I knocked one more time, opened the door, and walked over to the bed. The piece of binder paper stuck out from under the clothes on the pillow.

Dear Teresa,

Thank you for being my best friend. Tell Maria thank you for me too. And David, and even Luna, ha ha ha. I am going to find my rooster. I don't want to go home to my father until I have him. I hope I can get a ride to Sonoita, but I took some apples and bread just in case it takes longer, so tell Maria I'm sorry. I will see you again soon I hope.

Love, your friend Paco.

Tears happen, even if you don't think they will, when something hurts. And sometimes you can't believe what's hurting your heart is really true, so you don't cry until you know it for sure. But those tears make a letter from your best friend on a piece of notebook paper blotchy and hard to read, either way.

"What is it, Teresa?" Maria asked when she pulled up to the house and saw me crying.

I showed her the note.

"Shit," she said, "Come with me."

She called David's dispatcher and asked her to have David call back. "Teresa, did Paco call his parents this morning? Did you hear him on the phone?"

I told her I hadn't heard a phone call.

"He can't get far on foot. You stay here. I'll drive out to the road. Maybe I'll find him. Or maybe someone's seen him."

I had no idea what time of the night or morning Paco had left. He could have been far away for all I knew.

She got back in her car and was gone.

I cleared breakfast dishes. Salma said she wanted to watch television and look at one of her books, so I let her, while I sat at the dining room table and watched the hands of the clock on the wall.

Maria was back in a half hour and asked if the phone had rung.

She made another phone call to the dispatcher, who hadn't reached David. She seemed more angry than sad.

I guess I understood that. She was having to go look and worry and make phone calls because of my friend. She'd left Luna at the main house in the kitchen and needed to call Angela to go over and help get lunch fixed and served.

"Teresa, take Salma over to the little house closest to the school. Miss Suela lives there. Leave Salma with her, and you go and look in all the places you and Paco went. Maybe he's still here."

I jumped up, put Salma's shoes on her and hurried her out the door. When we got close to the school, she started pulling back and whining.

"No," I said, "you come on, we are not going to school."

Miss Suela's house was a square of adobe with deep-set windows, a scraggly wire fence that guarded four rows of withering vegetable plants in front, and a chicken coop with three yellow chickens on one side. On the other side was a shade for her old faded car. She was in the yard, pulling at a hose that didn't quite reach her garden. She hadn't combed her hair very well, and had put an elastic band around it to hold it back. Her loose hair waving around her head made her look like a wild woman, tugging at the green hose that was already stretched tight.

"Teresa!" she said when she saw us, "What are you doing here? Do you miss school already?" She was always cheerful and teasing. She was probably my grandmother's age, but Miss Suela seemed older.

"Maria told me to leave Salma here with you for a while, if that's all right," I told her.

"Of course, it's all right. Come on, Salma. What has you so out of breath?" she asked.

"Well, did you see me walking around with a boy?" She shook her head that she hadn't. "He's about as tall as me, black hair. He's my best friend from Centro, and he's missing."

"Missing!" she said. "What is his name?"

"Paco Dominguez," I said. "He's thirteen years old."

"I'll watch for him and I'll let Miss Connie know. She's going to town in a little while. What is he wearing?"

I had to think for a moment about the dirty clothes Paco was wearing when David Sanchez brought him to Maria's house. "A red and black striped T-shirt, and blue jeans, I think. Thank you. I have to go."

Salma had been standing happily with Miss Suela until I said I was going. Then she started fussing, wanting to go with me.

"Salma, you stay here with Miss Suela until I come back."

The windows at the school office reflected me walking fast, looking around the school building when I went by. I walked past Rafael's tool shed to the pond. No sign of Paco. The ranch had a water tower to the north side of the main house. I headed over to climb the ladder, so I could look across the acacia tops and rock piles. I had to jump to the first rung. Then it was an easy climb, except the sun had already made the metal bars hot. With my arms hooked around the top rung, I could turn and look in all directions but the one hidden behind the water tower. A narrow platform went all the way around the tower. I slid one foot at a time and got around the tower to look from the other side.

I was coming back down the ladder and saw Rafael coming my way, looking up. His age and stooped back were not slowing him down at all, and he was at the bottom of the ladder when I got there. "What are you doing, chica?" he said.

"My friend, Paco, ran away last night, or maybe this morning. He said he wants to find his rooster before Maria takes him to Nogales, to his father," I said.

Rafael put his hand on the side of the ladder. "I saw your friend this morning. He was on the gravel road. He was carrying a sack, maybe a pillow case."

"What time?" I asked.

"The sun was just up. I was coming out to get eggs when I saw him. He was getting in a car. Señor Ormond's car."

"Oh, good! Thank you, Rafael," I said. Maybe Señor Ormond had taken him to the main house and he was there.

I ran all the way back to Maria's house, but she wasn't there. By the time I got to the kitchen door at the Ormond's house, I was out of breath again. Maria came out of the kitchen and said, "What's up?"

"Rafael saw Paco!" I shouted. "He saw him get into Mr. Ormond's car, in the driveway. Early this morning!"

"Wait for me here," Maria said. She got in her car and drove away. She'd left the kitchen door open, and Luna had come over to listen to us.

"Come in and help me with these pots and pans," Luna said.

We watched Maria's car on the ranch road, driving toward the warehouse, and I guessed she'd gone to find Mr. Ormond. We could see her in the distance when she got out of her car and ran to the building. She'd only been inside for a few seconds and came back out, and there was a tall man in tan trousers, a white shirt, and a neck tie walking with her to her car. He put both hands on her shoulders, and she put her head back like she was looking at the sky, or maybe she was praying, or maybe she was relieved. She drove back to the main house.

"Mr. Ormond picked Paco up in the driveway about dawn. He was driving into town for a breakfast meeting and wondered why a boy he hadn't seen before was on the ranch. Paco didn't tell him he'd been staying at my house, just that he wanted to get to Sonoita," she said.

"Did he take him to Sonoita?" Luna asked.

"He took him to Tubac, and one of the men at the meeting was from Sonoita. He sent Paco with that man."

"How will we find him?" I said. Maria exhaled, I think for the first time since I'd told her Paco was missing.

"Mr. Ormond will call his friend and see where he dropped Paco off. We'll find him. I'll call the dispatcher, and David will find him if he's anywhere close. I don't want another agent picking him up."

Luna and I had finished the breakfast cleanup, so we went back to Maria's house with her. She called David's dispatcher, then sent me back to Miss Suela's to get Salma.

Rafael was in front of Suela's house when I walked up, shoveling chicken droppings onto her garden.

"Did you find your friend?" he asked.

"Not yet, but thank you for telling me you saw him." I got my little sister to let go of the doll Suela had given her to keep her happy and took her back to Maria's house.

It was two days before we saw Paco. David picked him up at the Santa Cruz County Sheriff's office, where he'd alerted the deputies that he was looking for a thirteen-year-old kid who might show up at one of the cockfights looking for a rooster. Paco had cuts and bruises on his face and arms. He didn't have his rooster.

Maria called Paco's father as soon as he and David walked in at her house. She told us she didn't want to be responsible for any more problems.

Paco and I went outside. He was so sad, I just wanted to hug him. He told me he'd come up on a cockfight the first night and told some men there that a guy named Favo had stolen his rooster and had maybe sold him in Sonoita. One of the men he was talking to led him to where the cars were parked, and two men took turns punching and kicking him. One of them was Favo.

We walked over to the pond and sat under the one tree that shaded the narrowest part of the water. Frogs scooted off the mud bank and back to safety. We watched one frog get eaten by the big catfish. Rafael must have seen us going there because, in a few minutes, he was there with his wheelbarrow and tools, checking on the sand he'd added, raking it a little more. I waved to him and he walked over to us.

"You found him. Welcome back, my young friend," he said.

"Yes, we found him," I answered.

Rafael eyed Paco's beat up face and said, "Who did this?" Paco pressed his bruised lip with two fingers to feel the cut there. It started bleeding.

"I was trying to find my rooster. Favo found me instead."

Rafael leaned closer to look at the damage to Paco's face. "Favo is the devil, young man. Someday, someone will kill him. I hope you will never have to see him again."

I could see something had broken in my friend, Paco. Maybe it was that he'd lost the rooster. Maybe it was that he'd been beaten up. Maybe he was just tired of trying to make something good happen, and it all goes bad, and it feels like nothing you do will ever be right.

AN ACT OF KINDNESS

The convent in Centro has a business to run.
It's an orphanage for children who have been
left alone in the world by fate,
and it provides an act of kindness that can be seen
and glorified in the community.
Therefore, donations are more plentiful.
Of course, there are actual orphans at the convent,
because it would only be right
that orphans would be a feature at an orphanage.
But the real business is
the exchange of money for rehoming
unwanted babies.

30

ANA 1949

Contractions

Ana went into labor one morning while she was whisking eggs. When her water broke, she kicked a towel under her feet, put the French toast in a skillet, and waited for Juanita to come back from setting the table.

"I will be in my room. You serve breakfast, then call Gabriella. Tell her to let the midwife know."

"Ana! I'm going to call her now!" Juanita exclaimed.

"No, there is time, just . . . " she waited out a short contraction, "just call her after the Ormonds leave." Ana went to her room and lay down.

Juanita served breakfast, then rushed back to check on her.

"Not yet," Ana told her.

She sent Juanita back to the kitchen to wait for the Ormonds to finish eating, then clear and wash dishes. By the time Juanita came back, the contractions were getting closer, and Juanita called Gabriella.

Gabriella pulled her car up to the kitchen door, and she and Juanita guided Ana into the back seat. Gabriella had the car in gear and rolling before she had her door closed. The midwife's house was a half mile away, and Gabriella drove across the lawn as though she were on the highway. She'd seen labor enough to know Ana was going to have this baby any moment. The old midwife helped Gabriella get Ana inside, and they unbuttoned and stripped off her fluid-streaked uniform.

Ana asked for help getting onto the cot where she squatted, facing and holding on to the iron bedpost. Twenty minutes later, the midwife held a beautiful caramel-haired baby girl for Ana to see. Gabriella told them she'd go back to the house to tell Juanita, and have her prepare lunch. The midwife brought Ana a glass of cinnamon-laced milk.

"Drink, and you will have good milk."

Ana watched the tiny lips making movements and pressed her baby to a breast. Without hesitation, the mouth found its place and Ana fell in love, the same way she'd fallen in love with Nina.

"She is so pretty!" the old midwife said. "What will you call her?"

Ana shifted on the bed and looked up at the nearly blind old woman standing at her side. She thought about the plaster face of the Blessed Virgin at the Convent chapel, and how she had been angry and defiant towards the Virgin, and how disappointed Jesus had been. Ana wanted to make amends with the holiest of mothers.

"I think I will name her . . . " she touched the tiny nose gingerly, "Maria."

Ana said she'd be ready to go home with her new daughter any time, but Gabriella insisted she stay the night at the midwife's house. Gabriella went to give Suela and Maya the news and to notify Stan Ormond that there was a pretty new baby girl on the ranch.

The old midwife took Ana some tea after she'd expelled the after-birth, and Ana eased herself into the rocking chair beside the dingy window to feed her daughter while Esme took the placenta out to bury in her garden. She had just planted corn and tomatoes and it would help them grow if the timing was right.

Esme prepared soup for later and left Ana alone to rest. Esme knew she didn't need to worry about Ana, since she was young and strong and only had one baby to feed.

Rosemary, who'd been there when Suela's babies were born, came to the door midafternoon.

"I hear there's a new baby girl!" she said in a shrill, grating voice.

The old midwife saw through clouded eyes that there was someone else in the car who hadn't come to the door. She squinted against the windshield glare and was able to make out Señora Ormond. Lorene Ormond hadn't been to the midwife's house to look at a baby for more than a year.

"I want to see the baby," Rosemary said, trying to push her way around Esme, "if you'll get out of my way."

Esme stepped aside and Rosemary walked into the birthing room.

Ana saw her coming, shifted her little Maria to her other arm, away from Rosemary, and the baby's mouth popped off her nipple with a soft sucking noise.

"Oh, she is a pretty one," Rosemary said. She went back out to the car, and leaned against the car door, talking through the open window to Señora Ormond, who still sat in the passenger seat. Rosemary straightened up, looked back at the house, and returned to the door.

"Si?" the midwife asked.

"Please bring the baby out, so Mrs. Ormond can see her."

Ana heard the conversation at the door. She rose, in the nightdress the midwife had loaned her, and walked barefooted to the front door, holding her baby.

"I'll take her out," Ana said, still feeling the sting of Mrs. Ormond's insistence that she didn't see a pregnant woman serving meals to her and her husband in her dining room. Ana walked past Esme and the open-mouthed Rosemary to the passenger side of the car. She held her baby up for a moment.

"This is Maria."

Lorene Ormond placed a hand at her smooth white throat and tried to compose herself. "Thank you, Ana, Mary is a lovely name," she said.

Ana took a step back and held her baby closer to her chest.

"Maria," Ana said, and turned to go back into the house.

"Esme, would you mind leaving Ana and me alone for a while?" Gabriella said. Esme shook the matted pillow into a clean case before she responded by shuffling out and closing the door behind her.

"Am I being scolded for telling Señora Ormond what my daughter's name is?"

"No, Ana." Gabriella glanced at the white curtain covering the half-opened window when it moved. "Would you like this window open or closed?"

"Open. I took her outside to the car myself. That woman wanted to take her, and I said no."

"Yes, believe me, I heard. I talked to them both. You are not in trouble." Gabriella's tone softened as she scooted the chair closer to the bed. "I need to tell you some things. And I want you to know, Ana, that I work for the Ormonds, but you and the other girls . . . " her voice dropped off and her eyes flicked to baby Maria when she made a tiny grunt. Gabriella's face looked older to Ana, just since yesterday. ". . . it's like you are my own family. And you are a part of the Ormond ranch. The Ormonds cannot have children. Maybe the other girls told you."

"No. They didn't tell me. Señor Ormond told me." Ana shifted under the sheet, to work the fresh nightgown over her thighs.

"I see. Well, I want you to know I'm not that much different from you or Maya or Suela, Ana. I have a job to do, just like you do."

"Except you can come and go any time," Ana said.

"Yes, I can. But I have worked for the Ormond family for thirty years. I worked for Señor Ormond's father. I'm not a very good cook, and can't sew, but I know how to keep books and keep the place running smoothly. Ana, I know what goes on in those back rooms when I'm not around."

"Are you going to fire me?"

"No, Ana, what has happened is something that happens. To Maya, to Suela, to other girls before them, and now to you."

"Why was I brought here, to this place, Gabriella?" Ana's eye met Gabriella's for an instant before she looked down to close the front of her nightgown.

"To cook. They really did need a cook. But also, because . . . " Gabriella cleared her throat softly. "Ana. This is hard for me to say. I like you, and the other girls. I'm from Mexico too. Juarez, Coahuila. My mother and father and my brother and I crossed the Rio Grande when I was Nina's age. They worked at a factory in El Paso. My parents wanted me to go to college. They worked at that factory, and lived with two other families in a two-room house, so they could save money for me to go to school. I know what it's like to not have anything of my own."

"You have a house and a car," Ana said.

"I do now. And I save my money, but the house and car belong to the Ormonds. I'd be an old woman doing books for a hotel or something if my parents had not come to work for the Ormond family when I was still in school. That's how I got hired just after college to work here. I'd studied hotel management, and I knew how to keep books. This job paid more than a hotel job."

Ana glanced at Gabriella's hands when she smoothed the bedsheet. She had never seen Gabriella ill at ease before.

"But I'm glad I was not pretty when I was young, I really am. What Señor's father did, you know, with the girls who worked here, it only happened with pretty girls, like you." Gabriella spoke rapidly, as though she wanted to get something out. "And his son does the same. Your and Maya's and Suela's babies are not the first babies. Do you understand, Ana? Those kind of men think it's their right to have the pretty girls who work for them. I guess they make girls think they love them. Did Stan Ormond do that to you?" Gabriella sat back a little but kept her knees touching the side of the mattress.

"Gabriella, why are you telling me this?" Ana lowered her eyes to the top of her new daughter's head.

"Because this is me, talking to you. Because I care what happens to you and your Nina, and this baby, and to Maya, and Suela."

"So, what do you want to tell me?" Ana said.

"Before all of you were here, he tried to have babies with those two women who were here when you helped Suela. They are sisters. Their father gave the Ormond family a loan to expand the business, if he would take those two as wives."

"Maya told me. But he has a wife. Here . . . can you . . . " she handed sleeping little Maria to Gabriella and indicated the cradle beside the cot. Gabriella laid the baby down gently, then took a deep breath.

"These people are not like us, Ana. Their church is not like the church you and I know. Men can have more than one wife. Not by law, but they do it anyway, and the women they marry don't know better. I think some of the women are not very smart. Maybe they're taught to be that way. But they look the other way when their husbands go to be with the other wives."

"So, he has babies with those two witches?" Ana said. Gabriella stifled a smile.

"They never got pregnant, and that's why he started hiring girls from Mexico. Always pretty girls. Pretty babies are kept."

"Where are all the babies, then?"

"Some live on the ranch with their mothers. Like Rudy. Some are adopted by other families from the Ormond's church, and from other churches like theirs."

"Gabriella, whose baby was in the dining room?" Ana said slowly and deliberately. "Was that Suela's baby girl? And Señor is the father?"

"Yes. She was a pretty baby, but not pretty enough for the Ormonds to keep."

"What do you mean? For them to keep?"

"I mean, Ana, that if Señora thinks they are pretty, she wants them. She wants to hold them, dress them up, show them off. There have been five she has wanted to keep since the Ormonds got married nine years ago."

"Then where are they? Because I have not seen any of them with them in the dining room." Ana's fists opened and closed, grasping at the sheet that covered her from the hips down.

"They've all been given back to their mothers to raise."

"Why? If they want children, why?

"Ana, Señor does not want children in the house. He only wants to—"

"To have his pants down in our rooms," Ana said. "And Señora only wants dolls to play with until she is tired of playing with them. Is that what you are telling me?"

"Yes. That's what I'm telling you. Ana, I wish this was not part of my job. But I want to go buy a house someday in California where my brother and his wife live. So, I do my job. But that doesn't mean I like my job all the time." Gabriella reached up to brush Ana's hair from her forehead. Ana was too tired to object. "Ana, this is the part I have to do, and I don't want to. But please, just let me say what I have to say."

"Say it, then." Ana leaned back against the pillows and waited.

"I have a proposal for you," Gabriella said. "Just let me say it before you say anything else."

"What is it?" Ana asked. The baby stirred and huffed, and Gabriella lifted her to put her back in Ana's arms.

"There's a little house near the main house that is available, and we, the Ormonds and I, would like to offer it to you. You and Nina and the baby can live there. Nina will be starting kindergarten in the fall and she can still walk to and from school with Maya. In fact, you'll be free to go get her at school in the afternoons. You'll have your job cooking. Nothing will change about that, but you'll have a key to the kitchen so you don't have to wait for me to get in and out."

Ana blinked a few times, taking the information in while she nursed her daughter.

"Why?" she asked, "Why would you give me a house and not Suela or Maya?"

Gabriella leaned forward and touched Ana's hand that lay over baby Maria's downy caramel-haired head. "They have an offer for you, and here is where I want you to hear what I'm telling you. Your baby is beautiful, and Señora Ormond wants to adopt your baby."

"No," said Ana.

"I understand, but just listen, all right?" Gabriella said.

Ana looked straight ahead but waved her hand at Gabriella to continue.

"Señor Ormond is willing to pay you extra if you let him and Mrs. Ormond adopt your Maria. She'll want to show her off to her friends and she'll want her at the table for meals sometimes, but the baby will be cared for by a nanny, and that nanny will be you. You'll still be cooking, and while she's a baby, if she's quiet, she can be in the kitchen with you. Maybe in the back room, but you can check on her any time."

"No," said Ana.

"Ana, in addition to the fifty dollars a week you're paid for cooking, plus room and board and your own house, you'll be paid fifty dollars a week more to be a caregiver for your own daughter. That will go up twenty-five dollars a week more when she starts first grade. But you'll raise her, and you'll just bring her in when Mrs. Ormond wants—"

"But she is mine—" Ana began.

"And she still will be. She will just be adopted by the Ormonds, and her name will be Ormond. They will send her to a good college. She'll mostly be with you, and what changes for you is making more money, and having your own house and more freedom. They just want Mrs. Ormond to feel like she has a baby."

"And if I don't want to cook for them anymore?" Ana asked.

"If you'd rather work at the warehouse, or at the school, we'll find you another job. But this offer is for you to be in the house during the day so you'd be able to take your daughter into the dining room for meals if Señora Ormond wants her there, and take her back to the kitchen when she's through. If you're working somewhere else, you won't be able to have her with you."

"And I get my own house?"

Gabriella nodded emphatically. "Yes, your own house, and a key to the kitchen."

"And I will have my baby with me and Nina, and she is still mine?" Ana asked.

"Well, in a way. Yours to raise, she'll just have a different last name."

"And I will get one hundred dollars a week?" Ana said, turning her head to study Gabriella's face.

"Yes," Gabriella said.

Ana kissed her baby on the head and shifted her to her other breast. "I'd also like to learn to drive and have a car to go to town, to the bank, and other things," she said.

"I think in your case, I can arrange that for you if the rest of this is agreeable."

Ana thought for a second. "Tell me, Gabriella, why does Suela still live in the room behind the kitchen? You tell me the truth."

Gabriella leaned closer and lowered her voice. "Suela's girl was not pretty enough. And the little boy was dark. The Ormonds don't want to adopt a dark baby."

"You let them tell Suela the little girl died! They gave Suela medicine to keep her from knowing they stole her baby. How could you do that to her?"

Gabriella stayed close to Ana and said, "The people who adopted that little girl can send her to college. They can give her things Suela can't. The father—"

"I know the father is the same father as my Maria. I knew when I saw the radio in Suela's room. I knew when I saw that baby's eyes in the kitchen. Suela thinks she has gone crazy." Ana talked through clenched teeth. "Did you know that? She thinks she must have dreamed she had two babies."

"Ana, I know you are smart and are not going to be fooled by promises and half-truths. Your baby is pretty. I know that seems like an unfair reason for someone to want a baby or not, but it's the truth. She'll get to go to college. She'll still have you for a mother, even if another woman is her mother on paper."

Ana pressed her head back against the pillows. "What about the car?" she said.

"I'll make that happen for you because you're a good cook and they want you to stay, and so do I."

"But I have to sign a paper that says she is not mine?"

"Yes, that's the way it will have to be," Gabriella said.

"What if I have another baby? Then what?" Ana asked.

"It depends on who the father is, Ana."

"And do I have to have another baby if I don't want to?"

Gabriella sighed, because she'd answered this question before. "No, you don't. It's your choice."

Ana swung her legs over the side of the cot, and stood, cradling her new daughter. "I will tell you tomorrow morning what my answer is. If I decide not to stay, I'll take my baby and Nina, and go back to Mexico."

"You'd be welcome to do that, and I'd take you back to the convent or where ever you wanted to go. But only you and Nina. The father of the baby would keep you from taking her to Mexico," Gabriella said.

Ana stood beside the crib, looking down at the baby she held. She thought about the ranch and the school and the warehouse, and all the people who worked for the Ormonds, and she knew what Gabriella was telling her was true.

"I'll do everything I can for you, Ana. I'll come get you in the morning and you can tell me then if you want to live in the quarters behind the kitchen with your daughters, and nothing changes, or in a house of your own with twice the pay, and an education for this little one."

"And a car to drive," Ana added. She might have been taken aback by the offer, but her head for business was working all the same. "I'll tell you in the morning."

Gabriella went to the warehouse office to inform her boss she'd made the offer and told him about the counteroffer from Ana. He laughed and told Gabriella that a car was not a problem. He'd have one sent from the used car lot he and another brother owned in St. George, Utah.

Then Gabriella went back to the main house to help Juanita get dinner ready. Juanita would be moving from the servant's quarters behind the kitchen to David Ormond's household a few miles away as soon as Ana was back in the kitchen. Maybe if Gabriella got Juanita moved away quickly, she wouldn't have to do this part of her job again for a while.

In the morning Ana signed the papers, allowing her baby daughter by Stan Ormond to be adopted by him and his vapid wife, Lorene.

PROFIT AND LOSS

Three o'clock in the morning.
The hare-lipped prostitute staggers in and lies down on the
bare mattress
in the rented room where she sleeps.
He gets up to collect his cut of her night's profits.
She is already passed out and won't remember anyway.
He helps himself to the coin pouch she wears tied at the waistband
of her filthy skirt.

He sees she has had another poor night out,
with only one or two customers.
Or she has accepted too little money for her various acts
in alleys behind the bars.
At the bottom of the pouch is a cheap gold-colored watch
with a broken wristband.
And a single, cross-shaped earring.
He leaves the watch on the floor beside her, takes all the money.
And puts the earring in his own ear.

Unburdened by a Child

At the convent in Centro, the most attractive young women
who come to the convent doors pregnant and alone are taken in.
They are given shelter, food, help with birthing, and privacy to leave quietly,
unburdened by a child they do not want and cannot support.

Such kindness is not extended to the homely girls,
who would not produce infants
that wealthy patrons looking for babies would want to take home.
Known prostitutes are turned away at the door by the nuns.
Children blinded and crippled by venereal diseases are not adoptable.

SALABLE PRODUCT

The young women who give birth at the convent
are asked to stay long enough to nurse their infants once.
The nuns are instructed to drape a sheet
over the heads of the pretty infants while they nurse,
to keep the girls from looking down and falling in love with them.
There is no profit in providing birthing services unless
there is a salable product at the end.
If a woman produces a damaged child,
she is strongly encouraged, by means of guilt,
to take it with her when she leaves the convent.

CREATED BY HER SINS

At the convent orphanage,
the occasional nun who succumbs to the temptations of the flesh
is provided hushed birthing
and is allowed to provide care for her own child
until an adoption takes place,
so long as she never acknowledges to anyone, including the child,
that she is the mother.
If a nun gives birth to a damaged child,
the mother superior herself makes sure the
nun sees the monster created by her sins,
then takes it away.
The physically inferior babies of wayward nuns are never seen again.

31

TERESA 1971

Rosary beads

"Only in Mexico, Teresa," was what my mother told me when I'd asked her if the rosary beads my grandmother had given me really worked. She had shown me that you slide them through your fingers while you pray. I got them out of the bottom of Mama's pack and said a prayer for my mother and for Paco and told God that if my grandmother was a good woman, that I wanted to pray for her too. But I was thinking that what my mother had said really was true, because here in the United States, things had not worked out. Maybe the rosary beads weren't any good here.

I told Luna I wanted to take Salma and go back to Centro. We could live with our grandmother.

Luna shook her head firmly and said, "If she really did that to Maria, if she really did leave her behind when she went back to Mexico, maybe she's not such a good person to live with." Luna and I lay awake that night and talked. For the first time since we'd been in Arizona, she was thinking like a normal person and making sense.

"She's our grandmother, and we don't know if she really did that," I said.

"Well, why would Maria lie?" Luna asked.

She had a point. It seemed terrible, if it was true, what Maria had told us about her mother leaving her behind. Maybe our own mother hadn't told us about Maria being her sister because it was too hard to explain why her mother took her back to Mexico and left Maria in Arizona.

Maria arranged to take Paco to Nogales the next day to hand him over to his father. I wanted to go along, but Maria said it was best if I didn't go, in case there were any questions at the border.

Early in the morning Luna and I hugged Paco, and I gave him Maria's address, so he could write. He said he'd go see my grandmother and tell her we were all right. He waved from behind the windshield as Maria backed out onto the road.

Maria had returned from her trip to Nogales before dinnertime. She didn't say anything more about Paco, and I knew better than to ask.

I did get a letter from Paco the next week though. He'd gotten in big trouble with his father and couldn't go anywhere but their own yard by himself for a month. He'd asked if his father would take him to our grandmother's husband's store to tell her we were all right in Arizona. His father walked with him to the store the next day. Paco said our grandmother had hugged him and cried when he told her. He didn't know if it was because she was happy or sad.

The summer monsoons had finally come. The mornings were clear and sunny, and then the wind would bring the clouds and enough rain to make small lakes in the yard and on the sides of the gravel roads every afternoon. Maria kept two umbrellas by the kitchen door, so we could use them if we were going somewhere. But I didn't use them. I liked the rain.

Just to get out of the house, I took Salma to the pond every morning. With all that rain, the pond was almost over its banks. The gulley that led to it was wide, full of muddy water. The sun bleached the lawn to tan-topped light green, and the rain could only keep the bottom layer of grass from drying out. When the sun got high, I'd take Salma back to the house and put her in front of the television while I fixed us some lunch.

About two weeks after I got the letter from Paco, a letter came addressed to Luna and Teresa Espinosa, c/o Maria Ormond. Maria handed it to Luna, with a questioning look, and Luna put it in her pocket until she and I got to our room.

Dear Luna, Teresa, and Salma,

Your friend, Paco, told me you were at the Ormond ranch. I didn't know your mother was going there. She didn't tell me. I wish she had told me so I could talk her out of it, but it's too late. I know you are with your mother's sister, Maria. I know you didn't know about her until you got to the ranch. Your friend told me you found out.

Please stay where you are. Call me and I'll come there to get you if you want to come home. Please don't be mad about things you didn't know. Your father has gotten married to another woman. You don't need to go back to him. You have a home here with me.

Love, your Grandmother,

Ana Lopez

I waited until the next night, at dinner, to tell Maria what the letter said. She acted like she hadn't even heard me. Then she told Luna that since she'd been doing well helping in the kitchen, she'd be paid now, and she could help with breakfast and dinner after school started back if she wanted to work.

And I was supposed to start the eighth grade, but I didn't really like the school because of the things about the Bible they were telling us. We hadn't gone to church very much in Centro, but I knew enough to know that the teacher in my class at this school at the ranch had to be making some of it up. Jesus was in Nazareth, not in the United States.

I dreamed of my mother that night, of how pretty she looked when she went to the market. We were setting up, and she kept putting out things to sell. Then she couldn't find Salma, and I wanted to look for her, but I couldn't move my arms and legs, and I saw a wolf walking on its hind legs, carrying Salma down the street. My mother was crawling after the wolf, crying, and I still couldn't move.

When I woke up my heart was beating fast, and I went to my little sister's bed to look at her. She was sound asleep. I touched the latch on the window beside her bed, to be sure it was locked, and it was. Luna sat up, looking at me strangely.

"What's wrong?" she asked.

"I dreamed about Mama and that a wolf had Salma."

She stared at me. Her face was pale grey in the moonlight.

"I dreamed about a wolf too," she said.

COCAINE AND A TATTOO

The border coyote has delivered a man, woman, and their two children
to a waiting truck.
He is on his way back to town to buy cocaine with the profits.
Maybe he'll get a new tattoo while he's there too.
He swings by the windmill and water tank where he sometimes finds
illegals who've crossed, gotten lost, and are desperate enough to hand
over their life savings for a ride out of the desert.

He hears a low moan and walks to a cover of brush.
A long-haired young man lies on the ground,
a belt wrapped tightly around his thigh.
He asks the man what's wrong, and the man tells him, through his pain,
that he is snake bit.
The coyote digs through the pack beside the man,
finds a few pesos, and pockets them.
The coyote sees that the young man is wearing almost-new hiking boots.
He can sell those at the market.
He pulls the belt off the man's swelling leg, takes his boots,
and drives on to Nogales.

32

ANA 1949-1954

Driving

Ana inched the car across the grass with her hands clenched on the steering wheel. Her fingers and wrists ached. After a few minutes of circling the lawn, Gabriella had her steer toward the ranch road and told her to speed up and stop a few times. Ana began to feel some freedom in Arizona for the first time.

Maya had come with Gabriella that afternoon, to babysit.

"There's something for you at your house," Gabriella said. Two cars were parked at Ana's little house, and two men stood waiting. When they saw Gabriella and Ana, one of them waved cheerfully, held up a set of keys, and walked over. He shook Gabriella's hand.

"Here you go. This is a good car. 1941 Oldsmobile. Hydromatic transmission, so it's easy to drive." He dropped the keys in Gabriella's hand, got in the other car, and the two men left.

"Time to have a driving lesson," Gabriella said.

Within a few days, Ana started driving over to pick up Maya, Rudy, Nina, and Suela's little son at school. Baby Maria would lie bundled between her and Maya on the front seat. Rudy kept the younger boy from pulling Nina's hair. Ana would drop them all off at the main house, let them in through the kitchen with her key, and then drive to the sewing room to pick up Suela. Suela and Maya were happy to have a ride from work, and the children loved to hang their heads out the window to feel the breeze.

Ana had moved into the little house after a tearful exchange with Maya and Suela, and things were settled. Juanita was sent to the other side of the ranch and, after a few days of Gabriella taking plates to the dining room, Ana was told she was to return to serving meals. Stan Ormond didn't look at her any more than he had before she'd had her brief affair with him. She kept the baby in the kitchen and, if requested, took her into the dining room with a bottle. She let Lorene Ormond hold and coo over her "sweet little baby." As soon as the bottle was empty, or the diaper was full, whichever came first, the bell would ring for the nanny to relieve Lorene of motherhood.

When Ana's first daughter, Nina, began kindergarten in the fall of 1954, little Maria had started standing up in the playpen Gabriella had brought over for her, trying to climb out. Gabriella told Ana it was time for Maria to go to the nursery anyway. Maya told Ana she didn't mind carrying Maria in the mornings, until she got big enough to walk.

On the days Señora Ormond wanted to have the adopted daughter she called Mary there for breakfast, Ana took Maria to the nursery later in the morning.

Ana was paid her extra fifty dollars a week. She put her cash in the bank and sometimes kept out a few dollars to buy a treat for her daughters if they rode to town with her. Gabriella told Ana she was nervous that Ana might get stopped in her car and get in trouble for not having a license, so she got a copy of the driver's license test for Ana. Ana took the test a few weeks later and was issued an Arizona driver's license. Gabriella thought it probably didn't matter that she'd faked a birth certificate for Ana, so long as the address shown as her home address matched the address of the owner of the car, "Ormond Manufacturing, Inc."

Ana cooked new dishes Lorene Ormond clipped from magazines. She had a nice home, made good money, and her girls were going to school. As far as Ana was concerned, life was good for the unmarried girl from Juarez who had, a few years before, been cooking over a fire at a convent and orphanage in Centro.

Ana hadn't heard anything from Aunt Pena, until a letter from the new Mother Superior at the convent came, addressed to "Ana Rosario, c/o The Ormond Ranch." Gabriella read it while Ana was rolling out a pie crust. Uncle Ancho had died, and Pena was helping at the convent with the babies to make a little money. Ana wrote to Pena to tell her to look under the loose floorboard in the little room where Ana had slept, to find the wooden box, and to take the twenty pesos she'd hidden there.

The year after Maria was born, Ana delivered Suela's pretty light-skinned daughter, who was named Angelina. Angelina was adopted by the Ormonds and was brought to the dining room for an occasional meal with her new parents, then returned to Suela. Suela finally got her house.

By the time Nina was in the sixth grade, she often came home telling Ana that Suela's son, Favorite, who was in the second grade, was in trouble at school. Gabriella moved Suela from her job in the sewing room, to the school, where she could help in the nursery and be close when her son got into trouble. Ana hoped he would not be held back a year in school, because then he'd be in Maria's class. Suela came to Ana many times, beside herself over Favorite's bad behavior because the boy threw things at teachers and his classmates and was spending as much time in the principal's office as he spent in class.

"The teacher says there is a doctor who can write a prescription for something that will make my son calmer at school," Suela told Ana one afternoon. "Can you take me to town to get it?" They filled the prescription at the pharmacy in Tubac, and the medication helped, but only when Favorite swallowed the pills.

Ana was parked at the school one afternoon waiting for Maria, Nina, Rudy, and Favorite to get out of school. Another car pulled up beside her. The couple who had adopted the baby named Gracie sat in the car. A caramel-skinned girl in school uniform came out with the second graders and ran to get in the car.

"Who's the new girl?" Ana asked when Nina got in the front seat.

"Gracie Smith," Nina said. "She just moved here from Colorado City. Why?"

"Just asking," Ana said. "Maria, will you sing that song you've been practicing for the school play?"

Six-year-old Maria launched into her solo just as Suela got in the car and was still singing when they dropped Suela and her children off at their house. Anything, Ana thought, to keep the children from talking about the new girl in front of Suela.

When Maya's son, Rudy, was a junior in high school, the room behind the kitchen was no longer big enough for a teenage boy and his mother to share. Gabriella asked Ana if she thought Maya would let him move to another house on the ranch, where the warehouse foreman and his wife were looking for extra help with their two sets of twin boys. What Gabriella really wanted, she said, was for Ana to help her convince Maya to let him take the job, which included a small salary for tutoring the boys with their schoolwork and a room of his very own.

Ana brought up the idea to Maya, who was surprisingly easy to convince, since she'd complained to Ana that sometimes cleaning up after a teenage boy was like trying to mop a floor with a pig living in the room. Rudy wanted to go, and peace was restored, once he was not under Maya's constant scrutiny.

When Rudy moved out, two young women from Mexico came to live in the rooms behind the kitchen. Rudy still walked over several times a week for dinner with his mother, Ana, Nina, Maria, and the two new women whom he helped with their English.

Ana was grateful that Rudy stood dutifully with thirteen-year-old Nina, eleven-year-old Favorite, nine-year-old Maria, and Suela's eight-year-old daughter Angelina while they waited for Ana to pick them up after school. Once they were in Ana's car, Rudy gathered up the four boys he watched and walked them to the home across the big field from their house.

Ana learned from Nina that Lorene Ormond was at school plays and choir performances, immaculately dressed and coifed, to watch Mary and Angela Ormond. Ana would have liked to go watch her daughters in school plays and in the choir, but she was not excused from work. None of the Mexican women were.

The more that Ana and Suela's daughters played outside in the sun, the more their skins darkened. By the time Maria was ten and Angelina was nine, The Ormonds hardly ever had their adopted daughters Mary and Angela brought to the dining room for meals. Newer, younger, lighter-skinned children took their places.

Ana was content enough in her work, in her home, in her life at the Ormond ranch. In the spring of Nina's eighth grade year at the ranch school, Rafael helped Ana put in a small garden on the sunny side of her house, so she could grow some spices and vegetables. When the jackrabbits ate all the newly sprouted corn and eggplant, he brought over some chicken wire to keep them out, then came by the next day with two young hens to put in the enclosure. Rafael assured Ana the hens would eat the pests and leave the plants alone. The hens ate every insect they found, plus the lizards, and all of the sweet peas. Ana didn't have the heart to send the hens back, and Rafael added a couple of nesting boxes in the corner of the garden for them.

Nina and Maria tended the garden early in the mornings before breakfast, and since Ana's garden wasn't visible from the Ormond house, Maria's adoptive parents couldn't see the gardening chores and object to their adopted daughter doing manual labor alongside her Mexican sister.

When the school year ended, Maria and Angelina were sent, with other children who'd been adopted by families from the temple, to a summer camp in northern Arizona. With Rudy on the other side of the ranch, the early evening kickball games had come to an end, and Nina was bored. Nina asked Ana if she could help in the kitchen for the summer between her eighth-grade year and the start of high school.

Ana told Nina to dress in her school uniform to help in the kitchen and told her she'd give her a dollar a week. After that, Nina seemed happy to be staying at the ranch while her sister got to go to camp.

Ana taught Nina to put her hair in a tidy bun and hair pins and fitted her with aprons over her school uniform. By the end of June, she let Nina go into the dining room to serve the Ormonds. Ana had her doing most of the prep work by July and some of the cooking by August.

After school started in September, Nina helped Ana get breakfast on the table then ran to school. Her grades were A's and B's, according to her first quarter report cards. Gabriella let Ana know Maria had also made good grades in the first quarter and that the Ormonds were rewarding Maria and Angelina with a Thanksgiving vacation trip with the Ormonds to Utah, along with another fifth-grade girl who Ana noticed looked eerily like ten-year-old Maria. If Nina ever felt hurt or slighted when Maria left with the Ormonds, she never told Ana.

Gabriella, Ana, and Nina spent Thanksgiving morning in the kitchen roasting two turkeys, with cornbread stuffing, tamales, and grilled vegetables for dinner in the school cafeteria for the warehouse, groundskeeping, and housekeeping staff and all their children.

Rafael had on a clean, pressed shirt when he arrived, escorting Suela and Maya. There was a round of applause when Ana and Gabriella set the turkeys on the cafeteria tables. Nina sat beside her best friend, Rudy, and grinned proudly.

"Nina, I want you to go to school," Ana said, the week after Thanksgiving, when Nina asked if she could work in the kitchen instead of continuing high school.

"But Mama, I'm learning here. It's like school, helping you," Nina said, hopefully. "I want to be a cook."

Ana's plans for her daughter's schooling were stopped short once Gabriella offered to pay Nina to be a cook's assistant in the Ormond kitchen with a salary of five dollars a week. In January fourteen-year-old Nina, like the other teenage Mexican girls at the ranch school, dropped out of school and went to work. Suela took a couple of the smaller sized uniforms over to the sewing room and made them into Nina's size.

Ana decided not to fight the new development, because she knew from experience how tempting the flattery of boys in high school could be to a teenage girl, especially one who was beginning to show some curves.

Ana runs toward the shrieking whine of an ambulance siren at the school, and stops to let the sheriff's car pass by. Suela's thirteen-year-old son's wild eyes stare out at her from the back seat of the patrol car.

She reaches the edge of the school yard as the ambulance driver and helper roll a gurney out of a classroom. Suela trots alongside with her hand on the railing, sobbing.

"I'm so sorry, I'm so sorry," Suela cried, as the gurney was lifted into the ambulance. One of the teachers stepped in before the doors closed.

Ana looked frantically for Maria and found her with her friends, huddled against the lockers in the hallway.

"What happened?" she said to the girls.

"That crazy kid, the one with the funny name?" A blonde girl gasped, "He stabbed Gracie Smith with a pencil. Right in the neck."

"Yeah," said another girl. "Blood was going everywhere."

"Who?" Ana asked, "Who stabbed her?" Maria was not jabbering from the excitement. She looked pale and solemn.

"It was Favorite," Maria told Ana quietly. "He stabbed Gracie. He went crazy and he stabbed her."

"You stay right here until I come back, Maria" Ana said.

"Who's Maria?" the gasping blonde girl said.

"That's Mexican for Mary," said the girl with a halo of strawberry curls.

"Hey, Mary, why is your nanny calling you Maria?" said the blonde girl.

Ana turned to look for Suela. Her jaw hardened at the stinging words from the little savages in school uniforms.

"How do I know?" Maria said. "She doesn't know better."

Ana's attention snapped back to Maria.

"You will not talk that way."

Maria looked at her defiantly and whispered something to one of the girls.

"You are going with me," Ana said, and grabbed Maria's arm.

Maria's classmates watched in horror as Mary Ormond's nanny dragged her away.

Suela was on her knees where the ambulance had been parked when Ana found her, mopping at a spray of blood on the sidewalk with a handkerchief.

"Suela, come with me," Ana said, helping her up. Maria stayed by Ana's side, her head hanging. Ana could guess what was going through her daughter's head. She probably hated her mother for humiliating her in front of her friends who only knew her as Mary Ormond. She hated her friends for humiliating her mother. And she hated Suela's son, for stabbing that girl Gracie.

Suela wept silently as Ana led her away from the crowd of children.

"Maria, you help Suela back to the house. I'll be back soon," Ana said. She walked into the school office.

"I'm sorry, we're rather busy right now," said the woman at the desk.

"Where did the sheriff take the boy?" Ana demanded.

"I'm afraid this is a private matter," the woman said curtly.

"I'm taking my daughter home, and I want to know where my friend's son has been taken."

"Who is your daughter?" the woman at the desk asked, looking over the top of her glasses.

"Mary, Mary Ormond," Ana said.

"Now, miss, Mrs. Ormond will come to get Mary if she feels there's a reason, but I can't release her to you," the woman said.

"Then please call Mrs. Ormond now and tell her what has happened," Ana said.

"And you are?"

"Her nanny," Ana seethed, "Ana. Tell her Ana took her home."

"All right, I'll give her a call. But please don't take her from—" the woman said to Ana's back while Ana stormed out the door to hide her tears of anger.

Back at the house, Ana went in to help an inconsolable Suela change out of her blood-smeared dress. "You stay here, Suela. Nina will bring some lunch in a little while."

She stopped in the kitchen to see that Nina had looked at the menu on the counter and was already working on preparation.

"I'll be right back," Ana told her oldest daughter. Ana found Maria in the back room, slumped at the table, sulking.

"What happened? Why did Favorite hurt Gracie?" she asked her younger daughter.

"Well, Gracie, she's snotty," Maria said.

"Maria! He could have killed her!"

"But he didn't. She was screaming her head off so she's alive," Maria said sullenly.

"Why did he do that?" Ana asked.

Maria sat up straight and sighed. "Gracie told some of the kids that she was lucky she was adopted, because her real mother was a dumb Mexican. She said her parents told her that her real mother's name was Suela and that her twin brother was retarded."

"Did she? Well that is a terrible thing to say," Ana said, taking a seat beside Maria.

"And, Mama, she said her parents told her she was special and blessed and all that. She thinks she's so much better than the rest of us. I hate her."

"Shame on her for saying that. Suela is a good woman. Gracie sounds like she has no manners at all."

"Yes, but my friends will be mean to me now if I tell them I know Suela, and I like her," Maria said, as tears slid down her cheeks.

"Maria, maybe you need better friends."

Suela's son spent eighteen months in juvenile hall, then was sent to a school for troubled boys in Tucson. The adoptive parents of Gracie Smith hired an attorney and threatened a lawsuit if the boy who'd attacked their daughter showed up at the school, or anywhere within a half mile of Gracie again. Suela was allowed visits with her son once a month but she seldom asked to go.

33

ANA 1959

Nothing

"Nina," Ana called into the pantry one morning, "Is there more flour in there?"

"No, Mama. Remember, we used it all for those cupcakes Señora took to the school." Ana went to the pantry door. Her daughter was arranging cans on a shelf.

"Then I'll go to town. She wants two pies to take to a party tomorrow."

"Isn't Gabriella coming with groceries this afternoon?" Nina asked.

"She had to drive Señora to Phoenix to go shopping. I'll go get flour. You peel those peaches. Put some lemon juice on them to keep them from browning and peel the potatoes for tonight. I'll be back in an hour," Ana said, taking her apron off. She locked the side door to the kitchen on her way out. She was backing her Oldsmobile out of the drive when Stan Ormond pulled up and rolled his window down.

"Hello, Ana, where are you off to this morning?"

"Gabriella is in Phoenix, and I need flour to make Señora Ormond's pies," she explained.

He studied her for a moment, and if she'd been the naive woman she'd been eleven years before, she'd have been happy to be looked at that way.

"Here, take some letters to the post office for me, then," he said.

She took the bundle of envelopes and drove to Tubac.

There were two grocery stores in town. The first had only one-pound sacks of flour, so she went to the other store, and while she was there, she got an extra can of lard for pie crusts and some spices she knew were running low. She dropped the letters at the post office and got back to the house an hour and a half after she'd left.

The kitchen door was unlocked. Ana replayed her movements, knowing she'd locked it. She thought, *Gabriella must have come by.* She set the flour and lard on the counter and looked in the pantry for Nina, and then pushed the back room door open. Her fourteen-year-old daughter, Nina, was sitting on the edge of the table. Stan Ormond was standing close to Nina with his back to the door. Ana froze when she saw the look on Nina's face. It was the look of a girl caught doing something she knew was wrong.

"Nina, go measure and sift the flour," Ana said.

Nina slid down from the table. Ormond had to step back to make room for her to get by.

Ana stepped closer as her daughter went into the kitchen. She stood a foot away from him and felt the familiar heat, smelled his aftershave.

"What are you doing in here?" she asked quietly.

"Well, Ana, I own this kitchen and I own this room. So, I have every right to be here." He smirked down at Ana.

"She is my daughter," Ana snarled. "She is fourteen years old. Maybe she doesn't know she shouldn't be in here with you or any man. But you know, Señor Ormond. You know it's wrong." Ana was struggling to keep her voice down.

"How old were you when you had her, Ana? Sixteen? Seventeen? You sure have been a good mother, now, haven't you? Unmarried, two children out of wedlock. You girls from Centro never change. I could fire you for talking to me like that," Ormond said, grinning profanely at Ana. He ambled through the back room and out the kitchen door.

Ana followed him and locked the door behind him, knowing it was futile. He had a key. She spun on her white kitchen shoes back to her daughter.

Nina stood at the sink, holding a paring knife over a peach.

"Nina, what was going on?"

"Nothing, Mama."

"Nina, that was not nothing. Your face is red. That was not nothing."

"We were just talking, Mama."

"No, Nina, you do NOT go into the back room and sit like that on the table to just talk. You just talk in the kitchen," she said. Her anger rose with her voice. "Peel those peaches and don't you ever do something like that again. You are too young to understand."

Nina started peeling peaches. Ana got the sifter and a bowl out of the cabinet and slapped them down to emphasize her fury at her daughter, but even more, at Stan Ormond.

"Mama?" Nina said, putting down the paring knife, "He told me that Señora Ormond doesn't love him like a wife should love a husband."

Ana's blood felt like ice in her heart.

"Nina! Did he touch you? Did he try to kiss you?" Panic closed her throat.

"Mama, he told me I am so special, and he wants me to have my own house if I want."

"You stay right here, don't you leave. Do you understand?" Ana choked the words out.

Ana opened the kitchen door, started for her car, then came back to the kitchen, and stood in the doorway. She looked around the kitchen where she'd worked for eleven years.

"Nina, put those things down. You come with me. Right now."

Nina obeyed. Her mother was angrier than she'd ever seen her.

"Get in the car," Ana said. She drove to her house.

Nina followed her mother into the house and headed for her room.

"You put your clothes in a box, or a pillowcase. I don't care, but you get what you want and be ready to go," Ana said. Ana went to her room, stripped off the grey cook's uniform and shoes, and put on her own blouse and skirt. She shoved her other clothes into two pillowcases. In Maria's room, she found a suitcase Maria had been given when she'd gone to Utah with the Ormonds and crammed as many of Maria's clothes in it as she could.

"Are you ready?" Ana shouted toward Nina's bedroom door. Nina opened the door slowly and peered out. Her face was streaked from crying.

"Ready for what, Mama?"

"We are going to get Maria at school and we are leaving here right now."

"But WHY, Mama?" Nina wailed.

"Get in the car, Nina," Ana said, lifting her two pillowcases and Maria's suitcase. "Take your things and put them in the trunk."

"No, Mama, I'm not leaving," Nina protested. "I have a job here, and . . . " she put her hands over her eyes and sobbed. "Mama, you don't understand, I love him."

Ana slapped her daughter's face.

"Get in the car now." Her crying daughter ran to the car, put her things in the trunk, and got in the front seat.

Ana drove to the school and parked in front of the office. She strode by the office window. She didn't look at the woman in the office who'd been rude to her the day Gracie Smith had been stabbed by her twin brother.

The woman followed her down the hall.

"May I help you?" the woman called.

"Where is sixth grade?" Ana asked, opening doors.

"It's right there, but—"

Ana yanked the door open and looked across the children at their desks for her daughter. "Where is Mary Ormond?" she asked the teacher.

"Her mother took her to Phoenix today. Aren't you the nanny?" the teacher asked.

Ana stormed back to her car. Nina had stayed put.

"I need to stop in town at the bank," she said. She spun her tires on the pavement leaving the school. She drove faster than she'd ever driven on the road to Tubac, left the car running in front of the bank, and told Nina to wait for her.

She showed her bank book and asked to withdraw her money.

The new bank manager came over to the window when the teller asked how to issue that large a transaction. He looked over her bank book and driver's license. The manager gave her ten thousand dollars and a promissory note for the rest.

"Call me when you get to your new bank," he said and added his home number to his business card. "I'll be sure your money gets to you."

Ana drove south out of Tubac like a woman possessed. She watched her rearview mirror for Ormond's car, and the side roads for police. Nina was shrieking for her mother to stop and cursing in language that should have made Ana stop to punish her. Ana had a full tank of gas and no intention of stopping.

She had no idea how to explain why she had her boss's car and a sack of money if she got stopped on her way to Nogales. The agent at the border gate waved the Mexican woman and her daughter through, admiring her nice car. Ana breathed a sigh of relief.

She realized as she entered the Mexican side of Nogales that she wasn't sure how to get from there to Centro. She stopped to buy a map from a roadside vendor.

"Look at this and tell me where to turn," she said, and threw the map at Nina. Nina stopped crying and opened the map.

When Ana passed the convent where she'd worked and raised Nina, she knew she was home.

Pena was feeding her little flock of chickens when the big car with Arizona license plates stopped in front of her house.

"Aunt Pena, it's me, Ana," she said.

The old women peered into Ana's face and embraced her.

"Ana? Is it you?" she cried.

"Pena, there is not much time. Here is Nina." she said. Nina got out of the car, brooding. "Nina, bring your things."

Nina obeyed.

"Aunt Pena, will you keep her? I need to go back to Arizona. I'll explain later." Ana turned, took her daughter's shoulders, and shook her. "Nina, stay here with Pena. Stay here. I will be back with Maria." She handed the pillowcases and suitcase stuffed with clothing to Nina, the bank bag to Pena, and got back in the Oldsmobile.

Stan Ormond had seen Ana driving from her house to the school, then going toward town in a hurry. He called the bank, and the new manager, whom Stan did not know, confirmed that Ana had withdrawn money from her account, but would not tell him how much, no matter how Ormond threatened to call the main branch manager in Phoenix.

He knew that Lorene had his and Ana's daughter, Mary, with her in Phoenix. He guessed Ana would come back for her. He called his friend with the Arizona Highway Patrol and had a Highway Patrol officer waiting for Ana at the border in Nogales.

The Highway Patrol officer pulled his car in front of Ana's to keep her from driving through the border stop. He told Ana if she surrendered the car that belonged to Ormond Manufacturing peacefully, she could go back into Sonora on foot.

Ana slid out of the car. Her world was spinning out from under her feet. She watched as the officer instructed his partner to take the car back to the Ormond ranch.

"My daughter," she pleaded with the officer, "I need to get my daughter."

The officer opened a spiral notebook from his shirt pocket.

"It says here that you tried to abduct the daughter of Stan and Lorene Ormond, Mary Ormond, from her school." He tucked the book back into his pocket.

"I don't want to arrest you, miss, and I don't want trouble from the Ormonds. And there would be trouble if you were to go back there. Please don't make more trouble. Please."

Ana backed away from him, and started walking, dazed, into No-gales.

Maria was told, when she and Lorene were brought back from Phoe-nix, that Ana and Nina had left. Had run off to Mexico without her. Lorene and Stan Ormond assured her that she'd be well taken care of by Maya, and that they loved her. After all, she was their daughter.

For the first day Ana stayed close to Pena's house with Nina, wonder-ing if Ormond would come looking for her. He didn't. She took out her rosary for the first time in years and said a prayer for help getting her money out of Arizona. She walked to the bank in Centro and opened an account with her ten thousand dollars. When the bank manager asked if there was anything else he could do to help, Ana showed him the promissory note for the balance in her account in Tubac. Ana told him she needed to use the phone to make a call to the United States. She called the home number for the bank manager in Tubac, and the manager's wife, Juanita, who'd seen more than her share of dirty laun-dry at the Ormond ranch when she'd worked for both Stan and David Ormond, answered the phone.

Juanita told Ana she could only guess what had happened and she'd do anything she could to help. Juanita said she'd call her husband at work. Less than five minutes later, Juanita's husband called to assure the Centro bank manager that the note was legitimate, and he would have the funds transferred in pesos to Ana's new account. Juanita's hus-band made good on his promise to Ana.

The next time Ana was at the bank in Centro, the bank manager told her he'd heard back from Juanita's husband a few days after he'd transferred the money. Juanita's husband got a visit from the main branch manager from Phoenix who happened to be Lorene Ormond's first cousin. He was fired.

Luna was born and named on a moonlit night to fifteen-year-old Nina eight months after Ana and Nina left the Ormond Ranch, and twelve years after they'd left the convent.

Ana hadn't seen the signs before that day she'd walked into the back room of the kitchen. Or maybe she had not wanted to see. But when she held her granddaughter for the first time, she loved her as she loved her own daughters.

A young man named Carlos Espinosa came to do some repairs on Pena's fence and chicken coop. He seemed taken with Nina and her child. He asked Ana's permission to marry Nina and promised to take care of her and the baby. It seemed like the right thing, for Nina to at least be married, even if the man didn't have much ambition.

Ana couldn't forgive herself for being too late to keep her daughter from being stalked and used by Ormond. She wrote letters to her younger daughter, Maria, to explain what had happened and sent them to the ranch in care of Gabriella.

Maya wrote to Ana telling her she'd gotten Ana's address in Centro from the stack of unopened letters to Gabriella from Ana she'd found in the trash. In her letter, which she told Ana she was sending from town, instead of the ranch mailbox, she said she was in the back room of the kitchen when Stan Ormond stormed in and ordered Gabriella to go after Ana and bring back the mother of his and Lorene's next baby. Gabriella refused, and Ormond threatened to fire her. Maya said Gabriella told him she was quitting right then.

34

TERESA 1971

The pond

When the rainy season started, Rafael added sandbags to the pond banks to keep his catfish from washing out onto the ground. The fish had been staying close to where the gulley washed in to eat the bugs and mice, and other things that rode the flood of muddy water to the pond. Salma and I had Rafael's pole and some earthworms we'd found half drowned on the lawn. Rafael waved to us from across the water and kept working while we ran back and forth to dangle the poor worms in front of shadows in the muddy water.

Rafael stood up stiffly to look across the ranch toward Suela's house. A red car had pulled up in front. A man in a white undershirt got out and walked to the door and went right in like he was supposed to. Rafael left the sandbags he'd filled on the bank, put his shovel and hoe in his wheelbarrow and pushed it toward Suela's house. He seemed to be in a hurry, and I got a bad feeling that something was very wrong. I took Salma by the hand, and we followed him, but stayed back. That way if Rafael turned around and saw us, I could pretend we were going somewhere else.

When Rafael got to Suela's crooked little gate, he stopped and tipped his head like he was listening. Then he was walking fast toward the door, and the screen door slammed open against the house and the man who'd gone in walked out, cursing loud enough we could hear him. Suela was following him, trying to grab his arm. The man shoved her hard. She fell to her knees. I was too far away to hear what she was saying. Rafael rushed to Suela to help her, and the man got in his car and started it. He drove right over Rafael's wheelbarrow and dragged it until it got mashed out the back end of the car.

The car turned and headed toward Salma and me. Salma stood like she was frozen, watching the car come at us and I didn't know where to go because the car was faster than we could run. He drove straight at us and swerved and turned his head to look at me as he went by us. I was looking right into the angry, mad dog, grey-green eyes of Favo. He was so close I could see the cross-shaped gold earring in his left ear.

I grabbed Salma's hand, and ran toward Suela's house. Rafael had gotten Suela up on her feet. They both stood and stared at Salma and me running. Favo turned the car around, and the engine roared like an animal as he came up behind us. He was shrieking and howling like a wild man when he veered around to block us from the house.

Salma was old enough to have her own sense to survive, and she pulled away from me. Favo threw the car door open and ran after her. I screamed. He got hold of her and dragged her toward the car under his tattooed arm. She kicked and yelled, "Teresa! Teresa!"

He was almost to the car door and I was running toward them. I didn't know what I was going to do. Rafael stepped into view, swung his shovel and connected with Favo's forehead.

Salma dropped to the ground and crawled under the car. I ran to the other side of the car and shouted, "Here, come here," and she crawled out from under the car to me.

I grabbed Salma by her arm, and we ran to Suela. Salma put her head against Suela's waist and clung to her. Suela stood by the gate holding on to Salma, crying, "Rafael, no, no."

I couldn't make sense of the sound coming from behind me until I looked back at the car. The sound was the heavy shunk-shunk-shunk-shunk of Rafael's newly sharpened shovel on Favo's head.

Rafael stopped, and jammed his shovel into the wet ground beside Favo. He raised his old grey head to tell Suela to go in the house. She didn't. I told Salma to go inside. She did.

Suela walked to the side of the car and knelt beside the bloody mess that had been Favo. Rafael took a step backwards, and sat down on the ground, just staring at Suela while she made the sign of the cross over Favo.

Suela wiped her face on her arm and walked past me into the house. She came back out with an old striped blanket and helped Rafael wrap it around Favo. Neither one of them said anything to me. They dragged him to the car. Rafael got in the back seat and dragged Favo in, then came out the other side and closed the door. He opened the front door on the passenger side and looked around for a few seconds. He tossed a wallet, a yellow folder, and a packet of papers toward the gate.

"Teresa, take those. Keep them until I get back," he said.

Rafael touched Suela's arm, and she got behind the wheel and Rafael got in the passenger seat. She drove to the pond and stopped by the tree where we'd sat so many times, watching fish and frogs and dragon-flies and birds. I started walking toward the pond carrying the things Rafael had given me to keep. The two of them dragged the blanket with Favo in it out of the back seat, and Rafael looked at the sandbags he'd left by the pond. Then Rafael dragged Favo to the middle of the pond and let go. He waded out to the bank, lifted a sandbag on each shoul-der, and went back where the air bubbles were coming up. He dropped the sandbags in the middle of the bubbles.

Suela stood for a few minutes, staring at the water, until Rafael cleared his throat.

"I know, Rafael," she said. She and I walked back to her house. Salma had been watching from the window. Her face was still pale with fear.

Rafael drove the car to the Ormond's house, left it parked in the driveway in front of the garage, then walked back to Suela's house. He pulled his shovel up from where he'd left it with its blade in the ground. He dug a hole in Suela's yard beside the water pan for the chickens.

I looked down at the envelope from the car, opened it and read.

Make: Chev
Model: Impala
Year 1967
License # AZ FMA665
Color: Red
Owner: Ormond Manufacturing, Tubac, AZ.

I opened the wallet. The grey-green eyes glared at me even from the photo on the Arizona driver's license for Favorite Ormond from Tubac, Arizona.

Rafael took the wallet and envelope from me, took the money out of the wallet, and put it in Suela's hand. She tried to hand it back, but Rafael gently closed her fingers over the bills.

"Please, Suela, please take it."

I opened the yellow folder I was still holding, and saw that it was the folder Paco, Luna and I had seen in the school office. The folder with Salma's pictures. The folder that said, "Date of Availability: June 1971."

There were four one-hundred-dollar bills in a paper clip inside the folder with Salma's pictures. I handed the money to Suela. Rafael pointed at the hole he'd dug in Suela's garden. I dropped the wallet, the car registration, and the folder into the hole. Rafael used his shovel to cover the last of Favo.

⸎

When Luna got back from working in the kitchen, I took her into our room and told her about Favo hurting Suela, and chasing us, and grabbing Salma. How Rafael had killed him and had gotten rid of Favo for good. I told her that the car Favo was driving belonged to Mr. Ormond, and that Favo's name was Favorite Ormond. And I told her Favo had the folder with our sister's pictures in the car and four hundred dollars.

Luna went to the dresser and got out the paper with the map and the phone numbers. She dialed for long distance and gave the operator the number for Alisio Lopez' store and asked Alisio to have our grand-mother come to the phone.

"Grandmother, will you come get us?" was all Luna said. She listened for a few seconds and hung up the phone. "She and Alisio will come get us early tomorrow."

I told Salma to take a bath. Maria came in, tired from running errands, and was glad that we'd started cooking. David Sanchez arrived a while later. We had fried pork chops and rice, and salad for dinner.

Salma was quieter than usual, and Maria asked, "You feel okay, honey?"

I don't know why I didn't want to tell Maria about what happened.

But she did ask David if he'd seen Favo around, and he said, "No, why do you ask?"

"Just wondering," she said. Maybe she recognized the red car that had been left parked at the Ormond's house. Maybe she knew why Favo had come to the ranch. I didn't want to know if she knew.

Luna and I excused ourselves from watching television and went to our room. Luna had outgrown the clothes she'd worn when we came up from Mexico, so I took hers for myself, put them in Mama's pack, and she stuffed a few things from the closet that fit her into a cardboard box. We put some of Salma's clothes into her little pack. When Salma got in bed, we both kissed her goodnight.

WINDMILL CHECK

A Border Patrol agent stops to check a windmill and tank
along the human-traffic highway of sand.
He catches the sickly-sweet odor of a carcass.
Sometimes out here it's a chicken, or a dog, but this is stronger.
Today it is a human corpse with a swollen, unrecognizable face
and a mop of unruly black hair that waves eerily in the breeze.
The white topstitching on the pants is stretched tight.

This man was probably thin.
Before the body bloated.
The pants are torn at the calf on the balloon-like right leg.
The tightly stretched black T-Shirt is adorned with a pair of huge red lips.
The agent nudges the swollen leg,
and an army of beetles scurries for new cover.
Someone has taken the shoes.

35

TERESA 1971

To leave Arizona

Even Luna was ready to leave Arizona. We agreed we'd act like nothing was different in the morning and told Salma not to tell. We were up at six o'clock. Just before seven, we heard a car stop outside.

Maria went to the window to see who was coming to the house that early and said, "Oh, God, I think it's my mother." David walked over to the window to look. Maria opened the door and waited for our grandmother to walk from the car. Grandmother's husband Alisio sat behind the wheel.

"What are you doing here?" Maria said.

"The girls wanted me to come get them," Grandmother Ana said.

Maria turned slowly and looked at Luna and me.

We went to our room and got the things we'd packed.

"Just a minute," Maria said, putting a hand on my chest while she talked. "What makes you want to take care of your grandchildren, when you didn't take care of me?"

"Maria, I took care of you, I raised you," Grandmother Ana said.

"YOU LEFT ME. I DIDN'T KNOW WHERE YOU WENT!" Maria shouted. David stepped closer to Maria and touched her arm. She jerked away. "Mr. Ormond told me everything. He told me you ran away and took Nina, and stole a car, and that you weren't ever coming back," she said, sputtering to get the words out.

"Is that what he told you?" Grandmother Ana asked. "That I left you and stole a car? It's not true. It was my car. I tried to come back for you and your father had someone waiting for me at the border, and they took my car, and told me if I came back, they'd arrest me. I sent you letters, I told you everything. I sent you a letter every week for years. I did."

"What father, Mama? I didn't have a father. I never got any letters from you."

"Yes, you did, Maria. I did what I thought was best for you. I raised you," Grandmother said.

"Yes, thank goodness the Ormonds adopted me. Because you left me here. But thanks to you, I never knew my father!" she sneered.

"Maria, Stan Ormond is your father. And he is Luna's father too."

Maria burst into tears and backed away from the door. She leaned against David.

Luna clutched her bundle of clothes.

"No, that's not true!" Luna cried

Grandmother leaned toward Luna and said, "Yes, Luna, it is true. That's why I took your mother back to Centro as soon as I found out something was . . . I was too late."

Luna and I looked at each other.

"Well, who's MY father?" I said.

"Carlos Espinosa," Grandmother said. Salma came from our room carrying her little backpack and ran to our grandmother.

"Let's go, girls," Grandmother Ana said, "Maria, you can come with us if you want, but I don't expect you to. You've been told a lie all this time." Maria reached out and almost touched our grandmother's cheek. We got into the car, and Alisio drove us to Mexico.

We stopped for lunch at a restaurant in Nogales, then went on to Centro.

A week after we'd gotten settled in, I remembered the pack I'd brought back with me from Arizona was Mama's pack. I held it and breathed in the scent of Mama's hair. I remembered when Mama died trying to do something for us. When my sisters and I were in the desert, lost, looking for water, hiding from Favo and the border patrol. I wondered what happened to the man in the charro shirt and his handsome brother who'd walked with me while I looked for my sisters, and the crow that had followed me. Maybe that crow was trying to warn me all along.

I saw some frayed stitching while I looked in Mama's pack, and when I pulled at it, a slit in the lining opened. Inside that slit, and four other slits, I found the money Mama had hidden before we'd left Centro. Enough money to get a new wagon and a tarp, and some things to sell at the market. I showed Luna, and we showed our grandmother. She said she would help us connect with sellers of the goods we needed.

Another week later we were back at our old spot and our old business. Paco came over sometimes to help us push and pull the wagon.

Salma still knew how to charm the customers, Luna still knew how to hum "Celito Lindo," and we were right back where we'd started, selling cotton blankets, castanets, and brightly painted maracas to tourists on the market street in Centro.

THE GOLDEN TREASURE

The elderly gardener takes his cane fishing pole to the pond he has
tended for five decades.
He spears chicken livers on the hook, slings the weighted bait to the deep
middle of the pond,
and sits down to wait.
His bobber twitches, then disappears.
He counts "uno—dos—tres," and sets the hook.
Half an hour later, the twenty-five-pound behemoth from the depths of
the mossy green water
gives up and rises to the surface.

The gardener finds a gold earring in the shape of a cross in the stomach
of the catfish.
He recalls when he last saw that earring, more than a decade ago,
and he leaves it among the fish guts at the edge of the pond.

The crow watches from the tree that shades the pond.
When the man has gone,
she claims the cross-shaped golden treasure for her nest.

36

TERESA 1983

Mexico

When I passed the bar exam on my second try, my grandmother had a celebration at the clothing store. She and Alisio moved mannequins to the dressing rooms to make room for tables. Luna catered the party.

When I got hired at the law firm, the first case I was given was a woman whose daughter was taken from her by her wealthy husband's family. We won the case for her and she got her daughter back.

I love my work. There are a lot of people who don't know what to do, like when Grandmother had Maria taken from her, or when our Mama got pregnant—when she was only fourteen—by a grown-up man, and now, I know how to help them.

Luna studied business management at the University, and then went to study at the culinary institute in El Paso. There, she met a man whose family has restaurants in Coahuila and Monterrey. After she graduated, they got married. She and her husband, Raul, hope to buy one of the restaurants sometime next year. They take turns cooking so one of them can be home with their young son and daughter.

Paco is a school teacher now. He teaches math, because he was always good at math. He coaches the school soccer team too. This year my boss at the law firm sponsored them and got them matching uniforms and new shoes.

Paco is still my best friend. I should probably marry him someday.

I live in Centro, near my grandmother. It's my home, and I can be near the people I love. I still keep a close eye on Salma. She starts at the University next fall. I want my little sister to know that she can be anything she wants to be in this world.

The same women still sell goods at the market and their sons and daughters learn the trade from them. Men raise fighting cocks to watch them win or die. Damaged children will always offer candies for sale at the edge of town. Border patrol agents keep finding the bodies of those who don't survive the desert and leave them for the crows. Nuns at the orphanage take in children and hope they can feed them until they're sent back out to the streets to make room for the next crop of the unplanned and unwanted. And gringo couples go to the convent orphanage to get girls from Centro to take back to America, where they promise something better than life on the streets of Nogales.

There's a crow that is always sitting on the side mirror on my car when I leave for work. He squawks and purrs at me when I say, "Good Morning" to him.

And every day I say a prayer with the rosary my grandmother gave me, because now I know Mama was right.

It does work in Mexico.

ABOUT THE AUTHOR

 Juni Fisher is a multi-award-winning singer, songwriter, and producer. She's been the Western Music Association's (WMA) Entertainer of the Year, four-time Female Performer of the Year, (WMA and AWA), three-time Song of the Year winner, and is a two-time True West Magazine Best Solo Musician. Juni was the first woman to win the National Cowboy Museum's Wrangler Award in 2009 for her landmark CD, *Gone For Colorado*, which was also the 2009 WMA Album of the year. Her songs have appeared in feature film and documentary sound tracks and have been recorded by artists in folk and western music circles.

Before embarking on writing her first full-length novel, she had articles published in *Equus Magazine, The Trout Unlimited Newsreel, The Western Way,* and *True West Magazine.*

Fisher splits her time between the outskirts of Nashville, Tennessee, and her hometown in Tulare County, in central California. When she's on the west coast between concert tours, she rides and shows her cow horse, nicknamed Dee Jay, who sports Juni's 2NZ (which reads "tunes") brand on her hip.

And when she takes an incognito break from the road with husband Rusty, they head for places where waters run clear and cold, and trout rise to well-tied flies. She has a wicked double haul cast and has been known to have to be coaxed out of the water at the end of the day. After all, she is a Fisher.

Visit Juni at:

www.JuniFisher.com

www.facebook.com/JAJuniFisherAuthor

Instagram: Juni_Fisher

Dear Reader,
If you enjoyed this
book enough to review
it for Goodreads, B&N,
or Amazon.com, I'd
appreciate it!
Thanks, Juni

Find more great reads at
Pen-L.com

26259356R00190

Made in the USA
Lexington, KY
21 December 2018